Lamb

 Also by CHRISTOPHER MOORE

You Suck: A Love Story

A Dirty Job

The Stupidest Angel

Fluke: Or, I Know Why the Winged Whale Sings

The Lust Lizard of Melancholy Cove

Island of the Sequined Love Nun

Bloodsucking Fiends

Coyote Blue

Practical Demonkeeping

Lamb

The Gospel According to Biff, Christ's Childhood Pal

CHRISTOPHER MOORE

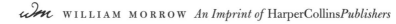 WILLIAM MORROW *An Imprint of* HarperCollins*Publishers*

HarperCollins books may be purchased for educational, business, or sales promotional use. For information please write: Special Markets Department, HarperCollins Publishers, 10 East 53rd Street, New York, NY 10022.

FIRST EDITION

Designed by Shubhani Sarkar

Library of Congress Cataloguing-in-Publication Data has been applied for.

ISBN: 978-0-06-143859-2
ISBN-10: 0-06-143859-6

07 08 09 10 11   RRD   10 9 8 7 6 5 4 3 2

Contents

PROLOGUE   1

PART I: *The Boy*   5
PART II: *Change*   99
PART III: *Compassion*   183
PART IV: *Spirit*   233
PART V: *Lamb*   273
PART VI: *Passion*   365

EPILOGUE   401
AFTERWORD: *Teaching Yoga to an Elephant*   403
AFTERWORD II: *When the Muse Sneezed*   409

Author's blessing

If you have come to these pages for laughter,
may you find it.

If you are here to be offended, may your ire rise
and your blood boil.

If you seek an adventure, may this story sing you
away to blissful escape.

If you need to test or confirm your beliefs, may
you reach comfortable conclusions.

All books reveal perfection, by what they are or
what they are not.

May you find that which you seek, in these pages
or outside them.

May you find perfection, and know it
by name.

Lamb

Prologue

The angel was cleaning out his closets when the call came. Halos and moonbeams were sorted into piles according to brightness, satchels of wrath and scabbards of lightning hung on hooks waiting to be dusted. A wineskin of glory had leaked in the corner and the angel blotted it with a wad of fabric. Each time he turned the cloth a muted chorus rang from the closet, as if he'd clamped the lid down on a pickle jar full of Hallelujah Chorus.

"Raziel, what in heaven's name are you doing?"

The archangel Stephan was standing over him, brandishing a scroll like a rolled-up magazine over a piddling puppy.

"Orders?" the angel asked.

"Dirt-side."

"I was just there."

"Two millennia ago."

"Really?" Raziel checked his watch, then tapped the crystal. "Are you sure?"

"What do you think?" Stephan held out the scroll so Raziel could see the Burning Bush seal.

"When do I leave? I was almost finished here."

"Now. Pack the gift of tongues and some minor miracles. No weapons, it's not a wrath job. You'll be undercover. Very low profile, but important. It's all in the orders." Stephan handed him the scroll.

"Why me?"

"I asked that too."

"And?"

"I was reminded why angels are cast out."

"Whoa! That big?"

Stephan coughed, clearly an affectation, since angels didn't breathe. "I'm not sure I'm supposed to know, but the rumor is that it's a new book."

"You're kidding. A sequel? Revelation 2, just when you thought it was safe to sin?"

"It's a Gospel."

"A Gospel, after all this time? Who?"

"Levi who is called Biff."

Raziel dropped his rag and stood. "This has to be a mistake."

"It comes directly from the Son."

"There's a reason Biff isn't mentioned in the other books, you know? He's a total—"

"Don't say it."

"But he's such an asshole."

"You talk like that and you wonder why you get dirt-duty."

"Why now, after so long, the four Gospels have been fine so far, and why him?"

"Because it's some kind of anniversary in dirt-dweller time of the Son's birth, and he feels it's time the whole story is told."

Raziel hung his head. "I'd better pack."

"Gift of tongues," Stephan reminded.

"Of course, so I can take crap in a thousand languages."

"Go get the good news, Raziel. Bring me back some chocolate."

"Chocolate?"

"It's a dirt-dweller snack. You'll like it. Satan invented it."

"Devil's food?"

"You can only eat so much white cake, my friend."

Midnight. The angel stood on a barren hillside on the outskirts of the holy city of Jerusalem. He raised his arms aloft and a dry wind whipped his white robe around him.

"Arise, Levi who is called Biff."

A whirlwind formed before him, pulling dust from the hillside into a column that took the shape of a man.

"Arise, Biff. Your time has come."

The wind whipped into a fury and the angel pulled the sleeve of his robe across his face.

"Arise, Biff, and walk again among the living."

The whirlwind began to subside, leaving the man-shaped column of dust standing on the hillside. In moment, the hillside was calm again. The angel pulled a gold vessel from his satchel and poured it over the column. The dust washed away, leaving a muddy, naked man sputtering in the starlight.

"Welcome back to the living," the angel said.

The man blinked, then held his hand before his eyes as if he expected to see through it.

"I'm alive," he said in a language he had never heard before.

"Yes," the angel said.

"What are these sounds, these words?"

"You have been given the gift of tongues."

"I've always had the gift of tongues, ask any girl I've known. What are these words?"

"Languages. You've been given the gift of languages, as were all the apostles."

"Then the kingdom has come."

"Yes."

"How long?"

"Two thousand years ago."

"You worthless bag of dog shit," said Levi who was called Biff, as he punched the angel in the mouth. "You're late."

The angel picked himself up and gingerly touched his lip. "Nice talk to a messenger of the Lord."

"It's a gift," Biff said.

Part I

The Boy

God is a comedian playing to an audience that is afraid
to laugh.

VOLTAIRE

Chapter 1

You think you know how this story is going to end, but you don't. Trust me, I was there. I know.

The first time I saw the man who would save the world he was sitting near the central well in Nazareth with a lizard hanging out of his mouth. Just the tail end and the hind legs were visible on the outside; the head and forelegs were halfway down the hatch. He was six, like me, and his beard had not come in fully, so he didn't look much like the pictures you've seen of him. His eyes were like dark honey, and they smiled at me out of a mop of blue-black curls that framed his face. There was a light older than Moses in those eyes.

"Unclean! Unclean!" I screamed, pointing at the boy, so my mother would see that I knew the Law, but she ignored me, as did all the other mothers who were filling their jars at the well.

The boy took the lizard from his mouth and handed it to his younger brother, who sat beside him in the sand. The younger boy played with the lizard for a while, teasing it until it reared its little head as if to bite, then he picked up a rock and mashed the creature's head. Bewildered, he pushed the dead lizard around in the sand, and once assured that it wasn't going anywhere on its own, he picked it up and handed it back to his older brother.

Into his mouth went the lizard, and before I could accuse, out it came again, squirming and alive and ready to bite once again. He handed it back to his younger brother, who smote it mightily with the rock, starting or ending the whole process again.

I watched the lizard die three more times before I said, "I want to do that too."

The Savior removed the lizard from his mouth and said, "Which part?"

by the way, his name was Joshua. Jesus is the Greek translation of the Hebrew *Yeshua,* which is Joshua. Christ is not a last name. It's the Greek for *messiah,* a Hebrew word meaning anointed. I have no idea what the "H" in Jesus H. Christ stood for. It's one of the things I should have asked him.

Me? I am Levi who is called Biff. No middle initial.

Joshua was my best friend.

The angel says I'm supposed to just sit down and write my story, forget about what I've seen in this world, but how am I to do that? In the last three days I have seen more people, more images, more wonders, than in all my thirty-three years of living, and the angel asks me to ignore them. Yes, I have been given the gift of tongues, so I see nothing without knowing the word for it, but what good does that do? Did it help in Jerusalem to know that it was a Mercedes that terrified me and sent me diving into a Dumpster? Moreover, after Raziel pulled me out and ripped my fingernails back as I struggled to stay hidden, did it help to know that it was a Boeing 747 that made me cower in a ball trying to rock away my own tears and shut out the noise and fire? Am I a little child, afraid of its own shadow, or did I spend twenty-seven years at the side of the Son of God?

On the hill where he pulled me from the dust, the angel said, "You will see many strange things. Do not be afraid. You have a holy mission and I will protect you."

Smug bastard. Had I known what he would do to me I would have hit him again. Even now he lies on the bed across the room, watching pictures move on a screen, eating the sticky sweet called Snickers, while I scratch out my tale on this soft-as-silk paper that reads *Hyatt Regency, St. Louis* at the top. Words, words, words, a million million words circle in my head like hawks, waiting to dive onto the page to rend and tear the only two words I want to write.

Why me?

There were fifteen of us—well, fourteen after I hung Judas—so why me? Joshua always told me not to be afraid, for he would always be with me. Where are you, my friend? Why have you forsaken me? You wouldn't be afraid here. The towers and machines and the shine and stink of this world would not daunt you. Come now, I'll order a pizza from room service. You would like pizza. The servant who brings it is named Jesus. And he's not even a Jew. You always liked irony. Come, Joshua, the angel says you are yet with us, you can hold him down while I pound him, then we will rejoice in pizza.

Raziel has been looking at my writing and is insisting that I stop whining and get on with the story. Easy for him to say, he didn't just spend the last two thousand years buried in the dirt. Nevertheless, he won't let me order pizza until I finish a section, so here goes . . .

I was born in Galilee, the town of Nazareth, in the time of Herod the Great. My father, Alphaeus, was a stonemason and my mother, Naomi, was plagued by demons, or at least that's what I told everyone. Joshua seemed to think she was just difficult. My proper name, Levi, comes from the brother of Moses, the progenitor of the tribe of priests; my nickname, Biff, comes from our slang word for a smack upside the head, something that my mother said I required at least daily from an early age.

I grew up under Roman rule, although I didn't see many Romans until I was ten. The Romans mostly stayed in the fortress city of Sepphoris, an hour's walk north of Nazareth. That's where Joshua and I saw a Roman soldier murdered, but I'm getting ahead of myself. For now, assume that the soldier is safe and sound and happy wearing a broom on his head.

Most of the people of Nazareth were farmers, growing grapes and olives on the rocky hills outside of town and barley and wheat in the valleys below. There were also herders of goats and sheep whose families lived in town while the men and older boys tended the flocks in the highlands. Our houses were all made of stone, and ours had a stone floor, although many had floors of hard-packed dirt.

I was the oldest of three sons, so even at an the age of six I was being prepared to learn my father's trade. My mother taught my spoken lessons, the Law and stories from the Torah in Hebrew, and my father took me to the synagogue to hear the elders read the Bible. Aramaic was my first language, but by the time I was ten I could speak and read Hebrew as well as most of the men.

My ability to learn Hebrew and the Torah was spurred on by my friendship with Joshua, for while the other boys would be playing a round of tease the sheep or kick the Canaanite, Joshua and I played at being rabbis, and he insisted that we stick to the authentic Hebrew for our ceremonies. It was more fun than it sounds, or at least it was until my mother caught us trying to circumcise my little brother Shem with a sharp rock. What a fit she threw. And my argument that Shem needed to renew his covenant with the Lord didn't seem to convince her. She beat me to stripes with an olive switch and forbade me to play with Joshua for a month. Did I mention she was besought with demons?

Overall, I think it was good for little Shem. He was the only kid I ever knew who could pee around corners. You can make a pretty good living as a beggar with that kind of talent. And he never even thanked me.

Brothers.

Children see magic because they look for it.

When I first met Joshua, I didn't know he was the Savior, and neither did he, for that matter. What I knew was that he wasn't afraid. Amid a race of conquered warriors, a people who tried to find pride while cowering before God and Rome, he shone like a bloom in the desert. But maybe only I saw it, because I was looking for it. To everyone else he seemed like just another child: the same needs and the same chance to die before he was grown.

When I told my mother of Joshua's trick with the lizard she checked me for fever and sent me to my sleeping mat with only a bowl of broth for supper.

"I've heard stories about that boy's mother," she said to my father. "She claims to have spoken to an angel of the Lord. She told Esther that she had borne the Son of God."

"And what did you say to Esther?"

"That she should be careful that the Pharisees not hear her ravings or we'd be picking stones for her punishment."

"Then you should not speak of it again. I know her husband, he is a righteous man."

"Cursed with an insane girl for a wife."

"Poor thing," my father said, tearing away a hunk of bread. His hands were as hard as horn, as square as hammers, and as gray as a leper's from the limestone he worked with. An embrace from him left scratches on my back that sometimes wept blood, yet my brothers and I fought to be the first in his arms when he returned from work each evening. The same injuries inflicted in anger would have sent us crying to our mother's skirts. I fell asleep each night feeling his hand on my back like a shield.

Fathers.

Do you want to mash some lizards?" I asked Joshua when I saw him again. He was drawing in the dirt with a stick, ignoring me. I put my foot on his drawing. "Did you know that your mother is mad?"

"My father does that to her," he said sadly, without looking up.

I sat down next to him. "Sometimes my mother makes yipping noises in the night like the wild dogs."

"Is she mad?" Joshua asked.

"She seems fine in the morning. She sings while she makes breakfast."

Joshua nodded, satisfied, I guess, that madness could pass. "We used to live in Egypt," he said.

"No, you didn't, that's too far. Farther than the temple, even." The Temple in Jerusalem was the farthest place I had been as a child. Every spring my family took the five-day walk to Jerusalem for the feast of Passover. It seemed to take forever.

"We lived here, then we lived in Egypt, now we live here again," Joshua said. "It was a long way."

"You lie, it takes forty years to get to Egypt."

"Not anymore, it's closer now."

"It says in the Torah. My abba read it to me. 'The Israelites traveled in the desert for forty years.' "

"The Israelites were lost."

"For forty years?" I laughed. "The Israelites must be stupid."

"We are the Israelites."

"We are?"

"Yes."

"I have to go find my mother," I said.

"When you come back, let's play Moses and Pharaoh."

The angel has confided in me that he is going to ask the Lord if he can become Spider-Man. He watches the television constantly, even when I sleep, and he has become obsessed with the story of the hero who fights demons from the rooftops. The angel says that evil looms larger now than it did in my time, and that calls for greater heroes. The children need heroes, he says. I think he just wants to swing from buildings in tight red jammies.

What hero could touch these children anyway, with their machines and medicine and distances made invisible? (Raziel: not here a week and he would trade the Sword of God to be a web slinger.) In my time, our heroes were few, but they were real—some of us could even trace our kinship to them. Joshua always played the heroes—David, Joshua, Moses—while I played the evil ones: Pharaoh, Ahab, and Nebuchadnezzar. If I had a shekel for every time I was slain as a Philistine, well, I'd not be riding a camel through the eye of a needle anytime soon, I'll tell you that. As I think back, I see that Joshua was practicing for what he would become.

"Let my people go," said Joshua, as Moses.

"Okay."

"You can't just say, 'Okay.' "

"I can't?"

"No, the Lord has hardened your heart against my demands."

"Why'd he do that?"

"I don't know, he just did. Now, let my people go."

"Nope." I crossed my arms and turned away like someone whose heart is hardened.

"Behold as I turn this stick into a snake. Now, let my people go!"

"Okay."

"You can't just say 'okay'!"

"Why? That was a pretty good trick with the stick."

"But that's not how it goes."

"Okay. No way, Moses, your people have to stay."

Joshua waved his staff in my face. "Behold, I will plague you with frogs. They will fill your house and your bedchamber and get on your stuff."

"So?"

"So that's bad. Let my people go, Pharaoh."

"I sorta like frogs."

"Dead frogs," Moses threatened. "Piles of steaming, stinking dead frogs."

"Oh, in that case, you'd better take your people and go. I have some sphinxes and stuff to build anyway."

"Dammit, Biff, that's not how it goes! I have more plagues for you."

"I want to be Moses."

"You can't."

"Why not?"

"I have the stick."

"Oh."

And so it went. I'm not sure I took to playing the villains as easily as Joshua took to being the heroes. Sometimes we recruited our little brothers to play the more loathsome parts. Joshua's little brothers Judah and James played whole populations, like the Sodomites outside of Lot's door.

"Send out those two angels so that we can know them."

"I won't do that," I said, playing Lot (a good guy only because Joshua wanted to play the angels), "but I have two daughters who don't know anyone, you can meet them."

"Okay," said Judah.

I threw open the door and led my imaginary daughters outside so they could know the Sodomites . . .

"Pleased to meet you."

"Charmed, I'm sure."

"Nice to meet you."

"THAT'S NOT HOW IT GOES!" Joshua shouted. "You're supposed to try to break the door down, then I will smite you blind."

"Then you destroy our city?" James said.

"Yes."

"We'd rather meet Lot's daughters."

"Let my people go," said Judah, who was only four and often got his stories confused. He particularly liked the Exodus because he and James got to throw jars of water on me as I led my soldiers across the Red Sea after Moses.

"That's it," Joshua said. "Judah, you're Lot's wife. Go stand over there."

Sometimes Judah had to play Lot's wife no matter what story we were doing. "I don't want to be Lot's wife."

"Be quiet, pillars of salt can't talk."

"I don't want to be a girl."

Our brothers always played the female parts. I had no sisters to torment, and Joshua's only sister at the time, Elizabeth, was still a baby. That was before we met the Magdalene. The Magdalene changed everything.

After I overheard my parents talking about Joshua's mother's madness, I often watched her, looking for signs, but she seemed to go about her duties like all the other mothers, tending to the little ones, working in the garden, fetching water, and preparing food. There was no sign of going about on all fours or foaming at the mouth as I had expected. She was younger than many of the mothers, and much younger than her husband, Joseph, who was an old man by the standards of our time. Joshua said that Joseph wasn't his real father, but he wouldn't say who his father was. When the subject came up, and Mary was in earshot, she would call to Josh, then put her finger to her lips to signal silence.

"Now is not the time, Joshua. Biff would not understand."

Just hearing her say my name made my heart leap. Early on I developed a little-boy love for Joshua's mother that sent me into fantasies of marriage and family and future.

"Your father is old, huh, Josh?"

"Not too old."

"When he dies, will your mother marry his brother?"

"My father has no brothers. Why?"

"No reason. What would you think if your father was shorter than you?"

"He isn't."

"But when your father dies, your mother could marry someone shorter than you, and he would be your father. You would have to do what he says."

"My father will never die. He is eternal."

"So you say. But I think that when I'm a man, and your father dies, I will take your mother as my wife."

Joshua made a face now as if he had bitten into an unripe fig. "Don't say that, Biff."

"I don't mind that she's mad. I like her blue cloak. And her smile. I'll be a good father, I'll teach you how to be a stonemason, and I'll only beat you when you are a snot."

"I would rather play with lepers than listen to this." Joshua began to walk away.

"Wait. Be nice to your father, Joshua bar Biff"—my own father used my full name like this when he was trying to make a point—"Is it not the word of Moses that you must honor me?"

Little Joshua spun on his heel. "My name is not Joshua bar Biff, and it is not Joshua bar Joseph either. It's Joshua bar Jehovah!"

I looked around, hoping that no one had heard him. I didn't want my only son (I planned to sell Judah and James into slavery) to be stoned to death for uttering the name of God in vain. "Don't say that again, Josh. I won't marry your mother."

"No, you won't."

"I'm sorry."

"I forgive you."

"She will make an excellent concubine."

Don't let anyone tell you that the Prince of Peace never struck anyone. In those early days, before he had become who he would be, Joshua smote me in the nose more than once. That was the first time.

Mary would stay my one true love until I saw the Magdalene.

If the people of Nazareth thought Joshua's mother was mad, there was little said of it out of respect for her husband, Joseph. He was wise in the Law, the Prophets, and the Psalms, and there were few wives in Nazareth who didn't serve supper in one of his smooth olive-wood bowls. He was fair, strong, and wise. People said that he had once been an Essene, one of the dour, ascetic Jews who kept to themselves and never married or cut their hair, but he did not congregate with them, and unlike them, he still had the ability to smile.

In those early years, I saw him very little, as he was always in Sepphoris, building structures for the Romans and the Greeks and the landed Jews of that city, but every year, as the Feast of Firsts approached, Joseph would stop his work in the fortress city and stay home carving bowls and spoons to give to the Temple. During the Feast of Firsts, it was the tradition to give first lambs, first grain, and first fruits to the priests of the Temple. Even first sons born during the year were dedicated to the Temple, either by promising them for labor when they were older, or by a gift of money. Craftsmen like my father and Joseph could give things that they made, and in some years my father fashioned mortars and pestles or grinding stones for the tribute, while in others he gave tithes of coin. Some people made the pilgrimage to Jerusalem for this feast, but since it fell only seven weeks after Passover, many families could not afford to make the pilgrimage, and the gifts went to our simple village synagogue.

During the weeks leading up to the feast, Joseph sat outside of his house in the shade of an awning he had made, worrying the gnarled olive wood with adze and chisel, while Joshua and I played at his feet. He wore the single-piece tunic that we all wore, a rectangle of fabric with neck hole in the middle, belted with a sash so that the sleeves fell to the elbows and the hem fell to the knees.

"Perhaps this year I should give the Temple my first son, eh, Joshua? Wouldn't you like to clean the altar after the sacrifices?" He grinned to himself without looking up from his work. "I owe them a first son, you know. We were in Egypt at the Firsts Feast when you were born."

The idea of coming in contact with blood clearly terrified Joshua, as it would any Jewish boy. "Give them James, Abba, he is your first son."

Joseph shot a glance my way, to see if I had reacted. I had, but it was because I was considering my own status as a first son, hoping that my father wasn't thinking along the same lines. "James is a second son. The priests don't want second sons. It will have to be you."

Joshua looked at me before he answered, then back at his father. Then he smiled. "But Abba, if you should die, who will take care of Mother if I am at the Temple?"

"Someone will look after her," I said. "I'm sure of it."

"I will not die for a long time." Joseph tugged at his gray beard. "My beard goes white, but there's a lot of life in me yet."

"Don't be so sure, Abba," Joshua said.

Joseph dropped the bowl he was working on and stared into his hands. "Run along and play, you two," he said, his voice little more than a whisper.

Joshua stood and walked away. I wanted to throw my arms around the old man, for I had never seen a grown man afraid before and it frightened me too. "Can I help?" I said, pointing to the half-finished bowl that lay in Joseph's lap.

"You go with Joshua. He needs a friend to teach him to be human. Then I can teach him to be a man."

Chapter 2

The angel wants me to convey more of Joshua's grace. Grace? I'm trying to write about a six-year-old, for Christ's sakes, how much grace could he have? It's not like Joshua walked around professing that he was the Son of God every day of the week. He was a pretty normal kid, for the most part. There was the trick he did with the lizards, and once we found a dead meadowlark and he brought it back to life, and there was the time, when we were eight, when he healed his brother Judah's fractured skull after a game of "stone the adulteress" got out of hand. (Judah could never get the knack of being an adulteress. He'd stand there stiff as Lot's wife. You can't do that. An adulteress has to be wily and nimble-footed.) The miracles Joshua performed were small and quiet, as miracles tend to be, once you get used to them. But trouble came from the miracles that happened around him, without his volition, as it were. Bread and serpents come to mind.

It was a few days before the Passover feast, and many of the families of Nazareth were not making the pilgrimage to Jerusalem that year. There had been little rain through our winter season, so it was going to be a hard year. Many farmers could not afford the time away from their fields to travel to and from the holy city. My father and Joshua's were both working in Sepphoris, and the Romans wouldn't give them time off work beyond the actual feast days. My mother had been making the unleavened bread when I came in from playing in the square.

She held a dozen sheets of the flatbread before her and she

looked as if she was going to dash it to the floor any second. "Biff, where is your friend Joshua?" My little brothers grinned at me from behind her skirts.

"At home, I suppose. I just left him."

"What have you boys been doing?"

"Nothing." I tried to remember if I had done anything that should make her this angry, but nothing came to mind. It was a rare day and I'd made no trouble. Both my little brothers were unscathed as far as I knew.

"What have you done to cause this?" She held out a sheet of the flatbread, and there, in crispy brown relief on the golden crust, was the image of my friend Joshua's face. She snatched up another sheet of bread, and there, again, was my friend Josh. Graven images—big sin. Josh was smiling. Mother frowned on smiling. "Well? Do I need to go to Joshua's house and ask his poor, insane mother?"

"I did this. I put Joshua's face on the bread." I just hoped that she didn't ask me how I had done it.

"Your father will punish you when he comes home this evening. Now go, get out of here."

I could hear my little brother's giggling as I slunk out the door, but once outside, things worsened. Women were coming away from their baking stones, and each held a sheet of unleavened bread, and each was muttering some variation of "Hey, there's a kid on my bread."

I ran to Joshua's house and stormed in without knocking. Joshua and his brothers were at the table eating. Mary was nursing Joshua's newest little sister, Miriam.

"You are in big trouble," I whispered in Josh's ear with enough force to blow out an eardrum.

Joshua held up the flatbread he was eating and grinned, just like the face on his bread. "It's a miracle."

"Tastes good too," said James, crunching a corner off of his brother's head.

"It's all over town, Joshua. Not just your house. Everyone's bread has your face on it."

"He is truly the Son of God," Mary said with a beatific smile.

"Oh, jeez, Mother," James said.

"Yeah, jeez Mom," said Judah.

"His mug is all over the Passover feast. We have to do something." They didn't seem to get the gravity of the situation. I was already in trouble, and my mother didn't even suspect anything supernatural. "We have to cut your hair."

"What?"

"We cannot cut his hair," Mary said. She had always let Joshua wear his hair long, like an Essene, saying that he was a Nazarite like Samson. It was just another reason why many of the townspeople thought her mad. The rest of us wore our hair cut short, like the Greeks who had ruled our country since the time of Alexander, and the Romans after them.

"If we cut his hair he looks like the rest of us. We can say it's someone else on the bread."

"Moses," Mary said. "Young Moses."

"Yes!"

"I'll get a knife."

"James, Judah, come with me," I said. "We have to tell the town that the face of Moses has come to visit us for the Passover feast."

Mary pulled Miriam from her breast, bent, and kissed me on the forehead. "You are a good friend, Biff."

I almost melted in my sandals, but I caught Joshua frowning at me. "It's not the truth," he said.

"It will keep the Pharisees from judging you."

"I'm not afraid of them," said the nine-year-old. "I didn't do this to the bread."

"Then why take the blame and the punishment for it?"

"I don't know, seems like I should, doesn't it?"

"Sit still so your mother can cut your hair." I dashed out the door, Judah and James on my heels, the three of us bleating like spring lambs.

"Behold! Moses has put his face on the bread for Passover! Behold!"

Miracles. She kissed me. Holy Moses on a matzo! She kissed me.

The miracle of the serpent? It was an omen, in a way, although I can only say that because of what happened between Joshua and the Pharisees later on. At the time, Joshua thought it was the fulfillment of a prophecy, or that's how we tried to sell it to his mother and father.

It was late summer and we were playing in a wheat field outside of town when Joshua found the nest of vipers.

"A nest of vipers," Joshua shouted. The wheat was so tall I couldn't see where he was calling from.

"A pox on your family," I replied.

"No, there's a nest of vipers over here. Really."

"Oh, I thought you were taunting me. Sorry, a pox off of your family."

"Come, see."

I crashed through the wheat to find Joshua standing by a pile of stones a farmer had used to mark the boundary of his field. I screamed and backpedaled so quickly that I lost my balance and fell. A knot of snakes writhed at Joshua's feet, skating over his sandals and wrapping themselves around his ankles. "Joshua, get away from there."

"They won't hurt me. It says so in Isaiah."

"Just in case they haven't read the Prophets . . ."

Joshua stepped aside, sending the snakes scattering, and there, behind him, was the biggest cobra I had ever seen. It reared up until it was taller than my friend, spreading a hood like a cloak.

"Run, Joshua."

He smiled. "I'm going to call her Sarah, after Abraham's wife. These are her children."

"No kidding? Say good-bye now, Josh."

"I want to show mother. She loves prophecy." With that, he was off toward the village, the giant serpent following him like a shadow. The baby snakes stayed in the nest and I backed slowly away before running after my friend.

I once brought a frog home, hoping to keep him as a pet. Not a large frog, a one-handed frog, quiet and well mannered. My mother made me release him, then cleanse myself in the immersion pool (the mikveh) at the synagogue. Still she wouldn't let me in the house until after sunset because I was unclean. Joshua led a fourteen-foot-long cobra into his house and his mother squealed with joy. My mother never squealed.

ℳary slung the baby to her hip, kneeled in front of her son, and quoted Isaiah: " 'The wolf also shall dwell with the lamb, and the leopard shall lie down with the kid; and the calf and the young lion and the fatling together; and a little child shall lead them. And the cow and the bear shall feed; their young ones shall lie down together: and the lion shall eat straw like the ox. And the sucking child shall play on the hole of the asp, and the weaned child shall put his hand on the cockatrice's den.' "

James, Judah, and Elizabeth cowered in the corner, too frightened to cry. I stood outside the doorway watching.

The snake swayed behind Joshua as if preparing to strike. "Her name is Sarah."

"They were cobras, not asps," I said. "A whole pile of cobras."

"Can we keep her?" Joshua asked. "I'll catch rats for her, and make a bed for her next to Elizabeth's."

"Definitely not asps. I'd know an asp if I saw one. Probably not a cockatrice either. I'd say a cobra." (Actually, I didn't know an asp from a hole in the ground.)

"Shush, Biff," Mary said. My heart broke with the harshness in my love's voice.

Just then Joseph rounded the corner and went through he door before I could catch him. No worry, he was back outside in an instant. "Jumpin' Jehoshaphat!"

I checked to see if Joseph's heart had failed, having quickly decided that once Mary and I were married the snake would have to go, or at least sleep outside, but the burly carpenter seemed only shaken, and a little dusty from his backward dive through the door.

"Not an asp, right?" I asked. "Asps are made small to fit the breasts of Egyptian queens, right?"

Joseph ignored me. "Back away slowly, son. I'll get a knife from my workshop."

"She won't hurt us," Joshua said. "Her name is Sarah. She's from Isaiah."

"It is in the prophecy, Joseph," Mary said.

I could see Joseph searching his memory for the passage. Although only a layman, he knew his scripture as well as anyone. "I don't remember the part about Sarah."

"I don't think it's prophecy," I offered. "It says asps, and that is definitely not an asp. I'd say she's going to bite Joshua's ass off if you don't grab her, Joseph." (A guy has to try.)

"Can I keep her?" Joshua asked.

Joseph had regained his composure by now. Evidently, once you accept that your wife slept with God, extraordinary events seem sort of commonplace.

"Take her back where you found her, Joshua, the prophecy has been fulfilled now."

"But I want to keep her."

"No, Joshua."

"You're not the boss of me."

I suspected that Joseph had heard that before. "Just so," he said, "please take Sarah back where you found her."

Joshua stormed out of the house, his snake following close behind. Joseph and I gave them a wide berth. "Try not to let anyone see you," Joseph said. "They won't understand."

He was right, of course. On our way out of the village we ran into a gang of older boys, led by Jakan, the son of Iban the Pharisee. They did not understand.

There were perhaps a dozen Pharisees in Nazareth: learned men, working-class teachers, who spent much of their time at the synagogue debating the Law. They were often hired as judges and scribes, and this gave them great influence over the people of the village. So much influence, in fact, that the Romans often used them as mouthpieces to our people. With influence comes power, with power, abuse. Jakan was only the son of a Pharisee. He was only two years older than Joshua and me, but he was well on his way to mastering cruelty. If there is a single joy in having everyone you have ever known two thousand years dead, it is that Jakan is one of them. May his fat crackle in the fires of hell for eternity!

Joshua taught us that we should not hate—a lesson that I was never able to master, along with geometry. Blame Jakan for the former, Euclid for the latter.

Joshua ran behind the houses and shops of the village, the snake behind him by ten steps, and me behind her ten steps more. As he rounded the corner by the smith's shop, Joshua ran into Jakan, knocking him to the ground.

"You idiot!" Jakan shouted, rising and dusting himself off. His three friends laughed and he spun on them like an angry tiger. "This one needs to have his face washed in dung. Hold him."

The boys turned their focus on Joshua, two grabbing his arms while the third punched him in the stomach. Jakan turned to look for a pile to rub Joshua's face in. Sarah slithered around the corner and reared up behind Joshua, spreading her glorious hood wide above our heads.

"Hey," I called as I rounded the corner. "You guys think this is an asp?" My fear of the snake had changed into a sort of wary affection. She seemed to be smiling. I know I was. Sarah swayed from side to side like a wheat stalk in the wind. The boys dropped Joshua's arms and ran to Jakan, who had turned and slowly backed away.

"Joshua was talking about asps," I continued, "but I'd have to say that this here is a cobra."

Joshua was bent over, still trying to catch his breath, but he looked back at me and grinned.

"Of course, I'm not the son of a Pharisee, but—"

"He's in league with the serpent!" Jakan screamed. "He consorts with demons!"

"Demons!" the other boys shouted, trying to crowd behind their fat friend.

"I will tell my father of this and you'll be stoned."

A voice from behind Jakan said, "What is all this shouting?" And a sweet voice it was.

She came out of the house by the smith's shop. Her skin shone like copper and she had the light blue eyes of the northern desert people. Wisps of reddish-brown hair showed at the edges of her purple shawl. She couldn't have been more than nine or ten, but there was something very old in her eyes. I stopped breathing when I saw her.

Jakan puffed up like a toad. "Stay back. These two are consorting with a demon. I will tell the elders and they will be judged."

She spit at his feet. I had never seen a girl spit before. It was charming. "It looks like a cobra to me."

"See there, I told you."

She walked up to Sarah as if she were approaching a fig tree looking for fruit, not a hint of fear, only interest. "You think this is a demon?" she said, without looking back at Jakan. "Won't you be embarrassed when the elders find that you mistook a common snake of the field for a demon?"

"It *is* a demon."

The girl reached her hand up, and the snake made as if to strike, then lowered its head until its forked tongue was brushing the girl's fingers. "This is definitely a cobra, little boy. And these two were probably leading it back to the fields where it would help the farmers by eating rats."

"Yep, that's what we were doing," I said.

"Absolutely," Joshua said.

The girl turned to Jakan and his friends. "A demon?"

Jakan stomped like an angry donkey. "You are in league with them."

"Don't be silly, my family has only just arrived from Magdala, I've never seen these two before, but it's obvious what they were doing. We do it all the time in Magdala. But then, this is a backwater village."

"We do it here too," Jakan said. "I was—well—these two make trouble."

"Trouble," his friends said.

"Why don't we let them get on with what they were doing."

Jakan, his eyes bouncing from the girl to the snake to the girl again, began to lead his friends away. "I will deal with you two another time."

As soon as they were around the corner, the girl jumped back from the snake and ran toward the door of her house.

"Wait," Joshua called.

"I have to go."

"What is your name?"

"I'm Mary of Magdala, daughter of Isaac," she said. "Call me Maggie."

"Come with us, Maggie."

"I can't, I have to go."

"Why?"

"Because I've peed myself."

She disappeared through the door.

Miracles.

Once we were back in the wheat field Sarah headed for her den. We watched from a distance as she slid down the hole.

"Josh. How did you do that?"

"I have no idea."

"Is this kind of thing going to keep happening?"

"Probably."

"We are going to get into a lot of trouble, aren't we?"

"What am I, a prophet?"

"I asked you first."

Joshua stared into the sky like a man in a trance. "Did you see her? She's afraid of nothing."

"She's a giant snake, what's to be afraid of?"

Joshua frowned. "Don't pretend to be simple, Biff. We were saved by a serpent and a girl, I don't know what to think about that."

"Why think about it at all? It just happened."

"Nothing happens but by God's will," Joshua said. "It doesn't fit with the testament of Moses."

"Maybe it's a new testament," I said.

"You aren't pretending, are you?" Joshua said. "You really are simple."

"I think she likes you better than she likes me," I said.

"The snake?"

"Right, I'm the simple one."

I don't know if now, having lived and died the life of a man, I can write about little-boy love, but remembering it now, it seems the cleanest pain I've known.

Love without desire, or conditions, or limits—a pure and radiant glow in the heart that could make me giddy and sad and glorious all at once. Where does it go? Why, in all their experiments, did the Magi never try to capture that purity in a bottle? Perhaps they couldn't. Perhaps it is lost to us when we become sexual creatures, and no magic can bring it back. Perhaps I only remember it because I spent so long trying to understand the love that Joshua felt for everyone.

In the East they taught us that all suffering comes from desire, and that rough beast would stalk me through my life, but on that afternoon, and for a time after, I touched grace. At night I would lie awake, listening to my brothers' breathing against the silence of the house, and in my mind's eye I could see her eyes like blue fire in the dark. Exquisite torture. I wonder now if Joshua didn't make her whole life like that. Maggie, she was the strongest of us all.

After the miracle of the serpent, Joshua and I made up excuses to pass by the smith's shop where we might run into Maggie. Every morning we would rise early and go to Joseph, volunteering to run to the smith for some nails or the repair of a tool. Poor Joseph took this as enthusiasm for carpentry.

"Would you boys like to come to Sepphoris with me tomorrow?" Joseph asked us one day when we were badgering him about fetching nails. "Biff, would your father let you start learning the work of a carpenter?"

I was mortified. At ten a boy was expected to start learning his father's trade, but that was a year away—forever when you're nine. "I—I am still thinking about what I will do when I grow up," I said. My own father had made a similar offer to Joshua the day before.

"So you won't become a stonecutter?"

"I was thinking about becoming the village idiot, if my father will allow it."

"He has a God-given talent," Joshua said.

"I've been talking to Bartholomew the idiot," I said. "He's going to teach me to fling my own dung and run headlong into walls."

Joseph scowled at me. "Perhaps you two *are* yet too young. Next year."

"Yes," Joshua said, "next year. May we go now, Joseph? Biff is meeting Bartholomew for his lesson."

Joseph nodded and we were off before he inflicted more kindness upon us. We actually had befriended Bartholomew, the village idiot. He was foul and drooled a lot, but he was large, and offered some protection against Jakan and his bullies. Bart also spent most of his time begging near the town square, where the women came to fetch water from the well. From time to time we caught a glimpse of Maggie as she passed, a water jar balanced on her head.

"You know, we are going to have to start working soon," Joshua said. "I won't see you, once I'm working with my father."

"Joshua, look around you, do you see any trees?"

"No."

"And the trees we do have, olive trees—twisted, gnarly, knotty things, right?"

"Right."

"But you're going to be a carpenter like your father?"

"There's a chance of it."

"One word, Josh: rocks."

"Rocks?"

"Look around. Rocks as far as the eye can see. Galilee is nothing but rocks, dirt, and more rocks. Be a stonemason like me and my father. We can build cities for the Romans."

"Actually, I was thinking about saving mankind."

"Forget that nonsense, Josh. Rocks, I tell you."

Chapter 3

The angel will tell me nothing of what happened to my friends, of the twelve, of Maggie. All he'll say is that they are dead and that I have to write my own version of the story. Oh, he'll tell me useless angel stories—of how Gabriel disappeared once for sixty years and they found him on earth hiding in the body of a man named Miles Davis, or how Raphael snuck out of heaven to visit Satan and returned with something called a cell phone. (Evidently everyone has them in hell now.) He watches the television and when they show an earthquake or a tornado he'll say, "I destroyed a city with one of those once. Mine was better." I am awash in useless angel prattle, but about my own time I know nothing but what I saw. And when the television makes mention of Joshua, calling him by his Greek name, Raziel changes the channel before I can learn anything.

He never sleeps. He just watches me, watches the television, and eats. He never leaves the room.

Today, while searching for extra towels, I opened one of the drawers and there, beneath a plastic bag meant for laundry, I found a book: *Holy Bible,* it said on the cover. Thank the Lord I did not take the book from the drawer, but opened it with my back to the angel. There are chapters there that were in no Bible I know. I saw the names of Matthew and John, I saw Romans and Galatians—this is a book of my time.

"What are you doing?" the angel asked.

I covered the Bible and closed the drawer. "Looking for towels. I need to bathe."

"You bathed yesterday."

"Cleanliness is important to my people."

"I know that. What, you think I don't know that?"

"You're not exactly the brightest halo in the bunch."

"Then bathe. And stand away from the television."

"Why don't you go get me some towels?"

"I'll call down to the desk."

And he did. If I am to get a look at that book, I must get the angel to leave the room.

It came to pass that in the village of Japhia, the sister village of Nazareth, that Esther, the mother of one of the priests of the Temple, died of bad air. The Levite priests, or Sadducees, were rich from the tributes we paid to the Temple, and mourners were hired from all the surrounding villages. The families of Nazareth made the journey to the next hill for the funeral, and for the first time, Joshua and I were able to spend time with Maggie as we walked along the road.

"So," she said without looking at us, "have you two been playing with any snakes lately?"

"We've been waiting for the lion to lay down with the lamb," Joshua said. "That's the next part of the prophecy."

"What prophecy?"

"Never mind," I said. "Snakes are for boys. We are almost men. We will begin work after the Feast of Tabernacles. In Sepphoris." I was trying to sound worldly. Maggie seemed unimpressed.

"And you will learn to be a carpenter?" she asked Joshua.

"I will do the work of my father, eventually, yes."

"And you?" she asked me.

"I'm thinking of being a professional mourner. How hard can it be? Tear at your hair, sing a dirge or two, take the rest of the week off."

"His father is a stonemason," Joshua said. "We may both learn that skill." At my urging, my father had offered to take Joshua on as an apprentice if Joseph approved.

"Or a shepherd," I added quickly. "Being a shepherd seems easy. I went with Kaliel last week to tend his flock. The Law says that two must go with the flock to keep an abomination from happening. I can spot an abomination from fifty paces."

Maggie smiled. "And did you prevent any abominations?"

"Oh yes, I kept all of the abominations at bay while Kaliel played with his favorite sheep behind the bushes."

"Biff," Joshua said gravely, "that was the abomination you were supposed to prevent."

"It was?"

"Yes."

"Whoops. Oh well, I think I would make an excellent mourner. Do you know the words to any dirges, Maggie? I'm going to need to learn some dirges."

"I think that when I grow up," Maggie announced, "I shall go back to Magdala and become a fisherman on the Sea of Galilee."

I laughed, "Don't be silly, you are a girl. You can't be a fisherman."

"Yes I can."

"No, you can't. You have to marry and have sons. Are you betrothed, by the way?"

Joshua said: "Come with me, Maggie, and I will make you a fisher of men."

"What the hell does that mean?" Maggie asked.

I grabbed Joshua by the back of his robe and began to drag him away. "Don't pay any attention to him. He's mad. He gets it from his mother. Lovely woman, but a loony. Come now, Josh, let's sing a dirge."

I began improvising what I thought was a good funeral song.

"*La-la-la. Oh, we are really, really sad that your mom is dead. Too bad you're a Sadducee and don't believe in an afterlife and your mom is just going to be worm food, la-la. Makes you think that you might want to reconsider, huh? Fa-la-la-la-la-la-wacka-wacka.*" (It sounded great in Aramaic. Really.)

"You two are silly."

"Gotta go. Mourning to do. See you."

"A fisher of women?" Josh said.

"*Fa-la-la-la, don't feel bad—she was old and had no teeth left, la-la-la.* Come on, people, you know the words!"

Later, I said, "Josh, you can't keep saying creepy things like that. 'Fisher of men,' you want the Pharisees to stone you? Is that what you want?"

"I'm only doing my father's work. Besides, Maggie is our friend, she wouldn't say anything."

"You're going to scare her away."

"No I won't. She's going to be with us, Biff."

"Are you going to marry her?"

"I don't even know if I'm allowed to marry at all, Biff. Look."

We were topping the hill into Japhia, and we could see the crowd of mourners gathering around the village. Joshua was pointing to a red crest that stood out above the crowd—the helmet crest of a Roman centurion. The centurion was talking to the Levite priest, who was arrayed in white and gold, his white beard reaching past his belt. As we moved into the village we could see twenty or thirty other soldiers watching the crowd.

"Why are they here?"

"They don't like it when we gather," Joshua said, pausing to study the centurion commander. "They are here to see that we don't revolt."

"Why is the priest talking to him?"

"The Sadducee wants to assure the Roman of his influence over us. It wouldn't do to have a massacre on the day of his mother's funeral."

"So he's watching out for us."

"He's watching out for himself. Only for himself."

"You shouldn't say that about a priest of the Temple, Joshua." It was the first time I ever heard Joshua speak against the Sadducees, and it frightened me.

"Today, I think this priest will learn who the Temple belongs to."

"I hate it when you talk like that, Josh. Maybe we should go home."

"Do you remember the dead meadowlark we found?"

"I have a really bad feeling about this."

Joshua grinned at me. I could see gold flecks shining in his eyes. "Sing your dirge, Biff. I think Maggie was impressed by your singing."

"Really? You think so?"

"Nope."

There was a crowd of five hundred outside the tomb. In the front, the men had draped striped shawls over their heads and rocked as they prayed. The women were separated to the back, and except for the wailing of the hired mourners, it was as if they didn't exist. I tried to catch a glimpse of Maggie, but couldn't see her through the crowd. When I turned again, Joshua had wormed his way to the front of the men, where the Sadducee stood beside the corpse of his dead mother, reading from a scroll of the Torah.

The women had wrapped the corpse in linen and anointed it with fragrant oils. I could smell sandalwood and jasmine amid the acrid sweat of the mourners as I made my way to the front and stood by Joshua. He looked past the priest and was staring at the corpse, his eyes narrowed in concentration. He was trembling as if taken by a chill wind.

The priest finished his reading and began to sing, joined by the voices of hired singers who had made the journey all the way from the Temple in Jerusalem.

"It's good to be rich, huh?" I whispered to Joshua, elbowing him in the ribs.

He ignored me and balled up his fists at his sides. A vein stood out on his forehead as he burned his gaze on the corpse.

And she moved.

Just a twitch at first. The jerk of her hand under the linen shroud. I think I was the only one who noticed. "No, Joshua, don't," I said.

I looked for the Romans, who were gathered in groups of five at different points around the perimeter of the crowd looking bored, their hands resting on the hilts of their short swords.

The corpse twitched again and raised her arm. There was a gasp in the crowd and a boy screamed. The men started backing away and the women pushed forward to see what was happening. Joshua fell to his knees and pressed his fists to his temples. The priest sang on.

The corpse sat up.

The singers stopped and finally the priest turned to look behind him at his dead mother, who had swung her legs off of the slab and looked as if she was trying to stand. The priest stumbled back into the crowd, clawing at the air before his eyes as if it some vapor was causing this horrible vision.

Joshua was rocking on his knees, tears streaming down his cheeks. The corpse stood, and still covered by the shroud, turned as if she was looking around. I could see that several of the Romans had drawn their swords. I looked around and found the commanding centurion standing on the back of a wagon, giving signals to his men to stay calm. When I looked back I realized that Joshua and I had been deserted by the mourners and we stood out in the empty space.

"Stop it, now, Josh," I whispered in his ear, but he continued to rock and concentrate on the corpse, who took her first step.

The crowd seemed to be transfixed by the walking corpse, but we were too isolated, too alone now with the dead, and I knew it would only be seconds before they noticed Joshua rocking in the dirt. I threw my arm around his throat and dragged him back away from the corpse and into a group of men who were wailing as they backed away.

"Is he all right?" I heard at my ear, and turned to see Maggie standing beside me.

"Help me get him away."

Maggie took one of Joshua's arms and I took the other as we dragged him away. His body was as stiff as a walking staff, and he kept his gazed trained on the corpse.

The dead woman was walking toward her son, the priest, who was backing away, brandishing the scroll like a sword, his eyes as big as saucers.

Finally the woman fell in the dirt, twitched, then lay still. Joshua went limp in our arms.

"Let's get him out of here," I said to Maggie. She nodded and helped me drag him behind the wagon where the centurion was directing his troops.

"Is he dead?" the centurion asked.

Joshua was blinking as if he'd just been awakened from a deep sleep. "We're never sure, sir," I said.

The centurion threw his head back and laughed. His scale armor rattled with the tossing of his shoulders. He was older than the other soldiers, gray-haired, but obviously lean and strong, and totally unconcerned with the histrionics of the crowd. "Good answer, boy. What is your name?"

"Biff, sir. Levi bar Alphaeus, who is called Biff, sir. Of Nazareth."

"Well, Biff, I am Gaius Justus Gallicus, under-commander of Sepphoris, and I think that you Jews should make sure your dead are dead before you bury them."

"Yes sir," I said.

"You, girl. You are a pretty little thing. What is your name?"

I could see that Maggie was shaken by the attention of the Roman. "I am Mary of Magdala, sir." She wiped at Joshua's brow with the edge of her shawl as she spoke.

"You will break someone's heart someday, eh, little one?"

Maggie didn't answer. But I must have shown some reaction to the question, because Justus laughed again. "Or perhaps she already has, eh, Biff?"

"It is our way, sir. That's why we Jews bury our women when they are still alive. It cuts down on the heartbreak."

The Roman took off his helmet, ran his hand over his short hair, and flung sweat at me. "Go on, you two, get your friend into the shade. It's too hot out here for a sick boy. Go on."

Maggie and I helped Joshua to his feet and began to lead him away, but when we had gone only a few steps, Joshua stopped and looked back over his shoulder at the Roman. "Will you slay my people if we follow our God?" he shouted.

I cuffed him on the back of the head. "Joshua, are you insane?"

Justus narrowed his gaze at Joshua and the smile went out of his eyes. "Whatever they tell you, boy, Rome has only two rules: pay your taxes and don't rebel. Follow those and you'll stay alive."

Maggie yanked Joshua around and smiled back at the Roman. "Thank you, sir, we'll get him out of the sun." Then she turned back to Joshua. "Is there something you two would like to tell me?"

"It's not me," I said. "It's him."

the next day we met the angel for the first time. Mary and Joseph said that Joshua had left the house at dawn and they hadn't seen him since. I wandered around the village most of the morning, looking for Joshua and hoping to run into Maggie. The square was alive with talk of the walking dead woman, but neither of my friends was to be found. At noon my mother recruited me to watch my little brothers while she went to work with the other women in the vineyard. She returned at dusk, smelling of sweat and sweet wine, her feet purple from walking in the winepress. Cut loose, I ran all over the hilltop, checking in our favorite places to play, and finally found Joshua on his knees in an olive grove, rocking back and forth as he prayed. He was soaked in sweat and I was afraid he might have a fever. Strange, I never felt that sort of concern for my own brothers, but from the beginning, Joshua filled me with divinely inspired worry.

I watched, and waited, and when he stopped his rocking and sat back to rest, I faked a cough to let him know I was coming.

"Maybe you should stick with lizards for a while longer."

"I failed. I have disappointed my father."

"Did he tell you that, or do you just know it?"

He thought for a moment, made as if to brush his hair away from his face, then remembered that he no longer wore his hair long and dropped his hands in his lap. "I ask for guidance, but I get no answer. I can feel that I am supposed to do things, but I don't know what. And I don't know how."

"I don't know, I think the priest was surprised. I certainly was. Maggie was. People will be talking about it for months."

"But I wanted the woman to live again. To walk among us. To tell of the miracle."

"Well, it is written, two out of three ain't bad."

"Where is that written?"

"Dalmatians 9:7, I think—doesn't matter, no one else could have done what you did."

Joshua nodded. "What are people saying?"

"They think that it was something the women used to prepare the corpse. They are still going through purification for two more days, so no one can ask them."

"So they don't know that it was me?"

"I hope not. Joshua, don't you understand that you can't do that sort of thing in front of people? They aren't ready for it."

"But most of them want it. They talk about the Messiah coming to deliver us all the time. Don't I have to show them that he has come?"

What do you say to that? He was right, since I could remember there was always talk of the coming of the Messiah, of the coming of the kingdom of God, of the liberation of our people from the Romans—the hills were full of different factions of Zealots who skirmished with the Romans in hope that they could bring about the change. We were the chosen of God, blessed and punished like no other on earth. When the Jews spoke, God listened, now it was God's turn to speak. Evidently, my best friend was supposed to be the mouthpiece. But at that moment, I just didn't believe it. Despite what I'd seen, Joshua was my pal, not the Messiah.

I said, "I'm pretty sure the Messiah is supposed to have a beard."

"So, it's not time yet, is that what you're saying?"

"Right, Josh, I'm going to know when you don't. God sent a messenger to me and he said, 'By the way, tell Joshua to wait until he can shave before he leads my people out of bondage.' "

"It could happen."

"Don't ask me, ask God."

"That's what I've been doing. He's not answering."

It had been getting darker by the minute in the olive grove, and I could barely see the shine in Josh's eyes, but suddenly the area around us was lit up like daylight. We looked up to see the dreaded Raziel descending on us from above the treetops. Of course I didn't know he was the dreaded Raziel at the time, I was just terrified. The angel shone like a star above us, his features so perfect that even my beloved Maggie's beauty paled by comparison. Joshua hid his face and huddled against the trunk of an olive tree. I guess he was more easily surprised by the supernatural than I was. I just stood there staring with my mouth open, drooling like the village idiot.

"Fear not, for behold, I bring you tidings of great joy, which shall be to all men. For on this day, in the city of David, is born a Savior, which is Christ the Lord." Then he hovered for a second, waiting for his message to sink in.

Joshua uncovered his face and risked a glance at the angel.

"Well?" the angel said.

It took me a second to digest the meaning of the words, and I waited for Joshua to say something, but he had turned his face skyward and seemed to be basking in the light, a silly smile locked on his face.

Finally I pointed a thumb at Josh and said, "He was born in the city of David."

"Really?" said the angel.

"Yep."

"His mother's name is Mary?"

"Yep."

"She a virgin?"

"He has four brothers and sisters now, but at one time, yes."

The angel looked around nervously, as if he might expect a multitude of the heavenly host to show up at some point. "How old are you, kid?"

Joshua just stared, smiling.

"He's ten."

The angel cleared his throat and fidgeted a bit, dropping a few feet toward the ground as he did so. "I'm in a lot of trouble. I stopped to chat with Michael on the way here, he had a deck of cards. I knew some time had passed, but . . ." To Joshua he said, "Kid, were you born in a stable? Wrapped in swaddling cloths and lying in a manger?"

Joshua said nothing.

"That's the way his mom tells it," I said.

"Is he retarded?"

"I think you're his first angel. He's impressed, I think."

"What about you?"

"I'm in trouble because I'm going to be an hour late for dinner."

"I see what you mean. I'd better get back and check on this. If you see some shepherds watching over their flocks by night would you tell them—uh, tell them—that at some point, probably, oh—ten years or so ago, that a Savior was born? Could you do that?"

"Sure."

"Okey-dokey. Glory to God in the highest. Peace on earth, goodwill toward men."

"Right back at you."

"Thanks. Bye."

And as quickly as he had come, the angel was gone in a shooting star and the olive grove went dark again. I could just make out Joshua's face as he turned to look at me.

"There you go," I said. "Next question?"

I suppose that every boy wonders what he will be when he grows up. I suppose that many watch their peers accomplish great things and wonder, "Could I have done that?" For me, to know at ten that my best friend was the Messiah, while I would live and die a stonecutter, seemed too much of a curse for a ten-year-old to bear. The morning after we met the angel, I went to the square and sat with Bartholomew the village idiot, hoping that Maggie would come to the well. If I had to be a stonecutter, at least I might have the love of an enchanting woman. In those days, we started training for our life's work at ten, then received the prayer shawl and phylacteries at thirteen, signifying our entry into manhood. Soon after we were expected to be betrothed, and by fourteen, married and starting a family. So you see, I was not too young to consider Maggie as a wife (and I might always have the fallback position of marrying Joshua's mother when Joseph died).

The women would come and go, fetching water, washing clothes, and as the sun rose high and the square cleared, Bartholomew sat in the shade of tattered date palm and picked his nose. Maggie never appeared. Funny how easy heartbreak can come. I've always had a talent for it.

"Why you cry?" said Bartholomew. He was bigger than any man in the village, his hair and beard were wild and tangled, and the yellow dust that covered him from head to toe gave him the appearance of an incredibly stupid lion. His tunic was ragged and he wore no sandals. The only thing he owned was a wooden bowl that he ate from and licked clean. He lived off of the charity of the village, and by gleaning the grain fields (there was always some grain left in the fields for the poor—it was dictated by the Law). I never knew how old he was. He spent his days in the square, playing with the village dogs, giggling to himself, and scratching his crotch. When the women passed he would stick out his tongue and say, "Bleh." My mother said he had the mind of a child. As usual, she was wrong.

He put his big paw on my shoulder and rubbed, leaving a dusty circle of affection on my shirt. "Why you cry?" he asked again.

"I'm just sad. You wouldn't understand."

Bartholomew looked around, and when he saw that we were alone in the square except for his dog pals, he said, "You think too much. Thinking will bring you nothing but suffering. Be simple."

"What?" It was the most coherent thing I'd ever heard him say.

"Do you ever see me cry? I have nothing, so I am slave to nothing. I have nothing to do, so nothing makes me its slave."

"What do you know?" I snapped. "You live in the dirt. You are unclean! You do nothing. I have to begin working next week, and work for a lifetime until I die with a broken back. The girl I want is in love with my best friend, and he's the Messiah. I'm nothing, and you, you—you're an idiot."

"No, I'm not, I'm a Greek. A Cynic."

I turned and really looked at him. His eyes, normally as dull as mud, shone like black jewels in the dusty desert of his face. "What's a Cynic?"

"A philosopher. I am a student of Diogenes. You know Diogenes?"

"No, but how much could he have taught you? Your only friends are dogs."

"Diogenes went about Athens with a lamp in broad daylight, holding it in people's faces, saying he was looking for an honest man."

"So, he was like the prophet of the idiots?"

"No, no, no." Bart picked up a small terrier and was gesturing with him to make his point. The dog seemed to enjoy it. "They were all fooled by their culture. Diogenes taught that all affectations of modern life were false, that a man must live simply, outdoors, carry nothing, make no art, no poetry, no religion . . ."

"Like a dog," I said.

"Yes!" Bart described a flourish in the air with the rat dog. "Exactly!" The little dog made as if to upchuck from the motion. Bart put him down and he wobbled away.

A life without worry: right then it sounded wonderful. I mean, I didn't want to live in the dirt and have other people think me mad, like Bartholomew, but a dog's life really didn't sound bad. The idiot had been hiding a deep wisdom all these years.

"I'm trying to learn to lick my own balls," Bart said.

Maybe not. "I have to go find Joshua."

"You know he is the Messiah, don't you?"

"Wait a minute, you're not a Jew—I thought you didn't believe in any religion."

"The dogs told me he was the Messiah. I believe them. Tell Joshua I believe them."

"The dogs told you?"

"They're Jewish dogs."

"Right, let me know how the ball licking works out."

"Shalom."

Who would have thought that Joshua would find his first apostle among the dirt and dogs of Nazareth. Bleh.

Í found Joshua at the synagogue, listening to the Pharisees lecture on the Law. I stepped though the group of boys sitting on the floor and whispered to him.

"Bartholomew says that he knows you are the Messiah."

"The idiot? Did you ask him how long he's known?"

"He says the village dogs told him."

"I never thought to ask the dogs."

"He says that we should live simply, like dogs, carry nothing, no affectations—whatever that means."

"Bartholomew said that? Sounds like an Essene. He's much smarter than he looks."

"He's trying to learn to lick his own balls."

"I'm sure there's something in the Law that forbids that. I'll ask the rabbi."

"I'm not sure you want to bring that up to the Pharisee."

"Did you tell your father about the angel?"

"No."

"Good. I've spoken to Joseph, he's going to let me learn to be a stonecutter with you. I don't want your father to change his mind about teaching me. I think the angel would frighten him." Joshua looked at me for the first time, turning from the Pharisee, who droned on in Hebrew. "Have you been crying?"

"Me? No, Bart's stench made my eyes water."

Joshua put his hand on my forehead and all the sadness and trepidation seemed to drain out of me in an instant. He smiled. "Better?"

"I'm jealous of you and Maggie."

"That can't be good for your neck."

"What?"

"Trying to lick your own balls. It's got to be hard on your neck."

"Did you hear me? I'm jealous of you and Maggie."

"I'm still learning, Biff. There are things I don't understand yet. The Lord said, 'I am a jealous God.' So jealousy should be a good thing."

"But it makes me feel so bad."

"You see the puzzle, then? Jealousy makes you feel bad, but God is jealous, so it must be good, yet when a dog licks its balls it seems to enjoy it, but it must be bad under the Law."

Suddenly Joshua was yanked to his feet by the ear. The Pharisee glared at him. "Is the Law of Moses too boring for you, Joshua bar Joseph?"

"I have a question, Rabbi," Joshua said.

"Oh, jeez." I hid my head in my arms.

Chapter 4

Yet another reason that I loathe the heavenly scum with
whom I share this room: today I found that I had offended
our intrepid room service waiter, Jesus. How was I to
know? When he brought our pizza for dinner, I gave him
one of the American silver coins that we received from the
airport sweet shop called Cinnabon. He scoffed at me—
scoffed—then, thinking better of it, he said, "Señor, I know
you are foreign, so you do not know, but this is a very insulting tip. Better you just sign the room service slip so I get the
fee that is added automatically. I tell you this because you
have been very kind, and I know you do not mean to offend,
but another of the waiters would spit in your food if you
should offer him this."

I glared at the angel, who, as usual, was lying on the bed
watching television, and for the first time I realized that he
did not understand Jesus' language. He did not possess the
gift of tongues he had bestowed on me. He spoke Aramaic
to me, and he seemed to know Hebrew and enough English
to understand television, but of Spanish he understood not
a word. I apologized to Jesus and sent him on his way with a
promise that I would make it up to him, then I wheeled on
the angel.

"You fool, these coins, these dimes, are nearly worthless
in this country."

"What do you mean, they look like the silver dinars we
dug up in Jerusalem, they are worth a fortune."

He was right, in a way. After he called me up from the
dead I led him to a cemetery in the valley of Ben Hiddon,

and there, hidden behind a stone where Judas had put it two thousand years ago, was the blood money—thirty silver dinars. But for a little tarnish, they looked just as they did on the day I had taken them, and they were almost identical to the coin this country calls the dime (except for the image of Tiberius on the dinars, and some other Caesar on the dime). We had taken the dinars to an antiquities dealer in the old city (which looked nearly the same as it did when I'd last walked there, except that the Temple was gone and in its place two great mosques). The merchant gave us twenty thousand dollars in American money for them. It was this money that we had traveled on, and deposited at the hotel desk for our expenses. The angel told me the dimes must have the same worth as the dinars, and I, like a fool, believed him.

"You should have told me," I said to the angel. "If I could leave this room I would know myself."

"You have work to do," the angel said. Then he leapt to his feet and shouted at the television, "The wrath of the Lord shall fall upon ye, Stephanos!"

"What in the hell are you shouting at?"

The angel wagged a finger at the screen, "He has exchanged Catherine's baby for its evil twin, which he fathered with her sister while she was in a coma, yet Catherine does not realize his evil deed, as he has had his face changed to impersonate the bank manager who is foreclosing on Catherine's husband's business. If I was not trapped here I would personally drag the fiend straight to hell."

For days now the angel had been watching serial dramas on television, alternately shouting at the screen or bursting into tears. He had stopped reading over my shoulder, so I had just tried to ignore him, but now I realized what was going on.

"It's not real, Raziel."

"What do you mean?"

"It's drama, like the Greeks used to do. They are actors in a play."

"No, no one could pretend to such evil."

"That's not all. Spider-Man and Doctor Octopus? Not real. Characters in a play."

"You lying dog!"

"If you'd ever leave the room and look at how real people talk you'd know that, you yellow-haired cretin. But no, you stay here perched on my shoulder like a trained bird. I am dead two thousand years and even I know better." (I still need to get a look at that book in the dresser. I thought maybe, just maybe, I could goad the angel into giving me five minutes privacy.)

"You know nothing," said Raziel. "I have destroyed whole cities in my time."

"Sort of makes me wonder if you destroyed the right ones. That'd be embarrassing, huh?"

Then an advertisement came on the screen for a magazine that promised to "fill in all the blanks" and give the real inside story to all of soap operas: *Soap Opera Digest*. I watched the angel's eyes widen. He grabbed the phone and rang the front desk.

"What are you doing?"

"I need that book."

"Have them send up Jesus," I said. "He'll help you get it."

On our first day of work, Joshua and I were up before dawn. We met near the well and filled the waterskins our fathers had given us, then ate our breakfasts, flatbread and cheese, as we walked together to Sepphoris. The road, although packed dirt most of the way, was smooth and easy to walk. (If Rome saw to anything in its territories, it was the lifelines of its army.) As we walked we watched the rock-strewn hills turn pink under the rising sun, and I saw Joshua shudder as if a chill wind had danced up his spine.

"The glory of God is in everything we see," he said. "We must never forget that."

"I just stepped in camel dung. Tomorrow let's leave after it's light out."

"I just realized it, that is why the old woman wouldn't live again. I forgot that it wasn't my power that made her arise, it was the Lord's. I brought her back for the wrong reason, out of arrogance, so she died a second time."

"It squished over the side of my sandal. Well, that's going to smell all day."

"But perhaps it was because I did not touch her. When I've brought other creatures back to life, I've always touched them."

"Is there something in the Law about taking your camel off the road to do his business? There should be. If not the Law of Moses, then the Romans should have one. I mean, they won't hesitate to crucify a Jew who rebels, there should be some punishment for messing up their roads. Don't you think? I'm not saying crucifixion, but a good smiting in the mouth or something."

"But how could I have touched the corpse when it is forbidden by the Law? The mourners would have stopped me."

"Can we stop for a second so I can scrape off my sandal? Help me find a stick. That pile was as big as my head."

"You're not listening to me, Biff."

"I am listening. Look, Joshua, I don't think the Law applies to you. I mean, you're the Messiah, God is supposed to tell you what he wants, isn't he?"

"I ask, but I receive no answer."

"Look, you're doing fine. Maybe that woman didn't live again because she was stubborn. Old people are that way. You have to throw water on my grandfather to get him up from his nap. Try a young dead person next time."

"What if I am not really the Messiah?"

"You mean you're not sure? The angel didn't give it away? You think that God might be playing a joke on you? I don't think so. I don't know the Torah as well as you, Joshua, but I don't remember God having a sense of humor."

Finally, a grin. "He gave me you as a best friend, didn't he?"

"Help me find a stick."

"Do you think I'll make a good stonemason?"

"Just don't be better at it than I am. That's all I ask."

"You stink."

"What have I been saying?"

"You really think Maggie likes me?"

"Are you going to be like this every morning? Because if you are, you can walk to work alone."

The gates of Sepphoris were like a funnel of humanity. Farmers poured out into their fields and groves, craftsmen and builders crowded in, while merchants hawked their wares and beggars moaned at the roadside. Joshua and I stopped outside the gates to marvel and were nearly run down by a man leading a string of donkeys laden with baskets of stone.

It wasn't that we had never seen a city before. Jerusalem was fifty times larger than Sepphoris, and we had been there many times for feast days, but Jerusalem was a Jewish city—it was *the* Jewish city. Sepphoris was the Roman fortress city of Galilee, and as soon as we saw the statue of Venus at the gates we knew that this was something different.

I elbowed Joshua in the ribs. "Graven image." I had never seen the human form depicted before.

"Sinful," Joshua said.

"She's naked."

"Don't look."

"She's completely naked."

"It is forbidden. We should go away from here, find your father." He caught me by my sleeve and dragged me through the gates into the city.

"How can they allow that?" I asked. "You'd think that our people would tear it down."

"They did, a band of Zealots. Joseph told me. The Romans caught them and crucified them by this road."

"You never told me that."

"Joseph told me not to speak of it."

"You could see her breasts."

"Don't think about it."

"How can I not think about it? I've never seen a breast without a baby attached to it. They're more—more friendly in pairs like that."

"Which way to where we are supposed to work?"

"My father said to come to the western corner of the city and we would see where the work was being done."

"Then come along." He was still dragging me, his head down, stomping along like an angry mule.

"Do you think Maggie's breasts will look like that?"

My father had been commissioned to build a house for a wealthy Greek on the western side of the city. When Joshua and I arrived my father was already there, directing the slaves who were hoisting a cut stone into place on the wall. I suppose I expected something different. I suppose I was surprised that anyone, even a slave, would do as my father instructed. The slaves were Nubians, Egyptians, Phoenicians, criminals, debtors, spoils of war, accidents of birth; they were wiry, filthy men, many wearing nothing more than sandals and a loincloth. In another life they might have commanded an army or lived in a palace, but now they sweated in the morning chill, moving stones heavy enough to break a donkey.

"Are these your slaves?" Joshua asked my father.

"Am I a rich man, Joshua? No, these slaves belong to the Romans. The Greek who is building this house has hired them for the construction."

"Why do they do as you ask? There are so many of them. You are only one man."

My father hung his head. "I hope that you never see what the lead tips of a

Roman whip do to a man's body. All of these men have, and even seeing it has broken their spirit as men. I pray for them every night."

"I hate the Romans," I said.

"Do you, little one, do you?" A man's voice from behind.

"Hail, Centurion," my father said, his eyes going wide.

Joshua and I turned to see Justus Gallicus, the centurion from the funeral at Japhia, standing among the slaves. "Alphaeus, it seems you are raising a litter of Zealots."

My father put his hands on my and Joshua's shoulders. "This is my son, Levi, and his friend Joshua. They begin their apprenticeship today. Just boys," he said, by way of apology.

Justus approached, looked quickly at me, then stared at Joshua for a long time. "I know you, boy. I've seen you before."

"The funeral at Japhia," I said quickly. I couldn't take my eyes off of the wasp-waisted short sword that hung from the centurion's belt.

"No," the Roman seemed to be searching his memory. "Not Japhia. I've seen this face in a picture."

"That can't be," my father said. "We are forbidden by our faith from depicting the human form."

Justus glared at him. "I am not a stranger to your people's primitive beliefs, Alphaeus. Still, this boy is familiar."

Joshua stared up at the centurion with a completely blank expression.

"You feel for these slaves, boy? You would free them if you could?"

Joshua nodded. "I would. A man's spirit should be his own to give to God."

"You know, there was a slave about eighty years ago who talked like you. He raised an army of slaves against Rome, beat back two of our armies, took over all the territories south of Rome. It's a story every Roman soldier must learn."

"Why, what happened?" I asked.

"We crucified him," Justus said. "By the side of the road, and his body was eaten by ravens. The lesson we all learn is that nothing can stand against Rome. A lesson you need to learn, boy, along with your stonecutting."

Just then another Roman soldier approached, a legionnaire, not wearing the cape or the helmet crest of the centurion. He said something to Justus in Latin, then looked at Joshua and paused. In rough Aramaic he said, "Hey, didn't I see that kid on some bread once?"

"Wasn't him," I said.

"Really? Sure looks like him."

"Nope, that was another kid on the bread."

"It was me," said Joshua.

I backhanded him across the forehead, knocking him to the ground. "No it wasn't. He's insane. Sorry."

The soldier shook his head and hurried off after Justus.

I offered a hand to help Joshua up. "You're going to have to learn to lie."

"I am? But I feel like I'm here to tell the truth."

"Yeah, sure, but not now."

Í don't exactly know what I expected it would be like working as a stonemason, but I know that in less than a week Joshua was having second thoughts about not becoming a carpenter. Cutting great stones with small iron chisels was very hard work. Who knew?

"Look around, do you see any trees?" Joshua mocked. "Rocks, Josh, rocks."

"It's only hard because we don't know what we're doing. It will get easier."

Joshua looked at my father, who was stripped to the waist, chiseling away on a stone the size of a donkey, while a dozen slaves waited to hoist it into place. He was covered with gray dust and streams of sweat drew dark lines between cords of muscle straining in his back and arms. "Alphaeus," Joshua called, "does the work get easier once you know what you are doing?"

"Your lungs grow thick with stone dust and your eyes bleary from the sun and fragments thrown up by the chisel. You pour your lifeblood out into works of stone for Romans who will take your money in taxes to feed soldiers who will nail your people to crosses for wanting to be free. Your back breaks, your bones creak, your wife screeches at you, and your children torment you with open, begging mouths, like greedy baby birds in the nest. You go to bed every night so tired and beaten that you pray to the Lord to send the angel of death to take you in your sleep so you don't have to face another morning. It also has its downside."

"Thanks," Joshua said. He looked at me, one eyebrow raised.

"I for one, am excited," I said. "I'm ready to cut some stone. Stand back, Josh, my chisel is on fire. Life is stretched out before us like a great bazaar, and I can't wait to taste the sweets to be found there."

Josh tilted his head like a bewildered dog. "I didn't get that from your father's answer."

"It's sarcasm, Josh."

"Sarcasm?"

"It's from the Greek, *sarkasmos*. To bite the lips. It means that you aren't really saying what you mean, but people will get your point. I invented it, Bartholomew named it."

"Well, if the village idiot named it, I'm sure it's a good thing."

"There you go, you got it."

"Got what?"

"Sarcasm."

"No, I meant it."

"Sure you did."

"Is that sarcasm?"

"Irony, I think."

"What's the difference?"

"I haven't the slightest idea."

"So you're being ironic now, right?"

"No, I really don't know."

"Maybe you should ask the idiot."

"Now you've got it."

"What?"

"Sarcasm."

"Biff, are you sure you weren't sent here by the Devil to vex me?"

"Could be. How am I doing so far? You feel vexed?"

"Yep. And my hands hurt from holding the chisel and mallet." He struck the chisel with his wooden mallet and sprayed us both with stone fragments.

"Maybe God sent me to talk you into being a stonemason so you would hurry up and go be the Messiah."

He struck the chisel again, then spit and sputtered through the fragments that flew. "I don't know how to be the Messiah."

"So what, a week ago we didn't know how to be stonemasons and look at us now. It gets easier once you know what you're doing."

"Are you being ironic again?"

"God, I hope not."

Ít was two months before we actually saw the Greek who had commissioned my father to build the house. He was a short, soft-looking little man, who wore a robe that was as white as any worn by the Levite priests, with a border of interlocking rectangles woven around the hem in gold. He arrived in a pair of chariots, followed on foot by two body slaves and a half-dozen bodyguards who looked like Phoenicians. I say a pair of chariots because he rode with a driver in the lead chariot, but behind them they pulled a second chariot in which stood the ten-foot-tall marble statue of a naked man. The Greek climbed down from his chariot and went directly to my father. Joshua and I were mixing a batch of mortar at the time and we paused to watch.

"Graven image," Joshua said.

"Saw it," I said. "As graven images go, I like Venus over by the gate better."

"That statue is not Jewish," Joshua said.

"Definitely not Jewish," I said. The statue's manhood, although abundant, was not circumcised.

"Alphaeus," the Greek said, "why haven't you set the floor of the gymnasium yet? I've brought this statue to display in the gymnasium, and there's just a hole in the ground instead of a gymnasium."

"I told you, this ground is not suitable for building. I can't build on sand. I've had the slaves dig down in the sand until they hit bedrock. Now it has to be back-filled in with stone, then pounded."

"But I want to place my statue," the Greek whined. "It's come all the way from Athens."

"Would you rather your house fall down around your precious statue?"

"Don't talk to me that way, Jew, I am paying you well to build this house."

"And I am building this house well, which means not on the sand. So store your statue and let me do my work."

"Well, unload it. You, slaves, help unload my statue." The Greek was talking to Joshua and me. "All of you, help unload my statue." He pointed to the slaves who had been pretending to work since the Greek arrived, but who weren't sure that it was in their best interest to look like a part of a project about which the master seemed displeased. They all looked up with a surprised "Who, me?" expression on their faces, which I noticed was the same in any language.

The slaves moved to the chariot and began untying the ropes that held the statue in place. The Greek looked to us. "Are you deaf, slaves? Help them!" He stormed back to his chariot and grabbed a whip out of the driver's hand.

"Those are not slaves," my father said. "Those are my apprentices."

The Greek wheeled on him. "And I should care about that? Move, boys! Now!"

"No," Joshua said.

I thought the Greek would explode. He raised the whip as if to strike. "What did you say?"

"He said, no." I stepped up to Joshua's side.

"My people believe that graven images, statues, are sinful," my father said, his voice on the edge of panic. "The boys are only being true to our God."

"Well, that is a statue of Apollo, a real god, so they will help unload it, as will you, or I'll find another mason to build my house."

"No," Joshua repeated. "We will not."

"Right, you leprous jar of camel snot," I said.

Joshua looked at me, sort of disgusted. "Jeez, Biff."

"Too much?"

The Greek screeched and started to swing the whip. The last thing I saw as I covered my face was my father diving toward the Greek. I would take a lash for Joshua, but I didn't want to lose an eye. I braced for the sting that never came. There was a thump, then a twanging sound, and when I uncovered my face, the Greek was lying on his back in the dirt, his white robe covered with dust, his face red with rage. The whip was extend out behind him, and on its tip stood the armored hobnail boot of Gaius Justus Gallicus, the centurion. The Greek rolled in the dirt, ready to vent his ire on whoever had stayed his hand, but when he saw who it was, he went limp and pretended to cough.

One of the Greek's bodyguards started to step forward. Justus pointed a finger at the guard. "Will you stand down, or would you rather feel the foot of the Roman Empire on *your* neck?"

The guard stepped back into line with his companions.

The Roman was grinning like a mule eating an apple, not in the least concerned with allowing the Greek to save face. "So, Castor, am I to gather that you need to conscript more Roman slaves to help build your house? Or is it true what I hear about you Greeks, that whipping young boys is an entertainment for you, not a disciplinary action?"

The Greek spit out a mouthful of dust as he climbed to his feet. "The slaves I have will be sufficient for the task, won't they, Alphaeus?" He turned to my father, his eyes pleading.

My father seemed to be caught between two evils, and unable to decide which was the lesser of them. "Probably," he said, finally.

"Well, good, then," Justus said. "I will expect a bonus payment for the extra work they are doing. Carry on."

Justus walked through the construction site, acting as if every eye was not on him, or not caring, and paused as he passed Joshua and me.

"Leprous jar of camel snot?" he said under his breath.

"Old Hebrew blessing?" I ventured.

"You two should be in the hills with the other Hebrew rebels." The Roman laughed, tousled our hair, then walked away.

the sunset was turning the hillsides pink as we walked home to Nazareth that evening. In addition to being almost exhausted from the work, Joshua seemed vexed by the events of the day.

"Did you know that—about not being able to build on sand?" he asked.

"Of course, my father's been talking about it for a long time. You can build on sand, but what you build will fall down."

Joshua nodded thoughtfully. "What about soil? Dirt? Is it okay to build on that?"

"Rock is best, but I suppose hard dirt is good."

"I need to remember that."

We seldom saw Maggie in those days after we began working with my father. I found myself looking forward to the Sabbath, when we would go to the synagogue and I would mill around outside, among the women, while the men were inside listening to the reading of the Torah or the arguments of the Pharisees. It was one of the few times I could talk to Maggie without Joshua around, for though he resented the Pharisees even then, he knew he could learn from them, so he spent the Sabbath listening to their teachings. I still wonder if this time I stole with Maggie somehow represented a disloyalty to Joshua, but later, when I asked him about it, he said, "God is willing to forgive you the sin that you carry for being a child of man, but you must forgive yourself for having once been a child."

"I suppose that's right."

"Of course it's right, I'm the Son of God, you dolt. Besides, Maggie always wanted to talk about me anyway, didn't she?"

"Not always," I lied.

On the Sabbath before the murder, I found Maggie outside the synagogue, sitting by herself under a date palm tree. I shuffled up to her to talk, but kept looking at my feet. I knew that if I looked into her eyes I would forget what I was talking about, so I only looked at her in brief takes, the way a man will glance up at the sun on a sweltering day to confirm the source of the heat.

"Where's Joshua?" were the first words out of her mouth, of course.

"Studying with the men."

She seemed disappointed for a moment, but then brightened. "How is your work?"

"Hard, I like playing better."

"What is Sepphoris like? Is it like Jerusalem?"

"No, it's smaller. But there are a lot of Romans there." She'd seen Romans. I needed something to impress her. "And there are graven images—statues of people."

Maggie covered her mouth to stifle a giggle. "Statues, really? I would love to see them."

"Then come with us, we are leaving tomorrow very early, before anyone is awake."

"I couldn't. Where would I tell my mother I was going?"

"Tell her that you are going to Sepphoris with the Messiah and his pal."

Her eyes went wide and I looked away quickly, before I was caught in their spell. "You shouldn't talk that way, Biff."

"I saw the angel."

"You said yourself that we shouldn't say it."

"I was only joking. Tell your mother that I told you about a beehive that I found and that you want to go find some honey while the bees are still groggy from the morning cold. It's a full moon tonight, so you'll be able to see. She just might believe you."

"She might, but she'll know I was lying when I don't bring home any honey."

"Tell her it was a hornets' nest. She thinks Josh and I are stupid anyway, doesn't she?"

"She thinks that Joshua is touched in the head, but you, yes, she thinks you're stupid."

"You see, my plan is working. For it is written that 'if the wise man always appears stupid, his failures do not disappoint, and his success gives pleasant surprise.' "

Maggie smacked me on the leg. "That is not written."

"Sure it is, Imbeciles three, verse seven."

"There is no book of Imbeciles."

"Drudges five-four?"

"You're making that up."

"Come with us, you can be back to Nazareth before it's time to fetch the morning water."

"Why so early? What are you two up to?"

"We're going to circumcise Apollo."

She didn't say anything, she just looked at me, as if she would see "Liar" written across my forehead in fire.

"It wasn't my idea," I said. "It was Joshua's."

"I'll go then," she said.

Chapter 5

Well, it worked, I finally got the angel to leave the room. It went like this:

Raziel called down to the front desk and asked him to send Jesus up. A few minutes later our Latin pal stood at attention at the foot of the angel's bed.

Raziel said, "Tell him I need a *Soap Opera Digest*."

In Spanish, I said, "Good afternoon, Jesus. How are you today?"

"I am well, sir, and you?"

"As good as can be expected, considering this man is holding me prisoner."

"Tell him to hurry," said Raziel.

"He doesn't understand Spanish?" Jesus asked.

"Not a word of it, but don't start speaking Hebrew or I'm sunk."

"Are you really a prisoner? I wondered why you two never left the room. Should I call the police?"

"No, that won't be necessary, but please shake your head and look apologetic."

"What is taking so long?" Raziel said. "Give him the money and tell him to go."

"He said he is not allowed to buy publications for you, but he can direct you to a place where you can purchase them yourself."

"That's ridiculous, he's a servant, isn't he? He will do as I ask."

"Oh my, Jesus, he has asked if you would like to feel the power of his manly nakedness."

"Is he crazy? I have a wife and two children."

"Sadly, yes. Please show him that you are offended by his offer by spitting on him and storming out of the room."

"I don't know, sir, spitting on a guest . . ."

I handed him a handful of the bills that he'd taught me were appropriate gratuities. "Please, it will be good for him."

"Very well, Mister Biff." He produced an impressive loogie and launched it at the front of the angel's robe, where it splatted and ran.

Raziel leapt to his feet.

"Well done, Jesus, now curse."

"You fuckstick!"

"In Spanish."

"Sorry, I was showing off my English. I know many swear words."

"Well done. Spanish please."

"Pendejo!"

"Splendid, now storm out."

Jesus turned on his heel and left the room, slamming the door behind him.

"He spit on me?" Raziel said, still not believing it. "An angel of the Lord, and he spit on me."

"Yes, you offended him."

"He called me a fuckstick. I heard him."

"In his culture, it is an affront to ask another man to buy a *Soap Opera Digest* for you. We'll be lucky if he ever brings us a pizza again."

"But I want a *Soap Opera Digest.*"

"He said you can buy one just down the street, I will be happy to go get one for you."

"Not so fast, Apostle, none of your tricks. I'll get it myself, you stay here."

"You'll need money." I handed him some bills.

"If you leave the room I will find you in an instant, you know that?"

"Absolutely."

"You cannot hide from me."

"Wouldn't dream of it. Hurry now."

He sort of shuffled sideways toward the door. "Don't try to lock me out, I'm taking a key with me. Not that I need it or anything, being an angel of the Lord."

"Not to mention a fuckstick."

"I don't even know what that means."

"Go, go, go." I shooed him through the door. "Godspeed, Raziel."

"Work on your Gospel while I'm gone."

"Right." I slammed the door in his face and threw the safety lock. Raziel has now watched hundreds of hours of American television, you'd think he would have noticed that people wear shoes when they go outside.

The book is exactly as I suspected, a Bible, but written in a flowery version of this English I've been writing in. The translation of the Torah and the prophets from the Hebrew is muddled sometimes, but the first part seems to be our Bible. This language is amazing—so many words. In my time we had very few words, perhaps a hundred that we used all the time, and thirty of them were synonyms for guilt. In this language you can curse for an hour and never use the same word twice. Flocks and schools and herds of words, that's why I'm supposed to use this language to tell Joshua's story.

I've hidden the book in the bathroom, so I can sneak in and read it while the angel is in the room. I didn't have time to actually read much of the part of the book they call the New Testament, but it's obvious that it is the story of Joshua's life. Or parts of it, anyway.

I'll study it later, but now I should go on with the real story.

I suppose I should have considered the exact nature of what we were doing before I invited Maggie to join us. I mean, there is some difference between the circumcision of an eight-day-old baby boy, which she had seen before, and the same operation on the ten-foot statue of a Greek god.

"My goodness, that is, uh, impressive," Maggie said, staring up at the marble member.

"Graven image," Joshua said under his breath. Even in the moonlight I could tell he was blushing.

"Let's do it." I pulled a small iron chisel from my pouch. Joshua was wrapping the head of his mallet with leather to deaden its sound. Sepphoris slept around us, the silence broken only by the occasional bleat of a sheep. The evening cook fires had long since gone to coals, the dust cloud that stirred through the city during the day had settled, and the night air was clean and still. From time to time I would catch a sweet whiff of sandalwood coming from Maggie and I would lose my train of thought. Funny the things you remember.

We found a bucket and turned it upside down for Joshua to stand on while he worked. He set the tip of my chisel on Apollo's foreskin and ventured a light tap with the mallet. A tiny fragment of marble flaked away.

"Give it a good whack," I said.

"I can't, it will make too much noise."

"No, it won't, the leather will cover it."

"But I might take the whole end of it off."

"He can spare it," Maggie said, and we both turned to her with our mouths hanging open. "Probably," she added quickly. "I'm only guessing. What do I know, I'm just a girl. Do you guys smell something?"

We smelled the Roman before we heard him, heard him before we saw him. The Romans covered themselves with olive oil before they bathed, so if the wind was right or if it was an especially hot day you could smell a Roman coming at thirty paces. Between the olive oil they bathed with and the garlic and dried paste of anchovies they ate with their barley, when the legions marched into battle it must have smelled like an invasion of pizza people. If they'd had pizzas back then, which they didn't.

Joshua took a quick swipe with the mallet and the chisel slipped, neatly severing Apollo's unit, which fell to the dirt with a dull thud.

"Whoops," said the Savior.

"Shhhhhhhh," I shushed.

We heard the hobnails of the Roman's boots scraping on stone. Joshua jumped down from the bucket and looked frantically for a place to hide. The walls of the Greek's bathhouse were almost completed around the statue, so really, except for the entrance where the Roman was coming, there was no place to run.

"Hey, what are you doing there?"

We stood as still as the statue. I could see that it was the legionnaire that had been with Justus our first day in Sepphoris.

"Sir, it's us, Biff and Joshua. Remember? The kid from the bread?"

The soldier moved closer, his hand on the haft of his half-drawn short sword. When he saw Joshua he relaxed a bit. "What are you doing here so early? No one is to be about at this hour."

Suddenly, the soldier was yanked backward off of his feet and a dark figure fell on him, thrusting a blade into his chest over and over. Maggie screamed and the figure turned to us. I started to run.

"Stop," the murderer hissed.

I froze. Maggie threw her arms around me and hid her face in my shirt as I trembled. A gurgling sound came from the soldier, but he lay still. Joshua made to step toward the murderer and I threw an arm across his chest to stop him.

"That was wrong," Joshua said, almost in tears. "You are wrong to kill that man."

The murderer held his bloody blade up by his face and grinned at us. "Is it not written that Moses became a prophet only after killing an Egyptian slave driver? No master but God!"

"Sicarii," I said.

"Yes boy, Sicarii. Only when the Romans are dead will the Messiah come to set us free. I serve God by killing this tyrant."

"You serve evil," Joshua said. "The Messiah didn't call for the blood of this Roman."

The assassin raised his blade and came at Joshua. Maggie and I leapt back, but Joshua stood his ground. The assassin grabbed him by the front of his shirt and pulled him close. "What do you know of it, boy?"

We could clearly see the murderer's face in the moonlight. Maggie gasped, "Jeremiah."

His eyes went wide, with fear or recognition, I don't know which. He released Joshua and made as if to grab Maggie. I pulled her away.

"Mary?" The anger had left his voice. "Little Mary?"

Maggie said nothing, but I could feel her shoulders heave as she began to sob.

"Tell no one of this," the murderer said, now talking as if he were in a trance. He backed away and stood beside the dead soldier. "No master but God," he said, then he turned and ran into the night.

Joshua put his hand on Maggie's head and she immediately stopped crying.

"Jeremiah is my father's brother," she said.

before I go on you should know about the Sicarii, and to know about them, you have to know about the Herods. So here you go.

About the time that Joshua and I were meeting for the first time, King Herod the Great died after ruling Israel (under the Romans) for over forty years. It was, in fact, the death of Herod that prompted Joseph to bring his family back to Nazareth from Egypt, but that's another story. Now you need to know about Herod.

Herod wasn't called "the Great" because he was a beloved ruler. Herod the Great, was, in fact, a fat, paranoid, pox-ridden tyrant who murdered thousands of Jews, including his own wife and many of his sons. Herod was called "the Great" because he built things. Amazing things: fortresses, palaces, theaters, harbors—a whole city, Caesarea, modeled on the Roman ideal of what a city should be. The one thing he did for the Jewish people, who hated him, was to rebuild the Temple of Solomon on Mount Moriah, the center of our faith. When H. the G. died, Rome divided his kingdom among three of his sons, Archelaus, Herod Philip, and Herod Antipas. It was Antipas who ultimately passed sentence on John the Baptist and gave Joshua over to Pilate. Antipas, you sniveling fuckstick (if only we'd had the word back then). It was Antipas whose toady pandering to the Romans caused bands of Jewish rebels to rise up in the hills by the hundreds. The Romans called all of these rebels Zealots, as if they were all united in method as well as cause, but, in fact, they were as fragmented as Jews of the villages. One of the bands that rose in Galilee called themselves the Sicarii. They showed their disapproval of Roman rule by the assassination of Roman soldiers and officials. Although certainly not the largest group of Zealots by number, they were the most conspicuous by their actions. No one knew where they came from, and no one knew where they went to after they killed, but every time they struck, the Romans did their best to make our lives hell to get us to give the killers up. And when the Romans caught a Zealot, they didn't just crucify the leader of the band, they crucified the whole band, their families, and anyone suspected of helping them. More than once we saw the road out of Sepphoris lined with crosses and corpses. My people.

We ran through the sleeping city, stopping only after we had passed through the Venus Gate, where we fell in a heap on the ground, gasping.

"We have to take Maggie home and get back here for work," Joshua said.

"You can stay here," Maggie said. "I can go by myself."

"No, we have to go." Joshua held his arms out to his sides and we saw the bloody handprints the killer had left on his shirt. "I have to clean this before someone sees it."

"Can't you just make it go away?" Maggie asked. "It's just a stain. I'd think the Messiah could get a stain out."

"Be nice," I said. "He's not that good at Messiah stuff yet. It was your uncle, after all . . ."

Maggie jumped to her feet. "You were the one who wanted to do this stupid thing . . ."

"Stop!" Joshua said, holding his hand up as if he were sprinkling us with silence. "If Maggie hadn't been with us, we might be dead now. We may still not be safe when the Sicarii realize that three witnesses live."

An hour later Maggie was home safe and Joshua emerged from the ritual bath outside the synagogue, his clothes soaked and rivulets running out of his hair. (Many of us had these mikvehs outside of our homes—and there were hundreds outside the Temple in Jerusalem—stone pits with steps leading down both sides into the water so one might walk in over one's head on one side, then out on the other after the ritual cleansing was done. According to the Law, any contact with blood called for a cleansing. Joshua thought it would be a good opportunity to scrub the stain out of his shirt as well.)

"Cold." Joshua was shivering and hopping from foot to foot as if on hot coals. "Very cold."

(There was a small stone hut built over the baths so they never got the direct light of the sun, consequently they never warmed up. Evaporation in the dry Galilee air chilled the water even more.)

"Maybe you should come to my house. My mother will have a breakfast fire going by now, you can warm yourself."

He wrung out the tail of his shirt and water cascaded down his legs. "And how would I explain this?"

"Uh, you sinned, had an emergency cleansing to do."

"Sinned? At dawn? What sin could I have done before dawn?"

"Sin of Onan?" I said.

Joshua's eyes went wide. "Have you committed the sin of Onan?"

"No, but I'm looking forward to it."

"I can't tell your mother that I've committed the sin of Onan. I haven't."

"You could if you're fast."

"I'll suffer the cold," Joshua said.

The good old sin of Onan. That brings back memories.

The sin of Onan. Spilling the old seed on the ground. Cuffing the camel. Dusting the donkey. Flogging the Pharisee. Onanism, a sin that requires hundreds of hours of practice to get right, or at least that's what I told myself. God slew Onan for spilling his seed on the ground (Onan's seed, not God's. God's seed turned out to be my best pal. Imagine the trouble you'd be in if you actually spilled God's seed. Try explaining that). According to the Law, if you had any contact with "nocturnal emissions" (which are not what come out of your tailpipe at night—we didn't have cars then), you had to purify yourself by baptism and you weren't allowed to be around people until the next day. Around the age of thirteen I spent a lot of time in and out of our mikveh, but I fudged on the solitary part of penance. I mean, it's not like that was going to help the problem.

Many a morning I was still dripping and shivering from the bath when I met Joshua to go to work.

"Spilled your seed upon the ground again?" he'd ask.

"Yep."

"You're unclean, you know?"

"Yeah, I'm getting all wrinkly from purifying myself."

"You could stop."

"I tried. I think I'm being vexed by a demon."

"I could try to heal you."

"No way, Josh, I'm having enough trouble with laying on of my own hands."

"You don't want me to cast out your demon?"

"I thought I'd try to exhaust him first."

"I could tell the scribes and they would have you stoned." (Always trying to be helpful, Josh was.)

"That would probably work, but it is written that 'when the oil of the lamp is used up, the wanker shall light his own way to salvation.'"

"That is not written."

"It is to. In, uh, Isaiah."

"Is not."

"You need to study your Prophets, Josh. How are you going to be the Messiah if you don't know your Prophets?"

Joshua hung his head. "You are right, of course."

I clapped him on the shoulder. "You'll have time to learn the Prophets. Let's cut through the square and see if there are any girls gathering water."

Of course it was Maggie I was looking for. It was always Maggie.

By the time we got back to Sepphoris the sun was well up, but the stream of merchants and farmers that normally poured through the Venus Gate was not there. Roman soldiers were stopping and searching everyone who was trying to leave the city, sending them back the way they came. A group of men and women were waiting outside the gate to go in, my father and some of his helpers among them.

"Levi!" my father called. He ran to us and herded us to the side of the road.

"What's going on?" I asked, trying to look innocent.

"A Roman soldier was murdered last night. There will be no work today, now you both go home and stay there. Tell your mothers to keep the children in today. If the Romans don't find the killer there'll be soldiers in Nazareth before noon."

"Where is Joseph?" Joshua asked.

My father put his arm around Joshua's shoulder. "He's been arrested. He must have come to work very early. They found him at first light, near the body of the dead soldier. I only know what has been shouted from inside the gate, the Romans aren't letting anyone in or out of the city. Joshua, tell your mother not to worry. Joseph is a good man, the Lord will protect him. Besides, if the Romans thought he was the killer he would have been tried already."

Joshua backed away from my father in stiff, stumbling steps. He stared straight ahead, but obviously saw nothing.

"Take him home, Biff. I'll be along as soon as I can. I'm going to try to find out what they've done with Joseph."

I nodded and led Joshua away by the shoulders.

When we were a few steps down the road, he said, "Joseph came looking for me. He was working on the other side of the city. The only reason he was near the Greek's house is that he was looking for me."

"We'll tell the centurion we saw who killed the soldier. He'll believe us."

"And if he believes us, believes it was Sicarii, what will happen to Maggie and her family?"

I didn't know what to say. Joshua was right and my father was wrong, Joseph was not fine. The Romans would be questioning him right now, maybe torturing him to find out who his accomplices were. That he didn't know anything would not save him. And a testimony from his son not only wouldn't save him, but would send more people to the cross to join him. Jewish blood was going to be spilled one way or the other over this.

Joshua shook off my hands and ran off the road into an olive grove. I started to follow, but he suddenly spun on me and the fury of his gaze stopped me in midstride.

"Wait," he said. "I need to talk to my father."

Í waited by the road for nearly an hour. When Joshua walked out of the olive grove he looked as if a shadow had fallen permanently on his face.

"I am lost," he said.

I pointed over my shoulder. "Nazareth that way, Sepphoris the other way. You're in the middle. Feel better?"

"You know what I mean."

"No help from your father, then?" I always felt strange asking about Joshua's prayers. You had to see him pray, especially in those days, before we had traveled. There was a lot of strain and trembling, like someone trying to force a fever to break by sheer will. There was no peace in it.

"I am alone," Joshua said.

I punched him in the arm, hard. "Then you didn't feel that."

"Ouch. What'd you do that for?"

"Sorry, no one around to answer you. You're sooooooooo alone."

"I am alone!"

I wound up for a full-body-powered roundhouse punch. "Then you won't mind if I smite the bejeezus out of you."

He threw up his hands and jumped back. "No, don't."

"So you're not alone?"

"I guess not."

"Good, then wait here. I'm going to go talk to your father myself." I tramped off into the olive grove.

"You don't have to go in there to talk to him. He is everywhere."

"Yeah, right, like you know. If he's everywhere then how are you alone?"

"Good point."

I left Joshua standing by the road and went off to pray.

And thus did I pray:

"Heavenly Father, God of my father and my father's father, God of Abraham and Isaac, God of Moses, who did lead our people out of Egypt, God of David and Solomon—well, you know who you are. Heavenly Father, far be it from me to question your judgment, being as you are all powerful and the God of Moses and all of the above, but what exactly are you trying to do to this poor kid? I mean, he's your son, right? He's the Messiah, right? Are you pulling one of those Abraham faith-test things on him? In case you didn't notice, he's in quite a pickle here, having witnessed a murder and his stepfather under arrest by the Romans, and in all likelihood, a lot of our people, who you have mentioned on more than one occasion are your favorites and the chosen (and of which I am one, by the way) are going to be tortured and killed unless we—I mean he—does something. So, what I'm saying here is, could you, much as you did with

Samson when he was backed into a corner weaponless against the Philistines, throw the kid a bone here?

"With all due respect. Your friend, Biff. Amen."

Í was never very good at prayer. Storytelling, I'm fine with. I, in fact, am the originator of a universal story that I know has survived to this time because I have heard it on TV.

It begins: "Two Jews go into a bar . . ."

Those two Jews? Me and Josh. No kidding.

Anyway, I'm not good at prayer, but before you think I was a little rough on God, there's another thing you need to know about my people. Our relationship with God was different from other people and their Gods. Sure there was fear and sacrifice and all, but essentially, we didn't go to him, *he* came to *us*. *He* told *us* we were the chosen, *he* told *us* he would help us to multiply to the ends of the earth, *he* told *us* he would give us a land of milk and honey. We didn't go to him. We didn't ask. And since he came to us, we figure we can hold him responsible for what he does and what happens to us. For it is written that "he who can walk away, controls the deal." And if there's anything you learn from reading the Bible, it's that my people walked away a lot. You couldn't turn around that we weren't off in Babylon worshiping false gods, building false altars, or sleeping with unsuitable women. (Although the latter may be more of a guy thing than a Jewish thing.) And God pretty much didn't mind throwing us into slavery or simply massacring us when we did that. We have that kind of relationship with God. We're family.

So I'm not a prayer-master, so to speak, but that particular prayer couldn't have been that bad, because God answered. Well, he left me a message, anyway.

as I emerged from the olive grove, Joshua held out his hand and said, "God left a message."

"It's a lizard," I said. It was. Joshua was holding a small lizard in his outstretched hand.

"Yes, that's the message, don't you see?"

How was I to know what was going on? Joshua had never lied to me, never. So if he said that this lizard was a message from God, who was I to dispute him? I fell to my knees and bowed my head under Josh's outstretched hand. "Lord have mercy on me, I was expecting a burning bush or something. Sorry. Really." Then to Josh, I said, "I'm not so sure you should take that seriously, Josh. Reptiles don't tend to have a great record for getting the message right. Like for instance, oh, let's see, that Adam and Eve thing."

"It's not that kind of message, Biff. My father hasn't spoken in words, but this message is as clear as if his voice had come down from the heavens."

"I knew that." I stood up. "And the message is?"

"In my mind. When you had been gone only a few minutes this lizard ran up my leg and perched on my hand. I realized that it was my father giving me the solution to our problem."

"And the message is?"

"You remember when we were little, the game we used to play with the lizards?"

"Sure I do. But the message is?"

"You remember how I was able to bring them back to life."

"A great trick, Josh. But getting back to the message . . ."

"Don't you see? If the soldier isn't dead, than there was no murder. If there was no murder, than there is no reason for the Romans to harm Joseph. So all we have to do is see that the soldier is not dead. Simple."

"Of course, simple." I studied the lizard for a minute, looking at it from a number of different angles. It was brownish green and seemed quite content to sit there on Joshua's palm. "Ask him what we're supposed to do now."

# Chapter 6

When we got back to Nazareth we expected to find Joshua's mother hysterical with worry, but on the contrary, she had gathered Joshua's brothers and sisters outside of their house, lined them up, and was washing their faces and hands as if preparing them for the Sabbath meal.

"Joshua, help me get the little ones ready, we are all going to Sepphoris."

Joshua was shocked. "We are?"

"The whole village is going to ask the Romans to release Joseph."

James was the only one of the children who seemed to understand what had happened to their father. There were tear tracks on his cheeks. I put my arm around his shoulders. "He'll be fine," I said, trying to sound cheerful. "Your father is strong, they'll have to torture him for days before he gives up the ghost." I smiled encouragingly.

James broke out of my embrace and ran into the house crying. Mary turned and glared at me. "Shouldn't you be with your family, Biff?"

Oh my breaking heart, my bruised ego. Even though Mary had taken position as my emergency backup wife, I was crestfallen at her disapproval. And to my credit, not once during that time of trouble did I wish harm to come to Joseph. Not once. After all, I was still too young to take a wife, and some creepy elder would swoop Mary up before I had a chance to rescue her if Joseph died before I was fourteen.

"Why don't you go get Maggie," Joshua suggested, taking only a second from his mission of scrubbing the skin off his brother Judah's face. "Her family will want to go with us."

"Sure," I said, and I scampered off to the blacksmith's shop in search of approval from my primary wife-to-be.

When I arrived, Maggie was sitting outside of her father's shop with her brothers and sisters. She looked as frightened as she had when we first witnessed the murder. I wanted to throw my arms around her to comfort her.

"We have a plan," I said. "I mean, Joshua has a plan. Are you going to Sepphoris with everyone else?"

"The whole family," she said. "My father has made nails for Joseph, they're friends." She tossed her head, pointing toward the open shed that housed her father's forge. Two men were working over the forge. "Go ahead, Biff. You and Joshua go on ahead. We'll be along later." She started waving me away and mouthing words silently to me, which I didn't pick up.

"What are you saying? What? What?"

"And who is your friend, Maggie?" A man's voice, coming from near the forge. I looked over and suddenly realized what Maggie had been trying to tell me.

"Uncle Jeremiah, this is Levi bar Alphaeus. We call him Biff. He has to go now."

I started backing away from the killer. "Yes, I have to go." I looked at Maggie, not knowing what to do. "I'll—we—I have to—"

"We'll see you in Sepphoris," Maggie said.

"Right," I said, then I turned and dashed away, feeling more like a coward than I ever have in my life.

When we got back to Sepphoris there was a large gathering of Jews, perhaps two hundred, outside of the city walls, most I recognized as being from Nazareth. No mob mentality here, more a fearful gathering. More than half of those gathered were women and children. In the middle of the crowd, a contingent of a dozen Roman soldiers pushed back the onlookers while two slaves dug a grave. Like my own people, the Romans did not dally with their dead. Unless there was a battle ongoing, Roman soldiers were often put in the ground before the corpse was cool.

Joshua and I spotted Maggie standing between her father and her murderous uncle at the edge of the crowd. Joshua took off toward her. I followed, but before I got close, Joshua had taken Maggie's hand and dragged her into the midst of the crowd. I could see Jeremiah trying to follow them. I dove into the mass and crawled under people's feet until I came upon a pair of hobnail boots which indicated the lower end of a Roman soldier. The other end, equally Roman, was scowling at me. I stood up.

"*Semper fido*," I said in my best Latin, followed by my most charming smile.

The soldier scowled further. Suddenly there was a smell of flowers in my nose and sweet, warm lips brushed my ear. "I think you just said 'always dog,' " Maggie whispered.

"That would be why he's looking so unpleasant then?" I said out the side of my charming smile.

In my other ear another familiar, if not so sweet whisper, "Sing, Biff. Remember the plan," Joshua said.

"Right." And so I let loose with one of my famous dirges. "*La-la-la. Hey Roman guy, too bad about your getting stabbed. La-la-la. It's probably not a message from God or nothing. La-la-la. Telling you that maybe you should have gone home, la, la, la. Instead of oppressing the chosen people who God hisownself has said that he likes better than you. Fa, la, la, la.*"

The soldier didn't speak Aramaic, so the lyrics didn't move him as I had hoped. But I think the hypnotic toe-tappiness of the melody was starting to get him. I plunged into my second verse.

"*La-la-la, didn't we tell you that you shouldn't eat pork, la-la. Although looking at wounds in your chest, a dietary change might not have made that big a difference. Boom shaka-laka-laka-laka, boom shaka-laka-lak.* Come on, you know the words!"

"Enough!"

The soldier was yanked aside and Gaius Justus Gallicus stood before us, flanked by two of his officers. Behind him, stretched out on the ground, was the body of the dead soldier.

"Well done, Biff," Joshua whispered.

"We're offering our services as professional mourners," I said with a grin, which the centurion was eager not to return.

"That soldier doesn't need mourners, he has avengers."

A voice from the crowd. "See here, Centurion, release Joseph of Nazareth. He is no murderer."

Justus turned and the crowd parted, leaving a path between him and the man who had spoken up. It was Iban the Pharisee, standing with several other Pharisees from Nazareth.

"Would you take his place?" Justus asked.

The Pharisee backed away, his resolve melting quickly under the threat.

"Well?" Justus stepped forward and the crowd parted around him. "You speak for your people, Pharisee. Tell them to give me a killer. Or would you rather I crucify Jews until I get the right one?"

Iban was flustered now, and began jabbering a mishmash of verses from the Torah. I looked around and saw Maggie's uncle Jeremiah standing only a few paces behind me. When I caught his eye he slipped his hand under his shirt—to the haft of a knife, I had no doubt.

"Joseph didn't kill that soldier!" Joshua shouted.

Justus turned to him and the Pharisees took the opportunity to scramble to the back of the crowd. "I know that," Justus said.

"You do?"

"Of course, boy. No carpenter killed that soldier."

"How do you know that?" I asked.

Justus motioned to one of his legionnaires and the soldier came forward carrying a small basket. The centurion nodded and the soldier upended the basket. The stone effigy of Apollo's severed penis thudded to the ground in front of us.

"Uh-oh," I said.

"Because it was a stonecutter," Justus said.

"My, that *is* impressive," Maggie said.

I noticed that Joshua was edging toward the body of the soldier. I needed to distract Justus. "Aha," I said, "someone beat the soldier to death with a stone willie. Obviously the work of a Greek or a Samaritan—no Jew would touch such a thing."

"They wouldn't?" Maggie asked.

"Jeez, Maggie."

"I think you have something to tell me, boy," Justus said.

Joshua had laid hands on the dead soldier.

I could feel everyone's eyes on me. I wondered where Jeremiah was now. Was he behind me, ready to silence me with a knife, or had he made his escape? Either way, I couldn't say a word. The Sicarii did not work alone. If I gave up Jeremiah I'd be dead by a Sicarii dagger before the Sabbath.

"He can't tell you, Centurion, even if he knew," said Joshua, who had moved back to Maggie's side. "For it is written in our holy books that no Jew shall rat out another Jew, regardless of what a weasel one or the other shall be."

"Is that written?" Maggie whispered.

"Is now," Joshua whispered back.

"Did you just call me a weasel?" I asked.

"Behold!" A woman at the front of the crowd was pointing to the dead soldier. Another screamed. The corpse was moving.

Justus turned toward the commotion and I took the opportunity to look around for Jeremiah. He was still there behind me, only a few people back, but he was staring gape-jawed at the dead soldier, who was currently standing up and dusting off his tunic.

Joshua was concentrating intently on the soldier, but there was none of the sweating or trembling that we had seen at the funeral in Japhia.

To his credit, Justus, although he seemed frightened at first, stood his ground as the corpse ambled stiff-legged toward him. The other soldiers were backing away, along with all of the Jews except Maggie, Joshua, and me.

"I need to report an attack, sir," the once-dead soldier said, performing a very jerky Roman salute.

"You're—you're dead," Justus said.

"Am not."

"You have knife wounds all over your chest."

The soldier looked down, touched the wounds gingerly, then looked back to his commander. "Seems I have been nicked, sir."

"Nicked? Nicked? You've been stabbed half a dozen times. You're dead as dirt."

"I don't think so, sir. Look, I'm not even bleeding."

"That's because you've bled out, son. You're dead."

The soldier began to stagger now, started to fall, and caught himself. "I am feeling a little woozy. I was attacked last night sir, near where they are building that Greek's house. There, he was there." He pointed to me.

"And him too." He pointed to Joshua.

"And the little girl."

"These boys attacked you?"

I could hear scuffling behind me.

"No, not them, that man over there." The solder pointed to Jeremiah, who looked around like a trapped animal. Everyone was so intent on watching the miracle of the talking corpse that they had frozen in place. The killer couldn't push his way through the crowd to get away.

"Arrest him!" Justus commanded, but his soldiers were equally stunned by the resurrection of their cohort.

"Now that I think of it," the dead soldier said, "I do remember being stabbed."

No outlet from the crowd, Jeremiah turned toward his accuser and drew a blade from under his shirt. This seemed to snap the other soldiers out of their trance, and they began advancing on the killer from different angles, swords drawn.

At the sight of the blade, everyone had moved away from the killer, leaving him isolated with no path open but toward us.

"No master but God!" he shouted, then three quick steps and he leapt toward us, his knife raised. I dove on top of Maggie and Joshua, hoping to shield them, but even as I waited for the sharp pain between my shoulder blades, I heard the killer scream, then a grunt, then a protracted moan that ran out of air with a pathetic squeal.

I rolled over to see Gaius Justus Gallicus with his short sword sunk to the hilt in the solar plexus of Jeremiah. The killer had dropped his knife and was standing there looking at the Roman's sword hand, looking somewhat offended by it. He sank to his knees. Justus yanked his sword free, then wiped the blade on Jeremiah's shirt before stepping back and letting the killer fall forward.

"That was him," the dead soldier said. "Bastard kilt me." He fell forward next to his killer and lay still.

"Much better than last time, Josh," I said.

"Yes, much better," Maggie said. "Walking and talking. You had him going."

"I felt good, confident, but it was a team effort," Joshua said. "I couldn't have done it without everyone giving it their all, including God."

I felt something sharp against my cheek. With the tip of his sword, Justus guided my gaze to Apollo's stone penis, which lay in the dirt next to the two corpses. "And do you want to explain how that happened?"

"The pox?" I ventured.

"The pox can do that," Maggie said. "Can rot it right off."

"How do you know that?" Joshua asked her.

"Just guessing. I'm sure glad that's all over."

Justus let his sword fall to his side with a sigh. "Go home. All of you. By order of Gaius Justus Gallicus, under-commander of the Sixth Legion, commander of the Third and Fourth Centuries, under authority of Emperor Tiberius and the Roman Empire, you are all commanded to go home and perpetrate no weird shit until I have gotten well drunk and had several days to sleep it off."

"So you're going to release Joseph?" Maggie asked.

"He's at the barracks. Go get him and take him home."

"Amen," said Joshua.

"*Semper fido,*" I added in Latin.

Joshua's little brother Judah, who was seven by then, ran around the Roman barracks screaming "Let my people go! Let my people go!" until he was hoarse. (Judah had decided early on that he was going to be Moses when he grew up, only this time Moses would get to enter the promised land—on a pony.) As it turned out, Joseph had been waiting for us at the Venus Gate. He looked a little confused, but otherwise unharmed.

"They say that a dead man spoke," Joseph said.

Mary was ecstatic. "Yes, and walked. He pointed out his murderer, then he died again."

"Sorry," Joshua said, "I tried to make him live on, but he only lasted a minute."

Joseph frowned. "Did everyone see what you did, Joshua?"

"They didn't know it was my doing, but they saw it."

"I distracted everyone with one of my excellent dirges," I said.

"You can't risk yourself like that," Joseph said to Joshua. "It's not the time yet."

"If not to save my father, when?"

"I'm not your father." Joseph smiled.

"Yes you are." Joshua hung his head.

"But I'm not the boss of you." Joseph's smile widened to a grin.

"No, I guess not," Joshua said.

"You needn't have worried, Joseph," I said. "If the Romans had killed you I would have taken good care of Mary and the children."

Maggie punched me in the arm.

"Good to know," Joseph said.

On the road to Nazareth, I got to walk with Maggie a few paces behind Joseph and his family. Maggie's family was so distraught over what had happened to Jeremiah that they didn't even notice she wasn't with them.

"He's much stronger than he was the last time," Maggie said.

"Don't worry, he'll be a mess tomorrow: '*Oh, what did I do wrong. Oh, my faith wasn't strong enough. Oh, I am not worthy of my task.*' He'll be impossible to be around for a week or so. We'll be lucky if he stops praying long enough to eat."

"You shouldn't make fun of him. He's trying very hard."

"Easy for you to say, you won't have to hang out with the village idiot until Josh gets over this."

"But aren't you touched by who he is? What he is?"

"What good would that do me? If I was basking in the light of his holiness all of the time, how would I take care of him? Who would do all of his lying and cheating for him? Even Josh can't think about what he is all of the time, Maggie."

"I think about him all of the time. I pray for him all of the time."

"Really? Do you ever pray for me?"

"I mentioned you in my prayers, once."

"You did? How?"

"I asked God to help you not to be such a doofus, so you could watch over Joshua."

"You meant doofus in an attractive way, right?"

"Of course."

hapter 7

And the angel said, "What prophet has this written? For in this book is foretold all the events which shall come to pass in the next week in the land of *Days of Our Lives* and *All My Children.*"

And I said to the angel, "You fabulously feeble-minded bundle of feathers, there's no prophet involved. They know what is going to happen because they write it all down in advance for the actors to perform."

"So it is written, so it shall be done," said the angel.

I crossed the room and sat on the edge of the bed next to Raziel. His gaze never wavered from his *Soap Opera Digest.* I pushed the magazine down so the angel had to look me in the face.

"Raziel, do you remember the time before mankind, the time when there were only the heavenly host and the Lord?"

"Yes, those were the best of times. Except for the war, of course. But other than that, yes, wonderful times."

"And you angels were as strong and beautiful as divine imagination, your voices sang praise for the Lord and his glory to the ends of the universe, and yet the Lord saw fit to create us, mankind, weak, twisted, and profane, right?"

"That's when it all started to go downhill, if you ask me," Raziel said.

"Well, do you know why the Lord decided to create us?"

"No. Ours is not to question the Will."

"Because you are all dumbfucks, that's why. You're as mindless as the machinery of the stars. Angels are just pretty insects. *Days of Our Lives* is a show, Raziel, a play. It's not real, get it?'"

"No."

And he didn't. I've learned that there's a tradition in this time of telling funny stories about the stupidity of people with yellow hair. Guess where that started.

I think that we all expected everything to go back to normal after the killer was found, but it seemed that the Romans were much more concerned with the extermination of the Sicarii then they were with a single resurrection. To be fair, I have to say that resurrections weren't that uncommon in those days. As I mentioned, we Jews were quick to get our dead into the ground, and with speed, there's bound to be errors. Occasionally some poor soul would fall unconscious during a fever and wake to find himself being wrapped in linen and prepared for the grave. But funerals were a nice way to get the family together, and there was always a fine meal afterward, so no one really complained, except perhaps those people who didn't wake before they were buried, and if they complained—well, I'm sure God heard them. (It paid to be a light sleeper, in my time.) So, impressed as they might have been with the walking dead, the next day the Romans began to round up suspected conspirators. The men in Maggie's family were hauled off to Sepphoris at dawn.

No miracles would come to bring about the release of the prisoners, but neither were there any crucifixions announced in the days that followed. After two weeks had passed with no word of the fate or condition of the men, Maggie, her mother, her aunts, and her sisters went to the synagogue on the Sabbath and appealed to the Pharisees for help.

The next day, the Pharisees from Nazareth, Japhia, and Sepphoris appeared at the Roman garrison to appeal to Justus for the release of the prisoners. I don't know what they said, or what sort of leverage they could possibly have used to move the Romans, but the following day, just after dawn, the men of Maggie's family staggered back into our village, beaten, starving, and covered with filth, but very much alive.

There was no feast, no celebration for the return of the prisoners—we Jews walked softly for a few months to allow the Romans to settle down. Maggie seemed distant in the weeks that followed, and Josh and I never saw the smile that could make the breath catch in our throats. She seemed to be avoiding us, rushing out of the square whenever we saw her there, or on the Sabbath, staying so close to the women of her family that we couldn't talk to her. Finally, after a month had passed, with absolutely no regard for custom or common courtesy, Joshua insisted that we skip work and dragged me by the sleeve to Maggie's house. She was kneeling on the ground outside the door, grinding some barley with a millstone. We could see her mother moving around in the house and hear the sound of her father and older brother Simon (who was called Lazarus) working the forge next door. Maggie seemed to be lost in the rhythm of grinding the grain, so she didn't see us approach. Joshua put his hand on her shoulder, and without looking up, she smiled.

"You are supposed to be building a house in Sepphoris," she said.

"We thought it more important to visit a sick friend."

"And who would that be?"

"Who do you think?"

"I'm not sick. In fact, I've been healed by the touch of the Messiah."

"I think not," said Joshua.

She finally looked up at him and her smile evaporated. "I can't be friends with you two anymore," she said. "Things have changed."

"What, because your uncle was a Sicarii?" I said. "Don't be silly."

"No, because my mother made a bargain to get Iban to convince the other Pharisees to go to Sepphoris and plead for the men's lives."

"What kind of bargain?" Joshua asked.

"I am betrothed." She looked at the millstone again and a tear dripped into the powdered grain.

We were both stunned. Josh took his hand from her shoulder and stepped back, then looked at me as if there was something I could do. I felt as if I would start crying at any second myself. I managed to choke out, "Who to?"

"To Jakan," Maggie said with a sob.

"Iban's son? The creep? The bully?"

Maggie nodded. Joshua covered his mouth and ran a few steps away, then threw up. I was tempted to join him, but instead I crouched in front of Maggie.

"How long before you're married?"

"I'm to be married a month after the Passover feast. Mother made him wait six months."

"Six months! Six months! That's forever, Maggie. Why, Jakan could be killed in a thousand heinous ways in six months, and that's just the ones I can think of right now. Why, someone could turn him in to the Romans for being a rebel. I'm not saying who, but someone might. It could happen."

"I'm sorry, Biff."

"Don't be sorry for me, why would you be sorry for me?"

"I know how you feel, so I'm sorry."

I was thrown for a second. I glanced at Joshua to see if he could give me a clue, but he was still absorbed in splattering his breakfast in the dirt.

"But it's Joshua who you love?" I finally said.

"Does that make you feel any better?"

"Well, no."

"Then I'm sorry." She made as if to reach out to touch my cheek, but her mother called her before she made contact.

"Right now, Mary, in this house!"

Maggie nodded toward the barfing Messiah. "Take care of him."

"He'll be fine."

"And take care of yourself."

"I'll be fine too, Maggie. Don't forget I have an emergency backup wife. Besides, it's six months. A lot can happen in six months. It's not like we won't see you." I was trying to sound more hopeful than I felt.

"Take Joshua home," she said. Then she quickly kissed me on the cheek and ran into the house.

Joshua was completely against the idea of murdering Jakan, or even praying for harm to come to him. If anything, Joshua seemed more kindly disposed toward Jakan than he had been before, going as far as to seek him out and congratulate him on his betrothal to Maggie, an act that left me feeling angry and betrayed. I confronted Joshua in the olive grove, where he had gone to pray among the twisted tree trunks.

"You coward," I said, "you could strike him down if you wanted to."

"As could you," he replied.

"Yeah, but you can call the wrath of God down upon him. I'd have to sneak up behind him and brain him with a rock. There's a difference."

"And you would have me kill Jakan for what, your bad luck?"

"Works for me."

"Is it so hard for you to give up what you never had?"

"I had hope, Josh. You understand hope, don't you?" Sometimes he could be mightily dense, or so I thought. I didn't realize how much he was hurting inside, or how much he wanted to do something.

"I think I understand hope, I'm just not sure that I am allowed to have any."

"Oh, don't start with that 'Everyone gets something but me' speech. You've got plenty."

Josh wheeled on me, his eyes like fire, "Like what? What do I have?"

"Uh . . ." I wanted to say something about a really sexy mother, but that didn't seem like the sort of thing he wanted to hear. "Uh, you have God."

"So do you. So does everyone."

"Really?"

"Yes."

"Not the Romans."

"There are Roman Jews."

"Well, you've got, uh—that healing-raising-the-dead thing."

"Oh yeah, and that's working really well."

"Well, you're the Messiah, what's that? That's something. If you told people you were the Messiah they'd have to do what you say."

"I can't tell them."

"Why not?"

"I don't know how to be the Messiah."

"Well, at least do something about Maggie."

"He can't," came a voice from behind a tree. A golden glow emanated from either side of the trunk.

"Who's there?" Joshua called.

The angel Raziel stepped out from behind the tree.

"Angel of the Lord," I said under my breath to Josh.

"I know," he said, in a "you seen one, you seen 'em all" way.

"He can't do anything," the angel repeated.

"Why not?" I asked.

"Because he may not know any woman."

"I may not?" Joshua said, not sounding at all happy.

"He may not in that he *should* not, or that he *can*not?" I asked.

The angel scratched his golden head, "I didn't think to ask."

"It's kind of important," I said.

"Well, he can't do anything about Mary Magdalene, I know that. They told me to come and tell him that. That and that it is time for him to go."

"Go where?"

"I didn't think to ask."

I suppose I should have been frightened, but I seemed to have passed right through frightened to exasperated. I stepped up to the angel and poked him in the chest. "Are you the same angel that came to us before, to announce the coming of the Savior?"

"It was the Lord's will that I bring that joyful news."

"I just wondered, in case all of you angels look alike or something. So, after you showed up ten years late, they sent you with another message?"

"I am here to tell the Savior that it is time for him to go."

"But you don't know where?"

"No."

"And this golden stuff around you, this light, what is this?"

"The glory of the Lord."

"You're sure it's not stupidity leaking out of you?"

"Biff, be nice, he is the messenger of the Lord."

"Well, hell, Josh, he's no help at all. If we're going to get angels from heaven they should at least know what they are doing. Blow down walls or something, destroy cities, oh, I don't know—get the *whole* message."

"I'm sorry," the angel said. "Would you like me to destroy a city?"

"Go find out where Josh is supposed to go. How 'bout that?"

"I can do that."

"Then do that."

"I'll be right back."

"We'll wait."

"Godspeed," Joshua said.

In an instant the angel moved behind another tree trunk and the golden glow was gone from the olive grove with a warm breeze.

"You were sort of hard on him," Joshua said.

"Josh, being nice isn't always going to get the job done."

"One can try."

"Was Moses nice to Pharaoh?"

Before Joshua could answer me, the warm breeze blew into the olive grove again and the angel stepped out from behind a tree.

"To find your destiny," he said.

"What?" I said.

"What?" Joshua said.

"You are supposed to go find your destiny."

"That's it?" Joshua said.

"Yes."

"What about the 'knowing a woman' thing?" I asked.

"I have to go now."

"Grab him, Josh. You hold him and I'll hit him."

But the angel was gone with the breeze.

"My destiny?" Joshua looked at his open, empty palms.

"We should have pounded the answer out of him," I said.

"I don't think that would have worked."

"Oh, back to the *nice* strategy. Did Moses—"

"Moses should have said, 'Let my people go, *please*.' "

"That would have made the difference?"

"It could have worked. You don't know."

"So what do you do about your destiny?"

"I'm going to ask the Holy of Holies when we go to the Temple for the Passover."

a nd so it came to pass that in the spring all of the Jews from Galilee made the pilgrimage to Jerusalem for the Passover feast, and Joshua began the search for his destiny. The road was lined with families making their way to the holy city. Camels, carts, and donkeys were loaded high with provisions for the trip, and all along the column of pilgrims you could hear the bleating of the lambs that would be sacrificed for the feast. The road was dry that year, and a red-brown cloud of dust wound its way over the road as far as one could see in either direction.

Since we were each the eldest in our families, it fell on Joshua and me to keep track of all our younger brothers and sisters. It seemed that the easiest way to accomplish this was to tie them together, so we strung together, by height, my two brothers and Josh's three brothers and two sisters. I tied the rope loosely around their necks so it would only choke them if they got out of line.

"I can untie this," said James.

"Me too," said my brother Shem.

"But you won't. This is the part of the Passover where you reenact Moses leading you out of the Promised Land, you have to stay with the little ones."

"You're not Moses," said Shem.

"No—no, I'm not Moses. Smart of you to notice." I tied the end of the rope to a nearby wagon that was loaded high with jars of wine. "This wagon is Moses," I said. "Follow it."

"That wagon isn't—"

"It's symbolic, shut the hell up and follow Moses."

Thus freed of our responsibilities, Joshua and I went looking for Maggie and her family. We knew that Maggie and her clan had left after us, so we fought backward through the pilgrims, braving donkey bites and camel spit until we spotted her royal blue shawl on the hill behind us, perhaps a half-mile back. We had resolved to just sit by the side of the road to wait until she reached us, rather than battle the crowd, when suddenly the column of pilgrims started to leave the road altogether, moving to the sides in a great wave. When we saw the red crest of a centurion's helmet come over the top of the hill we understood. Our people were making way for the Roman army. (There would be nearly a million Jews in Jerusalem for Passover—a million Jews celebrating their liberation from oppression, a very dangerous mix from the Roman point of view. The Roman governor would come from Caesarea with his full legion of six thousand men, and each of the other barracks in Judea, Samaria, and Galilee would send a century or two of soldiers to the holy city.)

We used the opportunity to dash back to Maggie, arriving there at the same time as the Roman army. The centurion that led the cavalry kicked at me as he passed, his hobnail boot missing my head by a hair's breadth. I suppose I should be glad he wasn't a standard-bearer or I might have been conked with a Roman eagle.

"How long do I have to wait before you drive them from the land and restore the kingdom to our people, Joshua?" Maggie stood there with her hands on her hips, trying to look stern, but her blue eyes betrayed that she was about to burst into laughter.

"Uh, shalom to you too, Maggie," Joshua said.

"How about you, Biff, have you learned to be an idiot yet, or are you behind in your studies?" Those laughing eyes, even as the Romans passed by only an arm's length away. God, I miss her.

"I'm learning," I said.

Maggie put down the jar she'd been carrying and threw her arms out to embrace us. It had been months since we'd seen her other than passing in the square. She smelled of lemons and cinnamon that day.

We walked with Maggie and her family for a couple of hours, talking and joking and avoiding the subject that we were all thinking about until Maggie finally said, "Are you two coming to my wedding?"

Joshua and I looked at each other as if our tongues had suddenly been struck from our mouths. I saw that Josh was having no luck finding words, and Maggie seemed to be getting angry.

"Well?"

"Uh, Maggie, it's not that we're not overjoyed with your good fortune, but . . ."

She took the opportunity to backhand me across the mouth. The jar she carried on her head didn't even waver. Amazing grace that girl had.

"Ouch."

"Good fortune? Are you mad? My husband's a toad. I'm sick at the thought of him. I was just hoping you two would come to help me through the ceremony."

"I think my lip is bleeding."

Joshua looked at me and his eyes went wide. "Uh-oh." He cocked his head, as if listening to the wind.

"What, uh-oh?" Then I heard the commotion coming from ahead. There was a crowd gathered at a small bridge—a lot of shouting and waving. Since the Romans had long since passed, I assumed someone had fallen in the river.

"Uh-oh," Josh said again, and he began running toward the bridge.

"Sorry." I shrugged at Maggie, then followed Josh.

At the river's edge (no more than a creek, really) we saw a boy about our age, with wild hair and wilder eyes, standing waist-deep in the water. He was holding something under the water and shouting at the top of his lungs.

"You must repent and atone, atone and repent! Your sins have made you unclean. I cleanse you of the evil that you carry like your wallet."

"That's my cousin, John," Joshua said.

Trailing out of the water on either side of John stood our brothers and sisters, still tied together, but the missing link in the string of siblings was my brother Shem, who had been replaced by a lot of thrashing and bubbling muddy water in front of John. Onlookers were cheering on the Baptist, who was having a little trouble keeping Shem under water.

"I think he's drowning Shem."

"Baptizing," Joshua said.

"My mother will be happy that Shem's sins have been cleansed, but I have to think we're going to be in a lot of trouble if he drowns in the process."

"Good point," Josh said. He stepped into the water. "John! Stop that!"

John looked at him and seemed a little perplexed. "Cousin Joshua?"

"Yes. John, let him up."

"He has sinned," John said, as if that said it all.

"I'll take care of his sins."

"You think you're the one, don't you? Well, you're not. My birth was announced by an angel as well. It was prophesied that I would lead. You're not the one."

"We should talk about this in another place. Let him up, John. He's cleansed."

John let my brother pop out of the water and I ran down and dragged him and all the other kids out of the river.

"Wait, the others haven't been cleansed. They are filthy with sin."

Joshua stepped between his brother James, who would have been the next one dunked, and the Baptist. "You won't tell Mother about this, will you?"

Halfway between terrified and furious, James was tearing at the knots, trying to untie the rope from around his neck. He clearly wanted revenge on his big brother, but at the same time he didn't want to give up his brother's protection from John.

"If we let John baptize you long enough, you won't be able to tell your mother, will you, James?" Me, just trying to help out.

"I won't tell," James said. He looked back at John, who was still staring as if he'd dash out and grab someone to cleanse any second. "He's our cousin?"

"Yes," Joshua said. "The son of our mother's cousin Elizabeth."

"When did you meet him before?"

"I haven't."

"Then how did you know him."

"I just did."

"He's a loony," said James. "You're both loonies."

"Yes, a family trait. Maybe when you get older you can be a loony too. You won't tell Mother."

"No."

"Good," Joshua said. "You and Biff get the kids moving, will you?"

I nodded, shooting a glance back to John. "James *is* right, Josh. He is a loony."

"I heard that, sinner!" John shouted. "Perhaps you need to be cleansed."

John and his parents shared supper with us that evening. I was surprised that John's parents were older than Joseph—older than my grandparents even. Joshua told me that John's birth had been a miracle, announced by the angel. Elizabeth, John's mother, talked about it all through supper, as if it had happened yesterday instead of thirteen years ago. When the old woman paused to take a breath, Joshua's mother started in about the divine announcement of her own son's birth. Occasionally my mother, feeling the need to exhibit some maternal pride that she didn't really feel, would chime in as well.

"You know, Biff wasn't announced by an angel, but locusts ate our garden and Alphaeus had gas for a month around the time he would have been conceived. I think it might have been a sign. That certainly didn't happen with my other boys."

Ah, Mother. Did I mention that she was besought with a demon?

After supper, Joshua and I built our own fire, away from the others, hoping that Maggie would seek us out, but it turned out that only John joined us.

"You are not the anointed one," John said to Joshua. "Gabriel came to my father. Your angel didn't even have a name."

"We shouldn't be talking about these things," Joshua said.

"The angel told my father that his son would prepare the way for the Lord. That's me."

"Fine, I want nothing more than for you to be the Messiah, John."

"Really?" John asked. "But your mother seems so, so . . . ."

"Josh can raise the dead," I said.

John shifted his insane gaze to me, and I scooted away from him in case he tried to hit me. "He cannot," John said.

"Yep, I've seen it twice."

"Don't, Biff," Josh said.

"You're lying. Bearing false witness is a sin," John said. The Baptist started to look more panicked than angry.

"I'm not very good at it," Joshua said.

John's eyes went wide, now with amazement instead of madness. "You have done this? You have raised the dead?"

"And healed the sick," I said.

John grabbed me by the front of my tunic and pulled me close, staring into my eyes as if he was looking into my head. "You aren't lying, are you?" He looked at Joshua. "He's not lying, is he?"

Joshua shook his head. "I don't think so."

John released me, let out a long sigh, then sat back in the dirt. The firelight caught tears sparkling in his eyes as he stared at nothing. "I am so relieved. I didn't know what I would do. I don't know how to be the Messiah."

"Neither do I," said Joshua.

"Well, I hope you really can raise the dead," John said, "because this will kill my mother."

We walked with John for the next three days, through Samaria, into Judea, and finally into the holy city. Fortunately, there weren't many rivers or streams along the way, so we were able to keep his baptisms to a minimum. His heart was in the right place, he really did want to cleanse our people of their sins, it was just that no one would believe that God would give that responsibility to a thirteen-year-old. To keep John happy, Josh and I let him baptize our little brothers and sisters at every body of water we passed, at least until Josh's little sister Miriam developed the sniffles and Joshua had to perform an emergency healing on her.

"You really can heal," John exclaimed.

"Well, the sniffles are easy," Joshua said. "A little mucus is nothing against the power of the Lord."

"Would—would you mind?" John said, lifting up his tunic and showing his bare privates, which were covered with sores and greenish scales.

"Cover, please cover!" I yelled. "Drop the shirt and step away!"

"That's disgusting," Joshua said.

"Am I unclean? I've been afraid to ask my father, and I can't go to a Pharisee, not with my father being a priest. I think it's from standing in the water all of the time. Can you heal me?"

(I have to say here that I believe that this was the first time Joshua's little sister Miriam ever saw a man's privates. She was only six at the time, but the experience so frightened her that she never married. The last time anyone heard from her, she had cut her hair short, put on men's clothes, and moved to the Greek island of Lesbos. But that was later.)

"Have at it, Josh," I said. "Lay your hands upon the affliction and heal it."

Joshua shot me a dirty look, then looked back to his cousin John, with nothing but compassion in his eyes. "My mother has some salve you can put on it," he said. "Let's see if that works first."

"I've tried salve," John said.

"I was afraid you had," said Joshua.

"Have you tried rubbing it with olive oil?" I asked. "It probably won't cure you, but it might take your mind off of it."

"Biff, please. John is afflicted."

"Sorry."

Joshua said, "Come here, John."

"Oh, jeez, Joshua," I said. "You're not going to touch it, are you? He's unclean. Let him live with the lepers."

Joshua put his hands on John's head and the Baptist's eyes rolled back in his head. I thought he would fall, and he did waver, but remained standing.

"Father, you have sent this one to prepare the way. Let him go forth with his body as clean as his spirit."

Joshua released his cousin and stepped back. John opened his eyes and smiled. "I am healed!" he yelled. "I am healed."

John began to raise his shirt and I caught his arm. "We'll take your word for it."

The Baptist fell to his knees, then prostrated himself before Joshua, shoving his face against Josh's feet. "You are truly the Messiah. I'm sorry I ever doubted you. I shall declare your holiness throughout the land."

"Uh, maybe someday, but not now," Joshua said.

John looked up from where he had been grasping Josh's ankles. "Not now?"

"We're trying to keep it a secret," I said.

Josh patted his cousin's head. "Yes, it would be best not to tell anyone about the healing, John."

"But why?"

"We have to find out a couple of things before Joshua starts being the Messiah," I said.

"Like what?" John seemed as if he would start crying again.

"Well, like where Joshua left his destiny and whether or not he's allowed to, uh, have an abomination with a woman."

"It's not an abomination if it's with a woman," Josh added.

"It's not?"

"Nope. Sheep, goats, pretty much any animal—it's an abomination. But with a woman, it's something totally different."

"What about a woman and a goat, what's that?" asked John.

"That's five shekels in Damascus," I said. "Six if you want to help."

Joshua punched me in the shoulder.

"Sorry, old joke." I grinned. "Couldn't resist."

John closed his eyes and rubbed his temples, as if he might squeeze some understanding out of his mind if he applied enough pressure. "So you don't want anyone to know that you have the power to heal because you don't know if you can lie with a woman?"

"Well, that and I have no idea how to go about being the Messiah," Josh said.

"Yeah, and that," I said.

"You should ask Hillel," John said. "My father says he's the wisest of all of the priests."

"I'm going to ask the Holy of Holies," Joshua said. (The Holy of Holies was the Ark of the Covenant—the box containing the tablets handed down from God to Moses. No one I knew had ever seen it, as it was housed in the inner room at the Temple.)

"But it's forbidden. Only a priest may enter the chamber of the Ark."

"Yes, that's going to be a problem," I said.

the city was like a huge cup that had been filled to its brim with pilgrims, then spilled into a seething pool of humanity around it. When we arrived men were already lined up as far as the Damascus gate, waiting with their lambs to get to the Temple. A greasy black smoke was on the wind, coming from the Temple, where as many as ten thousand priests would be slaughtering the lambs and burning the blood and fatty parts on the altar. Cooking fires were burning all around the city as women prepared the lambs. A haze hung in the air, the steam and funk of a million people and as many animals. Stale breath and sweat and the smell of piss rose in the heat of the day, mixing with the bleating of lambs, the bellowing of camels, the crying of children, the ululations of women, and the low buzz of too many voices, until the air was thick with sounds and smells and God and history. Here Abraham received the word of God that his people would be the Chosen, here were the Hebrews delivered out of Egypt, here Solomon built the first Temple, here walked the prophets and the kings of the Hebrews, and here resided the Ark of the Covenant. Jerusalem. Here did I, the Christ, and John the Baptist come to find out the will of God and, if we were lucky, spot some really delicious girls. (What, you thought it was all religion and philosophy?)

Our families made camp outside the northern wall of the city, below the battlements of Antonia, the fortress Herod had built in tribute to his benefactor, Marc Antony. Two cohorts of Roman soldiers, some twelve hundred strong, watched the Temple courtyard from the fortress walls. The women fed and washed the children while Joshua and I carried lambs with our fathers to the Temple.

There was something unsettling about carrying an animal to its death. It wasn't that I hadn't seen the sacrifices before, nor even eaten the Passover lamb, but this was the first time I'd actually participated. I could feel the animal's breathing on my neck as I carried it slung over my shoulders, and amid all the noise and the smells and the movement around the Temple, there was, for a moment, silence, just the breath and heartbeat of the lamb. I guess I fell behind the others, because my father turned and said something to me, but I couldn't hear the words.

We went through the gates and into the outer courtyard of the Temple where merchants sold birds for the sacrifice and moneychangers traded shekels for a hundred different coins from around the world. As we passed through the enormous courtyard, where thousands of men stood with lambs on their shoulders waiting to get into the inner temple, to the altar, to the slaughter, I could see no man's face. I saw only the faces of the lambs, some calm and oblivious, others with their eyes rolled back, bleating in terror, still others seeming to be stunned. I swung the lamb from my own shoulders and cradled it in my arms like a child as I backed out toward the gate. I know my father and Joseph must have come after me, but I couldn't see their faces, just emptiness where their eyes should have been, just the eyes of the lambs they carried. I couldn't breathe, and I couldn't get out of the Temple fast enough. I didn't know where I was going, but I wasn't going inside to the altar. I turned to run, but a hand caught my shirt and pulled me back. I spun around and looked into Joshua's eyes.

"It's God's will," he said. He laid his hands on my head and I was able to breathe again. "It's all right, Biff. God's will." He smiled.

Joshua had put the lamb he'd been carrying on the ground, but it didn't run away. I suppose I should have known right then.

I didn't eat any of the lamb for that Passover feast. In fact, I've never eaten lamb since that day.

hapter 8

I've managed to sneak into the bathroom long enough to read a few chapters of this New Testament that they've added to the Bible. This Matthew fellow, who is obviously not the Matthew that we knew, seems to have left out quite a little bit. Like everything from the time Joshua was born to the time he was thirty!!! No wonder the angel brought me back to write this book. This Matthew fellow hasn't mentioned me yet, but I'm still in the early chapters. I have to ration myself to keep the angel from getting suspicious. Today he confronted me when I came out of the bathroom.

"You are spending a lot of time in there. You don't need to spend so much time in there."

"I told you, cleanliness is very important to my people."

"You weren't bathing. I would have heard the water running."

I decided that I needed to go on the offensive if I was going to keep the angel from finding the Bible. I ran across the room, leapt onto his bed, and fastened my hands around his throat—choking him as I chanted: "I haven't been laid in two thousand years. I haven't been laid in two thousand years. I haven't been laid in two thousand years." It felt good, there was a rhythm to it, I sort of squoze his throat a bit with every syllable.

I paused for a moment in choking the heavenly host to backhand him across his alabaster cheek. It was a mistake. He caught my hand. Then grabbed me by the hair with his other hand and calmly climbed to his feet, lifting me into the air by my hair.

"Ow, ow, ow, ow, ow," I said.

"So, you have not been laid in two thousand years? What does that mean?"

"Ow, ow, ow, ow," I replied.

The angel set me on my feet, but kept his grasp on my hair. "So?"

"It means that I haven't had a woman in two millennia, aren't you picking up any of the vocabulary from the television?"

He glanced at the TV, which, of course, was on. "I don't have your gift of tongues. What does that have to do with choking me?"

"I was choking you because you, once again, are as dense as dirt. I haven't had sex in two thousand years. Men have needs. What the hell do you think I'm doing in the bathroom all of that time?"

"Oh," the angel said, releasing my hair. "So you are . . . You have been . . . There is a . . ."

"Get me a woman and maybe I won't spend so much time in the bathroom, if you get my meaning." Brilliant misdirection, I thought.

"A woman? No, I cannot do that. Not yet."

"Yet? Does that mean . . ."

"Oh look," the angel said, turning from me as if I was no more than vapor, "*General Hospital* is starting."

And with that, my secret Bible was safe. What did he mean by "yet"?

At least this Matthew mentions the Magi. One sentence, but that's one more than I've gotten in his Gospel so far.

Our second day in Jerusalem we went to see the great Rabbi Hillel. (Rabbi means teacher in Hebrew—you knew that, right?) Hillel looked to be a hundred years old, his beard and hair were long and white, and his eyes were clouded over, his irises milk white. His skin was leathery-brown from sitting in the sun and his nose was long and hooked, giving him the aspect of a great, blind eagle. He held class all morning in the outer courtyard of the Temple. We sat quietly, listening to him recite from the Torah and interpret the verses, taking questions and engaging in arguments with the Pharisees, who tried to infuse the Law into every minute detail of life.

Toward the end of Hillel's morning lectures, Jakan, the camel-sucking husband-to-be of my beloved Maggie, asked Hillel if it would be a sin to eat an egg that had been laid on the Sabbath.

"What are you, stupid? The Lord doesn't give a damn what a chicken does on the Sabbath, you nimrod! It's a chicken. If a Jew lays an egg on the Sabbath, that's probably a sin, come see me then. Otherwise don't waste my friggin' time with that nonsense. Now go away, I'm hungry and I need a nap. All of you, scram."

Joshua looked at me and grinned. "He's not what I expected," he whispered.

"Knows a nimrod when he sees—uh—hears one, though," I said. (Nimrod was an ancient king who died of suffocation after he wondered aloud in front of his guards what it would be like to have your own head stuck up your ass.)

A boy younger than us helped the old man to his feet and began to lead him away toward the Temple gate. I ran up and took the priest's other arm.

"Rabbi, my friend has come from far away to talk to you. Can you help him?"

The old man stopped. "Where is your friend?"

"Right here."

"Then why isn't he talking for himself? Where do you come from, kid?"

"Nazareth," Joshua said, "but I was born in Bethlehem. I am Joshua bar Joseph."

"Oh yeah, I've talked to your mother."

"You have?"

"Sure, almost every time she and your father come to Jerusalem for a feast she tries to see me. She thinks you're the Messiah."

Joshua swallowed hard. "Am I?"

Hillel snorted. "Do you want to be the Messiah?"

Joshua looked at me as if I might have the answer. I shrugged. "I don't know," Josh finally said. "I thought I was just supposed to do it."

"Do you think you're the Messiah?"

"I'm not sure I should say."

"That's smart," Hillel said. "You shouldn't say. You can think you're the Messiah all that you want, just don't tell anyone."

"But if I don't tell them, they won't know."

"Exactly. You can think you're a palm tree if you want, just don't tell anyone. You can think you're a flock of seagulls, just don't tell anyone. You get my meaning? Now I have to go eat. I'm old and I'm hungry and I want to go eat now, so just in case I die before supper I won't go hungry."

"But he really is the Messiah," I said.

"Oh yeah," Hillel said, grabbing my shoulder, then feeling for my head so he could scream into my ear. "What do you know? You're an ignorant kid. How old are you? Twelve? Thirteen?"

"Thirteen."

"How could you, at thirteen, know anything? I'm eighty-four and I don't know shit."

"But you're wise," I said.

"I'm wise enough to know that I don't know shit. Now go away."

"Should I ask the Holy of Holies?" Joshua said.

Hillel swung at the air, as if to slap Joshua, but missed by a foot. "It's a box. I saw it when I could still see, and I can tell you that it's a box. And you know what else, if there were tablets in it, they aren't there now. So if you want to talk to a box, and probably be executed for trying to get into the chamber where it's kept, you go right ahead."

The breath seemed to be knocked out of Joshua's body and I thought he would faint on the spot. How could the greatest teacher in all of Israel speak of the Ark of the Covenant in such a way? How could a man who obviously knew every word of the Torah, and all the teachings written since, how could he claim not to know anything?

Hillel seemed to sense Joshua's distress. "Look, kid, your mother says that some very wise men came to Bethlehem to see you when you were born. They obviously knew something that no one else knew. Why don't you go see them? Ask them about being the Messiah."

"So you aren't going to tell him how to be the Messiah?" I asked.

Again Hillel reached out for Joshua, but this time without any anger. He found Joshua's cheek, and stroked it with his palsied hand. "I don't believe there will be a Messiah, and at this point, I'm not sure it would make a difference to me. Our people have spent more time in slavery or under the heels of foreign kings than we have spent free, so who is to say that it is God's will that we be free at all? Who is to say that God concerns himself with us in any way, beyond allowing us to be? I don't think that he does. So know this, little one. Whether you are the Messiah, or you become a rabbi, or even if you are nothing more than a farmer, here is the sum of all I can teach you, and all that I know: treat others as you would like to be treated. Can you remember that?"

Joshua nodded and the old man smiled. "Go find your wise men, Joshua bar Joseph."

What we did was stay in the Temple while Joshua grilled every priest, guard, even Pharisee about the Magi who had come to Jerusalem thirteen years before. Evidently it wasn't as big an event for others as it was for Josh's family, because no one had any idea what he was talking about.

By the time he'd been at it for a couple of hours he was literally screaming into the faces of a group of Pharisees. "Three of them. Magicians. They came because they saw a star over Bethlehem. They were carrying gold, frankincense, and myrrh. Come on, you're all old. You're supposed to be wise. Think!"

Needless to say, they weren't pleased. "Who is this boy who would question our knowledge? He knows nothing of the Torah and the prophets and yet berates us for not remembering three insignificant travelers."

It was the wrong thing to say to Joshua. No one had studied the Torah harder. No one knew scripture better. "Ask me any question, Pharisee," Joshua said. "Ask anything."

In retrospect, after having grown up, somewhat, and having lived, died, and been resurrected from the dust, I realize that there may be nothing more obnoxious than a teenager who knows everything. Certainly, it is a symptom of the age that they think they know everything, but now I have some sympathy for those poor men who challenged Joshua that day at the Temple. Of course, at the time, I shouted, "Smite the sons-a-bitches, Josh."

He was there for days. Joshua wouldn't even leave to eat, and I went out into the city to bring him back food. First the Pharisees, but later even some of the priests came to quiz Joshua, to try to throw him some question about some obscure Hebrew king or general. They made him recite the lineages from all the books of the Bible, yet he did not waver. Myself, I left him there to argue while I wandered through the holy city looking for Maggie, then, when I couldn't find her, for girls in general. I slept at the camp of my parents, assuming all the time that Joshua was returning each night to his own family, but I was wrong. When the Passover feast was over and we were packing up to leave, Mary, Joshua's mother, came to me in a panic.

"Biff. Have you seen Joshua?"

The poor woman was distraught. I wanted to comfort her so I held my arms out to give her a comforting embrace. "Poor Mary, calm down. Joshua is fine. Come, let me give you a comforting embrace."

"Biff!" I thought she might slap me.

"He's at the Temple. Jeez, a guy tries to be compassionate and what does he get?"

She had already taken off. I caught up to her as she was dragging Joshua out of the Temple by the arm. "You worried us half to death."

"You should have known you would find me in my father's house," Joshua said.

"Don't you pull that 'my father' stuff on me, Joshua bar Joseph. The commandment says honor thy father *and thy mother*. I'm not feeling honored right now, young man. You could have sent a message, you could have stopped by the camp."

Joshua looked at me, his eyes pleading for me to help him out.

"I tried to comfort her, Josh, but she wouldn't have it."

Later I found the two of them on the road to Nazareth and Joshua motioned for me to walk with them.

"Mother thinks we may be able to find at least one of the Magi, and if we find that one, he may know where the others are."

Mary nodded, "The one named Balthasar, the black one, he said he came from a village north of Antioch. He was the only one of the three that spoke any Hebrew."

I didn't feel confident. Although I'd never seen a map, "north of Antioch" sounded like a large, unspecific, and scary place. "Is there more?"

"Yes, the other two had come from the East by the Silk Road. Their names were Melchior and Gaspar."

"So it's off to Antioch," Joshua said. He seemed completely satisfied with the information his mother had given him, as if all he needed were the three Magi's names and he'd as much as found them.

I said, "You're going to go to Antioch assuming that someone there will remember a man who may have lived north of there thirteen years ago?"

"A magician," Mary said. "A rich, Ethiopian magician. How many can there be?"

"Well, there might not be any, did you think of that? He might have died. He might have moved to another city."

"In that case, I will be in Antioch," Joshua said. "From there I can travel the Silk Road until I find the other two."

I couldn't believe my ears. "You're not going alone."

"Of course."

"But Josh, you're helpless out in the world. You only know Nazareth, where people are stupid and poor. No offense, Mary. You'll be like—uh—like a lamb among wolves. You need me along to watch out for you."

"And what do you know that I don't? Your Latin is horrible, your Greek is barely passable, and your Hebrew is atrocious."

"Yeah. If a stranger comes up to you on the road to Antioch and asks you how much money you are carrying, what do you tell him?"

"That will depend on how much I am carrying."

"No it won't. You haven't enough for a crust of bread. You are a poor beggar."

"But that's not true."

"Exactly."

Mary put her arm around her son's shoulders. "He has a point, Joshua."

Joshua wrinkled his brow as if he had to think about it, but I could tell that he was relieved that I wanted to go along. "When do you want to leave?"

"When did Maggie say she was getting married?"

"In a month."

"Before then. I don't want to be here when it happens."

"Me either," Joshua said.

And so we spent the next few weeks preparing for our journey. My father thought I was crazy, but my mother seemed happy to have the extra space in the house and pleased that the family wouldn't have to put up a bride price to marry me off right away.

"So you'll be gone how long?" Mother asked.

"I don't know. It's not a terribly long journey to Antioch, but I don't know how long we'll be there. Then we'll be traveling the Silk Road. I'm guessing that that's a long journey. I've never seen any silk growing around here."

"Well, take a wool tunic in case it gets cold."

And that was all I heard from my mother. Not "Why are you going?" Not "Who are you looking for?" Just "Take a wool tunic." Jeez. My father was more supportive.

"I can give you a little money to travel with, or we could buy you a donkey."

"I think the money would be better. A donkey couldn't carry both of us."

"And who are these fellows you're looking for?"

"Magicians, I think."

"And you want to talk to magicians because . . . ?"

"Because Josh wants to know how to be the Messiah."

"Oh, right. And you believe that Joshua is the Messiah?"

"Yes, but more important than that, he's my friend. I can't let him go alone."

"And what if he's not the Messiah? What if you find these magicians and they tell you that Joshua is not what you think he is, that he's just a normal boy?"

"Well, he'll really need me to be there, then, won't he?"

My father laughed. "Yes, I guess he will. You come back, Levi, and bring your friend the Messiah with you. Now we'll have to set three empty places at the table on Passover. One for Elijah, one for my lost son, and one for his pal the Messiah."

"Well, don't seat Joshua next to Elijah. If those guys start talking religion we'll never have any peace."

It came down to only four days before Maggie's wedding before Joshua and I accepted that one of us would have to tell her we were leaving. After nearly a whole day of arguing, it fell upon me to go to her. I saw Joshua face down fears in himself that would have broken other men, but taking bad news to Maggie was one he couldn't overcome. I took the task on myself and tried to leave Joshua with his dignity.

"You wuss!"

"How can I tell her that it's too painful to watch her marry that toad?"

"First, you're insulting toads everywhere, and second, what makes you think it's any easier for me?"

"You're tougher than I am."

"Oh, don't try that. You can't just roll over and expect me to not notice that I'm being manipulated. She's going to cry. I hate it when she cries."

"I know," Josh said. "It hurts me too. Too much." Then he put his hand on my head and I suddenly felt better, stronger.

"Don't try your Son of God mumbo jumbo on me, you're still a wuss."

"If it be so, so be it. So it shall be written."

Well, it is now, Josh. It's written now. (It's strange, the word "wuss" is the same in my ancient Aramaic tongue as it is in this language. Like the word waited for me these two thousand years so I could write it down here. Strange.)

Maggie was washing clothes in the square with a bunch of other women. I caught her attention by jumping on the shoulders of my friend Bartholomew, who was gleefully exposing himself for the viewing pleasure of the Nazarene wives. With a subtle toss of my head I signaled to Maggie to meet me behind a nearby stand of date palms.

"Behind those trees?" Maggie shouted.

"Yeah," I replied.

"You bringing the idiot?"

"Nope."

"Okay," she said, and she handed her washing to one of her younger sisters and scampered to the trees.

I was surprised to see her smiling so close to the time of her wedding. She hugged me and I could feel the heat rise in my face, either from shame or love, like there was a difference.

"Well, you're in a good mood," I said.

"Why not? I'm using them all up before the wedding. Speaking of which, what are you two bringing me for a present? It had better be good if it's going to make up for who I have to marry."

She was joyful and there was music and laughter in her voice, pure Maggie, but I had to turn away.

"Hey, I was only joking," she said. "You guys don't need to bring me anything."

"We're leaving, Maggie. We won't be there."

She grabbed my shoulder and forced me to face her. "You're leaving? You and Joshua? You're going away?"

"Yes, before your wedding. We're going to Antioch, and from there far into the East along the Silk Road."

She said nothing. Tears welled up in her eyes and I could feel them rising in mine as well. This time she turned away.

"We should have told you before, I know, but really we only decided at Passover. Joshua is going to find the Magi who came to his birth, and I'm going with him because I have to."

She wheeled on me. "You have to? You have to? You don't have to. You can stay and be my friend and come to my wedding and sneak down to talk to me here or in the vineyard and we can laugh and tease and no matter how horrible it is being married to Jakan, I'll have that. I'll at least have that!"

I felt as if I'd be sick to my stomach any second. I wanted to tell her that I'd stay, that I'd wait, that if there was the slightest chance that her life wasn't going to be a desert in the arms of her creep husband that I could hold hope. I wanted to do whatever I could to take away even a little bit of her pain, even up to letting Joshua go by himself, but in thinking that, I realized that Joshua must have been feeling the same thing, so all I said was "I'm sorry."

"And what about Joshua, wasn't he even going to say good-bye?"

"He wanted to, but he couldn't. Neither of us can, I mean, we didn't want to have to watch you marry Jakan."

"Cowards. You two deserve each other. You can hide behind each other like Greek boys. Just go. Get away from me."

I tried to think of something to say, but my mind was a soup of confusion so I hung my head and walked away. I was almost out of the square when Maggie caught up to me. I heard her footsteps and turned.

"Tell him to meet me behind the synagogue, Biff. The night before my wedding, an hour after sunset."

"I'm not sure, Maggie, he—"

"Tell him," she said. She ran back to the well without looking back.

So I told Joshua, and on the night before Maggie's wedding, the night before we were to leave on our journey, Joshua packed some bread and cheese and a skin of wine and told me to meet him by the date palms in the square where we would share supper together.

"You have to go," Joshua said.

"I'm going. In the morning, when you do. What, you think I'd back out now?"

"No, tonight. You have to go to Maggie. I can't go."

"What? I mean, why?" Sure I'd been heartbroken when Maggie had asked to see Joshua and not me, but I'd come to terms with it. Well, as well as one ever comes to terms with an ongoing heartbreak.

"You have to take my place, Biff. There's almost no moon tonight, and we are about the same size. Just don't say much and she'll think it's me. Maybe not as smart as normal, but she can put that down to worry over the upcoming journey."

"I'd love to see Maggie, but she wants to see you, why can't you go?"

"You really don't know?"

"Not really."

"Then just take my word for it. You'll see. Will you do this for me, Biff? Will you take my place, pretend to be me?"

"That would be lying. You never lie."

"Now you're getting righteous on me? I won't be lying. You will be."

"Oh. In that case, I'll go."

But there wasn't even time to deceive. It was so dark that night that I had to make my way slowly through the village by starlight alone, and as I rounded the corner to the back of our small synagogue I was hit with a wave of sandalwood and lemon and girl sweat, of warm skin, a wet mouth over mine, arms around my back and legs around my waist. I fell backward on the ground and there was in my head a bright light, and the rest of the world existed in the senses of touch and smell and God. There, on the ground behind the synagogue, Maggie and I indulged desires we had carried for years, mine for her, and hers for Joshua. That neither of us knew what we were doing made no difference. It was pure and it happened and it was marvelous. And when we finished we lay there holding each other, half dressed, breathless, and sweating, and Maggie said, "I love you, Joshua."

"I love you, Maggie," I said. And ever so slightly she loosened her embrace.

"I couldn't marry Jakan without—I couldn't let you go without—without letting you know."

"He knows, Maggie."

Then she really pulled away.

"Biff?"

"Uh-oh." I thought she might scream, that she might leap up and run away, that she might do any one of a hundred things to take me from heaven to hell, but after only a second she nuzzled close to me again.

"Thank you for being here," she said.

We left at dawn, and our fathers walked with us as far as the gates of Sepphoris. When we parted at the gates my father gave me a hammer and chisel to carry with me in my satchel. "With that you can make enough for a meal anywhere you go," my father said. Joseph gave Joshua a wooden bowl. "Out of that you can eat the meal that Biff earns." He grinned at me.

By the gates of Sepphoris I kissed my father for the last time. By the gates of Sepphoris we left our fathers behind and went out into the world to find three wise men.

"Come back, Joshua, and make us free," Joseph shouted to our backs.

"Go with God," my own father said.

"I am, I am," I shouted. "He's right here."

Joshua said nothing until the sun was high in the sky and we stopped to share a drink of water. "Well?" Joshua said. "Did she know it was you?"

"Yes. Not at first, but before we parted. She knew."

"Was she angry at me?"

"No."

"Was she angry at you?"

I smiled. "No."

"You dog!" he said.

"You really should ask that angel what he meant about you not knowing a woman, Joshua. It's really important."

"You know now why I couldn't go."

"Yes. Thanks."

"I'll miss her," Joshua said.

"You have no idea," I said.

"Every detail. I want to know every detail."

"But you aren't supposed to know."

"That's not what the angel meant. Tell me."

"Not now. Not while I can still smell her on my arms."

Joshua kicked at the dirt. "Am I angry with you, or happy for you, or jealous of you? I don't know? Tell me!"

"Josh, right now, for the first time I can remember, I'm happier being your friend than I would be being you. Can I have that?"

Now, thinking about that night with Maggie behind the synagogue, where we stayed together until it was nearly dawn, where we made love again and again and fell asleep naked on top of our clothes—now, when I think of that, I want to run away from here, this room, this angel and his task, find a lake, dive down, and hide from the eye of God in the dark muck on the bottom.

Strange.

Part II

Change

Jesus was a good guy, he didn't need this shit.

JOHN PRINE

Chapter 9

I should have had a plan before I tried to escape from the
hotel room, I see that now. At the time, dashing out the door
and into the arms of sweet freedom seemed like plan
enough. I got as far as the lobby. It is a fine lobby, as grand as
any palace, but in the way of freedom, I need more. I noticed
before Raziel dragged me back into the elevator, nearly dis-
locating my shoulder in the process, that there were an inordinate number of old people in the lobby. In fact, compared
to my time, there are inordinate numbers of old people
everywhere—well, not on TV, but everywhere else. Have
you people forgotten how to die? Or have you used up all of
the young people on television so there's nothing left but
gray hair and wrinkled flesh? In my time, if you had seen
forty summers it was time to start thinking about moving on,
making room for the youngsters. If you lasted to fifty the
mourners would give you dirty looks when they passed, as if
you were purposely trying to put them out of business. The
Torah says that Moses lived to be 120 years old. I'm guessing that the children of Israel were following him just to see
when he would drop. There was probably betting.

If I do manage to escape the angel, I'm not going to be
able to make my living as a professional mourner, not if you
people don't have the courtesy to die. Just as well, I suppose,
I'd have to learn all new dirges. I've tried to get the angel to
watch MTV so I can learn the vocabulary of your music, but
even with the gift of tongues, I'm having trouble learning to
speak hip-hop. Why is it that one can busta rhyme or busta
move anywhere but you must busta cap in someone's ass? Is

"ho" always feminine, and "muthafucka" always masculine, while "bitch" can be either? How many peeps in a posse, how much booty before baby got back, do you have to be all that to get all up in that, and do I need to be dope and phat to be da bomb or can I just be "stupid"? I'll not be singing over any dead mothers until I understand.

The journey. The quest. The search for the Magi.

We traveled first to the coast. Neither Joshua nor I had ever seen the sea before, so as we topped a hill near the city of Ptolomais, and the endless aquamarine of the Mediterranean stretched before us, Joshua fell to his knees and gave thanks to his father.

"You can almost see the edge of the world," Joshua said.

I squinted into the dazzling sun, really looking for the edge of the world. "It looks sort of curved," I said.

"What?" Joshua scanned the horizon, but evidently he didn't see the curve.

"The edge of the world looks curved. I think it's round."

"What's round?"

"The world. I think it's round."

"Of course it's round, like a plate. If you go to the edge you fall off. Every sailor knows that," Joshua said with great authority.

"Not round like a plate, round like a ball."

"Don't be silly," Joshua said. "If the world was round like a ball then we would slide off of it."

"Not if it's sticky," I said.

Joshua lifted his foot and looked at the bottom of his sandal, then at me, then at the ground. "Sticky?"

I looked at the bottom of my own shoe, hoping to perhaps see strands of stickiness there, like melted cheese tethering me to the ground. When your best friend is the son of God, you get tired of losing every argument. "Just because you can't see it, doesn't mean the world is not sticky."

Joshua rolled his eyes. "Let's go swimming." He took off down the hill.

"What about the God?" I asked. "You can't see him."

Joshua stopped halfway down the hill and held his arms out to the shining, aquamarine sea. "You can't?"

"That's a crappy argument, Josh." I followed him down the hill, shouting as I went. "If you're not going to try, I'm not going to argue with you anymore. So, what if stickiness is like God? You know, how He abandons our people and leads them into slavery whenever we stop believing in Him. Stickiness could be like that. You could float off into the sky any time now because you don't believe in stickiness."

"It's good that you have something to believe in, Biff. I'm going in the water." He ran down the beach, shedding his clothes as he went, then dove into the surf, naked.

Later, after we'd both swallowed enough salt water to make us sick, we headed up the coast to the city of Ptolemais.

"I didn't think it would be so salty," Joshua said.

"Yeah," I said, "you'd never know it by looking at it."

"Are you still angry about your round-earth-stickiness theory?"

"I don't expect you to understand," I said, sounding very mature, I thought. "You being a virgin and all."

Joshua stopped and grabbed my shoulder, forcing me to wheel around and face him. "The night you spent with Maggie I spent praying to my father to take away the thoughts of you two. He didn't answer me. It was like trying to sleep on a bed of thorns. Since we left I was beginning to forget, or at least leave it behind, but you keep throwing it in my face."

"You're right," I said. "I forgot how sensitive you virgins can be."

Then, once again, and not for the last time, the Prince of Peace coldcocked me. A bony, stonecutter's fist just over my right eye. He hit harder than I remembered. I remember white seabirds in the sky above me, and just a wisp of clouds across the sky. I remember the frothy surf sloshing over my face, leaving sand in my ears. I remember thinking that I should get up and smite Josh upside the head. I remember thinking then that if I got up, Josh might hit me again, so I lay there for a moment, just thinking.

"So, what do you want?" I said, finally, from my wet and sandy supinity.

He stood over me with his fists balled. "If you're going to keep bringing it up, you have to tell me the details."

"I can do that."

"And don't leave anything out."

"Nothing?"

"I've got to know if I'm going to understand sin."

"Okay, can I get up? My ears are filling with sand."

He helped me to my feet and as we entered the seaside city of Ptolomais, I taught Josh about sex.

Down narrow stone streets between high stone walls.

"Well, most of what we learned from the rabbis was not exactly accurate."

Past men sitting outside their houses, mending their nets. Children selling cups of pomegranate juice, women hanging strings of fish from window to window to dry.

"For instance, you know that part right after Lot's wife gets turned to stone and then his daughters get drunk and fornicate with him?"

"Right, after Sodom and Gomorrah are destroyed."

"Well, that's not as bad as it sounds," I said.

We passed Phoenician women who sang as they pounded dried fish into meal. We passed evaporation pools where children scraped the encrusted salt from the rocks and put it into bags.

"But fornication is a sin, and fornication with your daughters, well, that's a, I don't know, that's a double-dog sin."

"Yeah, but if you put that aside for a second, and you just focus on the two young girls aspect of it, it's not nearly as bad as it sounds initially."

"Oh."

We passed merchants selling fruit and bread and oil, spices and incense, calling out claims of quality and magic in their wares. There was a lot of magic for sale in those days.

"And the Song of Solomon, that's a lot closer, and you can sort of understand Solomon having a thousand wives. In fact, with you being the Son of God and all, I don't think you'd have any problem getting that many girls. I mean, after you figure out what you're doing."

"And a lot of girls is a good thing?"

"You're a ninny, aren't you?"

"I thought you'd be more specific. What does Maggie have to do with Lot and Solomon?"

"I can't tell you about me and Maggie, Josh. I just can't."

We were passing a lick of prostitutes gathered outside the door of an inn. Their faces were painted, their skirts slit up the side to show their legs glistening with oil, and they called to us in foreign languages and made tiny dances with their hands as we passed.

"What the hell are they saying?" I asked Joshua. He was better with languages. I think they were speaking Greek.

"They said something about how they like Hebrew boys because we can feel a woman's tongue better without our foreskins." He looked at me as if I might confirm or deny this.

"How much money do we have?" I asked.

The inn rented rooms, stalls, and space under the eave to sleep. We rented two adjacent stalls, which was a bit of a luxury for us, but an important one for Joshua's education. After all, weren't we on this journey so he could learn to take his rightful place as the Messiah?

"I'm not sure if I should watch," Joshua said. "Remember David was running over the roofs and happened onto Bathsheba in her bath. That set a whole chain of sin in motion."

"But listening won't be a problem."

"I don't think it's the same thing."

"Are you sure that you don't want to try this yourself, Josh? I mean, the angel was never clear about your being with a woman." To be honest, I was a little frightened myself. My experience with Maggie hardly qualified me to be with a harlot.

"No, you go ahead. Just describe what's happening and what you're feeling. I have to understand sin."

"Okay, if you insist."

"Thank you for doing this for me, Biff."

"Not just for you, Josh, for our people."

So that's how we ended up with the two stalls. Josh would be in one while I, along with the harlot of my choice, instructed him from the other in the fine art of fornication.

Back out at the front of the inn I shopped for my teaching assistant. It was an eight-harlot inn, if that's how you measure an inn. (I understand that now they measure inns in stars. We are in a four-star inn right now. I don't know what the conversion from harlots to stars is.) Anyway, there were eight harlots outside the inn that day. They ranged in age from only a few years older than us to older than our mothers. And they ran the gamut of shapes and sizes, having in common only that they were all highly painted and well oiled.

"They're all so . . . so nasty-looking."

"They're harlots, Biff. They're supposed to be nasty-looking. Pick one."

"Let's go look at some different harlots." We had been standing a few doors down from the harlots, but they knew we were watching. I walked over and stopped close to a particularly tall harlot and said, "Excuse me, do you know where we might find a different selection of harlots? No offense, it's just that my friend and I . . ."

And she pulled open her blouse, exposing full breasts that were glistening with oil and flecks of mica, and she threw her skirt aside and stepped up so a long leg slid behind me and I could feel the rough hair between her legs grinding against my hip and her rouged nipples brushed my cheek and in that instant profound wood did from my person protrude.

"This one will be fine, Josh."

The other harlots let loose with an exaltation of ululation as we led my harlot away. (You know ululation as the sound an ambulance makes. That I get an erection every time one passes the hotel would seem morbid if you didn't know this story of how Biff Hires a Harlot.) The harlot's name was Set. She was a head and half taller than me, with skin the color of a ripe date, wide brown eyes flecked with gold, and hair so black that it reflected blue in the dim light of the stable. She was the perfect harlot design, wide where a harlot should be wide, narrow where a harlot should be narrow, delicate of ankle and neck, sturdy of conscience, intrepid and single-minded of goal once she was paid. She was an Egyptian, but she had learned Greek and a little Latin to help lubricate the discourse of her trade. Our situation required more creativity than she seemed accustomed to, but after a heavy sigh she mumbled something about "if you fuck a Hebrew, make room in the bed for his guilt," then pulled me into my stall and closed the gate. (Yes, the stalls were used for animals. There was a donkey in the stall opposite Josh's.)

"So what's she doing?" Josh asked.

"She's taking off my clothes."

"What now."

"She's taking off her clothes. Oh jeez. Ouch."

"What? Are you fornicating?"

"No. She's rubbing her whole body over mine, sort of lightly. When I try to move she smacks me in the face."

"How does it feel?"

"How do you think? It feels like someone smacking you, you twit."

"I mean how does her body feel? Do you feel sinful? Is it like Satan rubbing against you? Does it burn like fire?"

"Yeah, you got it. That pretty much has it."

"You're lying."

"Oh wow."

Then Josh said something in Greek that I didn't catch all of and the harlot answered, sort of.

"What did she say?" Josh asked.

"I don't know, you know my Greek is bad."

"Mine isn't, I couldn't understand what she said."

"Her mouth is full."

Set raised up. "Not full," she said in Greek.

"Hey, I understood that!"

"She has you in her mouth?"

"Yeah."

"That's heinous."

"It doesn't feel heinous."

"It doesn't?"

"No, Josh, I gotta tell you, this really is—oh my God!"

"What? What's happening?"

"She's getting dressed."

"Are you done sinning? That's it?"

The harlot said something in Greek that I didn't understand.

"What did she say?" I asked.

"She said that for the amount of money we gave her, you're finished."

"Do you think you understand fornication now?"

"Not really."

"Well then, give her some more money, Joshua. We're going to stay here until you learn what you need to know."

"You're a good friend to suffer this for me."

"Don't mention it."

"No, really," Joshua said. "Greater love hath no man, than he lay down for his friend."

"That's a good one, Josh. You should remember that one for later."

The harlot then spoke at length. "You want to know what this is like for me, kid? This is like a job. Which means that if you want it done, you need to pay for it. That's what it's like." (Joshua would translate for me later.)

"What'd she say?" I asked.

"She wants the wages of sin."

"Which are?"

"In this case, three shekels."

"That's a bargain. Pay her."

much as I tried—and I did try—I didn't seem able to convey to Joshua what it was he wanted to know. I went through a half-dozen more harlots and a large portion of our traveling money over the next week, but he still didn't understand. I suggested that perhaps this was one of the things that the magician Balthasar was supposed to teach Joshua. Truth be told, I'd developed a burning sensation when I peed and I was ready for a break from tutoring my friend in the fine art of sinning.

Ít's a week or less by sea if we go to Selucia, then it's less than a day's walk inland to Antioch," Joshua said, after he had been talking to some sailors who were drinking at the inn. "Overland it's two to three weeks."

"By sea, then," I said. Pretty brave, I thought, considering I'd never set foot in a boat in my life.

We found a wide-beamed, raised-stern Roman cargo ship bound for Tarsus that would stop at all the ports along the way, including Selucia. The ship's master was a wiry, hatchet-faced Phoenician named Titus Inventius, who claimed to have gone to sea when he was four and sailed to the edge of the world twice before his balls dropped, although what one had to do with the other I never figured out.

"What can you do? What's your trade?" Titus asked, from under a great straw hat he wore while watching the slaves load jars of wine and oil onto the ship. His eyes were black beads set back in caves of wrinkles formed by a lifetime of squinting into the sun.

"Well, I'm a stonemason and he's the Son of God." I grinned. I thought that would give us more diversity than just saying we were two stonemasons.

Titus pushed the straw hat back on his head and looked Joshua up and down. "Son of God, huh? How's that pay?"

Joshua scowled at me. "I know stone work and carpentry, and we both have strong backs."

"There's not a lot of call for stone work aboard a ship. Have you been to sea before?"

"Yes," I said.

"No," Joshua said.

"He was sick that day," I said. "I've been to sea."

Titus laughed. "Fine, you go help get those jars on board. I'm taking a load of pigs as far as Sidon, you two keep them calm and keep them alive in the heat and by that time maybe you'll be something of use to me. But it costs you as well."

"How much?" Joshua asked.

"How much do you have?"

"Five shekels," I said.

"Twenty shekels," Joshua said.

I elbowed the Messiah in the ribs hard enough to bend him over. "Ten shekels," I said. "Five each, I meant before when I said five." I felt as if I was negotiating with myself, and not doing that well.

"Then ten shekels plus any work I can find for you. But if you puke on my ship, you're over the side, you hear me? Ten shekels or not."

"Absolutely," I said, pulling Joshua down the dock to where the slaves were loading jars.

When we were out of earshot of Captain Titus, Joshua said, "You have to tell him that we're Jews, we can't tend pigs."

I grabbed one of the huge wine jars by the ears and started to drag it toward the ship. "It's okay, they're Roman pigs. They don't care."

"Oh, all right," Joshua said, latching onto a jar of his own and hoisting it onto his back. Then it hit him and he set the jar down again. "Hey, wait, that's not right."

the next morning we sailed with the tide. Joshua, me, a crew of thirty, Titus, and fifty allegedly Roman pigs.

Until we cast off from the dock—Josh and I manning one of the long oars— and we were well out of the harbor; until we had shipped the oars and the great square sail was ballooned over the deck like the belly of a gluttonous genie; until Joshua and I climbed to the rear of the ship where Titus stood on the raised deck manning one of the two long steering oars and I looked back toward land, and could see not a city but a speck on the horizon; until then, I had no idea that I had a deep-seated fear of sailing.

"We are way too far away from land," I said. "Way too far. You really need to steer closer to the land, Titus." I pointed to land, in case Titus was unsure as to which way he should go.

It makes sense, don't you think? I mean, I grew up in an arid country, inland, where even the rivers are little more than damp ditches. My people come from the desert. The one time we actually had to cross a sea, we walked. Sailing seemed, well, unnatural.

"If the Lord had meant us to sail we would have been born with, uh, masts," I said.

"That's the dumbest thing you've ever said," said Joshua.

"Can you swim?" asked Titus.

"No," I said.

"Yes he can," Joshua said.

Titus grabbed me by the back of the neck and threw me over the stern of the ship.

Chapter 10

The angel and I had been watching a movie about Moses. Raziel was angry because there were no angels in it. No one in the movie looked like any Egyptian I ever met.

"Did Moses look like that?" I asked Raziel, who was worrying the crust off of a goat cheese pizza in between spitting vitriol at the screen.

"No," said Raziel, "but that other fellow looks like Pharaoh."

"Really?"

"Yep," said Raziel. He slurped the last of a Coke through a straw making a rude noise, then tossed the paper cup across the room into the wastebasket.

"So you were there, during the Exodus?"

"Right before. I was in charge of locusts."

"How was that?"

"Didn't care for it. I wanted the plague of frogs. I like frogs."

"I like frogs too."

"You wouldn't have liked the plague of frogs. Stephan was in charge. A seraphim." He shook his head as if I should know some sad inside fact about seraphim. "We lost a lot of frogs.

"I suppose it's for the best, though," Raziel said with a sigh. "You can't have a someone who likes frogs bring a plague of frogs. If I'd done it, it would have been more of a friendly gathering of frogs."

"That wouldn't have worked," I said.

"Well, it didn't work anyway, did it? I mean, Moses, a

Jew, thought it up. Frogs were unclean to the Jews. To the Jews it was a plague. To the Egyptians it was like having a big feast of frog legs drop from the sky. Moses missed it on that one. I'm just glad we didn't listen to him on the plague of pork."

"Really, he wanted to bring down a plague of pork? Pigs falling from the sky?"

"Pig pieces. Ribs, hams, feet. He wanted everything bloody. You know, unclean pork and unclean blood. The Egyptians would have eaten the pork. We talked him into just the blood."

"Are you saying that Moses was a dimwit?" I wasn't being ironic when I asked this, I was aware that I was asking the eternal dimwit of them all. Still . . .

"No, he just wasn't concerned with results," said the angel. "The Lord had hardened Pharaoh's heart against letting the Jews go. We could have dropped oxen from the sky and he wouldn't have changed his mind."

"That would have been something to see," I said.

"I suggested that it rain fire," the angel said.

"How'd that go?"

"It was pretty. We only had it rain on the stone palaces and monuments. Burning up all of the Jews would sort of defeated the purpose."

"Good thinking," I said.

"Well, I'm good with weather," said the angel.

"Yeah, I know," I said. Then I thought about it a second, about how Raziel nearly wore out our poor room service waiter Jesus delivering orders of ribs the day they were the special.

"You didn't suggest fire, initially, did you? You just suggested that it rain barbecued pork, didn't you?"

"That guy doesn't look anything like Moses," the angel said.

That day, thrashing in the sea, trying to swim to catch the merchant ship that plowed through the water under full sail, I first saw that Raziel was, as he claimed, "good with weather." Joshua was leaning over the aft rail of the ship, shouting alternately to me, then to Titus. It was pretty obvious that even under the light wind that day, I would never catch the ship, and when I looked in the direction of shore I could see nothing but water. Strange, the things you think of at times like that. What I thought first was "What an incredibly stupid way to die." Next I thought, "Joshua will never make it without me." And with that, I began to pray, not for my own salvation but for Joshua. I prayed for the Lord to keep him safe, then I prayed for Maggie's safety and happiness. Then, as I shrugged off my shirt and fell into a slow crawl in the direction of the shoreline, which I knew I would never see, the wind stopped. Just stopped. The sea flattened and the only sound I could hear was the frightened cries of the crew of Titus's ship, which had stopped in the water as if it had dropped anchor.

"Biff, this way!" Joshua called.

I turned in the water to see my friend waving to me from the stern of the becalmed ship. Beside him, Titus cowered like a frightened child. On the mast above them sat a winged figure, who after I swam to the ship and was hoisted out by a very frightened bunch of sailors, I recognized as the angel Raziel. Unlike the times when we had seen him before, he wore robes as black as pitch, and the feathers in his wings shone the blue-black of the sea under moonlight. As I joined Joshua on the raised poop deck at the stern of the ship, the angel took wing and gently landed on the deck beside us. Titus was shielding his head with his arms, as if to ward off an attacker, and he looked as if he were trying to dissolve between the deck boards.

"You," Raziel said to the Phoenician, and Titus looked up between his arms. "No harm is to come to these two."

Titus nodded, tried to say something, then gave up when his voice broke under the weight of his fear. I was a little frightened myself. Decked out in black, the angel was a fearsome sight, even if he was on our side. Joshua, on the other hand, seemed completely at ease.

"Thank you," Josh said to the angel. "He's a cur, but he's my best friend."

"I'm good with weather," the angel said. And as if that explained everything, he flapped his massive black wings and lifted off the deck. The sea was dead calm until the angel was out of sight over the horizon, then the breeze picked up, the sails filled, and waves began to lap at the bow. Titus ventured a peek from his cowed position, then stood up slowly and took one of the steering oars under his arm.

"I'm going to need a new shirt," I said.

"You can have mine," Titus said.

"We should sail closer along the coast, don't you think?" I said.

"On the way, good master," Titus said. "On the way."

"Your mother eats the fungus from the feet of lepers," I said.

"I've been meaning to speak to her about that," Titus said.

"So we understand each other," I said.

"Absolutely," Titus said.

"Crap," Joshua said. "I forgot to ask the angel about knowing women again."

For the rest of the journey Titus was much more agreeable, and strangely enough, we didn't have to man any of the huge oars when we pulled into port, nor did we have to help unload or load any cargo. The crew avoided us altogether, and tended the pigs for us without our even asking. My fear of sailing subsided after a day, and as the steady breeze carried us north, Joshua and I would watch the dolphins that came to ride the ship's bow wave, or lie on the deck at night, breathing in the smell of cedar coming off the ship's timbers, listening to the creaking of rope and rigging, and trying to imagine aloud what it would be like when we found Balthasar. If it hadn't been for Joshua's constant badgering about what sex was like, it would have been a pleasant journey indeed.

"Fornication isn't the only sin, Josh," I tried to explain. "I'm happy to help out, but are you going to have me steal so I can explain it to you? Will you have me kill someone next so you can understand it?"

"No, the difference is that I don't *want* to kill anyone."

"Okay, I'll tell you again. You got your loins, and she's got her loins. And even though you call them both loins, they're different—"

"I understand the mechanics of it. What I don't understand is the feeling of it."

"Well, it feels good, I told you that."

"But that doesn't seem right. Why would the Lord make sin feel good, then condemn man for it?"

"Look, why don't you try it?" I said. "It would be cheaper that way. Or better yet, get married, then it wouldn't even be sin."

"Then it wouldn't be the same, would it?" Josh asked.

"How would I know, I've never been married."

"Is it always the same for you?"

"Well, in some ways, yes."

"In what ways?"

"Well, so far, it seems to be moist."

"Moist?"

"Yeah, but I can't say it's always that way, just in my experience. Maybe we should ask a harlot?"

"Better yet," Joshua said, looking around, "I'll ask Titus. He's older, and he looks as if he's sinned a lot."

"Yeah, well, if you count throwing Jews in the sea, I'd say he's an expert, but that doesn't mean—"

Joshua had run to the stern of the ship, up a ladder to the raised poop deck, and to a small, open-sided tent that acted as the captain's quarters. Under the tent Titus reclined on a pile of rugs, drinking from a wineskin, which I saw him hand to Joshua.

By the time I caught up with him Titus was saying, "So you want to know about fucking? Well, son, you have come to the right place. I've fucked a thousand women, half again as many boys, some sheep, pigs, a few chickens, and the odd turtle. What is it you want to know?"

"Stand away from him, Josh," I said, taking the wineskin and handing it back to Titus as I pushed Joshua back. "The wrath of God could hit him at any moment. Jeez, a turtle, that's got to be an abomination." Titus flinched when I mentioned the wrath of God, as if the angel might return to perch on his mast any second.

Joshua stood his ground. "Right now let's just stick with the women part of it, if that's all right." Joshua patted Titus's arm to reassure him. I knew how that touch felt: Titus would feel the fear run out of him like water.

"I've fucked every kind of woman there is. I've fucked Egyptians, Greeks, Romans, Jews, Ethiopians, and women from places that haven't even been named yet. I've fucked fat ones, skinny ones, women with no legs, women with—"

"Are you married?" Joshua interrupted before the sailor started into how he had fucked them in a box, with a fox, in a house, with a mouse . . .

"I have a wife in Rome."

"Is it the same with your wife and, say, a harlot?"

"What, fucking? No, it's not the same at all."

"It's moist," I said. "Right?"

"Well, yes, it's moist. But that's not—"

I grabbed Joshua's tunic and started to drag him away. "There you have it. Let's go, Josh. Now you know, sin is moist. Make a mental note. Let's get some supper."

Titus was laughing. "You Jews and your sin. You know if you had more gods you wouldn't have to be so worried about making one angry?"

"Right," I said, "I'm going to take spiritual advice from a guy who fucks turtles."

"You shouldn't be so judgmental, Biff," Joshua said. "You're not without sin yourself."

"Oh, you and your holier-than-thou attitude. You can just do your own sinning from now on if that's how you feel. You think I enjoy bedding harlots night after night, describing the whole process to you over and over?"

"Well, yeah," Joshua said.

"That's not the point. The point is, well . . . the point is . . . well. Guilt. I mean—turtles. I mean—" So I was flustered. Sue me. I'd never look at a turtle again without imagining it being molested by a scruffy Phoenician sailor. That's not disturbing to you? Imagine it right now. I'll wait. See?

"He's gone mad," Titus said.

"You shut up, you scurvy viper," Joshua said.

"What about not being judgmental?" Titus said.

"That's him," Josh said. "It's different for me." And suddenly, having said that, Joshua looked as sad as I had ever seen him. He slouched away toward the pigpen, where he sat down and cradled his head in his hands as if he'd just been crowned with the weight of all the worries of mankind. He kept to himself until we left the ship.

The Silk Road, the main vein of trade and custom and culture from the Roman world to the Far East, terminated where it met the sea at the port city of Selucia Pieria, the harbor city and naval stronghold that had fed and guarded Antioch since the time of Alexander. As we left the ship with the rest of the crew, Captain Titus stopped us at the gangplank. He held his hands, palm down. Joshua and I reached out and Titus dropped the coins we'd paid for passage into our palms. "I might have been holding a brace of scorpions, but you two reached out without a thought."

"It was a fair price to pay," Joshua said. "You don't have to return our money."

"I almost drowned your friend. I'm sorry."

"You asked if he could swim before you threw him in. He had a chance."

I looked at Joshua's eyes to see if he was joking, but it was obvious he wasn't.

"Still," Titus said.

"So perhaps you will be given a chance someday as well," Joshua said.

"A slim fucking chance," I added.

Titus grinned at me. "Follow the shore of the harbor until it becomes a river. That's the Onrontes. Follow its left bank and you'll be in Antioch by nightfall.

In the market there will be an old woman who sells herbs and charms. I don't remember her name, but she has only one eye and she wears a tunic of Tyran purple. If there is a magician in Antioch she will know where to find him."

"How do you know this old woman?" I asked.

"I buy my tiger penis powder from her."

Joshua looked at me for explanation. "What?" I said. "I've had a couple of harlots, I didn't exchange recipes." Then I looked to Titus. "Should I have?"

"It's for my knees," the sailor said. "They hurt when it rains."

Joshua took my shoulder and started to lead me away. "Go with God, Titus," he said.

"Put in a good word with the black-winged one for me," Titus said.

Once we were into the wash of merchants and sailors around the harbor, I said, "He gave us the money back because the angel scared him, you know that?"

"So his kindness allayed his fear as well as benefiting us," Joshua said. "All the better. Do you think the priests sacrifice the lambs at Passover for better reasons?"

"Oh, right," I said, having no idea what one had to do with the other, wondering still if tigers didn't object to having their penises powdered. (Keeps them from chafing, I guess, but that's got to be a dangerous job.) "Let's go find this old crone," I said.

The shore of the Onrontes was a stream of life and color, textures and smells, from the harbor all the way into the marketplace at Antioch. There were people of every size and color that I had ever imagined, some shoeless and dressed in rags, others wearing expensive silks and the purple linen from Tyre, said to be dyed with the blood of a poisonous snail. There were ox carts, litters, and sedan chairs carried by as many as eight slaves. Roman soldiers on horseback and on foot policed the crowd, while sailors from a dozen nations reveled in drink and noise and the feel of land beneath their feet. Merchants and beggars and traders and whores scurried for the turn of a coin, while self-appointed prophets spouted dogma from atop the mooring posts where ships tied off along the river—holy men lined up and preaching like a line of noisy Greek columns. Smoke rose fragrant and blue over the streaming crowd, carrying the smell of spice and grease from braziers in the food booths where men and women hawked their fare in rhythmic, haunting songs that all ran together as you walked along—as if one passed his song to the next so you might never experience a second of silence.

The only thing I had ever seen that approached this was the line of pilgrims leading into Jerusalem on the feast days, but there we never saw so much color, heard so much noise, felt so much excitement.

We stopped at a stand and bought a hot black drink from a wrinkled old man wearing a tanned bird carcass as a hat. He showed us how he made the drink from the seeds of berries that were first roasted, then ground into powder, then mixed with boiling water. We got this whole story by way of pantomime, as the man spoke none of the languages we were familiar with. He mixed the drink with honey and gave it to us, but when I tasted it, it still didn't seem to taste right. It seemed, I don't know, too dark. I saw a woman leading a nanny goat nearby, and I took Joshua's cup from him and ran after the woman. With the woman's permission, I squirted a bit of milk from the nanny goat's udder onto the top of each of our cups. The old man protested, making it seem as if we'd committed some sort of sacrilege, but the milk had come out warm and frothy and it served to take away the bitterness of the black drink. Joshua downed his, then asked the old man for two more, as well as handing the woman with the goat a small brass coin for her trouble. Josh gave the second drink back to the old man to taste, and after much grimacing, he took a sip. A smile crossed his toothless mouth and before we left he seemed to be striking some sort of deal with the woman with the goat. I watched the old man grind beans in a copper cylinder while the woman milked her goat into a deep clay bowl. There was a spice vendor next door and I could smell the cinnamon, cloves, and allspice that lay loose in baskets on the ground.

"You know," I said to the woman in Latin, "when you two get this all figured out, try sprinkling a little ground cinnamon on it. It just might make it perfect."

"You're losing your friend," she said.

I turned and looked around, catching the top of Joshua's head just as he turned a corner into the Antioch market and a new push of people. I ran to catch up to him.

Joshua was bumping people in the crowd as he passed, seemingly on purpose, and murmuring just loud enough so I could hear him each time he hit someone with a shoulder or an elbow. "Healed that guy. Healed her. Stopped her suffering. Healed him. Comforted him. Ooo, that guy was just stinky. Healed her. Whoops, missed. Healed. Healed. Comforted. Calmed."

People were turning to look back at Josh, the way one will when a stranger steps on one's foot, except these people all seemed to be either smiling or baffled, not annoyed as I expected.

"What are you doing?" I asked.

"Practicing," Joshua said. "Whoa, bad toe-jam." He spun on his heel, nearly turning his foot out of his sandal, and smacked a short bald man on the back of the head. "All better now."

The bald guy turned and looked back to see who had hit him. Josh was backing down the street. "How's your toe?" Joshua asked in Latin.

"Good," the bald guy said, and he smiled, sorta goofy and dreamy, like his toe had just sent him a message that all was right with the world.

"Go with God, and—" Josh spun, jumped, came down with each hand on a stranger's shoulder and shouted, "Yes! Double healing! Go with God, friends, two times!"

I was getting sort of uncomfortable. People had started to follow us through the crowd. Not a lot of people, but a few. Maybe five or six, each of them with that dreamy smile on his face.

"Joshua, maybe you should, uh, calm down a little."

"Can you believe all of these people need healing? Healed him." Josh leaned back and whispered in my ear. "That guy had the pox. He'll pee without pain for the first time in years. 'Scuse me." He turned back into the crowd. "Healed, healed, calmed, comforted."

"We're strangers here, Josh. You're attracting attention to us. This might not be safe . . ."

"It's not like they're blind or missing limbs. We'll have to stop if we run into something serious. Healed! God bless you. Oh, you no speak Latin? Uh—Greek? Hebrew? No?"

"He'll figure it out, Josh," I said. "We should look for the old woman."

"Oh, right. Healed!" Josh slapped the pretty woman very hard in the face. Her husband, a large man in a leather tunic, didn't look pleased. He pulled a dagger from his belt and started to advance on Joshua. "Sorry, sir," Joshua said, not backing up. "Couldn't be helped. Small demon, had to be banished from her. Sent it into that dog over there. Go with God. Thank you, thank you very much."

The woman grabbed her husband by the arm and swung him around. She still had Joshua's handprint on her face, but she was smiling. "I'm back!" she said to her husband. "I'm back." She shook him and the anger seemed to drain out of him. He looked back at Joshua with an expression of such dismay that I thought he might faint. He dropped his knife and threw his arms around his wife. Joshua ran forward and threw his arms around them both.

"Would you stop it please?" I pleaded.

"But I love these people," Josh said.

"You do, don't you?"

"Yeah."

"He was going to kill you."

"It happens. He just didn't understand. He does now."

"Glad he caught on. Let's find the old lady."

"Yes, then let's go back and get another one of those hot drinks," Joshua said.

We found the hag selling a bouquet of monkey feet to a fat trader dressed in striped silks and a wide conical hat woven from some sort of tough grass.

"But these are all back feet," the trader protested.

"Same magic, better price," said the hag, pulling back a shawl she wore over one side of her face to reveal a milky white eye. This was obviously her intimidation move.

The trader wasn't having it. "It is a well-known fact that the front paw of a monkey is the best talisman for telling the future, but the back—"

"You'd think the monkey would see something coming," I said, and they both looked at me as if I'd just sneezed on their falafel. The old woman drew back as if to cast a spell, or maybe a rock, at me. "If that were true," I continued, "I mean—about telling the future with a monkey paw—I mean—because he would have four of them—paws, that is—and, uh—never mind."

"How much are these?" said Joshua, holding up a handful of dried newts from the hag's baskets. The old woman turned to Josh.

"You can't use that many," the hag said.

"I can't?" asked Joshua.

"These are useless," said the merchant, waving the hind legs and feet of two and a half former monkeys, which looked like tiny people feet, except that they were furry and the toes were longer.

"If you're a monkey I'll bet they come in handy to keep your butt from dragging on the ground," I said, ever the peacemaker.

"Well, how many do I need?" Joshua asked, wondering how his diversion to save me had turned into a negotiation for newt crispies.

"How many of your camels are constipated?" asked the crone.

Joshua dropped the dried newts back into their basket. "Well, uh . . ."

"Do those work?" asked the merchant. "For plugged-up camels, I mean."

"Never fails."

The merchant scratched his pointed beard with a monkey foot. "I'll meet your price on these worthless monkey feet if you throw in a handful of newts."

"Deal," said the crone.

The merchant opened a satchel he had slung around his shoulder and dropped in his monkey feet, then followed them with a handful of newts. "So how do these work? Make them into tea and have the camel drink it?"

"Other end," said the crone. "They go in whole. Count to one hundred and step back."

The merchant's eyes went wide, then narrowed into a squint and he turned to me. "Kid," he said, "if you can count to a hundred, I've got a job for you."

"He'd love to work for you, sir," Joshua said, "But we have to find Balthasar the magus."

The crone hissed and backed to the corner of her booth, covering all of her face but her milky eye. "How do you know of Balthasar?" She held her hands in front of her like claws and I could see her trembling.

"Balthasar!" I shouted at her, and the old woman nearly jumped through the wall behind her. I snickered and was ready to *Balthasar!* her again when Josh interrupted.

"Balthasar came from here to Bethlehem to witness my birth," said Joshua. "I'm seeking his counsel. His wisdom."

"You would hail the darkness, you would consort with demons and fly with the evil Djinn like Balthasar? I won't have you near my booth, be gone from here." She made the sign of the evil eye, which in her case was redundant.

"No, no, no," I said. "None of that. The magus left some, uh, frankincense at Joshua's house. We need to return it to him."

The old woman regarded me with her good eye. "You're lying."

"Yes, he is," said Josh.

"BALTHASAR!" I screamed in her face. It didn't have the same effect as the first time around and I was a little disappointed.

"Stop that," she said.

Joshua reached out to take her craggy hand. "Grandmother," he said, "our ship's captain, Titus Inventius, said you would know where to find Balthasar. Please help us."

The old woman seemed to relax, and just when I thought she was going to smile, she raked her nails across Joshua's hand and leapt back. "Titus Inventius is a scalawag," she shouted.

Joshua stared at the blood welling up in the scratches on the back of his hand and I thought for a second that he might faint. He never understood it when someone was violent or unkind. I'd probably be half a day explaining to him why the old woman scratched him, but right then I was furious.

"You know what? You know what? You know what?" I was waving my finger under her nose. "You scratched the Son of God. That's your ass, that's what."

"The magus is gone from Antioch, and good riddance to him," screeched the crone.

The fat trader had been watching this the whole time without saying a word, but now he began laughing so hard that I could barely hear the old woman wheezing out curses. "So you want to find Balthasar, do you, God's Son?"

Joshua came out of the stunned contemplation of his wounds and looked at the trader. "Yes, sir, do you know him?"

"Who do you think the monkey's feet are for? Follow me." He whirled on his heel and sauntered away without another word.

As we followed the trader into an alley so narrow that his shoulders nearly touched the sides, I turned back to the old crone and shouted, "Your ass, hag! Mark my words."

She hissed and made the sign of the evil eye again.

"She was a little creepy," Joshua said, looking at the scratches on his hand again.

"Don't be judgmental, Josh, you're not without creepiness yourself."

"Where do you think this guy is leading us?"

"Probably somewhere where he can murder and kill us."

"Yeah, at least one of those."

Chapter 11

Since my escape attempt, I can't get the angel to leave the room at all. Not even for his beloved *Soap Opera Digest*. (And yes, when he left to obtain the first one, it would have been a good time to make my escape, but I wasn't thinking that way then, so back off.) Today I tried to get him to bring me a map.

"Because no one is going to know the places I'm writing about, that's why," I told him. "You want me to write in this idiom so people will understand what I'm saying, then why use the names of places that have been gone for thousands of years? I need a map."

"No," said the angel.

"When I say the journey was two months by camel, what will that mean to these people who can cross an ocean in hours? I need to know modern distances."

"No," said the angel.

(Did you know that in a hotel they bolt the bedside lamp to the table, thereby making it an ineffective instrument of persuasion when trying to bring an obdurate angel around to your way of thinking? Thought you should know that. Pity too, it's such a substantial lamp.)

"But how will I recount the heroic acts of the archangel Raziel if I can't tell the locations of his deeds? What, you want me to write, 'Oh, then somewhere generally to the left of the Great Wall that rat-bastard Raziel showed up looking like hell considering he may have traveled a long distance or not?' Is that what you want? Or should it read, 'Then, only a mile out of the port of Ptolemais, we were once again graced with the shining magnificence of the archangel Raziel? Huh, which way do you want it?"

(I know what you're thinking, that the angel saved my life when Titus threw me off the ship and that I should be more forgiving toward him, right? That I shouldn't try to manipulate a poor creature who was given an ego but no free will or capacity for creative thought, right? Okay, good point. But do please remember that the angel only intervened on my behalf because Joshua was praying for my rescue. And do please remember that he could have saved us a lot of difficulty over the years if he had helped us out more often. And please don't forget that—despite the fact that he is perhaps the most handsome creature I've ever laid eyes on—Raziel is a stone doofus. Nevertheless, the ego stroke worked.)

"I'll get you a map."

And he did. Unfortunately the concierge was only able to find a map of the world provided by an airline that partners with the hotel. So who knows how accurate it is. On this map the next leg of our journey is six inches long and would cost thirty thousand Friendly Flyer Miles. I hope that clears things up.

The trader's name was Ahmad Mahadd Ubaidullaganji, but he said we could call him Master. We called him Ahmad. He led us through the city to a hillside where his caravan was camped. He owned a hundred camels which he drove along the Silk Road, along with a dozen men, two goats, three horses, and an astonishingly homely woman named Kanuni. He took us to his tent, which was larger than both the houses Joshua and I had grown up in. We sat on rich carpets and Kanuni served us stuffed dates and wine from a pitcher shaped like a dragon.

"So, what does the Son of God want with my friend Balthasar?" Ahmad asked. Before we could answer he snorted and laughed until his shoulders shook and he almost spilled his wine. He had a round face with high cheekbones and narrow black eyes that crinkled at the corners from too much laughter and desert wind. "I'm sorry, my friends, but I've never been in the presence of the son of a god before. Which god is your father, by the way?"

"Well, *the* God," I said.

"Yep," said Joshua. "That's the one."

"And what is your God's name?"

"Dad," said Josh.

"We're not supposed to say his name."

"Dad!" said Ahmad. "I love it." He started giggling again. "I knew you were Hebrews and weren't allowed to say your God's name, I just wanted to see if you would. Dad. That's rich."

"I don't mean to be rude," I said, "and we are certainly enjoying the refreshments, but it's getting late and you said you would take us to see Balthasar."

"And indeed I will. We leave in the morning."

"Leave for where?" Josh asked.

"Kabul, the city where Balthasar lives now."

I had never heard of Kabul, and I sensed that was not a good thing. "And how far is Kabul?"

"We should be there in less than two months by camel," Ahmad said.

If I knew then what I know now, I might have stood and exclaimed, "Tarnation, man, that's over six inches and thirty thousand Friendly Flyer Miles!" But since I didn't know that then, what I said was "Shit."

"I will take you to Kabul," said Ahmad, "but what can you do to help pay your way?"

"I know carpentry," Joshua said. "My stepfather taught me how to fix a camel saddle."

"And you?" He looked at me. "What can you do?"

I thought about my experience as a stonecutter, and immediately rejected it. And my training as a village idiot, which I thought I could always fall back on, wasn't going to help either. I did have my newfound skill as a sex educator, but somehow I didn't think there'd be call for that on a two-month trip with fourteen men and one homely woman. So what could I do, what skill had I to gentle the road to Kabul?

"If someone in the caravan croaks I'm a great mourner," I said. "Want to hear a dirge?"

Ahmad laughed until he shook, then called for Kanuni to bring him his satchel. Once he had it in hand, he dug inside and pulled out the dried newts he'd bought from the old hag. "Here, you'll be needing these," he said.

Camels bite. A camel will, for no reason, spit on you, stomp you, kick you, bellow, burp, and fart at you. They are stubborn at their best, and cranky beyond all belief at their worst. If you provoke them, they will bite. If you insert a dehydrated amphibian elbow deep in a camel's bum, he considers himself provoked, doubly so if the procedure was performed while he was sleeping. Camels are wise to stealth. They bite.

í can heal that," Joshua said, looking at the huge tooth marks on my forehead. We were following Ahmad's caravan along the Silk Road, which was neither a road nor made of silk. It was, in fact, a narrow path through the rocky inhospitable highland desert of what is now Syria into the low, inhospitable desert of what is now Iraq.

"He said sixty days by camel. Doesn't that mean that we should be riding, not walking?"

"You're missing your camel pals, aren't you?" Josh grinned, that snotty, Son-o'-God grin of his. Maybe it was just a regular grin.

"I'm just tired. I was up half the night sneaking up on these guys."

"I know," said Joshua. "I had to get up at dawn to fix one of the saddles before we left. Ahmad's tools leave something to be desired."

"You go ahead and be the martyr, Josh, just forget about what I was doing all night. I'm just saying that we should get to ride instead of walking."

"We will," Josh said. "Just not now."

The men in the caravan were all riding, although several of them, as well as Kanuni, were on horses. The camels were loaded down with great packs of iron tools, powdered dyes, and sandalwood bound for the Orient. At the first highland oasis we crossed, Ahmad traded the horses for four more camels, and Joshua and I were allowed to ride. At night we ate with the rest of the men, sharing boiled grain or bread with sesame paste, the odd bit of cheese, mashed chickpeas and garlic, occasionally goat meat, and sometimes the dark hot drink we had discovered in Antioch (mixed with date sugar and topped with foaming goat's milk and cinnamon at my suggestion). Ahmad dined alone in his tent, while the rest of us would dine under the open awning that we constructed to shelter us from the hottest part of the day. In the desert, the day gets warmer as it gets later, so the hottest part of the day will be in the late afternoon, just before sundown brings the hot winds to leach the last moisture from your skin.

None of Ahmad's men spoke Aramaic or Hebrew, but they had enough functional Latin and Greek to tease Joshua and me about any number of subjects, their favorite, of course, being my job as chief camel deconstipator. The men hailed from a half-dozen different lands, many we had never heard of. Some were as black as Ethiopians, with high foreheads and long, graceful limbs, while others were squat and bowlegged, with powerful shoulders, high

cheekbones, and long wispy mustaches like Ahmad's. Not one of them was fat
or weak or slow. Before we were a week out of Antioch we figured out that it
only took a couple of men to care for and guide a caravan of camels, so we were
perplexed at why someone as shrewd as Ahmad would bring along so many
superfluous employees.

"Bandits," Ahmad said, adjusting his bulk to find a more comfortable position atop his camel. "I'd need no more than a couple of dolts like you two if it
was just the animals that needed tending. They're guards. Why did you think
they were all carrying bows and lances?"

"Yeah," I said, giving Joshua a dirty look, "didn't you see the lances?
They're guards. Uh, Ahmad, shouldn't Josh and I have lances—I mean, when
we get to the bandit area?"

"We've been followed by bandits for five days now," Ahmad said.

"We don't need lances," Joshua said. "I will not make a man sin by committing an act of thievery. If a man would have something of mine, he need only ask
and I will give it to him."

"Give me the rest of your money," I said.

"Forget it," said Joshua.

"But you just said—"

"Yeah, but not to you."

most nights Joshua and I slept in the open, outside Ahmad's tent, or if the
night was especially cold, among the camels, where we would endure their
grunting and snorting to get out of the wind. The guards slept in two-man
tents, except for two who stood guard all night. Many nights, long after the
camp was quiet, Joshua and I would lie looking up at the stars and pondering
the great questions of life.

"Josh, do you think the bandits will rob us and kill us, or just rob us?"

"Rob us, then kill us, I would think," said Josh. "Just in case they missed
something that we had hidden, they could torture its whereabouts out of us."

"Good point," I said.

"Do you think Ahmad has sex with Kanuni?" Joshua asked.

"I know he does. He told me he does."

"What do you think it's like? With them I mean? Him so fat and her so, you
know?"

"Frankly, Joshua, I'd rather not think about it. But thanks for putting that
picture in my head."

"You mean you can imagine them together?"

"Stop it, Joshua. I can't tell you what sin is like. You're going to have to do it yourself. What's next? I'll have to murder someone so I can explain what it's like to kill?"

"No, I don't want to kill."

"Well, that might be one you have to do, Josh. I don't think the Romans are going to go away because you ask them to."

"I'll find a way. I just don't know it yet."

"Wouldn't it be funny if you weren't the Messiah? I mean if you abstained from knowing a woman your whole life, only to find out that you were just a minor prophet?"

"Yeah, that would be funny," said Josh. He wasn't smiling.

"Kind of funny?"

The journey seemed to go surprisingly fast once we knew we were being followed by bandits. It gave us something to talk about and our backs stayed limber, as we were always twisting in our saddles and checking the horizon. I was almost sad when they finally, after ten days on our trail, decided to attack.

Ahmad, who was usually at the front of the caravan, fell back and rode beside us. "The bandits will ambush us inside that pass just ahead," he said.

The road snaked into a canyon with steep slopes on either side topped by rows of huge boulders and wind-eroded towers. "They're hiding in those boulders on top of either ridge," Ahmad said. "Don't stare, you'll give us away."

Joshua said, "If you know that they're going to attack, why not pull up and defend ourselves?"

"They will attack one way or another anyway. Better an ambush we know about than one we don't. And they don't know we know."

I noticed the squat guards with the mustaches take short bows from pouches behind their saddles, and as subtly as a man might brush a cobweb from his eyelash, they strung the bows. If you'd been watching them from a distance you'd have hardly seen them move.

"What do you want us to do?" I asked Ahmad.

"Try not to get killed. Especially you, Joshua. Balthasar will be very angry indeed if I show up with you dead."

"Wait," said Joshua, "Balthasar knows we are coming?"

"Why, yes," laughed Ahmad. "He told me to look for you. What, you think I help every pair of runts that wander into the market at Antioch?"

"Runts?" I had momentarily forgotten about the ambush.

"How long ago did he tell you to look for us?"

"I don't know, right after he first left Antioch for Kabul, maybe ten years ago. It doesn't matter now, I have to get back to Kanuni, bandits scare her."

"Let them get a good look at her," I said. "We'll see who scares who."

"Don't look at the ridges," Ahmad said as he rode away.

The bandits came down the sides of the canyon like a synchronized avalanche, driving their camels to the edge of balance, pushing a river of rocks and sand before them. There were twenty-five, maybe thirty of them, all dressed in black, half of them on camels waving swords or clubs, the other half on foot with long spears for gutting a camel rider.

When they were committed to the charge, all of them sliding down the hillsides, the guards broke our caravan in the middle, leaving an empty spot in the road where the bandits' charge would culminate. Their momentum was so great that the bandits were unable to change direction. Three of their camels went down trying to pull back.

Our guards moved into two groups, three in the front with the long lances, the bowmen just behind them. When the bowmen were set they let arrows fly into the bandits, and as each fell he took two or three of his cohorts down with him, until in seconds the charge had turned into an actual avalanche of rolling stones and men and camels. The camels bellowed and we could hear bones snapping and men screaming as they rolled into a bloody mass on the Silk Road. As each man rose and tried to charge our guards an arrow would drop him in his tracks. One bandit came up mounted on a camel and rode toward the back of the caravan, where the three lancers drove him from his mount in a spray of blood. Every movement in the canyon was met with an arrow. One bandit with a broken leg tried to crawl back up the canyon wall, and an arrow in the back of his skull cut him down.

I heard a wailing behind me and before I could turn Joshua rode by me at full gallop, passing the bowmen and the lancers at our side of the caravan, bound for the mass of dead and dying bandits. He slung himself off his camel's back and was running around the bodies like a madman, waving his arms and screaming until I could hear the rasp as his throat went raw.

"Stop this! Stop this!"

One bandit moved, trying to get to his feet, and our bowmen drew back to cut him down. Joshua threw his body on top of the bandit and pushed him back to the ground. I heard Ahmad give the command to hold.

A cloud of dust floated out of the canyon on the gentle desert breeze. A camel with a broken leg bellowed and an arrow in the eye put the animal to rest. Ahmad snatched a lance out of one of the guard's hands and rode to where Joshua was shielding the wounded bandit.

"Move, Joshua," Ahmad said, holding the lance at ready. "This must be finished."

Joshua looked around him. All of the bandits and all of their animals were dead. Blood ran in rivulets in the dust. Already flies were collecting to feast. Joshua walked through the field of dead bandits until his chest was pressed against the bronze point of Ahmad's lance. Tears streamed down Joshua's face. "This was wrong!" he screeched.

"They were bandits. They would have killed us and stolen everything we had if we had not killed them. Does your own God, your father, not destroy those who sin? Now move aside, Joshua. Let this be finished."

"I am not my father, and neither are you. You will not kill this man."

Ahmad lowered the lance and shook his head balefully. "He will only die anyway, Joshua." I could sense the guards fidgeting, not knowing what to do.

"Give me your water skin," Joshua said.

Ahmad threw the water skin down to Joshua, then turned his camel and rode back to where the guards waited for him. Joshua took the water to the wounded bandit and held his head as he drank. An arrow protruded from the bandit's stomach and his black tunic was shiny with blood. Joshua put his hand gently over the bandit's eyes, as if he were telling him to go to sleep, then he yanked out the arrow and tossed it aside. The bandit didn't even flinch. Joshua put his hand over the wound.

From the time that Ahmad had ordered them to hold fire, none of the guards had moved. They watched. After a few minutes the bandit sat up and Joshua stepped away from him and smiled. In that instant an arrow sprouted from the bandit's forehead and he fell back, dead.

"No!" Joshua wheeled around to face Ahmad's side of the caravan. The guard who had shot still held the bow, as if he might have to let fly another arrow to finish the job. Howling with rage, Joshua made a gesture as if he were striking the air with his open hand and the guard was lifted back off his camel and slammed into the ground. "No more!" Joshua screamed. When the guard sat up in the dirt his eyes were like silver moons in their sockets. He was blind.

later, when neither of us had spoken for two days, and Joshua and I were relegated to riding far behind the caravan because the guards were afraid of us, I took a drink from my water skin, then handed it to Joshua. He took a drink and handed it back.

"Thank you," Josh said. He smiled and I knew he'd be all right.

"Hey Joshua, do me a favor."

"What?"

"Remind me not to piss you off, okay?"

The city of Kabul was built on five rugged hillsides, with the streets laid out in terraces and the buildings built partly into the hills. There was no evidence of Roman or Greek influence in the architecture, but instead the larger buildings had tile roofs that turned up at the corners, a style that Joshua and I would see all over Asia before our journey was finished. The people were mostly rugged, wiry people who looked like Arabs without the glow in their skin that came from a diet rich in olive oil. Instead their faces seemed leaner, drawn by the cold, dry wind of the high desert. In the market there were merchants and traders from China, and more men who looked like Ahmad and his bowmen guards, a race whom the Chinese referred to simply as barbarians.

"The Chinese are so afraid of my people that they have built a wall, as high as any palace, as wide as the widest boulevard in Rome, and stretching as far as the eye can see ten times over," Ahmad said.

"Uh-huh," I said, thinking, *you lying bag-o'-guts.*

Joshua hadn't spoken to Ahmad since the bandit attack, but he smirked at Ahmad's story of the great wall.

"Just so," said Ahmad. "We will stay at an inn tonight. Tomorrow I will take you to Balthasar. If we leave early we can be there by noon, then you'll be the magician's problem, not mine. Meet me in front at dawn."

That night the innkeeper and his wife served us a dinner of spiced lamb and rice, with some sort of beer made from rice, which washed two months of desert grit from our throats and put a pleasant haze over our minds. To save money, we paid for pallets under the wide curving eaves of the inn, and although it was some comfort to have a roof over my head for the first time in months, I found that I missed looking at the stars as I fell asleep. I lay awake, half drunk, for a long time. Joshua slept the sleep of the innocent.

The next day Ahmad met us in front of the inn with two of his African guards and two extra camels in tow. "Come on, now. This may be the end of your journey, but it is merely a detour for me," Ahmad said. He threw us each a crust of bread and a hunk of cheese, which I took to mean we were to eat our breakfast on the way.

We rode out of Kabul and into the hills until we entered a labyrinth of canyons, which meandered through rugged mountains that looked as if they might have been shaped by God out of clay, then left to bake in the sun until the clay had turned to a deep golden color that reflected light in a spray that ate up shadows and destroyed shade. By noon I had no sense whatsoever of what direction we were traveling, nor could I have sworn that we weren't retracing our path through the same canyons over and over, but Ahmad's black guards seemed to know their way. Eventually they led us around a bend to a sheer canyon wall, two hundred feet tall, that stood out from the other canyon walls in that there were windows and balconies carved into it. It was a palace hewn out of solid rock. At the base stood an ironclad door that looked as if it would take twenty men to move.

"Balthasar's house," Ahmad said, prodding his camel to kneel down so he might dismount.

Joshua nudged me with his riding stick. "Hey, is this what you expected?"

I shook my head. "I don't know what I expected. Maybe something a little— I don't know—smaller."

"Could you find your way back out of these canyons if you had to?" Joshua asked.

"Nope. You?"

"Not a chance."

Ahmad waddled over to the great door and pulled a cord that hung down from a hole in the wall. Somewhere inside we heard the ringing of some great bell. (Only later would we learn that it was the sound of a gong.) A smaller door within the door opened and a girl stuck her head out. "What?" She had the round face and high cheekbones of an Oriental, and there were great blue wings painted on her face above her eyes.

"It's Ahmad. Ahmad Mahadd Ubaidullaganji. I've brought Balthasar the boy he has been waiting for." Ahmad gestured in our direction.

The girl looked skeptical. "Scrawny. You sure that's the one?"

"That's the one. Tell Balthasar he owes me."

"Who's that with him?"

"That's his stupid friend. No extra charge for him."

"You bring the monkey's paws?" the girl asked.

"Yes, and the other herbs and minerals Balthasar asked for."

"Okay, wait here." She closed the door, was gone only a second, then returned. "Send just the two of them in, alone. Balthasar must examine them, then he will deal with you."

"There's no need to be mysterious, woman, I've been in Balthasar's house a hundred times. Now quit dilly-dallying and open the door."

"Silence!" the girl shouted. "The great Balthasar will not be mocked. Send in the boys, alone." Then she slammed the little door and we could hear her cackling echo out the windows above.

Ahmad shook his head in disgust and waved us over to the door. "Just go. I don't know what he's up to, but just go."

Joshua and I dismounted, took our packs off the camels, and edged over to the huge door. Joshua looked at me as if wondering what to do, then reached for the cord to ring the bell, but as he did, the door creaked open just wide enough for one of us to enter if we turned sideways. It was pitch black inside except for a narrow stripe of light, which told us nothing. Joshua again looked at me and raised his eyebrows.

"I'm just the stupid no-extra-charge friend," I said, bowing. "After you."

Joshua moved though the door and I followed. When we were inside only a few feet, the huge door slammed with a sound like thunder and we stood there in complete darkness. I'm sure I could feel things scurrying around my feet in the dark.

There was a bright flash and a great column of red smoke rose in front of us, illuminated by a light coming from the ceiling somewhere. It smelled of brimstone and stung my nose. Joshua coughed and we both backed against the door as a figure stepped out of the smoke. He—it—stood as tall as any two men, although he was thin. He wore a long purple robe, embroidered with strange symbols in gold and silver, hooded, so we saw no face, only glowing red eyes set back in a field of black. He held a bright lamp out as if to examine us by the light.

"Satan," I said under my breath to Joshua, pressing my back against the great iron door so hard that I could feel rust flakes imbedding in my skin through my tunic.

"It's not Satan," Joshua said.

"Who would disturb the sanctity of my fortress?" boomed the figure. I nearly wet myself at hearing his voice.

"I'm Joshua of Nazareth," Joshua said, trying to be casual, but his voice broke on *Nazareth*. "And this is Biff, also of Nazareth. We're looking for

Balthasar. He came to Bethlehem, where I was born, many years ago looking for me. I have to ask him some questions."

"Balthasar is no more of this world." The dark figure reached into his robe and pulled out a glowing dagger, which he held high, then plunged into his own chest. There was an explosion, a flash, and an anguished roar, as if someone had killed a lion. Joshua and I turned and frantically scratched at the iron door, looking for a latch. We were both making an incoherent terrorized sound that I can only describe as the verbal version of running, sort of an extended rhythmic howl that paused only when the last of each lungful of air squeaked out of us.

Then I heard the laughing and Joshua grabbed my arm. The laughing got louder. Joshua swung me around to face death in purple. As I turned the dark figure threw back his hood and I saw the grinning black face and shaved head of a man—a very tall man, but a man nonetheless. He threw open the robe and I could see that it was, indeed, a man. A man who had been standing on the shoulders of two young Asian women who had been hiding beneath the very long robe.

"Just fuckin' with you," he said. Then he giggled.

He leapt off of the women's shoulders and took a deep breath before doubling over and hugging himself with laughter. Tears streamed out of his big chestnut eyes.

"You should have seen the look on your faces. Girls, did you see that?" The women, who wore simple linen robes, didn't seem as amused as the man. They looked embarrassed and a little impatient, as if they'd rather be anywhere else, doing anything but this.

"Balthasar?" Joshua asked.

"Yeah," said Balthasar, who stood up now and was only a little taller than I was. "Sorry, I don't get many visitors. So you're Joshua?"

"Yes," Joshua said, an edge in his voice.

"I didn't recognize you without the swaddling clothes. And this is your servant?"

"My friend, Biff."

"Same thing. Bring your friend. Come in. The girls will attend to Ahmad for the time being." He stalked off down a corridor into the mountain, his long purple robe trailing behind him like the tail of a dragon.

We stood there by the door, not moving, until we realized that once Balthasar turned a corner with his lamp we'd be in darkness again, so we took off after him.

As we ran down the corridor, I thought of how far we had traveled, and what we had left behind, and I felt as if I was going to be sick to my stomach any second. "Wise man?" I said to Joshua.

"My mother has never lied to me," said Josh.

"That you know of," I said.

Chapter 12

Well, by pretending to have an overactive bladder, I've managed to sneak enough time in the bathroom to finish reading this Gospel of Matthew. I don't know who the Matthew is that wrote this, but it certainly wasn't our Matthew. While our Matthew was a whiz at numbers (as you might expect from a tax collector), he couldn't write his own name in the sand without making three mistakes. Whoever wrote this Gospel obviously got the information at least secondhand, maybe thirdhand. I'm not here to criticize, but please, he never mentions me. Not once. I know my protests go against the humility that Joshua taught, but please, I was his best friend. Not to mention the fact that this Matthew (if that really is his name) takes great care in describing Joshua's genealogy back to King David, but after Joshua is born and the three wise men show up at the stable in Bethlehem, then you don't hear from Joshua again until he's thirty. Thirty! As if nothing happened from the manger until John baptized us. Jeez.

Anyway, now I know why I was brought back from the dead to write this Gospel. If the rest of this "New Testament" is anything like the book of Matthew, they need someone to write about Joshua's life who was actually there: me.

I can't believe I wasn't even mentioned once. It's all I can do to keep from asking Raziel what in the hell happened. He probably showed up a hundred years too late to correct this Matthew fellow. Oh my, there's a frightening thought, edited by the moron angel. I can't let that happen.

And the ending? Where did he get that?

I'll see what this next guy, this Mark, has to say, but I'm not getting my hopes up.

The first thing that we noticed about Balthasar's fortress was that there were no right angles, no angles period, only curves. As we followed the magus through corridors, and from level to level, we never saw so much as a squared-off stair step, instead there were spiral ramps leading from level to level, and although the fortress spread all over the cliff face, no room was more than one doorway away from a window. Once we were above the ground level, there was always light from the windows and the creepy feeling we'd had when we entered quickly passed away. The stone of the walls was more yellow in color than the limestone of Jerusalem, yet it had the same smooth appearance. Overall it gave the impression that you were walking through the polished entrails of some huge living creature.

"Did you build this place, Balthasar?" I asked.

"Oh, no," he said, without turning around. "This place was always here, I simply had to remove the stone that occupied it."

"Oh," I said, having gained no knowledge whatsoever.

We passed no doors, but myriad open archways and round portals which opened into chambers of various shapes and sizes. As we passed one egg-shaped doorway obscured by a curtain of beads Balthasar mumbled, "The girls stay in there."

"Girls?" I said.

"Girls?" Joshua said.

"Yes, girls, you ninnies," Balthasar said. "Humans much like yourselves, except smarter and better smelling."

Well, I knew that. I mean, we'd seen the two of them, hadn't we? I knew what girls were.

He pressed on until we came to the only other door I had seen since we entered, this one another huge, ironclad monster held closed with three iron bolts as big around as my arm and a heavy brass lock engraved with strange characters. The magus stopped and tilted an ear to the door. His heavy gold earring clinked against one of the bolts. He turned to us and whispered, and for the first time I could clearly see that the magus was very old, despite the strength of his laugh and the spring in his step. "You may go anywhere you wish while you stay here, but you must never open this door. *Xiong zai*."

"*Xiong zai,*" I repeated to Joshua in case he'd missed it.

"*Xiong zai.*" He nodded with total lack of understanding.

mankind, I suppose, is designed to run on to be motivated by—temptation. If progress is a virtue then this is our greatest gift. (For what is curiosity if not intellectual temptation? And what progress is there without curiosity?) On the other hand, can you call such a profound weakness a gift, or is it a design flaw? Is temptation itself at fault for man's woes, or is it simply the lack of judgment in response to temptation? In other words, who is to blame? Mankind, or a bad designer? Because I can't help but think that if God had never told Adam and Eve to avoid the fruit of the tree of knowledge, that the human race would still be running around naked, dancing in wonderment and blissfully naming stuff between snacks, naps, and shags. By the same token, if Balthasar had passed that great ironclad door that first day without a word of warning, I might have never given it a second glance, and once again, much trouble could have been avoided. Am I to blame for what happened, or is it the author of temptation, God Hisownself?

balthasar led us into a grand chamber with silks festooned from the ceiling and the floor covered with fine carpets and pillows. Wine, fruit, cheese, and bread were laid out on several low tables.

"Rest and refresh," said Balthasar. "I'll be back after I finish my business with Ahmad." Then he hurried off, leaving us alone.

"So," I said, "find out what you need to from this guy, then we can get on the road and on to the next wise man."

"I'm not sure it's going to be that quick. In fact, we may be here quite some time. Maybe years."

"Years? Joshua, we're in the middle of nowhere, we can't spend years here."

"Biff, we grew up in the middle of nowhere. What's the difference?"

"Girls," I said.

"What about them?" Joshua asked.

"Don't start."

We heard laughter rolling down the corridor into the room and shortly it was followed by Balthasar and Ahmad, who threw themselves down among the pillows and began eating the cheeses and fruits that had been set out.

"So," Balthasar said, "Ahmad tells me that you tried to save a bandit, and in the process blinded one of his men, without so much as touching him. Very impressive."

Joshua hung his head. "It was a massacre."

"Grieve," Balthasar said, "but consider also the words of the master Lao-tzu: 'Weapons are instruments of misfortune. Those who are violent do not die naturally.' "

"Ahmad," Joshua said, "what will happen to the guard, the one I . . ."

"He is no good to me anymore," said Ahmad. "A shame too, he was the best bowman of the lot. I'll leave him in Kabul. He's asked me to give his pay to his wife in Antioch and his other wife in Dunhuang. I suppose he will become a beggar."

"Who is Lao-tzu?" I asked.

"You will have plenty of time to learn of master Lao-tzu," said Balthasar. "Tomorrow I will assign you a tutor to teach you *qi,* the path of the Dragon's Breath, but for now, eat and rest."

"Can you believe a Chinaman can be so black?" laughed Ahmad. "Have you ever seen such a thing?"

"I wore the leopard skin of the shaman when your father was just a twinkle in the great river of stars, Ahmad. I mastered animal magic before you were old enough to walk, and I had learned all the secrets of the sacred Egyptian magic texts before you could sprout a beard. If immortality is to be found among the wisdom of the Chinese masters, then I shall be Chinese as long as it suits me, no matter the color of my skin or the place of my birth."

I tried to determine Balthasar's age. From what he was claiming he would have to be very old indeed, as Ahmad was not young himself, yet his movements were spry and as far as I could see he had all of his teeth and they were perfect. There was none of the feeble dotage that I'd seen in our elders at home.

"How do you stay so strong, Balthasar?" I asked.

"Magic." He grinned.

"There is no magic but that of the Lord," Joshua said.

Balthasar scratched his chin and replied quietly, "Then presumably none without his consent, eh, Joshua?"

Joshua slouched and stared at the floor.

Ahmad burst out laughing. "His magic isn't so mysterious, boys. Balthasar has eight young concubines to draw the poisons from his old body, that's how he stays young."

"Holy moly! Eight?" I was astounded. Aroused. Envious.

"Does that room with the ironclad door have something to do with your magic?" Joshua asked gravely.

Balthasar stopped grinning. Ahmad looked from Joshua to the magus and back, bewildered.

"Let me show you to your quarters," said Balthasar. "You should wash and rest. Lessons tomorrow. Say good-bye to Ahmad, you'll not see him again soon."

Our quarters were spacious, bigger than the houses we'd grown up in, with carpets on the floor, chairs made of dark exotic hardwoods carved into the shapes of dragons and lions, and a table that held a pitcher and basin for washing. Each of our rooms held a desk and cabinet full of instruments for painting and writing, and something neither of us had ever seen, a bed. A half-wall divided the space between Joshua's room and mine, so we were able to lie in the beds and talk before falling asleep, just as we had in the desert. I could tell that Joshua was deeply troubled about something that first night.

"You seem, I don't know, deeply troubled, Josh."

"It's the bandits. Could I have raised them?"

"All of them? I don't know, could you?"

"I thought about it. I thought that I could make them all walk and breathe again. I thought I could make them live. But I didn't even try."

"Why?"

"Because I was afraid they would have killed us and robbed us if I had. It's what Balthasar said, 'Those who are violent do not die naturally.' "

"The Torah says, an eye for an eye, a tooth for a tooth. They were bandits."

"But were they bandits always? Would they have been bandits in the years to come?"

"Sure, once a bandit, always a bandit. They take an oath or something. Besides, you didn't kill them."

"But I didn't save them, and I blinded that bowman. That wasn't right."

"You were angry."

"That's no excuse."

"What do you mean, that's no excuse? You're God's Son. God wiped out everyone on earth with a flood because he was angry."

"I'm not sure that's right."

" 'Scuse me?"

"We have to go to Kabul. I need to restore that man's sight if I can."

"Joshua, this bed is the most comfortable place I've ever been. Can we wait to go to Kabul?"

"I suppose."

Joshua was quiet for a long time and I thought that he might have fallen asleep. I didn't want to sleep, but I didn't want to talk about dead bandits either.

"Hey Josh?"

"What?"

"What do you think is in that room with the iron door, what did he call it?"

"Xiong zai," said Josh.

"Yeah, *Xiong zai.* What do you think that is?"

"I don't know, Biff. Maybe you should ask your tutor."

Xiong zai means house of doom, in the parlance of feng shui," said Tiny Feet of the Divine Dance of Joyous Orgasm. She knelt before a low stone table that held an earthenware teapot and cups. She wore a red silk robe trimmed with golden dragons and tied with a black sash. Her hair was black and straight and so long that she had tied it in a knot to keep it from dragging on the floor as she served the tea. Her face was heart-shaped, her skin as smooth as polished alabaster, and if she'd ever been in the sun, the evidence had long since faded. She wore wooden sandals held fast by silk ribbons and her feet, as you might guess from her name, were tiny. It had taken me three days of lessons to get the courage up to ask her about the room.

She poured the tea daintily, but without ceremony, as she had each of the previous three days before my lessons. But this time, before she handed it to me, she added to my cup a drop of a potion from a tiny porcelain bottle that hung from a chain around her neck.

"What's in the bottle, Joy?" I called her Joy. He full name was too ungainly for conversation, and when I'd tried other diminutives (Tiny Feet, Divine Dance, and Orgasm), she hadn't responded positively.

"Poison," Joy said with a smile. The lips of her smile were shy and girlish, but the eyes smiled a thousand years sly.

"Ah," I said, and I tasted the tea. It was rich and fragrant, just as it had been before, but this time there was a hint of bitterness.

"Biff, can you guess what your lesson is today?" Joy asked.

"I thought you would tell me what's in that house of doom room."

"No, that is not the lesson today. Balthasar does not wish you to know what is in that room. Guess again."

My fingers and toes had begun to tingle and I suddenly realized that my scalp had gone numb. "You're going to teach me how to make the fire-powder that Balthasar used the day we arrived?"

"No, silly." Joy's laugh had the musical sound of a clear stream running over rocks. She pushed me lightly on the chest and I fell over backward, unable to move. "Today's lesson is—are you ready?"

I grunted. It was all I could do. My mouth was paralyzed.

"Today's lesson is, if someone puts poison in your tea, don't drink it."

"Uh-huh," I sort of slurred.

So," Balthasar said, "I see that Tiny Feet of the Divine Dance of Joyous Orgasm has revealed what she keeps in the little bottle around her neck." The magus laughed heartily and leaned back on some cushions.

"Is he dead?" asked Joshua.

The girls laid my paralyzed body on some pillows next to Joshua, then propped me up so I could look at Balthasar. Beautiful Gate of Heavenly Moisture Number Six, who I had only just met and didn't have a nickname for yet, put some drops on my eyes to keep them moist, as I seemed to have lost the ability to blink.

"No," said Balthasar, "he's not dead. He's just relaxed."

Joshua poked me in the ribs and, of course, I didn't respond. "Really relaxed," he said.

Beautiful Gate of Heavenly Moisture Number Six handed Joshua the little vial of eye drops and excused herself. She and the other girls left the room. "Can he see and hear us?" Joshua asked.

"Oh yes, he's completely alert."

"Hey Biff, I'm learning about Chi," Joshua shouted into my ear. "It flows all around us. You can't see it, or hear it, or smell it, but it's there."

"You don't need to shout," said Balthasar. Which is what I would have said, if I could have said anything.

Joshua put some drops in my eyes. "Sorry." Then to Balthasar, "This poison, where did it come from?"

"I studied under a sage in China who had been the emperor's royal poisoner. He taught me this, and many other of the magics of the five elements."

"Why would an emperor need a poisoner?"

"A question that only a peasant would ask."

"An answer that only an ass would give," said Joshua.

Balthasar laughed. "So be it, child of the star. A question asked in earnest deserves an earnest answer. An emperor has many enemies to dispatch, but more important, he has many enemies who would dispatch him. The sage spent most of his time concocting antidotes."

"So there's an antidote to this poison," Joshua said, poking me in the ribs again.

"In good time. In good time. Have some more wine, Joshua. I wish to discuss with you the three jewels of the Tao. The three jewels of the Tao are compassion, moderation, and humility . . ."

An hour later, four Chinese girls came and picked me up, wiped the floor where I had drooled, and carried me to our quarters. As they passed the great ironclad door I could hear scraping and a voice in my head that said, "Hey kid, open the door," but the girls made no notice of it. Back in my room, the girls bathed me and poured some rich broth into me, then put me to bed and closed my eyes.

I could hear Joshua enter the room and shuffle around preparing for bed. "Balthasar says he will have Joy give you the antidote to the poison soon, but first you have a lesson to learn. He says that this is the Chinese way of teaching. Strange, don't you think?"

Had I been able to make a sound, I would have agreed, yes, indeed it was strange.

So you know:
Balthasar's concubines were eight in number and their names were:

> *Tiny Feet of the Divine Dance of Joyous Orgasm,*
> *Beautiful Gate of Heavenly Moisture Number Six,*
> *Temptress of the Golden Light of the Harvest Moon,*
> *Delicate Personage of Two Fu Dogs Wrestling Under a Blanket,*
> *Feminine Keeper of the Three Tunnels of Excessive Friendliness,*
> *Silken Pillows of the Heavenly Softness of Clouds,*
> *Pea Pods in Duck Sauce with Crispy Noodle,*
> *and Sue.*

And I found myself wondering, as a man does, about origins and motivations and such—as each of the concubines was more beautiful than the last, regardless of what order you put them in, which was weird—so after several weeks passed, and I could no longer stand the curiosity scratching at my brain like a cat in a basket, I waited until one of the rare occasions when I was alone with Balthasar, and I asked.

"Why Sue?"

"Short for Susanna," Balthasar said.

So there you go.

Their full names were somewhat ungainly, and to try to pronounce them in Chinese produced a sound akin to throwing a bag of silverware down a flight of steps (ting, tong, yang, wing, etc.) so Joshua and I called the girls as follows:

> *Joy,*
> *Number Six,*
> *Two Fu Dogs,*
> *Moon,*
> *Tunnels,*
> *Pillows,*
> *Pea Pods,*
> *and, of course,*
> *Sue,*

which we couldn't figure out how to shorten.

Except for a group of men who brought supplies from Kabul every two weeks, and while there would do any heavy moving, the eight young women did everything around the fortress. Despite the remoteness and the obvious wealth that the fortress housed, there were no guards. I found that curious.

Over the next week Joy tutored me in the characters that I would need to know to read the *Book of the Divine Elixirs or the Nine Tripods of the Yellow Emperor*, and the *Book of Liquid Pearl in Nine Cycles and of the Nine Elixirs of the Divine Immortals.* The plan was that once I became conversant in these two ancient texts, I would be able to assist Balthasar in his quest for immortality. That, by the way, was the reason that we were there, the reason that Balthasar had followed the star to Bethlehem at Joshua's birth, and the reason that he had put Ahmad on notice to look for a Jew seeking the African magus. Balthasar sought immortality, and he believed that Joshua held the key to it. Of course we didn't know that at the time.

My concentration while studying the symbols was particularly acute, helped by the fact that I could not move a muscle. Each morning Two Fu Dogs and Pillows (both named for their voluptuousness, which evidently came with considerable strength) would pull me from bed, squeeze me over the latrine, bathe me, pour some broth into me, then take me to the library and prop me in a chair while Joy lectured on Chinese characters, which she painted with a wet brush on large sheets of slate set on easels. Sometimes the other girls would stay and pose my body into various positions that amused them, and as much as I should have been annoyed by the humiliation, the truth be told, watching Pillows and Two Fu Dogs jiggle in paroxysms of girlish laughter was fast becoming the high point of my paralyzed day.

At midday, Joy would take a break while two or more of the other girls squoze me over the latrine, poured more broth into me, and then teased me mercilessly until Joy returned, clapped her hands, and sent them away well scolded. (Joy was the bull-ox concubine of them all, despite her tiny feet.)

Sometimes during these breaks, Joshua would leave his own lessons and come to the library to visit.

"Why have you painted him blue?" asked Joshua.

"He looks good blue," said Pea Pods. Two Fu Dogs and Tunnels stood by with paintbrushes admiring their work.

"Well, he's not going to be happy with this when he gets the antidote, I can tell you that." Then to me Joshua said, "You know, you do sort of look good blue. Biff, I've appealed to Joy on your behalf, but she says she doesn't think you've learned your lesson yet. You have learned your lesson though, haven't you? Stop breathing for a second if the answer is yes."

I did.

"I thought so." Joshua bent and whispered in my ear. "It's about that room behind the iron door. That's the lesson they want you to learn. I got the feeling that if I asked about it I'd be propped up there next to you." He stood up. "I have to go now. The three jewels to learn, don't you know. I'm on compassion. It's not as hard as it sounds."

two days later Joy came to my room in the morning with some tea. She pulled the tiny bottle from inside her dragon robe and held it close in front of my eyes. "You see the two small corks, a white one on one side of the vessel and a black one on the other? The black one is the poison I gave you. The white one is the antidote. I think you've learned your lesson."

I drooled in response, while sincerely hoping she hadn't mixed up the corks.

She tipped the little bottle over a teacup, then poured some tea down my throat, with half of it going down the front of my shirt as well. "That will take a while to work. You may experience some discomfort as the poison wears off." Joy dropped the little bottle down into its nest of Chinese cleavage, then kissed me on the forehead and left. If I could, I would have snickered at the blue paint she had on her lips as she walked away. Ha!

Some discomfort," she had said. For the better part of ten days I'd had no sensation in my body at all, then suddenly things started to work again. Imagine rolling out of your warm bed in the morning into—oh, I don't know—a lake of burning oil.

"Jumpin' Jehoshaphat, Joshua, I'm about to crawl out of my skin here." We were in our quarters, about an hour after I'd taken the antidote. Balthasar had sent Joshua to find me and bring me to the library, supposedly to see how I was doing.

Josh put his hand on my forehead, but instead of the usual calm that accompanied that gesture, it felt as if he'd lain a hot branding iron across my skin. I knocked his hand aside. "Thanks, but it's not helping."

"Maybe a bath," Joshua suggested.

"Tried it. Jeez, this is driving me mad!" I hopped around in a circle because I didn't know what else to do.

"Maybe Balthasar has something that can help," Joshua said.

"Lead on," I said. "I can't just sit here."

We headed off down the corridor, going down several levels on the way to the library. As we descended one of the spiral ramps I grabbed Joshua's arm.

"Josh, look at this ramp, you notice anything?"

He considered the surface and leaned out to look at the sides of the tread. "No. Should I?"

"How about the walls and ceilings, the floors, you notice anything?"

Joshua looked around. "They're all solid rock?"

"Yes, but what else? Look hard. Think of the houses we built in Sepphoris. Now do you notice anything?"

"No tool marks?"

"Exactly," I said. "I spent a lot of time over the last two weeks staring at walls and ceilings with nothing much else to look at. There's not the slightest evidence of a chisel, a pick, a hammer, anything. It's as if these chambers had been carved by the wind over a thousand years, but you know that's not the case."

"So what's your point?" Joshua said.

"My point is that there's more going on with Balthasar and his girls than he lets on."

"We should ask them."

"No, we shouldn't, Josh. Don't you get it? We need to find out what's going on without them knowing that we know."

"Why?"

"Why? Why? Because the last time I asked a question I was poisoned, that's why. And I believe that if Balthasar didn't think you had something that he wants, I'd have never seen the antidote."

"But I don't have anything," said Joshua, honestly.

"You might have something you don't know you have, but you can't just go asking what it is. We need to be devious. Tricky. Sneaky."

"But I'm not good at any of those things."

I put my arm around my friend's shoulders. "Not always so great being the Messiah, huh?"

Chapter 13

"I could kick that punk's punk ass," the angel said, jumping on the bed, shaking a fist at the television screen.

"Raziel," I said, "you are an angel of the Lord, he is a professional wrestler, I think it's understood that you could kick his punk ass." This has gone on for a couple of days now. The angel has found a new passion. The front desk has called a dozen times and sent a bellman up twice to tell the angel to quiet down. "Besides, it's just pretend."

Raziel looked at me as if I had slapped him. "Don't start with that again, these are not actors." The angel back flipped on the bed. "Ooo, ooo, you see that? Ho popped him with a chair. Thaz right, you go girl. She nasty."

It's like that now. Talk shows featuring the screaming ignorant, soap operas, and wrestling. And the angel guards the remote control like it's the Ark of the Covenant.

"This," I told him, "is why the angels were never given free will. This right here. Because you would spend your time watching this."

"Really?" Raziel said, and he muted the TV for what seemed like the first time in days. "Then tell me, Levi who is called Biff, if by watching this I am abusing the little freedom I've been given while carrying out this task, then what would you say of your people?"

"By my people you mean human beings?" I was stalling. I didn't remember the angel ever making a valid point before and I wasn't prepared for it. "Hey, don't blame me, I've been dead for two thousand years. I wouldn't have let this sort of thing happen."

"Uh-huh," said the angel, crossing his arms and striking a pose of incredulity that he had learned from a gangster rapper on MTV.

If there was anything I learned from John the Baptist, it was that the sooner you confess a mistake, the quicker you can get on to making new and better mistakes. Oh, that and don't piss off Salome, that was a big one too. "Okay, we've fucked up," I said.

"Thaz whut I'm talkin' about," said the angel, entirely too satisfied with himself.

Yeah? Where was he when we needed him and his sword of justice at Balthasar's fortress? Probably in Greece, watching wrestling.

Meanwhile, when we got to the library, Balthasar was sitting before the heavy dragon table, eating a bit of cheese and sipping wine while Tunnels and Pea Pods poured a sticky yellow wax on his bald head, then spread it around with small wooden paddles. The easels and slates from my lessons had been stacked out of the way against the shelves full of scrolls and codices.

"You look good blue," Balthasar said.

"Yeah, everybody says that." The paint, once set, didn't wash off, but at least my skin had stopped itching.

"Come in, sit. Have wine. They brought cheese from Kabul this morning. Try some."

Joshua and I sat in chairs across the table from the magus. Josh, completely true to form, disregarded my advice and asked Balthasar outright about the iron door.

The aspect of the jolly wizard became suddenly grave. "There are some mysteries one must learn to live with. Did not your own God tell Moses that no one must look upon his face, and the prophet accepted that? So you must accept that you cannot know what is in the room with the iron door."

"He knows his Torah, and Prophets and Writings too," Joshua said to me. "Balthasar knows more about Solomon than any of the rabbis or priests in Israel."

"That's swell, Josh." I handed him a hunk of cheese to keep him amused. To Balthasar I said, "But you forget God's butt." You don't hang out with the Messiah for most of your life without picking up a little Torah knowledge yourself.

"What?" said the magus. Just then the girls grabbed the edges of the hardened wax shell they'd made on Balthasar's head and ripped it off in one swift movement. "Ouch, you vicious harpies! Can't you warn me when you're going to do that? Get out."

The girls tittered and hid their satisfied grins behind delicate fans painted with pheasants and plum blossoms. They fled the library leaving a trail of girlish laughter in the hall as they passed.

"Isn't there an easier way to do that?" asked Joshua.

Balthasar scowled at him. "Don't you think that after two hundred years, if there was an easier way to do it I would have found it?"

Joshua dropped his cheese. "Two hundred years?"

I chimed in. "You get a hairstyle you like, stick with it. Not that you could call that hair, per se."

Balthasar wasn't amused. "What's this about God's butt?"

"Or that you could call that style, for that matter," I added, rising and going to a copy of the Torah that I'd seen on the shelves. Fortunately it was a codex—like a modern book—otherwise I'd have been unwinding a scroll for twenty minutes and the drama would have been lost. I quickly flipped to Exodus. "Right, here's the part you were talking about. 'And he said, Thou canst not see my face: for there shall no man see me, and live.' Right? Well, then God puts his hand over Moses as he passes, but he says, 'I will take away mine hand, and thou shalt see my back parts: but my face shall not be seen.' "

"So?" said Balthasar.

"So, God let Moses see his butt, so using your example, you owe us God's butt. So tell us, what's going on with that room with the iron door?" Brilliant. I paused and studied the blueness of my fingernails while savoring my victory.

"That's the silliest thing I've ever heard," said Balthasar. His momentary loss of composure was replaced by the calm and slightly amused attitude of the master. "What if I told you that it is dangerous for you to know about what is behind that iron door now, but once you have training, you will not only know, but you will gain great power from the knowledge? When I think you are ready, I promise to show you what is behind that door. But you must promise to study and learn your lessons. Can you do that?"

"Are you forbidding us to ask questions?" asked Joshua.

"Oh no, I'm simply denying you some of the answers for the time being. And trust me, time is the one thing that I have plenty of."

Joshua turned to me. "I still don't know what I am supposed to learn here, but I'm sure I haven't learned it yet." He was pleading me with his eyes to not push the issue. I decided to let it drop; besides, I didn't relish the idea of being poisoned again.

"How long is this going to take?" I asked. "These lessons, I mean?"

"Some students take many years to learn the nature of Chi. You will be provided for while you are here."

"Years? Can we think about it?"

"Take as long as you like," Balthasar stood. "Now I must go to the girls' quarters. They like to rub their naked breasts over my scalp right after it's been waxed and is at its smoothest."

I gulped. Joshua grinned and looked at the table in front of him. I often wondered, not just then, but most of the time, if Joshua had the ability to turn off his imagination when he needed to. He must have. Otherwise I don't know how he would have ever triumphed over temptation. I, on the other hand, was a slave to my imagination and it was running wild with the image of Balthasar's scalp massage.

"We'll stay. We'll learn. We'll do what is needed," I said.

Joshua burst out laughing, then calmed himself enough to speak. "Yes, we will stay and learn, Balthasar, but first I have to go to Kabul and finish some business."

"Of course you do," said Balthasar. "You can leave tomorrow. I'll have one of the girls show you the way, but for now, I must say good night." The wizard stalked off, leaving Joshua to collapse into a fit of giggles and me to wonder how I might look with my head shaved.

In the morning Joy came to our rooms wearing the garb of a desert trader: a loose tunic, soft leather boots, and pantaloons. Her hair was tied up under a turban and she carried a long riding crop in her hand. She led us through a long narrow passageway that went deep into the mountain, then emerged out of the side of a sheer cliff. We climbed a rope ladder to the top of the plateau where Pillows and Sue waited with three camels saddled and outfitted for a short journey. There was a small farm on the plateau, with several pens full of chickens, some goats, and a few pigs in a pen.

"We're going to have a tough time getting these camels down that ladder," I said.

Joy scowled and wrapped the tail of her turban around her face so that only her eyes showed. "There's a path down," she said. Then she tapped her camel on the shoulder with her crop and rode off, leaving Joshua and me to scramble onto our animals and follow.

The road down from the plateau was just wide enough for a single camel to sway his way down without falling, but once down on the desert floor, much like the entrance to the canyon where the fortress's entrance lay, if you didn't know it was there, you would never have found it. An added measure of security for a fortress that had no guards, I thought.

Joshua and I tried to engage Joy in conversation several times during the journey to Kabul, but she was cranky and abrupt and often just rode away from us.

"Probably depressed that she's not torturing me," I speculated.

"I can see how that might bring her down," said Joshua. "Maybe if you could get your camel to bite you. I know that always brightens my mood."

I rode on ahead without another word. It's wildly irritating to have invented something as revolutionary as sarcasm, only to have it abused by amateurs.

Once in Kabul, Joy led the search for the blinded guard by asking every blind beggar that we passed in the marketplace. "Have you seen a blind bowman who arrived by camel caravan a little more than a week ago?"

Joshua and I trailed several steps behind her, trying desperately to keep from grinning whenever she looked back. Joshua had wanted to point out the flaw in Joy's method, while I, on the other hand, wanted to savor her doofuscosity as passive revenge for having been poisoned. There was none of the competence and self-assured nature she showed at the fortress. She was clearly out of her element and I was enjoying it.

"You see," I explained to Joshua, "what Joy is doing is ironic, yet that's not her intent. That's the difference between irony and sarcasm. Irony can be spontaneous, while sarcasm requires volition. You have to create sarcasm."

"No kidding?" said Josh.

"Why do I waste my time with you?"

We indulged Joy's search for the blind man for another hour before directing her inquiries to the sighted, and to men from the camel caravans in particular. Once she started asking sighted people, it was a short time before we were directed to a temple where the blinded guard was said to have staked his begging territory.

"There he is," said Joshua, pointing to a ragged pile of human being beckoning to the worshipers as they moved in and out of the temple.

"It looks like things have been tough on him," I said, amazed that the guard, who had been one of the most vital (and frightening) men I'd ever seen, had been reduced to such a pathetic creature in so short a time. Then again, I was discounting the theatrics of it all.

"A great injustice has been done here," said Josh. He moved to the guard and gently put his hand on the blind man's shoulder. "Brother, I am here to relieve your suffering."

"Pity on the blind," said the guard, waving around a wooden bowl.

"Calm now," said Joshua, placing his hand over the blind man's eyes. "When I remove my hand you will see again."

I could see the strain in Joshua's face as he concentrated on healing the guard. Tears trickled down his cheeks and dripped on the flagstones. I thought of how effortless his healings had been in Antioch, and realized that the strain was not coming from the healing, but from the guilt he carried for having blinded the man in the first place. When he removed his hand and stepped away, both he and the guard shivered.

Joy stepped away from us and covered her face as if to ward off bad air.

The guard stared into space just as he had while he had been begging, but his eyes were no longer white.

"Can you see?" Joshua said.

"I can see, but everything is wrong. People's skin appears blue."

"No, he *is* blue. Remember, my friend Biff."

"Were you always blue?"

"No, only recently."

Then the guard seemed to see Joshua for the first time and his expression of wonderment was replaced by hatred. He leapt at Joshua, drawing a dagger from his rags as he moved. He would have split my friend's rib cage in a single swift blow if Joy hadn't swept his feet out from under him at the last second. Even so, he was up in an instant, going for a second attack. I managed to get my hand up in time to poke him in the eyes, just as Joy kicked him in the back of the neck, driving him to the ground in agony.

"My eyes!" he cried.

"Sorry," I said.

Joy kicked the knife out of the guard's reach. I put an arm around Joshua's chest and pushed him back. "You need to put some distance between you and him before he can see again."

"But I only meant to help him," said Joshua. "Blinding him was a mistake."

"Josh, he doesn't care. All he knows is that you are the enemy. All he knows is that he wants to destroy you."

"I don't know what I'm doing. Even when I try to do the right thing it goes wrong."

"We need to go," said Joy. She took one of Joshua's arms while I took the other and we led him away before the guard could gather his senses for another attack.

Joy had a list of supplies that Balthasar wanted her to bring back to the fortress, so we spent some time tracking down large baskets of a mineral called cinnabar, from which we would extract quicksilver, as well as some spices and pigments. Joshua followed us through the market in a daze until we passed a merchant who was selling the black beans from which was made the dark drink we'd had in Antioch.

"Buy me some," Joshua said. "Joy, buy me some of those."

She did, and Joshua cradled the bag of beans like an infant all the way back to the fortress. We rode most of the way in silence, but when the sun had gone down and we were almost to the hidden road that led up to the plateau, Joy galloped up beside me.

"How did he do it?" she asked.

"What?"

"I saw him heal that man's eyes. How did he do it? I know many kinds of magic, but I saw no spells cast, no potions mixed."

"It's very powerful magic all right." I checked over my shoulder to see if Joshua was paying attention. He was hugging his coffee beans and mumbling to himself as he had for the whole trip. Praying, I presume.

"Tell me how it's done," Joy said. "I asked Joshua, but he's just chanting and looking stunned."

"Well, I could tell you how it's done, but you have to tell me what's going on behind the ironclad door."

"I can't tell you that, but perhaps we can trade other things." She pulled the tail of her turban away from her face and smiled. She was stunningly beautiful in the moonlight, even in men's clothes. "I know over a thousand ways to bring pleasure to a man, and that's only what I know personally. The other girls have as many tricks that they'd be willing to show you too."

"Yeah, but how is that useful to me? What do I need to know about pleasing a man?"

Joy ripped her turban off her head and smacked me across the back of the head with it, sending a small cloud of dust drifting into the night. "You're stupid and you're blue and the next time I poison you I will be sure to use something without an antidote."

Even the wise and inscrutable Joy could be goaded, I guess. I smiled. "I will accept your paltry offerings," I said with as much pomposity as an adolescent boy can muster. "And in return I will teach the greatest secret of our magic. A secret of my own invention. We call it sarcasm."

"Let's make coffee when we get home," said Joshua.

It was some challenge to try to drag out the process of how Joshua had returned the guard's sight, especially since I hadn't the slightest idea myself, but through careful misdirection, obfuscation, subterfuge, guile, and complete balderdash, I was able to barter that lack of knowledge into months of outrageous knob polishing by the beauteous Joy and her comely minions. Somehow, the urgency of knowing what was behind the ironclad door and the answers to other enigmas of Balthasar's fortress abated, and I found myself quite content pursuing the lessons the wizard assigned me during the day, while stretching my imagination to its limit with the mathematical combinations of the night. There was the drawback that Balthasar would kill me if he knew that I was availing myself of the charms of his concubines, but is the pilfered fruit not sweetened by the stealing? Oh, to be young and in love (with eight Chinese concubines).

Meanwhile Joshua took to his studies with characteristic zeal, fueled in no little bit by the coffee he drank every morning until he nearly vibrated through the floor with enthusiasm.

"Look at this, do you see, Biff? When asked, the master Confucius says, 'Recompense injury with justice, and kindness with kindness.' Yet Lao-tzu says, 'Recompense injury with kindness.' Don't you see?" Joshua would dance around, scrolls trailing out behind him, hoping that somehow I would share his enthusiasm for the ancient texts. And I tried. I really did.

"No, I don't see. The Torah says, 'an eye for an eye, a tooth for a tooth,' that is justice."

"Exactly," said Joshua. "I think Lao-tzu is correct. Kindness precedes justice. As long as you seek justice by punishment you can only cause more suffering. How can that be right? This is a revelation!"

"I learned how to boil down goat urine to make explosives today," I said.

"That's good too," said Joshua.

It could happen like that any time of the day or night. Joshua would come blazing out of the library in the middle of the night, interrupt me in the midst of some complex oily tangle of Pea Pod and Pillows and Tunnels—while Number Six familiarized us with the five hundred jade gods of various depths and textures—and he'd avert his eyes just long enough for me to towel off before he'd shove some codex in my hand and force me to read a passage while he waxed enthusiastic on the thoughts of some long-dead sage.

"The Master says that 'the superior man may indeed endure want, but the inferior man, when he experiences want, will give into unbridled excess.' He's talking about you, Biff. You're the inferior man."

"I'm so proud," I told him, as I watched Number Six forlornly pack her gods into the warmed brass case where they resided. "Thank you for coming here to tell me that."

I was given the task of learning *waidan,* which is the alchemy of the external. My knowledge would come from the manipulation of the physical elements. Joshua, on the other hand, was learning *neidan,* the alchemy of the internal. His knowledge would come from the study of his own inner nature through the contemplation of the masters. So while Joshua read scrolls and books, I spent my time mixing quicksilver and lead, phosphorous and brimstone, charcoal and philosopher's stone, trying somehow to divine the nature of the Tao. Joshua was learning to be the Messiah and I was learning to poison people and blow stuff up. The world seemed very much in order. I was happy, Joshua was happy, Balthasar was happy, and the girls—well, the girls were busy. Although I passed the iron door every day (and the niggling voice persisted), what was behind it wasn't important to me, and neither were the answers to the dozen or so questions that Joshua and I should have put to our generous master.

Before we knew it a year had passed, then two more, and we were celebrating the passage of Joshua's seventeenth birthday in the fortress. Balthasar had the girls prepare a feast of Chinese delicacies and we drank wine late into the night. (And long after that, and even when we had returned to Israel, we always ate Chinese food on Joshua's birthday. I'm told it became a tradition not only with those of us who knew Joshua, but with Jews everywhere.)

"Do you ever think of home?" Joshua asked me the night of his birthday feast.

"Sometimes," I said.

"What do you think of?"

"Maggie," I said. "Sometimes my brothers. Sometimes my mother and father, but always Maggie."

"Even with all your experiences since, you still think of Maggie?" Joshua had become less and less curious about the essence of lust. Initially I thought that his lack of interest had to do with the depth of his studies, but I then realized that his interest was fading along with the memory of Maggie.

"Joshua, my memory of Maggie isn't about what happened the night before we left. I didn't go to see her thinking that we would make love. A kiss was more than I expected. I think of Maggie because I made a place in my heart for her to live, and it's empty. It always will be. It always was. She loved you."

"I'm sorry, Biff. I don't know how to heal that. I would if I could."

"I know, Josh. I know." I didn't want to talk about home anymore, but Josh deserved to get off his chest whatever it was that was bothering him, and if not to me, to whom? "Do you ever think of home?"

"Yes. That's why I asked. You know, the girls were cooking bacon today, and that made me think of home."

"Why? I don't remember anyone ever cooking bacon at home."

"I know, but if we ate some bacon, no one at home would ever know."

I got up and walked over to the half-wall that divided our rooms. There was moonlight coming through the window and Joshua's face had caught it and was glowing in that annoying way that it sometimes did.

"Joshua, you're the Son of God. You're the Messiah. That implies—oh, I don't know—that you're a Jew! You can't eat bacon."

"God doesn't care if we eat bacon. I can just feel it."

"Really. He still feel the same way about fornication?"

"Yep."

"Masturbation?"

"Yep."

"Killing? Stealing? Bearing false witness? Coveting thy neighbor's wife, et cetera? No change of heart on those?"

"Nope."

"Just bacon. Interesting. You would have thought there'd be something about bacon in the prophecies of Isaiah."

"Yeah, makes you wonder, doesn't it?"

"You're going to need more than that to usher in the kingdom of God, Josh, no offense. We can't go home with, 'Hi, I'm the Messiah, God wanted you to have this bacon.' "

"I know. We have much more to learn. But breakfasts will be more interesting."

"Go to sleep, Josh."

𝖆s time passed, I seldom saw Joshua except at mealtimes and before we went to sleep. Nearly all my time was taken up with my studies and helping the girls maintain the fortress, while nearly all of Joshua's time was spent with Balthasar, which would eventually become a problem.

"This is not good, Biff," Joy said in Chinese. I'd learned to speak her language well enough that she seldom spoke Greek or Latin anymore. "Balthasar is getting too close with Joshua. He seldom sends for one of us to join him in his bed now."

"You're not implying that Joshua and Balthasar are, uh, playing shepherd, are you? Because I know that's not true. Joshua isn't allowed." Of course the angel had said he couldn't know a woman, he hadn't said anything about a creepy old African wizard.

"Oh, I don't care if they're buggering their eyeballs out," said Joy. "Balthasar mustn't fall in love. Why do you think that there are eight of us?"

"I thought it was a matter of budget," I said.

"You haven't noticed that one of us will never spend two nights in a row with Balthasar, or that we don't speak with him beyond what is required for our duties and lessons?"

I had noticed, but it never occurred to me that there was something out of the ordinary. We hadn't gotten to the chapter on wizard–concubine behavior in the book yet. "So?"

"So I think he is falling in love with Joshua. That is not good."

"Well, I'm with you on that one. I wasn't happy the last time someone fell in love with him. But why does it matter here?"

"I can't tell you. But there has been more commotion coming from the house of doom," said Joy. "You have to help me. If I'm right, we have to stop Balthasar. We'll observe them tomorrow while we adjust the flow of Chi in the library."

"No, Joy. Not library Chi. The stuff in the library is too heavy. I hate library Chi."

Chi or *Qi*: the breath of the dragon, the eternal energy that flows through all things; in balance, as it should be, it was half yin, half yang, half light, half dark, half male, half female. The Chi in the library was always getting fucked up, while the Chi in the rooms with just cushions, or with lightweight furniture, seemed well adjusted and balanced. I don't know why, but I suspected it had a lot to do with Joy's need to make me move heavy things.

The next morning Joy and I went to the library to spy on Joshua and Balthasar while we redirected the library's Chi. Joy carried a complex brass instrument she called a Chi clock, which was supposed to be able to detect the flow of Chi. The magus was noticeably irritated as soon as we entered the room.

"Must this be done now?"

Joy bowed. "Very sorry, master, but this is an emergency." She turned and barked commands at me like a Roman centurion. "Move that table over there, can't you see that it rests on the tiger's testicles? Then point those chairs so they face the doorway, they lie on the dragon's navel. We're lucky someone hasn't broken a leg."

"Yeah, lucky," I said, straining to move the huge carved table, wishing that Joy had recruited a couple of the other girls to help. I'd been studying feng shui for more than three years now and I still couldn't detect the least bit of Chi, coming or going. Joshua had reconciled the elusive energy by saying that it was just an Oriental way to express God all around us and in all things. That may have helped him toward some sort of spiritual understanding, but it was about as effective as trained sheep when it came to arranging furniture.

"Can I help?" Joshua asked.

"No!" shouted Balthasar, standing up. "We will continue in my quarters." The old wizard turned and glared at Joy and me. "And we are not to be disturbed, under any circumstances."

He took Joshua by the shoulder and led him out of the room.

"So much for spying," I said.

Joy consulted the Chi clock and patted a cabinet filled with calligraphy materials. "This most certainly rides on the horn of the ox, it must be moved," she pronounced.

"They are gone," I said. "We don't have to pretend at this anymore."

"Who is pretending? That cabinet channels all the yin into the hall, while the yang circles like a bird of prey."

"Joy, stop it. I know you're making this stuff up."

She dropped the brass instrument to her side. "I am not."

"Yes, you are." And here I thought I'd push my credibility a bit, just to see. "I checked the yang in this room yesterday. It is in perfect balance."

Joy dropped to her hands and knees, crawled under one of the huge carved dragon tables, curled up into a ball, and began to cry. "I'm no good at this. Balthasar wants us all to know it, but I've never understood it. If you want the Elegant Torture of a Thousand Pleasant Touches, I can do it, you want someone poisoned, castrated, or blown up, I'm your man, but this feng shui stuff is just, just . . ."

"Stupid?" I supplied.

"No, I was going to say difficult. Now I've angered Balthasar and we have no way of knowing what is happening between him and Joshua. And we must know."

"I can find out," I said, polishing my nails on my tunic. "But I have to know why I'm finding out."

"How will you find out?"

"I have ways that are more subtle and crafty than all your Chinese alchemy and direction of energies."

"Now who's making things up?" I'd lost most of my credibility by dragging out the arcane-Hebrew-knowledge-for-sexual-favors ruse until I had actually claimed credit for receiving the tablets of the Ten Commandments as well as constructing the Ark of the Covenant. (What? It's not my fault. Joshua was the one who would never let me be Moses when we were kids.)

"If I find out, will you tell me what is going on?"

The head concubine chewed at an elegantly lacquered nail as she thought about it. "You promise not to tell anyone if I tell you? Not even your friend Joshua?"

"I promise."

"Then do what you will. But remember your lessons from *The Art of War*."

I considered the words of Sun-tzu, which Joy had taught me: *Be extremely subtle, even to the point of formlessness. Be extremely mysterious, even to the point of soundlessness. Thereby, you can be the director of the opponent's fate.* So after considering strategy carefully, running and rejecting the various scenarios in my head, working out what seemed a nearly foolproof plan, and making sure the timing was perfect, I went into action. That very night, as I lay in my bed and Joshua in his, I called forth all my powers of subtlety and mysteriousness.

"Hey Josh," I said. "Balthasar sodomizing you?"

"No!"

"Vice versa?"

"Absolutely not!"

"You get the feeling he'd like to?"

He was quiet for a second, then he said, "He's been very attentive lately. And he giggles at everything I say, why?"

"Because Joy says it's not good if he falls in love with you."

"Well, it's not if he's expecting any sodomizing, I'll tell you that. That's going to be one disappointed magus."

"No, worse than that. She won't tell me what, but it's really, really bad."

"Biff, I realize you may not think so, but from my way of thinking, sodomizing the Son of God *is* really, really bad."

"Good point. But I think she means something to do with whatever is behind the iron door. Until I find out, you have to keep Balthasar from falling in love with you."

"I'll bet he was myrrh," said Josh. "Bastard, he brings the cheapest gift and now he wants to sodomize me. My mother told me the myrrh went bad after a week too."

Did I mention that Joshua was not a myrrh fan?

Chapter 14

Meanwhile, back at the hotel room, Raziel has given up his hopes to be a professional wrestler and has resumed his ambition to be Spider-Man. He made the decision after I pointed out that in Genesis, Jacob wrestles an angel and wins. In short, a human defeated an angel. Raziel kept insisting that he didn't remember that happening and I was tempted to bring the Gideon Bible in out of the bathroom and show him the reference, but I've just started reading the Gospel of Mark and I'd lose the book if the angel found out about it.

I thought Matthew was bad, skipping right from Joshua's birth to his baptism, but Mark doesn't even bother with the birth. It's as if Joshua springs forth full grown from the head of Zeus. (Okay, bad metaphor, but you know what I mean.) Mark begins with the baptism, at thirty! Where did these guys get these stories? "I once met a guy in a bar who knew a guy who's sister's best friend was at the baptism of Joshua bar Joseph of Nazareth, and here's the story as best as he could remember it."

Well, at least Mark mentions me, once. And then it's totally out of context, as if I was just sitting around doing nothing and Joshua happened by and asked me to tag along. And Mark tells of the demon named Legion. Yeah, I remember Legion. Compared to what Balthasar called up, Legion was a wuss.

"I asked Balthasar if he was smitten with me," Joshua said over supper.

"Oh no," said Joy. We were eating in the girls' quarters. It smelled really good and the girls would rub our shoulders while we ate. Just what we needed after a tough day of studying.

"You weren't supposed to let him know we were on to him. What did he say?"

"He said that he'd just come off of a hard breakup and he wasn't ready for a relationship because he just needed to spend a little time getting to know himself, but that he'd love it if we could just be friends."

"He lies," said Joy. "He hasn't had a breakup in a hundred years."

I said, "Josh, you are so gullible. Guys always lie about stuff like that. That's the problem with your not being allowed to know women, it means you don't understand the most fundamental nature of men."

"Which is?"

"We're lying pigs. We'll say anything to get what we want."

"That's true," said Joy. The other girls nodded in agreement.

"But," said Josh, "the superior man does not, even for the space of a single meal, act contrary to virtue, according to Confucius."

"Of course," said I, "but the superior man can get laid without lying. I'm talking about the rest of us."

"So should I be worried about this trip he wants me to take with him?"

Joy nodded gravely and the other girls nodded with her.

"I don't see why," I said. "What trip?"

"He says we'll only be gone a couple of weeks. He wants to go to a temple at a city in the mountains. He believes that the temple was built by Solomon, it's called the Temple of the Seal."

"And why do you have to go along?"

"He wants to show me something."

"Uh-oh," I said.

"Uh-oh," echoed the girls, not unlike a Greek chorus, except of course they were speaking Chinese.

In the week leading up to Joshua and Balthasar's departure, I managed to talk Pea Pods into taking on a huge risk during her shift in Balthasar's bed. I picked Pea Pods not because she was the most athletic and nimble of the girls, which she was; nor because she was the lightest of foot and most stealthy, which she was also; but because she was the one who had taught me to make bronze castings of the Chinese characters that were the mark of my name (my chop), and she could be trusted to get the most accurate impression of the key that Balthasar wore on the chain around his neck. (Oh yes, there was a key to the ironclad door. Joy had let it slip where Balthasar kept it, but I was sure that she was too loyal to him to steal it. Pea Pods, on the other hand, was more fickle in her loyalties, and lately I had been spending a lot of time with her on and off.)

"By the time you return, I'll know what's going on here," I whispered to Joshua as he climbed onto his camel. "Find out what you can from Balthasar."

"I will. But be careful. Don't do anything while I'm gone. I think this trip, whatever it is that we are going to see, has something to do with the house of doom."

"I'm just going to look around. You be careful."

The girls and I stood at the top of the plateau and waved until Joshua and the magus, leading the extra camel loaded with supplies, rode out of sight, then, one by one, we made our way down the rope ladder to the passageway in the cliff's face. The entrance to the passageway, and the tunnel for perhaps thirty cubits, were just wide enough for one man to pass through if he stooped, and I always managed to bruise an elbow or a shoulder along the way, which allowed me to show off my ability to curse in four languages.

By the time I got to the chamber of the elements, where we practiced the art of the Nine Elixirs, Pea Pods had the small furnace stoked to a red heat and was adding ingots of brass to a small stone crucible. From the wax impression we had made a wax duplicate of the key, from that we'd made a plaster mold, which we'd fired to melt out the wax. Now we'd have one chance to cast the key, because once the metal cooled in the plaster mold, the only way to release it was to break off the plaster.

When we broke off the mold Pea Pods held the end of what looked like a brass dragon on a stick.

"That's some key," I said. The only locks I'd ever seen were big bulky iron boys, nothing elegant enough for a key like this.

"When are you going to use it?" asked Pea Pods. Her eyes went wide like those of an excited child. Times like that I almost fell in love with her, but fortunately I was always distracted by Joy's sophistication, Pillow's maternal fussing, Number Six's dexterity, or any one of the other charms that were heaped upon me daily. I understood completely Balthasar's strategy to keep from falling in love with any one of them. Joshua's situation, on the other hand, was harder to figure, because he enjoyed spending time with the girls, trading stories from the Torah for legends of the storm dragons and the monkey king. He said that there was an innate kindness born in women that he'd never seen in a man, and he liked being around them. His strength in resisting their physical charms astounded me perhaps even more than the other miraculous things I'd seen him do over the years. I couldn't relate to the act of raising someone from the dead, but turning down a beautiful woman, that took courage beyond my understanding.

"I'll take it from here," I said to Pea Pods. I didn't want her to be involved any further in case things didn't turn out well.

"When?" asked Pea Pods, meaning when would I attempt to open the door.

"Tonight, when you have all gone to live in the world of pleasant dreams." I tweaked her nose affectionately and she giggled. It was the last time I ever saw her in one piece.

𝔞 t night the halls of the fortress were lit by the ambient light from the moon and the stars that filtered in from the windows. Everywhere we went we carried a clay oil lamp which made the serpentine curves of the passageways seem even more like the inside of a huge creature as they swallowed up the dim orange light. After several years with Balthasar, I could find my way through the main living quarters of the fortress without any light at all, so I carried an unlit lamp with me until I had passed the girls' quarters, stopping at the beaded doorway to listen for their gentle snores.

Once I was well away from the girls' door, I lit my lamp using one of the fire sticks that I'd invented using some of the same chemicals we used to make the explosive black powder. The fire stick made a soft pop as I struck it on the stone wall and I could swear I heard it echo from the hall up ahead. As I made my way to the ironclad door I could smell burning brimstone and I thought it strange that the smell of the fire stick had stayed with me. Then I saw Joy standing by the door holding an oil lamp and the charred remains of the fire stick she'd used to light it.

"Let me see the key," she said.

"What key?"

"Don't be foolish. I saw what was left of the mold in the room of the elements."

I took the key from where I'd tucked it in my belt and handed it to Joy. She examined it by lamplight, turning it this way and that. "Pea Pods cast this," she said matter-of-factly. "Did she take the impression as well?"

I nodded. Joy didn't seem angry, and Pea Pods was the only one of the girls skilled enough in metallurgy to have done the casting, so why deny it?

"Getting the impression must have been the hard part," Joy said. "Balthasar is fierce about guarding this key. I'll have to ask her what she did to distract him. Could be a good thing to know, huh? For both of us." She smiled seductively, then turned toward the door and pushed aside the brass plate that covered the keyhole. In that second I felt as if a frozen dagger had been dragged over my spine.

"No!" I grabbed her hand. "Don't." I was overcome with a feeling of revulsion that wrenched my insides. "We can't."

Joy smiled again and pushed my hand away. "I have seen many wondrous things since I came here, but there has never been anything that was harmful. You planned this, you must want to know what is in here as much as I do."

I wanted to stop her, I even tried to take the key away from her, but she grabbed my arm and pushed into a pressure point that made my whole left side go numb. She raised an eyebrow as if to ask, "Do you really want to try that, knowing what I can do to you?" And I stepped back.

She put the dragon key into the lock and turned it three times. There was a clicking of machinery finer than anything I had ever heard, then she withdrew the key and shot the three heavy iron bolts. As she pulled the door open there was a rush of air, as if something had moved by us very quickly, and my lamp went out.

Joshua told me what had happened later and I put the timing together myself. As Joy and I were opening the room they called the house of doom, Joshua and Balthasar were camped in the arid mountains of what is now Afghanistan. The night was crisp and the stars shone with a cold blue light like loneliness or infinity. They had eaten some bread and cheese, then settled in close to the fire to share the last of a flask of fortified wine, Balthasar's second that evening.

"Have I told you of the prophecy that sent me in search of you when you were born, Joshua?"

"You spoke of the star. My mother told me of the star."

"Yes, the three of us followed that star, and by chance we met up in the mountains east of Kabul and finished the journey together, but the star wasn't the reason we went, it was only our means of navigation. We made the journey because each of us was looking for something at the end."

"Me?" Joshua said.

"Yes, but not just you, but what it is said was brought with you. In the temple where we travel now, there lies a set of clay tablets—very old—the priests say that they date back to the time of Solomon, and they foretell the coming of a child who will have power over evil and victory over death. They say he will carry the key to immortality."

"Me? Immortality? Nope."

"I think you do, you just don't know it yet."

"Nope, I'm sure," said Joshua. "It's true that I have brought people back from the dead, but never for very long. I've gotten better at healing over the years, but my back-from-the-dead stuff still needs work. I need to learn more."

"Which is why I have taught you, and why I am taking you to the temple now, so you may read the tablets yourself, but you must have the power of immortality within you."

"No, really, I haven't a clue."

"I am two hundred and sixty years old, Joshua."

"I've heard that, but I still can't help you. You look good though, I mean for two hundred and sixty."

At this point Balthasar started to sound desperate. "Joshua, I know that you have power over evil. Biff has told me of you banishing demons in Antioch."

"Little ones," Joshua said modestly.

"You must have power over death as well or it does me no good."

"What I am able to do comes through my father, I didn't bargain for it."

"Joshua, I am preserved by a pact with a demon. If you do not have the powers foretold in the prophecy I will never be free, I will never have peace, I will never have love. Every minute of my life I must have my will focused on controlling the demon. Should my will fail, the destruction would be unlike anything the world has ever seen."

"I know how it is. I'm not allowed to know a woman," Joshua said. "Although it was an angel that told me, not a demon. But still, you know, it's hard sometimes. I really like your concubines. The other night Pillows was giving me a back rub after a long day of studying, and I started getting this massive—"

"By the Golden Tenderloin of the Calf!" Balthasar exclaimed, leaping to his feet, his eyes wide with terror. The old man began loading his camel, thrashing around in the darkness like a madman. Joshua was following him, trying to calm him down, fearing he might have a fit any second.

"What? What?"

"It is out!" the magus said. "Help me pack up. We must go back. The demon is out."

Í stood cringing in the dark, waiting for disaster to fall, for mayhem to reign, for pain and pestilence and no good to manifest, then Joy struck a fire stick and lit our lamps. We were alone. The iron door hung open into a very small room, it too lined with iron. The entire room was just big enough to contain a small bed and a chair. Every span of the black iron walls was inlaid with golden symbols: pentagrams and hex symbols and a dozen others I had never seen before. Joy held her lamp close to the wall.

"These are symbols of containment," Joy said.

"I used to hear voices coming from in here."

"There was nothing in here when I opened the door. I could see in the second before the lamp blew out."

"Then what blew it out?"

"The wind?"

"I don't think so. I felt something brush me as it passed."

Just then someone in the girls' quarters screamed, then a chorus of screams joined in, primal screams of absolute terror and pain. Instantly Joy's eyes filled with tears. "What have I done?"

I took her sleeve and dragged her down the passage toward the girls' quarters, snatching up two heavy lances that were supporting a tapestry as we passed and handing one to her. As we rounded the curves I could see an orange light ahead and soon I could see that it was fire blazing on the stone walls from broken oil lamps. The screaming was reaching a higher pitch, but every few seconds a voice was removed from the chorus, until there was only one. As we approached the beaded doorway into the concubines' chamber the screaming stopped and a severed human head rolled in front of us. The creature stepped through the curtain, oblivious to the flames that licked the walls around it, its massive body filling the passageway, the reptilian skin on its shoulders and its tall pointed ears grating against the walls and ceiling. In its talonlike hand it held the bloody torso of one of the girls.

"Hey, kid," it said, its voice like a sword point dragged across stone, a yellow light coming from behind its dinner-plate-sized cat's eyes, "it took you long enough."

As they rode back to the fortress, Balthasar explained to Joshua about the demon: "His name is Catch, and he is a demon of the twenty-seventh order, a destroyer angel before the fall. As far as I could tell, he was first called up to assist Solomon in building the great temple, but something got out of hand and with the help of a djinn, Solomon was able to send the demon back to hell. I found the seal of Solomon and the incantation for raising the demon almost two hundred years ago in the Temple of the Seal."

"Oh," Joshua said, "so that's why they call it that. I thought it had something to do with one of the barky sea animals."

"I had to become an acolyte and study with the priests there for years before I was allowed access to the seal, but what is a few years against immortality. I was given immortality, but only so long as the demon walks the earth. And as long as he is on earth he must be fed, Joshua. That's the curse that goes with being this destroyer's master. He must be fed."

"I don't understand, he feeds on your will?"

"No, he feeds on human beings. It is only my will that keeps him in check, or it was until I was able to build the iron room and put golden symbols on the wall that would hold the demon. I've been able to keep him in the fortress I made him build for twenty years now, and it has been some respite. Until then he was with me every minute, everywhere I went."

"Didn't that attract enemies to you?"

"No. Unless he is in his eating form, I am the only one who can see Catch. In his noneating form he's small, the size of a child, and he can do little harm (except for being incredibly irritating). When he feeds, however, he's fully ten cubits tall, and he can tear a man in half with the swipe of his claw. No, enemies are not a problem, Joshua. Why do you think there are no guards at the fortress? In those years before the girls came to live there, some bandits attacked. What happened to them is legend now in Kabul, and no one has tried since. The problem is that if my will were to fail, he would be set loose again on the world as he was in the time of Solomon. I don't know what could stop him."

"And you can't send him back to hell?" Joshua asked.

"I can with the seal and the right incantation, which is why I was going to the Temple of the Seal. Which is why you are here. If you are the Messiah predicted in Isaiah, and on the clay tablets in the temple, then you are the direct descendant of David, and therefore Solomon. I believe that you can send the demon back and keep me from suffering the fate of his return."

"Why, what happens to you if he is sent back to hell?"

"I will assume the aspect of my true age. Which I would guess, by this time, would be dust. But you have the gift of immortality. You can stop that from happening."

"So this demon from hell is loose, and we are returning to the fortress without the Seal of Solomon or this incantation to do exactly what?"

"I hope to bring him back under control of my will. The room has always held him before. I didn't know, I truly didn't know . . ."

"Know what?"

"That my will had been broken by my feelings for you."

"You love me?"

"How was I to know?" The magus sighed.

And Joshua laughed here, despite the dire circumstances. "Of course you do, but it is not me, it's what I represent. I am not sure yet what I am to do, but I know that I am here in the name of my father. You love life so much that you would brave hell to hold on to it, it's only natural that you would love the one who gave you that life."

"Then you can banish the demon and preserve my life?"

"Of course not, I'm just saying that I understand how you feel."

Í don't know where she found the strength, but the diminutive Joy came from behind me and hurled the heavy lance with as much power as any soldier. (I felt my own knees starting to buckle in the face of the demon.) The bronze tip of the lance seemed to find its way between two of the monster's armored chest scales and drove itself a span deep under the weight of the heavy shaft. The demon gasped, and roared, opening his massive maw to show rows of saw-edged teeth. He grabbed the shaft of the lance and attempted to pull it out, his huge biceps quivering with the strain. He looked sadly down at the spear, then at Joy, and said, "Oh, foul woe upon you, you have kilt me most dead," then he fell back and the floor shook with the impact of his huge body.

"What'd he say, what'd he say?" Joy asked, digging her nails into my shoulder. The demon had spoken in Hebrew.

"He said that you killed him."

"Well, duh," said the concubine. (Strangely enough, "duh" sounds exactly the same in all languages.)

I had started to inch forward to see if anyone was still alive in the girls quarters when the demon sat up. "Just kidding," he said. "I'm not kilt." And he plucked the spear from his chest with less effort than it might take to brush away a fly.

I threw my own lance, but didn't wait to see where it hit. I grabbed Joy and ran.

"Where?" she said.

"Far," I said.

"No," she said, grabbing my tunic and jerking me around a corner, causing me to nearly coldcock myself on the wall. "To the cliff passage." We were in total darkness now, neither one of us having thought to grab a lamp, and I was trusting my life to Joy's memory of these stone halls.

As we ran we could hear the demon's scales scraping the walls and the occasional curse in Hebrew as he found a low ceiling. Perhaps he could see in the dark somewhat, but not a lot better than we could.

"Duck," Joy said, pushing my head down as we entered the narrow passage that led to the cliff above. I crouched in this passage the way the monster had to crouch to move in the normal-sized halls and I suddenly realized the brilliance of Joy's choice in taking this route. We were just seeing the moonlight breaking in through the opening in the cliff's face when I heard the monster hit the bottleneck of the passage.

"Fuck! Ouch! You weasels! I'm going to crunch your little heads between my teeth like candied dates."

"What'd he say?" asked Joy.

"He says that you are a sweet of uncommon delicacy."

"He did not say that."

"Believe me, my translation is as close as you want to the truth."

I heard a horrible scraping noise from inside the passage as we climbed out on the ledge and up the rope ladder to the top of the plateau. Joy helped me up, then pulled the ladder up behind us. We ran to the stable where the camel saddles and other supplies were normally kept. There were only the three camels that Joshua and Balthasar had taken, and no horses, so I couldn't figure out why we were taking the time to stop until I saw Joy filling two water skins at the cistern behind the stable.

"We'll never make it to Kabul without water," Joy said.

"And what happens when we make it to Kabul? Can anyone there help? What in the hell is that thing?"

"If I knew, would I have opened that door?" She was remarkably calm for someone who had just lost her friends to a hideous beast.

"I guess not. But I didn't see it come out of there. I felt something, but nothing that size."

"Act, Biff, don't think. Act."

She handed me a water skin and I held it in the cistern, trying to listen for the sound of the monster over the bubbles as it filled. All I could hear was the occasional bleating of the goats and the sound of my own pulse in my ears. Joy corked her water skin, then went about opening the pig and goat pens, shooing the animals out onto the plateau.

"Let's go!" she shouted to me. She took off down the path toward the hidden road. I pulled the water skin from the cistern and followed as quickly as I could. There was enough moonlight to make traveling fairly easy, but since I hadn't even seen the road in daylight, I didn't want to try to negotiate its deadly cutbacks at night without a guide. We had almost made the first leg of the road when we heard a hideous wailing and something heavy landed in the dust in front of us. When I could get my breath again I stepped up to find the bloodied carcass of a goat.

"There," Joy said, pointing down the mountainside to something moving among the rocks. Then it looked up at us and there was no mistaking the glowing yellow eyes.

"Back," Joy said, pulling me back from the road.

"Is that the only way down?"

"That or diving off the edge. It's a fortress, remember—it's not supposed to be easy to get in and out of."

We made our way back to the rope ladder, tossed it over the side, and started down. As Joy made it to the ledge and ducked into the cave something heavy hit me on the right shoulder. My arm went numb with the impact and I let go of the ladder. Mercifully, my feet had tangled in the rungs as I fell, and I found myself hanging upside down looking into the cave entrance where Joy stood. I could hear the terrified goat that had hit me screaming as it fell into the abyss, then there was a distant thump and the screaming stopped.

"Hey, kid, you're a Jew, aren't you?" said the monster from above.

"None of your business," I said. Joy grabbed the ladder and pulled me inside the cave, ladder and all, just as another goat came screaming past. I fell on my face in the dust and sputtered, trying to breathe and spit at the same time.

"It's been a long time since I've eaten a Jew. A good Jew sticks to your ribs. That's the problem with Chinese, you eat six or seven of them and in a half hour you're hungry again. No offense, miss."

"What'd he say?" Joy asked.

"He says he likes kosher food. Will that ladder hold him?"

"I made it myself."

"Swell," I said. We heard the ropes creak with the strain as the monster climbed onto the ladder.

Chapter 15

Joshua and Balthasar rode into Kabul at a time of night when only cutthroats and whores were about (the whores offering the "cutthroat discount" after midnight to promote business). The old wizard had fallen asleep to the rhythm of his camel's loping gait, an act that nearly baffled Joshua as much as the whole demon business, as he spent most of his time on camelback trying not to upchuck—seasickness of the desert, they call it. Joshua flicked the old man's leg with the loose end of his camel's bridle, and the magus came awake snorting.

"What is it? Are we there?"

"Can you control the demon, old man? Are we close enough for you to regain control?"

Balthasar closed his eyes and Joshua thought that he might be going to sleep again, except his hands began to tremble with some unseen effort. After a few seconds he opened his eyes again. "I can't tell."

"Well, you could tell that he was out."

"That was like a wave of pain in my soul. I'm not in intimate contact with the demon at all times. We are probably too far away still."

"Horses," Joshua said. "They'll be faster. Let's go wake up the stable master." Joshua led them through the streets to the stable where we had boarded our camels when we came to town to heal the blinded bandit. There were no lamps burning inside, but a half-naked whore posed seductively in the doorway.

"Special for cutthroats," she said in Latin. "Two for one, but no refunds if the old man can't do the business."

It had been so long since he'd heard the language that it took Joshua a second to respond. "Thank you, but we're not cutthroats,"

Joshua said. He stepped past her and pounded on the door. She ran a fingernail down his back as he waited.

"What are you? Maybe there's another special."

Joshua didn't even look back. "He's a two-hundred-and-sixty-year-old wizard and I'm either the Messiah or a hopeless faker."

"Uh, yeah, I think there is a special rate for fakers, but the wizard has to pay full price."

Joshua could hear stirring inside of the stable master's house and a voice calling for him to hold his horses, which is what stable masters always say when they make you wait. Joshua turned to the whore and touched her gently on the forehead.

"Go, and sin no more," he said in Latin.

"Right, and what do I do for a living then, shovel shit?"

Just then the stable master threw open the door. He was short and bow-legged and wore a long mustache that made him look like a dried-up catfish. "What is so important that my wife couldn't handle it?"

"Your wife?"

The whore ran her nail across the back of Joshua's neck as she passed him and stepped into the house. "Missed your chance," she said.

"Woman, what are you doing out here anyway?" asked the stable master.

Joy scurried out onto the landing and pulled a short, broad-bladed black dagger from the folds of her robe. The ends of the rope ladder were swaying in front of her as the monster descended.

"No, Joy," I said, reaching out to pull her back into the cave. "You can't hurt it."

"Don't be so sure."

She turned and grinned at me, then ran the dagger twice over the thick ropes on one side leaving it attached by only a few fibers, then she reached up a few rungs and sliced most of the way through the other side of the ladder. I couldn't believe how easily she'd cut through the rope.

She stepped back into the passageway and held the blade up so it caught the starlight. "Glass," she said, "from a volcano. It's a thousand times sharper than any edge on an iron blade." She put the dagger away and pulled me back into the passageway, just far enough so we could see the entrance and the landing.

I could hear the monster coming closer, then a huge clawed foot appeared in silhouette in the entrance, then the other foot. We held our breath as the monster reached the cut section of the ladder. Nearly a whole massive thigh was visible now, and one of his talonlike hands was reaching down for a new hold when the ladder snapped. Suddenly the monster hung sideways, swinging from his hold on a single rope in front of the entrance. He looked right at us, the fury in his yellow eyes replaced for a moment by confusion. His leathery bat ears rose in curiosity, and he said, "Hey?" Then the second rope snapped and he plunged out of our view.

We ran out to the landing and looked over the edge. It was at least a thousand feet to the floor of the valley. We could only see several hundred feet down in the dark, but it was several hundred feet of cliff face that was conspicuously monsterless.

"Nice," I said to Joy.

"We need to go. Now."

"You don't think that did it?"

"Did you hear anything hit bottom?"

"No," I said.

"Neither did I," she said. "We had better get going."

We'd left the water skins at the top of the plateau and Joy wanted to grab some from the kitchen but I dragged her toward the front entrance by the collar. "We need to get as far away from here as we can. Dying of thirst is the least of my worries." Once we were in the main area of the fortress there was enough light to negotiate the hallways without a lamp, which was good, because I wouldn't let Joy stop to light one. As we rounded the stairway to the third level Joy jerked me back, almost off my feet, and I turned around as mad as a cat.

"What? Let's get out of here!" I screamed at her.

"No, this is the last level with windows. I'm not going through the front door not knowing if that thing is outside it."

"Don't be ridiculous, it would take a man on a fast horse a half hour to make it around from the other side."

"But what if it didn't fall all the way? What if it climbed back up?"

"That would take hours. Come on, Joy. We could be miles away from here by the time he gets here from the other side."

"No!" She swept my feet out from under me and I landed flat on my back on the stone floor. By the time I was on my feet again she had run through the front chamber and was hanging out the window. As I approached her she held her finger to her lips. "It's down there, waiting."

I pulled her aside and looked down. Sure enough, the beast was looming in front of the iron door, waiting to grab the edge in its claws and rip it open as soon as we threw the bolts.

"Maybe it can't get in," I whispered. "It couldn't get through the other iron door."

"You didn't understand the symbols all over that room, did you?"

I shook my head.

"They were containment symbols—to contain a djinn, or a demon. The front door doesn't have any on it. It won't hold him back."

"So why isn't he coming in?"

"Why chase us when we will come right to him?"

Just then the monster looked up and I threw myself back from the window.

"I don't think he saw me," I whispered, spraying Joy with spit.

Then the monster began to whistle. It was a happy tune, lighthearted, something like you might whistle while you were polishing the bleached skull of your latest victim. "I'm not stalking anyone or anything," the monster said, much louder than would have been required had he been talking to himself. "Nope, not me. Just standing here for a second. Oh well, no one is here, I guess I'll be on my way." He began to whistle again and we could hear footsteps getting quieter along with the whistling. They weren't moving away, they were just getting quieter. Joy and I looked out the window to see the huge beast doing an exaggerated pantomime of walking, just as his whistle fizzled.

"What?" I shouted down, angry now. "Did you think we wouldn't look?"

The monster shrugged. "It was worth a try. I figured I wasn't dealing with a genius when you opened the door in the first place."

"What'd he say? What'd he say?" Joy chanted behind me.

"He said he doesn't think you're very smart."

"Tell him that I'm not the one who has spent all these years locked in the dark playing with myself."

I pulled back from the window and looked at Joy. "Do you think he could fit though this window?"

She eyed the window. "Yes."

"Then I'm not going to tell him. It might make him angry."

Joy pushed me aside, stepped up on the windowsill, turned around and faced me, then pulled up her robe and peed backward out the window. Her balance was amazing. From the growling below, I gathered that her accuracy wasn't bad either. She finished and jumped down. I looked out the window at the monster, who was shaking urine from its his ears like a wet dog.

"Sorry," I said, "language problem. I didn't know how to translate."

The monster growled and the muscles in its shoulders tensed beneath the scales, then it he let loose with a punch that sent its fist completely through the iron skin of the door.

"Run," Joy said.

"Where?"

"The passage to the cliff."

"You cut the ladder."

"Just run." She pulled me along behind her, guiding us through the dark as she had before. "Duck," she shouted, just a second after I realized that we'd entered the smaller passageway by using the sensitive stone-ceiling-sensing nerves in my forehead. We made it halfway down the passageway to the cliff when I heard the monster hit and curse.

There was a pause, then a horrible grinding noise so intense that we had to shield our ears from the assault. Then came the smell of burning flesh.

Dawn broke just as Joshua and Balthasar rode into the canyon entrance to the fortress.

"How about now?" Joshua asked. "Do you feel the demon now?"

Balthasar shook his head balefully. "We're too late." He pointed to where the great round door had once stood. Now it was a pile of bent and broken pieces hanging on what was left of the huge hinges.

"What in the name of Satan have you done?" Joshua said. He jumped off his horse and ran into the fortress, leaving the old man to follow as best he could.

The noise in the narrow passageway was so intense that I cut pieces of cloth from my sleeves with Joy's dagger and stuffed them in our ears. Then I lit one of the fire sticks to see what the monster was doing. Joy and I stood there, gaped-jawed, watching as the beast worried away at the stone of the passage, his claws moving in a blur of speed, throwing smoke and dust and stone shards into the air as he went, his scales burning from the friction and growing back as fast as they burned away. He hadn't come far, perhaps five feet toward us, but eventually he would widen the passage enough and pull us out like a badger digging termites out of the nest. I could see now how the fortress had been built without tool marks. The creature moved so quickly—literally wearing away the walls with his claws and scales—that the stone was polished as it was cut.

We had already made two ascents up what was left of the ladder to the top of the plateau, only to have the monster come around and chase us back down it before we could get to the road down. The second time he pulled the ladder up, then returned to the interior of the fortress to resume his hellish digging.

"I'll jump before I'll let that thing get me," I said to Joy.

She looked over the edge of the cliff into the endless darkness below. "You do that," she said. "Let me know how it goes."

"I will, but first I'll pray." And I did. I prayed so hard that beads of sweat popped out on my forehead and ran over my tightly closed eyes. I prayed so hard that even the constant screeching of the monster's scales against the stone was drowned out. For a moment there, I was sure that it was just me and God. As was his habit with me, God remained quiet, and I suddenly realized how frustrated Joshua must have been, asking always for a path to follow, a course of action, and being answered by nothing but silence.

When I opened my eyes again dawn had broken over the cliff and light was streaming into the passageway. By full daylight the demon was even scarier. There was blood and gore all over him from the massacre of the girls, and even as he relentlessly wore away at the stone, flies buzzed around him, but as each tried to light on him it died instantly and fell to the floor. The stench of rotting flesh and burning scales was almost overwhelming, and that alone nearly sent me over the side of the cliff. The beast was only three or four cubits out of reach from us, and every few minutes he would rear back, then throw his claw forward to try and grab at us.

Joy and I huddled on the landing over the cliff face, looking for any purchase, any handhold that would get us away from the beast: up, down, or sideways across the cliff face. The fear of heights had suddenly become very minor.

I was beginning to be able to feel the breeze from the monster's talons as he lunged into the narrow opening at us when I heard Balthasar's deep bass shout from behind the beast. The monster filled the whole opening so I couldn't see behind it, but he turned around and his spade-tipped tail whipped around us, nearly lacerating our skin as it passed. Joy drew the glass knife from her robe and slashed at the tail, nicking the scales but apparently not causing the monster enough trouble to turn around.

"Balthasar will tame you, you son of a shit-eating lizard!" Joy screamed.

Just then something came shooting through the opening and we ducked out of the way as it sailed into space and fell out of sight to the canyon floor, screeching like a falcon on the dive.

"What was that?" Joy was trying to squint into infinity to see what the monster had thrown.

"That was Balthasar," I said.

"Oops," said Joy.

Joshua yanked the great spade-tipped tail and the demon swung around with a ferocious snarl. Joshua held on to the tail even as the demon's claws whistled by his face.

"What is your name, demon?" Joshua said.

"You won't live long enough to say it," said the demon. He raised his claw again to strike.

Joshua yanked his tail and the demon froze. "No. That's not right. What is your name?"

"My name is Catch," said the demon, dropping his arm to his side in surrender. "I know you. You're the kid, aren't you? They used to talk about you in the old days."

"Time for you to go home," Joshua said.

"Can't I eat those two outside on the ledge first?"

"No. Satan awaits you."

"They are really irritating. She peed on me."

"No."

"I'd be doing you a favor."

"You don't want to hurt them now, do you?"

The demon laid his ears back and bowed his enormous head. "No. I don't want to hurt them."

"You're not angry anymore," Joshua said.

The monster shook his head, he was already bent nearly double in the narrow passage, but now he prostrated himself before Joshua and covered his eyes with his claws.

"Well, I'm still angry!" Balthasar screamed. Joshua turned to see the old man covered with blood and dirt, his clothes torn from where his broken bones had ripped through them on impact. He was healed now, only minutes after the fall, but not much better for having made the trip.

"You survived that fall?"

"I told you, as long as the demon is on earth, I'm immortal. But that was a first, he's never been able to hurt me before."

"He won't again."

"You have control over him? Because I don't."

Joshua turned around and put his hand on the demon's head. "This evil creature once beheld the face of God. This monster once served in heaven, obtained beauty, lived in grace, walked in light. Now he is the instrument of suffering. He is hideous of aspect and twisted in nature."

"Hey, watch it," said the demon.

"What I was going to say is that you can't blame him for what he is. He has never had what you or any other human has had. He has never had free will."

"That is so sad," said the demon.

"One moment, Catch, I will let you taste that which you have never known. For one moment I will grant you free will."

The demon sobbed. Joshua took his hand from the demon's head, then dropped his tail and walked out of the narrow passageway into the fortress hall.

Balthasar stood beside him, waiting for the demon to emerge from the passageway.

"Are you really able to do that? Give him free will?"

"We'll see, won't we?"

Catch crawled out of the passageway and stood up, now just ducking his head. Great viscous tears rolled down his scaled cheeks, over his jaws, and dripped to the stone floor, where they sizzled like acid. "Thank you," he growled.

"Free will," Balthasar said. "How does that make you feel?"

The demon snatched up the old man like a rag doll and tucked him under his arm. "It makes me feel like throwing you off the fucking cliff again."

"No," said Joshua. He leapt forward and touched the demon's chest. In that instant the air popped as the vacuum where the demon had stood was filled. Balthasar fell to the floor and groaned.

"Well, that free will thing wasn't such a great idea," said Balthasar.

"Sorry. Compassion got the better of me."

"I don't feel well," the magus said. He sat down hard on the floor and let out a long dry rasp of breath.

Joy and I came out of the passage to find Joshua bent over Balthasar, who was actively aging as we looked on.

"He's two hundred and sixty years old," Joshua said. "With Catch gone, his age is catching up."

The wizard's skin had gone ashen and the whites of his eyes were yellow. Joy sat on the floor and gently cradled the old man's head in her lap.

"Where's the monster?" I asked.

"Back in hell," Joshua said. "Help me get Balthasar to his bed. I'll explain later."

We carried Balthasar to his bedchamber, where Joy tried to pour some broth into him, but he fell asleep with the bowl at his lips.

"Can you help him?" I asked no one in particular.

Joy shook her head. "He's not sick. He's just old."

"It is written, 'To every thing there is a season,' " Joshua said. "I can't change the seasons. Balthasar's time has come round at last." Then he looked at Joy and raised his eyebrows. "You peed on the demon?"

"He had no right to complain. Before I came here I knew a man in Hunan who'd pay good money for that."

balthasar lingered for ten more days, toward the end looking more like a skeleton wrapped in old leather than a man. In his last days he begged Joshua to forgive him his vanity and he called us to his bedside over and over to tell us the same things, as he would forget what he'd told us only a few hours before.

"You will find Gaspar in the Temple of the Celestial Buddha, in the mountains to the east. There is a map in the library. Gaspar will teach you. He is truly a wise man, not a charlatan like me. He will help you become the man you need to be to do what you must do, Joshua. And Biff, well, you might not turn out terrible. It's cold where you are going. Buy furs along the way, and trade the camels for the woolly ones with two humps."

"He's delirious," I said.

Joy said, "No, there really are woolly camels with two humps."

"Oh, sorry."

"Joshua," Balthasar called. "If nothing else, remember the three jewels." Then the old man closed his eyes and stopped breathing.

"He dead?" I asked.

Joshua put his ear to the old man's heart. "He's dead."

"What was that about three jewels?"

"The three jewels of the Tao: compassion, moderation, and humility. Balthasar said compassion leads to courage, moderation leads to generosity, and humility leads to leadership."

"Sounds wonky," I said.

"Compassion," Joshua whispered, nodding toward Joy, who was silently crying over Balthasar.

I put my arm around her shoulders and she turned and sobbed into my chest. "What will I do now? Balthasar is dead. All of my friends are dead. And you two are leaving."

"Come with us," Joshua said.

"Uh, sure, come with us."

but Joy did not come with us. We stayed in Balthasar's fortress for another six months, waiting for winter to pass before we went into the high mountains to the east. I cleaned the blood from the girls' quarters while Joy helped Joshua to translate some of Balthasar's ancient texts. The three of us shared our meals, and occasionally Joy and I would have a tumble for old times' sake, but it felt as if the life had gone out of the place. When it came time for us to leave, Joy told us of her decision.

"I can't go with you to find Gaspar. Women are not allowed in the monastery, and I have no desire to live in the backwater village nearby. Balthasar has left me much gold, and everything in the library, but it does me no good out here in the mountains. I will not stay in this tomb with only the ghosts of my friends for company. Soon Ahmad will come, as he does every spring, and I will have him help me take the treasure and the scrolls to Kabul, where I will buy a large house and hire servants and I will have them bring me young boys to corrupt."

"I wish I had a plan," I said.

"Me too," said Josh.

The three of us celebrated Joshua's eighteenth birthday with the traditional Chinese food, then the next morning Joshua and I packed up the camels and prepared to head east.

"Are you sure you'll be all right until Ahmad comes?" Joshua asked Joy.

"Don't worry about me, you go learn to be a Messiah." She kissed him hard on the lips. He squirmed to get loose from her and he was still blushing as he climbed onto his camel.

"And you," she said to me, "you will come to see me in Kabul on your way back to Israel or I will put such a curse on you as you'll never be free of it." She took the little ying-yang vial full of poison and antidote from around her neck and put it around mine. It might have seemed a strange gift to anyone else, but I was the sorceress's apprentice and it seemed perfect to me. She tucked the black glass knife into my sash. "No matter how long it takes, come back and see me. I promise I won't paint you blue again."

I promised her and we kissed and I climbed on my camel and Joshua and I rode off. I tried not to look back, once again, to another woman who had stolen my heart.

We rode a half a furlong apart, each of us considering the past and future of our lives, who we had been and who we were going to be, and it was a couple of hours before I caught up with Joshua and broke the silence.

I thought of how Joy had taught me to read and speak Chinese, to mix potions and poisons, to cheat at gambling, to perform sleight of hand, and where and how to properly touch a woman. All of it without expecting anything in return. "Are all women stronger and better than me?"

"Yes," he said.

It was another day before we spoke again.

Part III

Compassion

Torah! Torah! Torah!

WAR CRY OF THE KAMIKAZE RABBIS

Chapter 16

We were twelve days into our journey, following Balthasar's meticulously drawn map, when we came to the wall.

"So," I said, "what do you think of the wall?"

"It's great," said Joshua.

"It's not that great," I said.

There was a long line waiting to get through the giant gate, where scores of bureaucrats collected taxes from caravan masters as they passed through. The gatehouses alone were each as big as one of Herod's palaces, and soldiers rode horses atop the wall, patrolling far into the distance. We were a good league back from the gate and the line didn't seem to be moving.

"This is going to take all day," I said. "Why would they build such a thing? If you can build a wall like this then you ought to be able to raise an army large enough to defeat any invaders."

"Lao-tzu built this wall," Joshua said.

"The old master who wrote the Tao? I don't think so."

"What does the Tao value above all else?"

"Compassion? Those other two jewel things?"

"No, inaction. Contemplation. Steadiness. Conservatism. A wall is the defense of a country that values inaction. But a wall imprisons the people of a country as much as it protects them. That's why Balthasar had us go this way. He wanted me to see the error in the Tao. One can't be free without action."

"So he spent all that time teaching us the Tao so we could see that it was wrong."

"No, not wrong. Not all of it. The compassion, humility, and moderation of the Tao, these are the qualities of a righteous man, but not inaction. These people are slaves to inaction."

"You worked as a stonecutter, Josh," I said, nodding toward the massive wall. "You think this wall was built through inaction?"

"The magus wasn't teaching us about action as in work, it was action as in change. That's why we learned Confucius first—everything having to do with the order of our fathers, the law, manners. Confucius is like the Torah, rules to follow. And Lao-tzu is even more conservative, saying that if you do nothing you won't break any rules. You have to let tradition fall sometime, you have to take action, you have to eat bacon. That's what Balthasar was trying to teach me."

"I've said it before, Josh—and you know how I love bacon—but I don't think bacon is enough for the Messiah to bring."

"Change," Joshua said. "A Messiah has to bring change. Change comes through action. Balthasar once said to me, 'There's no such thing as a conservative hero.' He was wise, that old man."

I thought about the old magus as I looked at the wall stretching over the hills, then at the line of travelers ahead of us. A small city had grown up at the entrance to the wall to accommodate the needs of the delayed travelers along the Silk Road and it boiled with merchants hawking food and drink along the line.

"Screw it," I said. "This is going to take forever. How long can it be? Let's go around."

A month later, when we had returned to the same gate and we were standing in line to get through, Joshua asked: "So what do you think of the wall now? I mean, now that we've seen so much more of it?"

"I think it's ostentatious and unpleasant," I said.

"If they don't have a name for it, you should suggest that."

And so it came to pass that through the ages the wall was known as the Ostentatious and Unpleasant Wall of China. At least I hope that's what happened. It's not on my Friendly Flyer Miles map, so I can't be sure.

We could see the mountain where Gaspar's monastery lay long before we reached it. Like the other peaks around it, it cut the sky like a huge tooth. Below the mountain was a village surrounded by high pasture. We stopped there to rest and water our camels. The people of the village all came out to greet us and they marveled at our strange eyes and Joshua's curly hair as if we were gods that had been lowered out of the heavens (which I guess was true in Josh's case, but you forget about that when you're around someone a lot). An old toothless woman who spoke a dialect of Chinese similar to the one we had learned from

Joy convinced us to leave the camels in the village. She traced the path up the mountain with a craggy finger and it was obvious that the path was both too narrow and too steep to accommodate the animals.

The villagers served us a spicy meat dish with frothy bowls of milk to wash it down. I hesitated and looked at Joshua. The Torah forbade us to eat meat and dairy at the same meal.

"I'm thinking this is a lot like the bacon thing," Joshua said. "I really don't feel that the Lord cares if we wash down our yak with a bowl of milk."

"Yak?"

"That's what this is. The old woman told me."

"Well, sin or not, I'm not eating it. I'll just drink the milk."

"It's yak milk too."

"I'm not drinking it."

"Use your own judgment, it served you so well in the past, like, oh, when you decided we should go around the wall."

"You know," I said, weary of having the whole wall thing brought up again, "I never said you could use sarcasm whenever you wanted to. I think you're using my invention in ways that it was never intended to be used."

"Like against you?"

"See? See what I mean?"

We left the village early the next morning, carrying only some rice balls, our waterskins, and what little money we had left. We left our three camels in the care of the toothless old woman, who promised to take care of them until we returned. I would miss them. They were the spiffy double-humpers we'd picked up in Kabul and they were comfortable to ride, but more important, none of them had ever tried to bite me.

"They're going to eat our camels, you know? We won't be gone an hour before one of them is turning on a spit."

"They won't eat the camels." Joshua, forever believing in the goodness of human beings.

"They don't know what they are. They think that they're just tall food. They're going to eat them. The only meat they ever get is yak."

"You don't even know what a yak is."

"Do too," I said, but the air was getting thin and I was too tired to prove myself at the time.

The sun was going down behind the mountains when we finally reached the monastery. Except for a huge wooden gate with a small hatch in it, it was constructed entirely of the same black basalt as the mountain on which it stood. It looked more like a fortress than a place of worship.

"Makes you wonder if all three of your magi live in fortresses, doesn't it?"

"Hit the gong," said Joshua. There was a bronze gong hanging outside the door with a padded drumstick standing next to it and a sign in a language that we couldn't read.

I hit the gong. We waited. I hit the gong again. And we waited. The sun went down and it began to get very cold on the mountainside. I rang the gong three times loud. We ate our rice balls and drank most of our water and waited. I pounded the bejezus out of the gong and the hatch opened. A dim light from inside the gate illuminated the smooth cheeks of a Chinese man about our age. "What?" he said in Chinese.

"We are here to see Gaspar," I said. "Balthasar sent us."

"Gaspar sees no one. Your aspect is dim and your eyes are too round." He slammed the little hatch.

This time Joshua pounded on the gong until the monk returned.

"Let me see that drumstick," the monk said, holding his hand out through the little port.

Joshua gave him the drumstick and stepped back.

"Go away and come back in the morning," the monk said.

"But we've traveled all day," Joshua said. "We're cold and hungry."

"Life is suffering," the monk said. He slammed the little door, leaving us in almost total darkness.

"Maybe that's what you're supposed to learn," I said. "Let's go home."

"No, we wait," said Joshua.

In the morning, after Joshua and I had slept against the great gate, huddled together to conserve warmth, the monk opened the little hatch. "You still here?" He couldn't see us, as we were directly below the window.

"Yes," I said. "Can we see Gaspar now?"

He craned his neck out the hatch, then pulled it back in and produced a small wooden bowl, from which he poured water on our heads. "Go away. Your feet are misshapen and your eyebrows grow together in a threatening way."

"But . . ."

He slammed the hatch. And so we spent the day outside the gate, me wanting to go down the mountain, Joshua insisting that we wait. There was frost in our hair when we woke the next morning, and I felt my very bones aching. The monk opened the hatch just after first light.

"You are so stupid that the village idiots' guild uses you as a standard for testing," said the monk.

"Actually, I'm a member of the village idiots' guild," I retorted.

"In that case," said the monk, "go away."

I cursed eloquently in five languages and was beginning to tear at my hair in frustration when I spotted something large moving in the sky overhead. As it got closer, I saw that it was the angel, wearing his aspect of black robe and wings. He carried a flaming bundle of sticks and pitch, which trailed a trail of flames and thick black smoke behind him in the sky. When he had passed over us several times, he flew off over the horizon, leaving a smoky pattern of Chinese characters that spelled out a message across the sky: SURRENDER DOROTHY.

I was just fuckin' with you (as Balthasar used to say). Raziel didn't really write SURRENDER DOROTHY in the sky. The angel and I watched *The Wizard of Oz* together on television last night and the scene at the gates of Oz reminded me of when Joshua and I were at the monastery gate. Raziel said he identified with Glinda, Good Witch of the North. (I would have thought flying monkey, but I believe his choice was a blond one.) I have to admit that I felt some sympathy for the scarecrow, although I don't believe I would have been singing about the lack of a brain. In fact, amid all the musical laments over not having a heart, a brain, or the nerve, did anyone notice that they didn't have a penis among them? I think it would have shown on the Lion and the Tin Man, and when the Scarecrow has his pants destuffed, you don't see a flying monkey waving an errant straw Johnson around anywhere, do you? I think I know what song I'd be singing:

> *Oh, I would while away the hours,*
> *Wanking in the flowers, my heart all full of song,*
> *I'd be gilding all the lilies as I waved about my willie*
> *If I only had a schlong.*

And suddenly it occurred to me, as I composed the above opus, that although Raziel had always seemed to have the aspect of a male, I had no idea if there were even genders among the angels. After all, Raziel was the only one I'd ever seen. I leapt from my chair and confronted him in the midst of an afternoon Looney Tunes festival.

"Raziel, do you have equipment?"

"Equipment?"

"A package, a taliwacker, a unit, a dick—do you have one?"

"No," said the angel, perplexed that I would be asking. "Why would I need one?"

"For sex. Don't angels have sex?"

"Well, yes, but we don't use those."

"So there are female angels and male angels?"

"Yes."

"And you have sex with female angels."

"Correct."

"With what do you have sex?"

"Female angels. I just told you."

"No, do you have a sex organ?"

"Yes."

"Show me?"

"I don't have it with me."

"Oh." I realized that there are some things I'd really rather not know about.

Anyway, he didn't write in the sky, and, in fact, we didn't see Raziel again, but the monks did let us into the monastery after three days. They said that they made everybody wait three days. It weeded out the insincere.

The entire two-story structure that was the monastery was fashioned of rough stone, none larger than could have been lifted into place by a single man. The rear of the building was built right into the mountainside. The structure seemed to have been built under an existing overhang in the rock, so there was minimal roofing exposed to the elements. What did show was made of terra-cotta tiles that lay on a steep incline, obviously to shed any buildup of snow.

A short and hairless monk wearing a saffron-colored robe led us across an outer courtyard paved with flagstone through an austere doorway into the monastery. The floor inside was stone, and though immaculately clean, it was no more finished than the flagstone of the courtyard. There were only a few windows, more like arrow slits, cut high in the wall, and little light penetrated the interior once the front door was closed. The air was thick with incense and filled with a buzzing chorus of male voices producing a rhythmic chant that seemed to come from everywhere and nowhere at once and made it seem as if my ribs and kneecaps were vibrating from the inside. Whatever language they were chanting in I didn't understand, but the message was clear: these men were invoking something that transcended this world.

The monk led us up a narrow stairway into a long, narrow corridor lined with open doorways no higher than my waist. As we passed I could see that these must be the monks' cells, and each was just large enough to accommodate a small man lying down. There was a woven mat on the floor and a woolen blanket rolled up at the top of each cell, but there was no evidence of personal possessions nor storage for any. There were no doors to close for privacy. In short, it was very much like what I had grown up with, which didn't make me feel any better about it. Nearly five years of the relative opulence at Balthasar's fortress had spoiled me. I yearned for a soft bed and a half-dozen Chinese concubines to hand-feed me and rub my body with fragrant oils. (Well, I said I was spoiled.)

At last the monk led us into a large open chamber with a high stone ceiling and I realized that we were no longer in a man-made structure, but a large cave. At the far end of the cave was a stone statue of a man seated cross-legged, his eyes closed, his hands before him with the first fingers and thumbs forming closed circles. Lit by the orange light of candles, a haze of incense smoke hanging about his shaved head, he appeared to be praying. The monk, our guide, disappeared into the darkness at the sides of the cave and Joshua and I approached the statue cautiously, stepping carefully across the rough floor of the cave.

(We had long since lost our surprise and outrage at graven images. The world at large and the art we had seen in our travels served to dampen even that grave commandment. "Bacon," Joshua said when I asked him about it.)

This great room was the source of the chanting we had been hearing since entering the monastery, and after seeing the monks' cells we determined that there must be at least twenty monks adding their voices to the droning, although the way the cave echoed it might have been one or a thousand. As we approached the statue, trying to ascertain what sort of stone it was made from, it opened its eyes.

"Is that you, Joshua?" it said in perfect Aramaic.

"Yes," said Joshua.

"And who is this?"

"This is my friend, Biff."

"Now he will be called Twenty-one, when he needs to be called, and you shall be Twenty-two. While you are here you have no name." The statue wasn't a statue, of course, it was Gaspar. The orange light of the candles and his complete lack of motion or expression had only made him appear to be made of stone. I suppose we were also thrown off because we were expecting a Chinese. This man looked as if he was from India. His skin was even darker than ours and he wore the red dot on his head that we had seen on Indian traders in Kabul and Antioch. It was difficult to tell his age, as he had no hair or beard and there wasn't a line in his face.

"He's the Messiah," I said. "The Son of God. You came to see him at his birth."

Still no expression from Gaspar. He said, "The Messiah must die if you are to learn. Kill him tomorrow."

" 'Scuse me?" I said.

"Tomorrow you will learn. Feed them," said Gaspar.

Another monk, who looked almost identical to the first monk, came out of the dark and took Joshua by the shoulder. He led us out of the chapel chamber and back to the cells where he showed Joshua and me our accommodations. He took our satchels away from us and left. He returned in a few minutes with a bowl of rice and a cup of weak tea for each of us. Then he went away, having said nothing since letting us in.

"Chatty little guy," I said.

Joshua scooped some rice into his mouth and grimaced. It was cold and unsalted. "Should I be worried about what he said about the Messiah dying tomorrow, do you think?"

"You know how you've never been completely sure whether you were the Messiah or not?"

"Yeah."

"Tomorrow, if they don't kill you first thing in the morning, tell them that."

The next morning Number Seven Monk awakened Joshua and me by whacking us in the feet with a bamboo staff. To his credit, Number Seven was smiling when I finally got the sleep cleared from my eyes, but that was really a small consolation. Number Seven was short and thin with high cheekbones and widely set eyes. He wore a long orange robe woven from rough cotton and no shoes. He was clean-shaven and his head was also shaved except for a small tail that grew out at the crown and was tied with a string. He looked as if he could be anywhere from seventeen to thirty-five years old, it was impossible to tell. (Should you wonder about the appearance of Monks Two through Six, and Eight through Twenty, just imagine Number Seven Monk nineteen times. Or at least that's how they appeared to me for the first few months. Later, I'm sure, except that we were taller and round-eyed, Joshua and I, or Monks Twenty-one and Twenty-two, would have fit the same description. When one is trying to shed the bonds of ego, a unique appearance is a liability. That's why they call it a "uniform." But alas, I'm getting ahead of myself.)

Number Seven led us to a window that was obviously used as a latrine, waited while we used it, then took us to a small room where Gaspar sat, his legs crossed in a seemingly impossible position, with a small table before him. The monk bowed and left the room and Gaspar asked us to sit down, again in our native Aramaic.

We sat across from him on the floor—no, that's not right, we didn't actually sit, we lay on the floor on our sides, propped up on one elbow the way we would have been at the low tables at home. We sat after Gaspar produced a bamboo staff from under the table and, with a motion as fast as a striking cobra's, whacked us both on the side of the head with it. "I said sit!" he said.

Then we sat.

"Jeez," I said, rubbing the knot that was swelling over my ear.

"Listen," Gaspar said, holding the stick up to clarify exactly what he meant.

We listened as if they were going to discontinue sound any second and we needed to stock up. I think I even stopped breathing for a while.

"Good," said Gaspar, laying the stick down and pouring tea into three simple bowls on the table.

We looked at the tea sitting there, steaming—just looked at it. Gaspar laughed like a little boy, all the graveness and authority from a second ago gone from his face. He could have been a benevolent older uncle. In fact, except for the obviously Indian features, he reminded me a lot of Joseph, Joshua's stepfather.

"No Messiah," Gaspar said, switching to Chinese now. "Do you understand?"

"Yes," Joshua and I said in unison.

In an instant the bamboo stick was in his hand and the other end was bouncing off of Joshua's head. I covered my own head with my arms but the blow never came.

"Did I strike the Messiah?" Gaspar asked Joshua.

Joshua seemed genuinely perplexed. He paused, rubbing the spot on his head, when another blow caught him over his other ear, the sound of the impact sharp and harsh in the small stone room.

"Did I strike the Messiah?" Gaspar repeated.

Joshua's dark brown eyes showed neither pain nor fear, just confusion as deep as the confusion of a calf who has just had its throat cut by the Temple priest.

The stick whistled through the air again, but this time I caught it in mid-swing, wrenched it out of Gaspar's hand, and tossed it out the narrow window behind him. I quickly folded my hands and looked at the table in front of me. "Begging your pardon, master," I said, "but if you hit him again, I'll kill you."

Gaspar stood, but I was afraid to look at him (or Joshua, for that matter). "Ego," said the monk. He left the room without another word.

Joshua and I sat in silence for a few minutes, thinking and rubbing our goose eggs. Well, it had been an interesting trip and all, but Joshua wasn't very well going to learn much about being the Messiah from someone who hit him with a stick whenever it was mentioned, and that, I supposed, was the reason we were there. So, onward. I drank the bowl of tea in front of me, then the one that Gaspar had left. "Two wise men down, one to go," I said. "We'd better find some breakfast if we're going to travel."

Joshua looked at me as perplexed as he had at Gaspar a few minutes before. "Do you think he needs that stick?"

𝐧umber Seven Monk handed us our satchels, bowed deeply, then went back into the monastery and closed the door, leaving Joshua and me standing there by the gong. It was a clear morning and we could see the smoke of cook fires rising from the village below.

"We should have asked for some breakfast," I said. "This is going to be a long climb down."

"I'm not leaving," Josh said.

"You're kidding."

"I have a lot more to learn here."

"Like how to take a beating?"

"Maybe."

"I'm not sure Gaspar will let me back in. He didn't seem too pleased with me."

"You threatened to kill him."

"I did not, I *warned* that I'd kill him. Big difference."

"So you're not going to stay?"

And there it was, the question. Was I going to stay with my best friend, eat cold rice, sleep on a cold floor, take abuse from a mad monk, and very likely have my skull split open, or was I going to go? Go where? Home? Back to Kabul and Joy? Despite the long journey, it seemed easier to go back the way I had come. At least some level of familiarity would be waiting there. But if I was making easy choices, why was I there in the first place?

"Are you sure you have to stay here, Josh? Can't we go find Melchior?"

"I know I have things to learn here." Joshua picked up the drumstick and rang the gong. In a few minutes the little port opened in the door and a monk we had never seen before stuck his face in the opening. "Go away. Your nature is dense and your breath smells like a yak's ass." He slammed the hatch.

Joshua rang the gong again.

"I don't like that whole thing about killing the Messiah. I can't stay here, Joshua. Not if he's going to hit you."

"I have a feeling I'm going to get hit quite a few more times until I learn what he needs me to know."

"I have to go."

"Yes, you do."

"But I could stay."

"No. Trust me, you have to leave me now, so you won't later. I'll see you again." He turned away from me and faced the door.

"Oh, you don't know anything else, but you know that all of a sudden?"

"Yes. Go, Biff. Good-bye."

I walked down the narrow path and nearly stumbled over a precipice when I heard the hatch in the door open. "Where are you going?" shouted the monk.

"Home," I said.

"Good, go frighten some children with your glorious ignorance."

"I will." I tried to keep my shoulders steady as I walked away, but it felt like someone was ripping my soul through the muscles of my back. I would not turn around, I vowed, and slowly, painfully, I made my way down the path, convinced that I would never see Joshua again.

Chapter 17

I've settled into some sort of droning routine here at the hotel, and in that way it reminds me of those times in China. My waking hours are filled with writing these pages, watching television, trying to irritate the angel, and sneaking off to the bathroom to read the Gospels. And I think it's the latter that's sent my sleeping hours into a landscape of nightmare that leaves me spent even when I wake. I've finished Mark, and again this fellow talks of a resurrection, of acts beyond the time of my and Joshua's death. It's a similar story to that told by the Matthew fellow, the events jumbled somewhat, but basically the story of Joshua's ministry, but it's the telling of the events of that last week of Passover that chills me. The angel hasn't been able to keep the secret that Joshua's teachings survived and grew to vast popularity. (He's stopped even changing the channel at the mention of Joshua on television, as he did when we first arrived.) But is this the book from which Joshua's teachings are drawn? I dream of blood, and suffering, and loneliness so empty that an echo can't survive, and I wake up screaming, soaked in my own sweat, and even after I'm awake the loneliness remains for a while. Last night when I awoke I thought I saw a woman standing at the end of my bed, and beside her, the angel, his black wings spread and touching the walls of the room on either side. Then, before I could get my wits about me, the angel wrapped his wings around the woman and she disappeared in the darkness of them and was gone. I think I really woke up then, because the angel was lying there on the other bed, staring into the dark, his eyes like black pearls, catching the red blinking aircraft lights that shone dimly through the window from the tops of the buildings across the street. No wings, no black robe, no woman. Just Raziel, staring.

"Nightmare?" the angel asked.

"Memory," I said. Had I been asleep? I remember that same red blinking light, ever so dim, playing on the cheekbone and the bridge of the nose of the woman in my nightmare. (It was all I could see of her face.) And those elegant contours fit into the recesses of my memory like a key in the tumblers of a lock, releasing cinnamon and sandalwood and a laugh sweeter than the best day of childhood.

Two days after I had walked away, I rang the gong outside the monastery and the little hatch opened to reveal the face of a newly shaven monk, the skin of his bald scalp still a dozen shades lighter in color than that of his face. "What?" he said.

"The villagers ate our camels," I said.

"Go away. Your nostrils flare in an unpleasant manner and your soul is somewhat lumpy."

"Joshua, let me in. I don't have anywhere to go."

"I can't just let you in," Josh whispered. "You have to wait three days like everyone else." Then loudly, and obviously for someone inside's benefit, he said, "You appear to be infested by Bedouins! Now go away!" And he slammed the hatch.

I stood there. And waited. In a few minutes he opened the hatch.

"Infested by Bedouins?" I said.

"Give me a break. I'm new. Did you bring food and water to last you?"

"Yes, the toothless woman sold me some dried camel meat. There was a special."

"That's got to be unclean," said Josh.

"Bacon, Joshua, remember?"

"Oh yeah. Sorry. I'll try to sneak some tea and a blanket out to you, but it won't be right away."

"Then Gaspar will let me back in?"

"He was perplexed why you left in the first place. He said if anyone needed to learn some discipline, well, you know. There'll be punishment, I think."

"Sorry I left you."

"You didn't." He grinned, looking sillier than normal with his two-toned head. "I'll tell you one thing I've learned here already."

"What's that?"

"When I'm in charge, if someone knocks, they will be able to come in. Making someone who is seeking comfort stand out in the cold is a crock of rancid yak butter."

"Amen," I said.

Josh slammed the little hatch, obviously the prescribed way of closing it. I stood and wondered how Joshua, when he finally learned how to be the Messiah, would work the phrase "crock of rancid yak butter" into a sermon. Just what we Jews needed, I thought, more dietary restrictions.

The monks stripped me naked and poured cold water over my head, then brushed me vigorously with brushes made from boar's hair, then poured hot water on me, then scrubbed, then cold water, until I screamed for them to stop. At that point they shaved my head, taking generous nicks out of my scalp as they did so, rinsed away the hair that stuck to my body, and handed me a fresh orange robe, a blanket, and a wooden rice bowl. Later I was given a pair of slippers, woven from some sort of grass, and I made myself some socks from woven yak hair, but this was the measure of my wealth for six years: a robe, a blanket, a bowl, some slippers, and some socks.

As Monk Number Eight led me to meet with Gaspar, I thought of my old friend Bartholomew, and how much he would have loved the idea of my newfound austerity. He often told of how his Cynic patriarch Diogenes carried a bowl with him for years, but one day saw a man drinking from his cupped palm and declared, "I have been a fool, burdened all these years by the weight of a bowl when a perfectly good vessel lay at the end of my wrist."

Yeah, well, that's all well and good for Diogenes, but when it was all I had, if anyone had tried to take my bowl they would have lost the vessel at the end of their wrist.

Gaspar sat on the floor in the same small room, eyes closed, hands folded on his knees before him. Joshua sat facing him in the same position. Number Eight Monk bowed out of the room and Gaspar opened his eyes.

"Sit."

I did.

"These are the four rules for which you may be expelled from the monastery: one, a monk will have no sexual intercourse with anyone, even down to an animal."

Joshua looked at me and cringed, as if he expected me to say something that would anger Gaspar. I said, "Right, no intercourse."

"Two: a monk, whether in the monastery or in the village, shall take no thing that is not given. Three: if a monk should intentionally take the life of a human or one like a human, either by his hand or by weapon, he will be expelled."

"One like a human?" I asked.

"You shall see," said Gaspar. "Four, a monk who claims to have reached superhuman states, or claims to have attained the wisdom of the saints, having not done so, will be expelled. Do you understand these four rules?"

"Yes," I said. Joshua nodded.

"Understand that there are no mitigating circumstances. If you commit any of these offenses as judged by the other monks, you must leave the monastery."

Again I said yes and then Gaspar went into the thirteen rules for which a monk could be suspended from the monastery for a fortnight (the first of these was the heartbreaker, "no emission of semen except in a dream") and then the ninety offenses for which one would receive an unfavorable rebirth if the sins were not repented (these ranged from destroying any kind of vegetation or deliberately depriving an animal of life to sitting in the open with a woman or claiming to a layman to have superhuman powers, even if you had them). Overall, there was an extraordinary number of rules, over a hundred on decorum, dozens for settling disputes, but remember, we were Jews, raised under the influence of the Pharisees, who judged virtually every event of day-to-day life against the Law of Moses. And with Balthasar we had studied Confucius, whose philosophy was little more than an extensive system of etiquette. I had no doubt Joshua could do this, and there was a chance I could handle it too, if Gaspar didn't use that bamboo rod too liberally and if I could conjure enough wet dreams. (Hey, I was eighteen years old and had just lived five years in a fortress full of available concubines, I had a habit, okay?)

"Monk Number Twenty-two," Gaspar said to Joshua, "you shall begin by learning how to sit."

"I can sit," I said.

"And you, Number Twenty-one, will shave the yak."

"That's just an expression, right?"

It wasn't.

𝕬 yak is an extremely large, extremely hairy, buffalolike animal with dangerous-looking black horns. If you've ever seen a water buffalo, imagine it wearing a full-body wig that drags the ground. Now sprinkle it with musk, manure, and sour milk: you've got yourself a yak. In a cavelike stable, the monks kept one female yak, which they let out during the day to wander the mountain paths to graze. On what, I don't know. There didn't seem to be enough living plant life to support an animal of that size (the yak's shoulder was higher than my head), but there didn't seem to be enough plant life in all of Judea for a herd of goats, either, and herding was one of the main occupations. What did I know?

The yak provided just enough milk and cheese to remind the monks that they didn't get enough milk and cheese from one yak for twenty-two monks. The animal also provided a long, coarse wool which needed to be harvested twice a year. This venerated duty, along with combing the crap and grass and burrs out of the wool, fell to me. There's not much to know about yaks beyond that, except for one important fact that Gaspar felt I needed to learn through practice: yaks hate to be shaved.

It fell to Monks Eight and Seven to bandage me, set my broken legs and arm, and clean off the yak dung that had been so thoroughly stomped into my body. I would tell you the distinction of those two solemn students if I could think of any, but I can't. The goal of all of the monks was to let go of the ego, the self, and but for a few more lines on the faces of the older men, they looked alike, dressed alike, and behaved alike. I, on the other hand, was quite distinct from the others, despite my shaved head and saffron robe, as I had bandages over half of my body and three out of four limbs splinted with bamboo.

After the yak disaster, Joshua waited until the middle of the night to crawl down the hall to my cell. The soft snores of monks filled the halls, and the soft turbulence of the bats that entered their cave through the monastery echoed off the stone walls like the death panting of epileptic shadows.

"Does it hurt?" Joshua said.

Sweat streamed from my face despite the chilly temperature. "I can hardly breathe." Seven and Eight had wrapped my broken ribs, but every breath was a knife in the side.

Joshua put his hand on my forehead.

"I'll be all right, Josh, you don't have to do that."

"Why wouldn't I?" he said. "Keep your voice down."

In seconds my pain was gone and I could breathe again. Then I fell asleep or passed out from gratitude, I don't know which. When I awoke with the dawn Joshua was still kneeling beside me, his hand still pressed against my forehead. He had fallen asleep there.

I carried the combed yak wool to Gaspar, who was chanting in the great cavern temple. It amounted to a fairly large bundle and I set it on the floor behind the monk and backed away.

"Wait," Gaspar said, holding a single finger in the air. He finished his chant, then turned to me. "Tea," he said. He led and I followed to the room where he had received Joshua and me when we had first arrived. "Sit," he said. "Sit, don't wait."

I sat and watched him make a charcoal fire in a small stone brazier, using a bow and fire drill to start the flames first in some dried moss, then blowing it onto the charcoal.

"I invented a stick that makes fire instantly," I said. "I could teach—"

Gaspar glared at me and held up the finger again to poke my words out of the air. "Sit," he said. "Don't talk. Don't wait."

H e heated water in a copper pot until it boiled, then poured it over some tea leaves in a earthenware bowl. He set two small cups on the table, then proceeded to pour tea from the bowl.

"Hey, doofus!" I yelled. "You're spilling the fucking tea!"

Gaspar smiled and set the bowl down on the table.

"How can I give you tea if your cup is already full?"

"Huh?" I said eloquently. Parables were never my strong suit. If you want to say something, say it. So, of course, Joshua and Buddhists were the perfect people to hang out with, straight talkers that they were.

Gaspar poured himself some tea, then took a deep breath and closed his eyes. After perhaps a whole minute passed, he opened them again. "If you already know everything, then how will I be able to teach you? You must empty your cup before I can give you tea."

"Why didn't you say so?" I grabbed my cup, tossed the tea out the same window I'd tossed Gaspar's stick, then plopped the cup back on the table. "I'm ready," I said.

"Go to the temple and sit," Gaspar said.

No tea? He was obviously still not happy about my almost-threat on his life. I backed out of the door bowing (a courtesy Joy had taught me).

"One more thing," Gaspar said. I stopped and waited. "Number Seven said that you would not live through the night. Number Eight agreed. How is it that you are not only alive, but unhurt?"

I thought about it for a second before I answered, something I seldom do, then I said, "Perhaps those monks value their own opinions too highly. I can only hope that they have not corrupted anyone else's thinking."

"Go sit," Gaspar said.

Sitting was what we did. To learn to sit, to be still and hear the music of the universe, was why we had come halfway around the world, evidently. To let go of ego, not individuality, but that which distinguishes us from all other beings. "When you sit, sit. When you breathe, breathe. When you eat, eat," Gaspar would say, meaning that every bit of our being was to be in the moment, completely aware of the now, no past, no future, nothing dividing us from everything that is.

It's hard for me, a Jew, to stay in the moment. Without the past, where is the guilt? And without the future, where is the dread? And without guilt and dread, who am I?

"See your skin as what connects you to the universe, not what separates you from it," Gaspar told me, trying to teach me the essence of what enlightenment meant, while admitting that it was not something that could be taught. Method he could teach. Gaspar could sit.

The legend went (I pieced it together from bits dropped by the master and his monks) that Gaspar had built the monastery as a place to sit. Many years ago he had come to China from India, where he had been born a prince, to teach the emperor and his court the true meaning of Buddhism, which had been lost in years of dogma and overinterpretation of scripture.

Upon arriving, the emperor asked Gaspar, "What have I attained for all of my good deeds?"

"Nothing," said Gaspar.

The emperor was aghast, thinking now that he had been generous to his people all these years for nothing.

He said, "Well then, what is the essence of Buddhism?"

"Vast amphibians," said Gaspar.

The emperor had Gaspar thrown from the temple, at which time the young monk decided two things; one, that he would have a better answer the next time he was asked the question, and two, that he'd better learn to speak better Chinese before he talked to anyone of importance. He'd meant to say, "Vast emptiness," but he'd gotten the words wrong.

The legend went on to say that Gaspar then came to the cave where the monastery was now built and sat down to meditate, determined to stay there until enlightenment came to him. Nine years later, he came down from the mountain, and the people of the village were waiting for him with food and gifts.

"Master, we seek your most holy guidance, what can you tell us?" they cried.

"I really have to pee," said the monk. And with that all of the villagers knew that he had indeed achieved the mind of all Buddhas, or "no mind," as we called it.

The villagers begged Gaspar to stay with them, and they helped him build the monastery at the site of the very cave where he had achieved his enlightenment. During the construction, the villagers were attacked many times by vicious bandits, and although he believed that no being should be killed, he also felt that these people should have a way to defend themselves, so he meditated on the subject until he devised a method of self-defense based on various movements he learned from the yogis in his native India, which he taught to the villagers, then to each of the monks as they joined the monastery. He called this discipline kung fu, which translates, "method by which short bald guys may kick the bejeezus out of you."

Our training in kung fu began with the hopping posts. After breakfast and morning meditation, Number Three Monk, who seemed to be the oldest of the monks, led us to the monastery courtyard where we found a stack of posts, perhaps two feet long and about a span's width in diameter. He had us set the posts on end in a straight line, about a half a stride away from each other. Then he told us to hop up on one of the posts and balance there. After both of us spent most of the morning picking ourselves up off the rough stone paving, we each found ourselves standing on one foot on the end of a pole.

"Now what?" I asked.

"Now nothing," Number Three said. "Just stand."

So we stood. For hours. The sun crossed the sky and my legs and back began to ache and we fell again and again only to have Number Three bark at us and tell us to jump back up on the post. When darkness began to fall and we both had stood for several hours without falling, Number Three said, "Now hop to the next post."

I heard Joshua sigh heavily. I looked at the line of posts and could see the pain that lay ahead if we were going to have to hop this whole gauntlet. Joshua was next to me at the end of the line, so he would have to hop to the post I was standing on. Not only would I have to jump to the next post and land without falling, but I would have to make sure that my take-off didn't knock over the post I was leaving.

"Now!" said Number Three.

I leapt and missed the landing. The post tipped out from under me and I hit the stone headfirst, sending a white flash before my eyes and a bolt of fire down my neck. Before I could gather my wits Joshua tumbled over on top of me. "Thank you," he said, grateful to have landed on a soft Jew rather than hard flagstone.

"Back up," Number Three said.

We set up our posts again, then hopped up on them again. This time both of us made it on the first try. Then we waited for the command to take the next leap. The moon rose high and full and we both stared down the row of poles, wondering how long it would take us before we could hop the whole row, wondering how long Number Three would make us stay there, thinking about the story of how Gaspar had sat for nine years. I couldn't remember ever having felt so much pain, which is saying something if you've been yak-stomped. I was trying to imagine just how much fatigue and thirst I could bear before I fell when Number Three said, "Enough. Go sleep."

"That's it?" Joshua asked, as he hopped off his post and winced upon landing. "Why did we set up twenty posts if we were only going to use three?"

"Why were you thinking of twenty when you can only stand on one?" answered Three.

"I have to pee," I said.

"Exactly," said the monk.

So there you have it: Buddhism.

Each day we went to the courtyard and arranged the posts differently, randomly. Number Three added posts of different heights and diameters. Sometimes we had to hop from one post to the other as quickly as possible, other times we stood in one place for hours, ready to move in an instant, should Number Three command it. The point, it seemed, was that we could not anticipate anything, nor could we develop a rhythm to the exercise. We were forced to be ready to move in any direction, without forethought. Number Three called this controlled spontaneity, and for the first six months in the monastery we spent as much time atop the posts as we did in sitting meditation. Joshua took to the kung fu training immediately, as he did to the meditation. I was, as the Buddhists say, more dense.

In addition to the normal duties of tending the monastery, our gardens, and milking the yak (mercifully, a task I was never assigned), every ten days or so a group of six monks would go to the village with their bowls and collect alms from the villagers, usually rice and tea, sometimes dark sauces, yak butter, or cheese, and on rare occasions cotton fabric, from which new robes would be made. For the first year Joshua and I were not allowed to leave the monastery at all, but I started to notice a pattern of strange behavior. After each trip to the village for alms, four or five monks would disappear into the mountains for several days. Nothing was ever said of it, either when they left or when they returned, but it seemed that there was some sort of rotation, with each monk only leaving every third or fourth time, with the exception of Gaspar, who left more often.

Finally I worked up the courage to ask Gaspar what was going on and he said, "It is a special meditation. You are not ready. Go sit."

Gaspar's answer to most of my questions was "Go sit," and my resentment meant that I wasn't losing the attachment to my ego, and therefore I wasn't going anywhere in my meditation. Joshua, on the other hand, seemed completely at peace with what we were doing. He could sit for hours, not moving, and then perform the exercise on the posts as if he'd spent an hour limbering up.

"How do you do it?" I asked him. "How do you think of nothing and not fall asleep?" That had been one of the major barriers to my enlightenment. If I sat still for too long, I fell asleep, and evidently, the sound of snoring echoing through the temple disturbed the meditations of the other monks. The recommended cure for this condition was to drink huge quantities of green tea, which did, indeed, keep me alert, but also replaced my "no mind" state with constant thoughts of my bladder. In fact, in less than a year, I attained total bladder conciousness. Joshua, on the other hand, was able to completely let go of his ego, as he had been instructed. It was in our ninth month at the monastery, in the midst of the most bitter winter I can even imagine, when Joshua, having let go of all constructions of self and vanity, became invisible.

Chapter 18

I have been out among you, eating and talking and walking and walking and walking, for hours without having to turn because of a wall in my way. The angel woke me this morning with a new set of clothes, strange to the feel but familiar to the sight (from television). Jeans, sweatshirt, and sneakers, as well as some socks and boxer shorts.

"Put these on. I'm taking you out for a walk," said Raziel.

"As if I were a dog," I said.

"Exactly as if you were a dog."

The angel was also wearing modern American garb, and although he was still strikingly handsome, he looked so uncomfortable that the clothes might have been held to his body with flaming spikes.

"Where are we going?"

"I told you, out."

"Where did you get the clothes?"

"I called down and Jesus brought them up. There is a clothing store in the hotel. Come now."

Raziel closed the door behind us and put the room key in his jeans pocket with the money. I wondered if he'd ever had pockets before. I wouldn't have thought to use them. I didn't say a word as we rode the elevator down to the lobby and made our way out the front doors. I didn't want to ruin it, to say something that would bring the angel to his senses. The noise in the street was glorious: the cars, the jackhammers, the insane people babbling to themselves. The light! The smells! I felt as if I must have been in shock when we first traveled here from Jerusalem. I didn't remember it being so vivid.

I started to skip down the street and the angel caught me

by the shoulder; his fingers dug into my muscles like talons. "You know that you can't get away, that if you run I can catch you and snap your legs so you will never run again. You know that if you should escape even for a few minutes, you cannot hide from me. You know that I can find you, as I once found everyone of your kind? You know these things?"

"Yes, let go of me. Let's walk."

"I hate walking. Have you ever seen an eagle look at a pigeon? That's how I feel about you and your walking."

I should point out, I suppose, what Raziel was talking about when he said that he once found everyone of my kind. It seems that he did a stint, centuries ago, as the Angel of Death, but was relieved of his duties because he was not particularly good at them. He admits that he's a sucker for a hard-luck story (perhaps that explains his fascination with soap operas). Anyway, when you read in the Torah about Noah living to be nine hundred and Moses living to be a hundred and forty, well, guess who led the chorus line in the "Off This Mortal Coil" shuffle? That's where he got the black-winged aspect that I've talked about before. Even though they fired him, they let him keep the outfit. (Can you believe that Noah was able to postpone death for eight hundred years by telling the angel that he was behind in his paperwork? Would that Raziel could be that incompetent at his current task.)

"Look, Raziel! Pizza!" I pointed to a sign. "Buy us pizza!"

He took some money out of his pocket and handed it to me. "You do it. You can do it, right?"

"Yes, we had commerce in my time," I said sarcastically. "We didn't have pizza, but we had commerce."

"Good, can you use that machine?" He pointed to a box that held newspapers behind glass.

"If it doesn't open with that little handle, then no."

The angel looked perturbed. "How is it that you can receive the gift of tongues and suddenly understand all languages, and there is no gift that can tell you how things work in this time? Tell me that."

"Look, maybe if you didn't hog the remote all the time I would learn how to use these things." I meant that I could have learned more about the outside world from television, but Raziel thought I meant that I needed more practice pushing the channel buttons.

"Knowing how to use the television isn't enough. You have to know how everything in this world works." And with that the angel turned and stared through the window of the pizza place at the men tossing disks of dough into the air.

"Why, Raziel? Why do I need to know about how this world works? If anything, you've tried to keep me from learning anything."

"Not anymore. Let's go eat pizza."

"Raziel?"

He wouldn't explain any further, but for the rest of the day we wandered the city, spending money, talking to people, learning. In the late afternoon Raziel inquired of a bus driver as to where we might go to meet Spider-Man. I could have gone another two thousand years without seeing the kind of disappointment I saw on Raziel's face when the bus driver gave his answer. We returned here to the room where Raziel said, "I miss destroying cities full of humans."

"I know what you mean," I said, even though it was my best friend who had caused that sort of thing to go out of fashion, and not a moment too soon. But the angel needed to hear it. There's a difference between bearing false witness and saving someone's feelings. Even Joshua knew that.

"Joshua, you're scaring me," I said, talking to the disembodied voice that floated before me in the temple. "Where are you?"

"I am everywhere and nowhere," Joshua's voice said.

"How come your voice is in front of me then?" I didn't like this at all. Yes, my years with Joshua had jaded me in regard to supernatural experiences, but my meditation hadn't yet brought me to the place where I wouldn't react to my friend being invisible.

"I suppose it is the nature of a voice that it must come from somewhere, but only so that it may be let go."

Gaspar had been sitting in the temple and at the sound of our voices he rose and came over to me. He didn't appear to be angry, but then, he never did. "Why?" Gaspar said to me, meaning, *Why are you talking and disturbing everyone's meditation with your infernal noise, you barbarian?*

"Joshua has attained enlightenment," I said.

Gaspar said nothing, meaning, *So? That's the idea, you unworthy spawn of a razor-burned yak.* I could tell that's what he meant by the tone in his voice.

"So he's invisible."

"*Mu*," Joshua's voice said. *Mu* meaning *nothing beyond nothingness* in Chinese.

In an act of distinctly uncontrolled spontaneity, Gaspar screamed like a little girl and jumped four feet straight in the air. Monks stopped chanting and looked up. "What was that?"

"That's Joshua."

"I am free of self, free of ego," Joshua said. There was a little squeak and then a nasty stench infused us.

I looked at Gaspar and he shook his head. He looked at me and I shrugged.

"Was that you?" Gaspar asked Joshua.

"Me in the sense that I am part of all things, or me in the sense of I am the one who poofed the gefilte gas?" asked Josh.

"The latter," said Gaspar.

"No," said Josh.

"You lie," I said, as amazed at that as I was at the fact that I couldn't see my friend.

"I should stop talking now. Having a voice separates me from all that is." With that he was quiet, and Gaspar looked as if he were about to panic.

"Don't go away, Joshua," the abbot said. "Stay as you are if you must, but come to the tea chamber at dawn tomorrow." Gaspar looked to me. "You come too."

"I have to train on the poles in the morning," I said.

"You are excused," Gaspar said. "And if Joshua talks to you anymore tonight, try to persuade him to share our existence." Then he hurried off in a very unenlightened way.

That night I was falling asleep when I heard a squeak in the hall outside of my cell, then an incredibly foul odor jolted me awake.

"Joshua?" I crawled out of my cell into the hall. There were narrow slots high in the walls through which moonlight could sift, but I saw nothing but faint blue light on the stone. "Joshua, is that you?"

"How could you tell?" Joshua's disembodied voice said.

"Well, honestly, you stink, Josh."

"The last time we went to the village for alms, a woman gave Number Fourteen and me a thousand-year-old egg. It didn't sit well."

"Can't imagine why. I don't think you're supposed to eat an egg after, oh, two hundred years or so."

"They bury them, leave them there, then dig them up."

"Is that why I can't see you?"

"No, that's because of my meditation. I've let go of everything. I've achieved perfect freedom."

"You've been free ever since we left Galilee."

"It's not the same. That's what I came to tell you, that I can't free our people from the rule of Romans."

"Why not?"

"Because that's not true freedom. Any freedom that can be given can be taken away. Moses didn't need to ask Pharaoh to release our people, our people didn't need to be released from the Babylonians, and they don't need to be released from the Romans. I can't give them freedom. Freedom is in their hearts, they merely have to find it."

"So you're saying you're not the Messiah?"

"How can I be? How can a humble being presume to grant something that is not his to give?"

"If not you, who, Josh? Angels and miracles, your ability to heal and comfort? Who else is chosen if not you?"

"I don't know. I don't know anything. I wanted to say good-bye. I'll be with you, as part of all things, but you won't perceive me until you become enlightened. You can't imagine how this feels, Biff. You are everything, you love everything, you need nothing."

"Okay. You won't be needing your shoes then, right?"

"Possessions stand between you and freedom."

"Sounded like a yes to me. Do me one favor though, okay?"

"Of course."

"Listen to what Gaspar has to say to you tomorrow." *And give me time to think up an intelligent answer to someone who's invisible and crazy,* I thought to myself. Joshua was innocent, but he wasn't stupid. I had to come up with something to save the Messiah so he could save the rest of us.

"I'm going to the temple to sit. I'll see you in the morning."

"Not if I see you first."

"Funny," said Josh.

Gaspar looked especially old that morning when I met him in the tea room. His personal quarters consisted of a cell no bigger than my own, but it was located just off the tea room and had a door which he could close. It was cold in the morning in the monastery and I could see our breath as Gaspar boiled the water for tea. Soon I saw a third puff of breath coming from my side of the table, although there was no person there.

"Good morning, Joshua," Gaspar said. "Did you sleep, or are you free from that need?"

"No, I don't need sleep anymore," said Josh.

"You'll excuse Twenty-one and I, as we still require nourishment."

Gaspar poured us some tea and fetched two rice balls from a shelf where he kept the tea. He held one out for me and I took it.

"I don't have my bowl with me," I said, worried that Gaspar would be angry with me. How was I to know? The monks always ate breakfast together. This was out of order.

"Your hands are clean," said Gaspar. Then he sipped his tea and sat peacefully for a while, not saying a word. Soon the room heated up from the charcoal brazier that Gaspar had used to heat the tea and I was no longer able to see Joshua's breath. Evidently he'd also overcome the gastric distress of the thousand-year-old egg. I began to get nervous, aware that Number Three would be waiting for Joshua and me in the courtyard to start our exercises. I was about to say something when Gaspar held up a finger to mark silence.

"Joshua," Gaspar said, "do you know what a bodhisattva is?"

"No, master, I don't."

"Gautama Buddha was a bodhisattva. The twenty-seven patriarchs since Gautama Buddha were also bodhisattvas. Some say that I, myself, am a bodhisattva, but the claim is not mine."

"There are no Buddhas," said Joshua.

"Indeed," said Gaspar, "but when one reaches the place of Buddhahood and realizes that there is no Buddha because everything is Buddha, when one reaches enlightenment, but makes a decision that he will not evolve to nirvana until all sentient beings have preceded him there, then he is a bodhisattva. A savior. A bodhisattva, by making this decision, grasps the only thing that can ever be grasped: compassion for the suffering of his fellow humans. Do you understand?"

"I think so," said Joshua. "But the decision to become a bodhisattva sounds like an act of ego, a denial of enlightenment."

"Indeed it is, Joshua. It is an act of self-love."

"Are you asking me to become a bodhisattva?"

"If I were to say to you, love your neighbor as you love yourself, would I be telling you to be selfish?"

There was silence for a moment, and as I looked at the place where Joshua's voice was originating, he gradually started to become visible again. "No," said Joshua.

"Why?" asked Gaspar.

"Love thy neighbor as thou lovest thyself"—and here there was a long pause when I could imagine Joshua looking to the sky for an answer, as he so often did, then: "for he is thee, and thou art he, and everything that is ever worth loving is everything." Joshua solidified before our eyes, fully dressed, looking no worse for the wear.

Gaspar smiled and those extra years that he had been carrying on his face seemed to fade away. There was a peace in his aspect and for a moment he could have been as young as we were. "That is correct, Joshua. You are truly an enlightened being."

"I will be a bodhisattva to my people," Joshua said.

"Good, now go shave the yak," said Gaspar.

I dropped my rice ball. "What?"

"And you, find Number Three and commence your training on the posts."

"Let me shave the yak," I said. "I've done it before."

Joshua put his hand on my shoulder. "I'll be fine."

Gaspar said: "And on the next moon, after alms, you shall both go with the group into the mountains for a special meditation. Your training begins tonight. You shall receive no meals for two days and you must bring me your blankets before sundown.

"But I've already been enlightened," protested Josh.

"Good. Shave the yak," said the master.

Í suppose I shouldn't have been surprised when Joshua showed up the next day at the communal dining room with a bale of yak hair and not a scratch on him. The other monks didn't seem surprised in the least. In fact, they hardly looked up from their rice and tea. (In my years at Gaspar's monastery, I found it was astoundingly difficult to surprise a Buddhist monk, especially one who had been trained in kung fu. So alert were they to the moment that one had to become nearly invisible and completely silent to sneak up on a monk, and even then simply jumping out and shouting "boo" wasn't enough to shake their chakras. To get a real reaction, you pretty much had to poleax one of them with a fighting staff, and if he heard the staff whistling through the air, there was a good chance he'd catch it, take it away from you, and pound you into damp pulp with it. So, no, they weren't surprised when Joshua delivered the fuzz harvest unscathed.)

"How?" I asked, that being pretty much what I wanted to know.

"I told her what I was doing," said Joshua. "She stood perfectly still."

"You just told her what you were going to do?"

"Yes."

"She wasn't afraid, so she didn't resist. All fear comes from trying to see the future, Biff. If you know what is coming, you aren't afraid."

"That's not true. I knew what was coming—namely that you were going to get stomped by the yak and that I'm not nearly as good at healing as you are—and I was afraid."

"Oh, then I'm wrong. Sorry. She must just not like you."

"That's more like it," I said, vindicated. Joshua sat on the floor across from me. Like me, he wasn't permitted to eat anything, but we were allowed tea. "Hungry?"

"Yes, you?"

"Starving. How did you sleep last night, without your blanket, I mean?"

"It was cold, but I used the training and I was able to sleep."

"I tried, but I shivered all night long. It's not even winter yet, Josh. When the snow falls we'll freeze to death without a blanket. I hate the cold."

"You have to be the cold," said Joshua.

"I liked you better before you got enlightened," I said.

Now Gaspar started to oversee our training personally. He was there every second as we leapt from post to post, and he drilled us mercilessly through the complex hand and foot movements we practiced as part of our kung fu regimen. (I had a funny feeling that I'd seen the movements before as he taught them to us, then I remembered Joy doing her complex dances in Balthasar's fortress. Had Gaspar taught the wizard, or vice versa?) As we sat in meditation, sometimes all through the night, he stood behind us with his bamboo rod and periodically struck us on the back of the head for no reason I could discern.

"Why's he keep doing that? I didn't do anything," I complained to Joshua over tea.

"He's not hitting you to punish you, he's hitting you to keep you in the moment."

"Well, I'm in the moment now, and at the moment I'd like to beat the crap out of him."

"You don't mean that."

"Oh, what? I'm supposed to want to *be* the crap I beat out of him?"

"Yes, Biff," Joshua said somberly. "You must *be* the crap." But he couldn't keep a straight face and he started to snicker as he sipped his tea, finally spraying the hot liquid out his nostrils and collapsing into a fit of laughter. All of the other monks, who evidently had been listening in, started giggling as well. A couple of them rolled around on the floor holding their sides.

It's very difficult to stay angry when a room full of bald guys in orange robes start giggling. Buddhism.

Gaspar made us wait two months before taking us on the special meditation pilgrimage, so it was well into winter before we made that monumental trek. Snow fell so deep on the mountainside that we literally had to tunnel our way out to the courtyard every morning for exercise. Before we were allowed to begin, Joshua and I had to shovel all of the snow out of the courtyard, which meant that some days it was well past noon before we were able to start drilling. Other days the wind whipped down out of the mountains so viciously that we couldn't see more than a few inches past our faces, and Gaspar would devise exercises that we could practice inside.

Joshua and I were not given our blankets back, so I, for one, spent every night shivering myself to sleep. Although the high windows were shuttered and charcoal braziers were lit in the rooms that were occupied, there was never anything approaching physical comfort during the winter. To my relief, the other monks were not unaffected by the cold, and I noticed that the accepted posture for breakfast was to wrap your entire body around your steaming cup of tea, so not so much as a mote of precious heat might escape. Someone entering the dining hall, seeing us all balled up in our orange robes, might have thought he stumbled into a steaming patch of giant pumpkins. At least the others, including Joshua, seemed to find some relief from the chill during their meditations, having reached that state, I'm told, where they could, indeed, generate their own heat. I was still learning the discipline. Sometimes I considered climbing to the back of the temple where the cave became narrow and hundreds of fuzzy bats hibernated on the ceiling in a great seething mass of fur and sinew. The smell might have been horrid, but it would have been warm.

When the day finally came for us to take the pilgrimage, I was no closer to generating my own heat than I had been at the start, so I was relieved when Gaspar led five of us to a cabinet and issued yak-wool leggings and boots to each of us. "Life is suffering," said Gaspar as he handed Joshua his leggings, "but it is more expedient to go through it with one's legs intact." We left just after dawn on a crystal clear morning after a night of brutal wind that had blown much of the snow off the base of the mountain. Gaspar led five of us down the mountain to the village. Sometimes we trod in the snow up to our waists, other times we hopped across the tops of exposed stones, suddenly making our training on the tops of the posts seem much more practical than I had ever thought possible. On the mountainside, a slip from one of the stones might have sent us plunging into a powder-filled ravine to suffocate under fifty feet of snow.

The villagers received us with great celebration, coming out of their stone and sod houses to fill our bowls with rice and root vegetables, ringing small brass bells and blowing the yak horn in our honor before quickly retreating back to their fires and slamming their doors against the cold. It was festive, but it was brief. Gaspar led us to the home of the toothless old woman who Joshua and I had met so long ago and we all bedded down in the straw of her small barn amid her goats and a pair of yaks. (Her yaks were much smaller than the one we kept at the monastery, more the size of normal cattle. I found out later that ours was the progeny of the wild yaks that lived in the high plateaus, while hers were from stock that had been domesticated for a thousand years.)

After the others had gone to sleep, I snuck into the old woman's house in search of some food. It was a small stone house with two rooms. The front one was dimly lit by a single window covered with a tanned and stretched animal hide that transmitted the light of the full moon as a dull yellow glow. I could only make out shapes, not actual objects, but I felt my way around the room until I laid my hand on what had to be a bag of turnips. I dug one of the knobby vegetables from the bag, brushed the dirt from the surface with my palm, then sunk in my teeth and crunched away a mouthful of crisp, earthy bliss. I had never even cared for turnips up to that time, but I had just decided that I was going to sit there until I had transferred the entire contents of that bag to my stomach, when I heard a noise in the back room.

I stopped chewing and listened. Suddenly I could see someone standing in the doorway between the two rooms. I drew in my breath and held it. Then I heard the old woman's voice, speaking Chinese with her peculiar accent: "To take the life of a human or one like a human. To take a thing that is not given. To claim to have superhuman powers."

I was slow, but suddenly I realized that the old woman was reciting the rules for which a monk could be expelled from the monastery. As she came into the dim light from the window she said, "To have intercourse with anyone, even down to an animal." And at that second, I realized that the toothless old woman was completely naked. A mouthful of chewed turnip rolled out of my mouth and down the front of my robe. The old woman, close now, reached out, I thought to catch the mess, but instead she caught what was under my robe.

"Do you have superhuman powers?" the old woman said, pulling on my manhood, which, much to my amazement, nodded an answer.

I need to say here that it had been over two years since we had left Balthasar's fortress, and another six months before that since the demon had come and killed all of the girls but Joy—thus curtailing my regular supply of sexual companions. I want to go on record that I had been steadfast in adhering to the rules of the monastery, allowing only those nocturnal emissions as were expelled during dreams (although I had gotten pretty good in directing my dreams in that direction, so all that mental discipline and meditation wasn't completely useless). So, that said, I was in a weakened state of resistance when the old woman, leathery and toothless as she might have been, compelled me by threat and intimidation to share with her what the Chinese call the Forbidden Monkey Dance. Five times.

Imagine my chagrin when the man who would save the world found me in the morning with a twisted burl of Chinese crone-flesh orally affixed to my fleshy pagoda of expandable joy, even as I snored away in transcendent turnip-digesting oblivion.

"Ahhhhhhhhhhh!" said Joshua, turning to the wall and throwing his robe over his head.

"Ahhhhhhhhhhh!" I said, roused from my slumber by the disgusted exclamation of my friend.

"Ahhhhhhhhhh!" said the old woman, I think. (Her speech was generously obstructed, if I do say so myself.)

"Jeez, Biff," Joshua stuttered. "You can't . . . I mean . . . Lust is . . . Jeez, Biff!"

"What?" I said, like I didn't know what.

"You've ruined sex for me for all time," Joshua said. "Whenever I think of it, this picture will always come up in my mind."

"So," I said, pushing the old woman away and shooing her into the back room.

"So . . ." Joshua turned around and looked me in the eye, then grinned widely enough to threaten the integrity of his ears. "So thanks."

I stood and bowed. "I am here only to serve," I said, grinning back.

"Gaspar sent me to look for you. He's ready to leave."

"Okay, I'd better, you know, say good-bye." I gestured toward the back room.

Joshua shuddered. "No offense," he said to the old woman, who was out of sight in the other room. "I was just surprised."

"Want a turnip?" I said, holding up one of the knobby treats.

Joshua turned and started out the door. "Jeez, Biff," he was saying as he left.

Chapter 19

Another day spent wandering the city with the angel,
another dream of the woman standing at the foot of my bed,
and I awoke finally—after all these years—to understand
what Joshua must have felt, at least at times, as the only one
of his kind. I know he said again and again that he was the
son of man, born of a woman, one of us, but it was the pater-
nal part of his heritage that made him different. Now, since
I'm fairly sure I am the only person walking the earth who
was doing so two thousand years ago, I have an acute sense
of what it is to be unique, to be the one and only. It's lonely.
That's why Joshua went into those mountains so often, and
stayed so long in the company of the creature.

Last night I dreamed that the angel was talking to someone in the room while I slept. In the dream I heard him say,
"Maybe it would be best just to kill him when he finishes.
Snap his neck, shove him into a storm sewer." Strange,
though, there wasn't the least bit of malice in the angel's
voice. On the contrary, he sounded very forlorn. That's how
I know it was a dream.

I never thought I'd be happy to get to back to the monastery, but
after trudging through the snow for half the day, the dank stone walls
and dark hallways were as welcoming as a warmly lit hearth. Half of
the rice we had collected as alms was immediately boiled, then
packed into bamboo cylinders about a hand wide and as long as a
man's leg, then half of the root vegetables were stored away while the
rest were packed into satchels along with some salt and more bamboo
cylinders filled with cold tea. We had just enough time to chase the
chill out of our limbs by the cook fires, then Gaspar had us take up the

cylinders and the satchels and he led us out into the mountains. I had never noticed when the other monks left on the pilgrimage of secret meditation that they were carrying so much food. And with all this food, much more than we could eat in the four or five days we were gone, why had Joshua and I been training for this by fasting?

Traveling higher into the mountains was actually easier for a while, as the snow had been blown off the trail. It was when we came to the high plateaus where the yak grazed and the snow drifted that the going became difficult. We took turns at the head of the line, plowing a trail through the snow.

As we climbed, the air became so thin that even the highly conditioned monks had to stop frequently to catch their breaths. At the same time, the wind bit through our robes and leggings as if they weren't there. That there was not enough air to breath, yet the movement of the air would chill our bones, I suppose is ironic, yet I was having a hard time appreciating it even then.

I said, "Why couldn't you just go to the rabbis and learn to be the Messiah like everyone else? Do you remember any snow in the story of Moses? No. Did the Lord appear to Moses in the form of a snow bank? I don't think so. Did Elijah ascend to heaven on a chariot of ice? Nope. Did Daniel come forth unharmed from a blizzard? No. Our people are about fire, Joshua, not ice. I don't remember any snow in all of the Torah. The Lord probably doesn't even go to places where it snows. This is a huge mistake, we never should have come, we should go home as soon as this is over, and in conclusion, I can't feel my feet." I was out of breath and wheezing.

"Daniel didn't come forth from the fire," Joshua said calmly.

"Well, who can blame him, it was probably warm in there."

"He came forth unharmed from the lion's den," said Josh.

"Here," said Gaspar, stopping any further discussion. He put down his parcels and sat down.

"Where?" I said. We were under a low overhang, out of the wind, and mostly out of the snow, but it was hardly what you could call shelter. Still, the other monks, including Joshua, shed their packs and sat, affecting the meditation posture and holding their hands in the mudra of all-giving compassion (which, strangely enough, is the same hand gesture that modern people use for "okay." Makes you think).

"We can't be here. There's no here here," I said.

"Exactly," said Gaspar. "Contemplate that."

So I sat.

Joshua and the others seemed impervious to the cold and as frost formed on my eyelashes and clothing, the light dusting of ice crystals that covered the ground and rocks around each of them began to melt, as if there was a flame burning inside of them. Whenever the wind died, I noticed steam rising off of Gaspar as his damp robe gave up its moisture to the chill air. When Joshua and I first learned to meditate, we had been taught to be hyperaware of everything around us, connected, but the state that my fellow monks were in now was one of trance, of separation, of exclusion. They had each constructed some sort of mental shelter in which they were happily sitting, while I, quite literally, was freezing to death.

"Joshua, I need a little help here," I said, but my friend didn't move a muscle. If it weren't for the steady stream of his breath I would have thought him frozen himself. I tapped him on the shoulder, but received no response whatsoever. I tried to get the attention of each of the other four monks, but they too gave no reaction to my prodding. I even pushed Gaspar hard enough to knock him over, yet he stayed in the sitting position, looking like a statue of the Buddha that had tumbled from its pedestal. Still, as I touched each of my companions I could feel the heat coming off of him. Since it was obvious that I wasn't going to learn how to reach this trance state in time to save my own life, my only alternative was to take advantage of theirs.

At first I arranged the monks in a large pile, trying to keep the elbows and knees out of the eyes and yarbles, out of respect and in the spirit of the infinitely compassionate Buddha and stuff. Although the warmth coming off them was impressive, I found that I could only keep one side of me warm at a time. Soon, by arranging my friends in a circle facing outward, and sitting in the middle, I was able to construct an envelope of comfort that kept the chill at bay. Ideally, I could have used a couple of more monks to stretch over the top of my hut to block the wind, but as the Buddha said, life is suffering and all, so I suffered. After I heated some tea on Number Seven monk's head and tucked one of the cylinders of rice under Gaspar's arm until it was warm, I was able to enjoy a pleasant repast and dropped off to sleep with a full belly.

I awoke to what sounded like the entire Roman army trying to slurp the anchovies out of the Mediterranean Sea. When I opened my eyes I saw the source of the noise and nearly tumbled over backward trying to back away. A huge, furry creature, half again as tall as any man I had ever seen was trying to slurp the tea out of one of the bamboo cylinders, but the tea had frozen to slush and the creature looked as if he might suck the top of his head in if he continued. Yes, he looked sort of like a man, except his entire body was covered with a long white fur. His eyes were as large as a cow's, with crystal blue irises and pinpoint pupils. Thick black eyelashes knitted together when he blinked. He had long black nails on his hands, which were similar to a man's except twice the size, and the only clothing he wore at all were some sort of boots that looked to be made of yak skin. The impressive array of tackle swinging between the creature's legs tipped me off to his maleness.

I looked around at the circle of monks to see if anyone had noticed that our supplies were being raided by a woolly beast, but they were all deeply entranced. The creature slurped again from the cylinder, then pounded on the side of it with his hand, as if to dislodge the contents, then looked at me as if asking for help. Whatever terror I felt melted away the second I looked into the creature's eyes. There wasn't the hint of aggression there, not a glint of violence or threat. I picked up the cylinder of tea that I had heated on Number Three's head. It sloshed in my hand, indicating that it hadn't frozen during my nap, so I held it out to the creature. He reached over Joshua's head and took the cylinder, pulled the cork from the end, and drank greedily.

I took the moment to kick my friend in the kidney. "Josh, snap out of it. You need to see this." I got no response, so I reached around and pinched my friend's nostrils shut. To master meditation the student must first master his breath. The savior made a snorting sound and came out of his trance gasping and twisting in my grip. He was facing me when I finally let go.

"What?" Josh said.

I pointed behind him and Joshua turned around to witness the full glory of the big furry white guy. "Holy moly!"

Big Furry jumped back cradling his tea like a threatened infant and made some vocalization which wasn't quite language. (But if it had been, it would probably have translated as "Holy Moly," as well.)

It was nice to see Joshua's masterful control slip to reveal a vulnerable underbelly of confusion. "What . . . I mean who . . . I mean, what is that?"

"Not a Jew," I said helpfully, pointing to about a yard of foreskin.

"Well, I can see it's not a Jew, but that doesn't narrow it down much, does it?"

Strangely, I seemed to be enjoying this much more than my two semi-terrified cohorts. "Well, do you remember when Gaspar gave us the rules of the monastery, and we wondered about the one that said we were not to kill a human or someone like a human?"

"Yes?"

"Well, he's someone like a human, I guess."

"Okay." Joshua climbed to his feet and looked at Big Furry. Big Furry straightened up and looked at Joshua, tilting his head from side to side.

Joshua smiled.

Big Furry smiled back. Black lips, really long sharp canines.

"Big teeth," I said. "Very big teeth."

Joshua held his hand out to the creature. The creature reached out to Joshua and ever so gently took the Messiah's smaller hand in his great paw . . . and wrenched Joshua off his feet, catching him in a hug and squeezing him so hard that his beatific eyes started to bug out.

"Help," squeaked Joshua.

The creature licked the top of Joshua's head with a long blue tongue.

"He likes you," I said.

"He's tasting me," Joshua said.

I thought of how my friend had fearlessly yanked the tail of the demon Catch, of how he had faced so many dangers with total calm. I thought of the times he had saved me, both from outside dangers and from myself, and I thought of the kindness in his eyes that ran deeper than sea, and I said:

"Naw, he likes you." I thought I'd try another language to see if the creature might better comprehend my meaning: "You like Joshua, don't you? Yes you do. Yes you do. He wuvs his widdle Joshua. Yes he does." Baby talk is the universal language. The words are different, but the meaning and sound is the same.

The creature nuzzled Joshua up under its chin, then licked his head again, this time leaving a steaming trail of green-tea-stained saliva behind on my friend's scalp. "Yuck," said Joshua. "What is this thing?"

"It's a yeti," said Gaspar from behind me, obviously having been roused from his trance. "An abominable snowman."

"This is what happens when you fuck a sheep!?" I exclaimed.

"Not an *abomination*," Josh said, "*abominable*." The yeti licked him on the cheek. Joshua tried to push away. To Gaspar he said, "Am I in danger?"

Gaspar shrugged. "Does a dog have a Buddha nature?"

"Please, Gaspar," Joshua said. "This is a question of practical application, not spiritual growth." The yeti sighed and licked Josh's cheek again. I guessed that the creature must have a tongue as rough as a cat's, as Joshua's cheek was going pink with abrasion.

"Turn the other cheek, Josh," I said. "Let him wear the other one out."

"I'm going to remember this," Joshua said. "Gaspar, will he harm me?"

"I don't know. No one has ever gotten that close to him before. Usually he comes while we are in trance and disappears with the food. We are lucky to even get a glimpse of him."

"Put me down, please," said Josh to the creature. "Please put me down."

The yeti set Joshua back on his feet on the ground. By this time the other monks were coming out of their trances. Number Seventeen squealed like a frying squirrel when he saw the yeti so close. The yeti crouched and bared his teeth.

"Stop that!" barked Joshua to Seventeen. "You're scaring him."

"Give him some rice," said Gaspar.

I took the cylinder I had warmed and handed it to the yeti. He popped off the top and began scooping out rice with a long finger, licking the grains off his fingers like they were termites about to make their escape. Meanwhile Joshua backed away from the yeti so that he stood beside Gaspar.

"This is why you come here? Why after alms you carry so much food up the mountain?"

Gaspar nodded. "He's the last of his kind. He has no one to help him gather food. No one to talk to."

"But what is he? What is a yeti?"

"We like to think of him as a gift. He is a vision of one of the many lives a man might live before he reaches nirvana. We believe he is as close to a perfect being as can be achieved on this plane of existence."

"How do you know he is the only one?"

"He told me."

"He talks?"

"No, he sings. Wait."

As we watched the yeti eat, each of the monks came forward and put his cylinders of food and tea in front of the creature. The yeti looked up from his eating only occasionally, as if his whole universe resided in that bamboo pipe full of rice, yet I could tell that behind those ice-blue eyes the creature was counting, figuring, rationing the supplies we had brought.

"Where does he live?" I asked Gaspar.

"We don't know. A cave somewhere, I suppose. He has never taken us there, and we don't look for it."

Once all the food was put before the yeti, Gaspar signaled to the other monks and they started backing out from under the overhang into the snow, bowing to the yeti as they went. "It is time for us to go," Gaspar said. "He doesn't want our company."

Joshua and I followed our fellow monks back into the snow, following a path they were blazing back the way we had come. The yeti watched us leave, and every time I looked back he was still watching, until we were far enough away that he became little more than an outline against the white of the mountain. When at last we climbed out of the valley, and even the great sheltering overhang was out of sight, we heard the yeti's song. Nothing, not even the blowing of the ram's horn back home, not the war cries of bandits, not the singing of mourners, nothing I had ever heard had reached inside of me the way the yeti's song did. It was a high wailing, but with stops and pulses like the muted sound of a heart beating, and it carried all through the valley. The yeti held his keening notes far longer than any human breath could sustain. The effect was as if someone was emptying a huge cask of sadness down my throat until I thought I'd collapse or explode with the grief. It was the sound of a thousand hungry children crying, ten thousand widows tearing their hair over their husbands' graves, a chorus of angels singing the last dirge on the day of God's death. I covered my ears and fell to my knees in the snow. I looked at Joshua and tears were streaming down his cheeks. The other monks were hunched over as if shielding themselves from a hailstorm. Gaspar cringed as he looked at us, and I could see then that he was, indeed, a very old man. Not as old as Balthasar, perhaps, but the face of suffering was upon him.

"So you see," the abbot said, "he is the only one of his kind. Alone."

You didn't have to understand the yeti's language, if he had one, to know that Gaspar was right.

"No he's not," said Joshua. "I'm going to him."

Gaspar took Joshua's arm to stop him. "Everything is as it should be."

"No," said Joshua. "It is not."

Gaspar pulled his hand back as if he had plunged it into a flame—a strange reaction, as I had actually seen the monk put his hand in flame with less reaction as part of the kung fu regimen.

"Let him be," I said to Gaspar, not sure at the time why I was doing it.

Joshua headed back into the valley by himself, having not said another word to us.

"He'll be back when it's time," I said.

"What do you know?" snapped Gaspar in a distinctly unenlightened way. "You'll be working off your karma for a thousand years as a dung beetle just to evolve to the point of being dense."

I didn't say anything. I simply bowed, then turned and followed my brother monks back to the monastery.

It was a week before Joshua returned to us, and it was another day before he and I actually had time to speak. We were in the dining hall, and Joshua had eaten his own rice as well as mine. In the meantime, I had applied a lot of thought to the plight of the abominable snowman and, more important, to his origins.

"Do you think there were a lot of them, Josh?"

"Yes. Never as many as there are men, but there were many more."

"What happened to them?"

"I'm not sure. When the yeti sings I see pictures in my head. I saw that men came to these mountains and killed the yeti. They had no instinct to fight. Most just stood in place and watched as they were slaughtered. Perplexed by man's evil. Others ran higher and higher into the mountains. I think that this one had a mate and a family. They starved or died of some slow sickness. I can't tell."

"Is he a man?"

"I don't think he is a man," said Joshua.

"Is he an animal?"

"No, I don't think he's an animal either. He knows who he is. He knows he is the only one."

"I think I know what he is."

Joshua regarded me over the rim of his bowl. "Well?"

"Well, do you remember the monkey feet Balthasar bought from the old woman in Antioch, how they looked like little human feet?"

"Yes."

"And you have to admit that the yeti looks very much like a man. More like a man than he does any other creature, right? Well, what if he is a creature who is becoming a man? What if he isn't really the last of his kind, but the first of ours? What made me think of it was how Gaspar talks about how we work off our karma in different incarnations, as different creatures. As we learn more in each lifetime we may become a higher creature as we go. Well, maybe creatures do that too. Maybe as the yeti needs to live where it is warmer he loses his fur. Or as the monkeys need to, I don't know, run cattle and sheep, they become bigger. Not all at once, but through many incarnations. Maybe creatures evolve the way Gaspar believes the soul evolves. What do you think?"

Joshua stroked his chin for a moment and stared at me as if he was deep in thought, while at the same time I thought he might burst out laughing any second. I'd spent a whole week thinking about this. This theory had vexed me through all of my training, all of my meditations since we'd made the pilgrimage to the yeti's valley. I wanted some sort of acknowledgment from Joshua for my effort, if nothing else.

"Biff," he said, "That may be the dumbest idea you've ever had."

"So you don't think it's possible?"

"Why would the Lord create a creature only to have it die out? Why would the Lord allow that?" Joshua said.

"What about the flood? All but Noah and his family were killed."

"But that was because people had become wicked. The yeti isn't wicked. If anything, his kind have died out because they have no capacity for wickedness."

"So, you're the Son of God, you explain it to me."

"It is God's will," said Joshua, "that the yeti disappear."

"Because they had no trace of wickedness?" I said sarcastically. "If the yeti isn't a man, then he's not a sinner either. He's innocent."

Joshua nodded, staring into his now-empty bowl. "Yes. He's innocent." He stood and bowed to me, which was something he almost never did unless we were training. "I'm tired now, Biff. I have to sleep and pray."

"Sorry, Josh, I didn't mean to make you sad. I thought it was an interesting theory."

He smiled weakly at me, then bowed his head and shuffled off to his cell.

Over the next few years Joshua spent at least a week out of every month in the mountains with the yeti, going up not only with every group after alms, but often going up into the mountains by himself for days or, in the summer, weeks at a time. He never talked about what he did while in the mountains, except, he told me, that the yeti had taken him to the cave where he lived and had shown him the bones of his people. My friend had found something with the yeti, and although I didn't have the courage to ask him, I suspect the bond he shared with the snowman was the knowledge that they were both unique creatures, nothing like either of them walked the face of the earth, and regardless of the connection each might feel with God and the universe, at that time, in that place, but for each other, they were utterly alone.

Gaspar didn't forbid Joshua's pilgrimages, and indeed, he went out of his way to act as if he didn't notice when Twenty-Two Monk was gone, yet I could tell there was some unease in the abbot whenever Joshua was away.

We both continued to drill on the posts, and after two years of leaping and balancing, dancing and the use of weapons were added to our routine. Joshua refused to take up any of the weapons; in fact, he refused to practice any art that would bring harm to another being. He wouldn't even mimic the action of fighting with swords and spears with a bamboo substitute. At first Gaspar bristled at Joshua's refusal, and threatened to banish him from the monastery, but when I took the abbot aside and told him the story of the archer Joshua had blinded on the way to Balthasar's fortress, the abbot relented. He and two of the older monks who had been soldiers devised for Joshua a regimen of weaponless fighting that involved no offense or striking at all, but instead channeled the energy of an attacker away from oneself. Since the new art was practiced only by Joshua (and sometimes myself), the monks called it *Jew-dô,* meaning *the way of the Jew.*

In addition to learning kung fu and Jew-dô, Gaspar set us to learning to speak and write Sanskrit. Most of the holy books of Buddhism had been written in that language and had yet to be translated into Chinese, which Joshua and I had become fluent in.

"This is the language of my boyhood," Gaspar said before beginning our lessons. "You need to know this to learn the words of Gautama Buddha, but you will also need this language when you follow your dharma to your next destination."

Joshua and I looked at each other. It had been a long time since we had talked about leaving the monastery and the mention of it put us on edge. Routine feeds the illusion of safety, and if nothing else, there was routine at the monastery.

"When will we leave, master?" I asked.

"When it is time," said Gaspar.

"And how will we know it is time to leave?"

"When the time for staying has come to an end."

"And we will know this because you will finally give us a straight and concrete answer to a question instead of being obtuse and spooky?" I asked.

"Does the unhatched tadpole know the universe of the full-grown frog?"

"Evidently not," Joshua said.

"Correct," said the master. "Meditate upon it."

As Joshua and I entered the temple to begin our meditation I said, "When the time comes, and we know that the time has come for us to leave, I am going to lump up his shiny little head with a fighting staff."

"Meditate upon it," said Josh.

"I mean it. He's going to be sorry he taught me how to fight," I said.

"I'm sure of it. I'm sorry already."

"You know, he doesn't have to be the only one bopped in the noggin when noggin-boppin' time rolls around," I said.

Joshua looked at me as if I'd just awakened him from a nap. "All the time we spend meditating, what are you really doing, Biff?"

"I'm meditating—sometimes—listening to the sound of the universe and stuff."

"But mostly you're just sitting there."

"I've learned to sleep with my eyes open."

"That won't help your enlightenment."

"Look, when I get to nirvana I want to be well rested."

"Don't spend a lot of time worrying about it."

"Hey, I have discipline. Through practice I've learned to cause spontaneous nocturnal emissions."

"That's an accomplishment," the Messiah said sarcastically.

"Okay, you can be snotty if you want to, but when we get back to Galilee, you walk around trying to sell your 'love your neighbor because he is you' claptrap, and I'll offer the 'wet dreams at will' program and we'll see who gets more followers."

Joshua grinned: "I think we'll both do better than my cousin John and his 'hold them underwater until they agree with you' sermon."

"I haven't thought about him in years. Do you think he's still doing that?"

Just then, Number Two Monk, looking very stern and unenlightened, stood and started across the temple toward us, his bamboo rod in hand.

"Sorry, Josh, I'm going no-mind." I dropped to the lotus position, formed the mudra of the compassionate Buddha with my fingers, and lickity-split was on the sitting-still road to oneness with allthatness.

Despite Gaspar's veiled warning about our moving on, we again settled into a routine, this one including learning to read and write the sutras in Sanskrit, but also Joshua's time with the yeti. I had gotten so proficient in the martial arts that I could break a flagstone as thick as my hand with my head, and I could sneak up on even the most wary of the other monks, flick him on the ear, and be back in lotus position before he could spin to snatch the still-beating heart from my chest. (Actually, no one was really sure if anyone could do that. Every day Number Three Monk would declare it time for the "snatching the still-beating heart from the chest" drill, and every day he would ask for volunteers. After a brief wait, when no one volunteered, we'd move onto the next drill, usually the "maiming a guy with a fan" drill. Everyone wondered if Number Three could really do it, but no one wanted to ask. We knew how Buddhist monks liked to teach. One minute you're curious, the next a bald guy is holding a bloody piece of pulsating meat in your face and you're wondering why the sudden draft in the thorax area of your robe. No thanks, we didn't need to know that badly.)

Meanwhile, Joshua became so adept at avoiding blows that it was as if he'd become invisible again. Even the best fighting monks, of whom I was not one, had trouble laying a hand on my friend, and often they ended up flat on their backs on the flagstones for their trouble. Joshua seemed his happiest during these exercises, often laughing out loud as he narrowly dodged the thrust of a sword that would have taken his eye. Sometimes he would take the spear away from Number Three, only to bow and present it to him with a grin, as if the grizzled old soldier had dropped it instead of having it finessed from his grip. When Gaspar witnessed these displays he would leave the courtyard shaking his head and mumbling something about ego, leaving the rest of us to collapse into paroxysms of laughter at the abbot's expense. Even Numbers Two and Three, who were normally the strict disciplinarians, managed to mine a few smiles from their ever-so furrowed brows. It was a good time for Joshua. Meditation, prayer, exercise, and time with the yeti seemed to have helped him to let go of the colossal burden he'd been given to carry. For the first time he seemed truly happy, so I was stunned the day my friend entered the courtyard with tears streaming down his cheeks. I dropped the spear I was drilling with and ran to him.

"Joshua?"

"He's dead," Joshua said.

I embraced him and he collapsed into my arms sobbing. He was wearing wool leggings and boots, so I knew immediately that he'd just returned from one of his visits into the mountains.

"A piece of ice fell from over his cave. I found him under it. Crushed. He was frozen solid."

"So you couldn't . . ."

Joshua pushed me back and held me by the shoulders. "That's just it. I wasn't there in time. I not only couldn't save him, I wasn't even there to comfort him."

"Yes you were," I said.

Joshua dug his fingers into my shoulders and shook me as if I was hysterical and he was trying to get my attention, then suddenly he let go of me and shrugged. "I'm going to the temple to pray."

"I'll join you soon. Fifteen and I have three more movements to practice." My sparring partner waited patiently at the edge of the courtyard, spear in hand, watching.

Joshua got almost to the doors before he turned. "Do you know the difference between praying and meditating, Biff?"

I shook my head.

"Praying is talking to God. Meditating is listening. I've spent most of these last six years listening. Do you know what I've heard?"

Again I said nothing.

"Not a single thing, Biff. Now I have some things I want to say."

"I'm sorry about your friend," I said.

"I know." He turned and started inside.

"Josh," I called. He paused and looked over his shoulder at me.

"I won't let that happen to you, you know that, right?"

"I know," he said, then he went inside to give his father a divine ass-chewing.

The next morning Gaspar summoned us to the tea room. The abbot looked as if he had not slept in days and whatever his age, he was carrying a century of misery in his eyes.

"Sit," he said, and we did. "The old man of the mountain is dead."

"Who?"

"That's what I called the yeti, the old man of the mountain. He has passed on to his next life and it is time for you to go."

Joshua said nothing, but sat with his hands folded in his lap, staring at the table.

"What does one have to do with the other?" I asked. "Why should we leave because the yeti has died? We didn't know he even existed until we had been here for two years."

"But I did," said Gaspar.

I felt a heat rising in my face—I'm sure that my scalp and ears must have flushed, because Gaspar scoffed at me. "There is nothing else here for you. There was nothing here for *you* from the beginning. I would not have allowed you to stay if you weren't Joshua's friend." It was the first time he'd used either of our names since we'd arrived at the monastery. "Number Four will meet you at the gate. He has the possessions you arrived with, as well as some food for your journey."

"We can't go home," Joshua said at last. "I don't know enough yet."

"No," said Gaspar, "I suspect that you don't. But you know all that you will learn here. If you come to a river and find a boat at the edge, you will use that boat to cross and it will serve you well, but once across the river, do you put the boat on your shoulders and carry it with you on the rest of your journey?"

"How big is the boat?" I asked.

"What color is the boat?" asked Joshua.

"How far is the rest of the journey?" I queried.

"Is Biff there to carry the oars, or do I have to carry everything?" asked Josh.

"No!" screamed Gaspar. "No, you don't take the boat along on the journey. It has been useful but now it's simply a burden. It's a parable, you cretins!"

Joshua and I bowed our heads under Gaspar's anger. As the abbot railed, Joshua smiled at me and winked. When I saw the smile I knew that he'd be okay.

Gaspar finished his tirade, then caught his breath and resumed in the tone of the tolerant monk that we were used to. "As I was saying, there is no more for you to learn. Joshua, go be a bodhisattva for your people, and Biff, try not to kill anyone with what we have taught you here."

"So do we get our boat now?" Joshua asked.

Gaspar looked as if he were about to explode, then Joshua held his hand up and the old man remained silent.

"We are grateful for our time here, Gaspar. These monks are noble and honorable men, and we have learned much from them. But you, honorable abbot, are a pretender. You have mastered a few tricks of the body, and you can reach a trance state, but you are not an enlightened being, though I think you have glimpsed enlightenment. You look everywhere for answers but where they lie. Nevertheless, your deception hasn't stopped you from teaching us. We thank you, Gaspar. Hypocrite. Wise man. Bodhisattva."

Gaspar sat staring at Joshua, who had spoken as if he were talking to a child. The old man went about fixing the tea, more feebly now, I thought, but maybe that was my imagination.

"And you knew this?" Gaspar asked me.

I shrugged. "What enlightened being travels halfway around the world following a star on the rumor that a Messiah has been born?"

"He means *across* the world," said Josh.

"I mean *around* the world." I elbowed Joshua in the ribs because it was easier than explaining my theory of universal stickiness to Gaspar. The old guy was having a rough day as it was.

Gaspar poured tea for all of us, then sat down with a sigh. "You were not a disappointment, Joshua. The three of us knew as soon as we saw you that you were a being unlike any other. Brahman born to flesh, my brother said."

"What gave it away," I said, "the angels on the roof of the stable?"

Gaspar ignored me. "But you were still an infant, and whatever it was that we were looking for, you were not it—not yet, anyway. We could have stayed, I suppose, and helped to raise you, protect you, but we were all dense. Balthasar wanted to find the key to immortality, and there was no way that you could give him that, and my brother and I wanted the keys to the universe, and those were not to be found in Bethlehem either. So we warned your father of Herod's intent to have you killed, we gave him gold to get you out of the country, and we returned to the East."

"Melchior is your brother?"

Gaspar nodded. "We were princes of Tamil. Melchior is the oldest, so he would have inherited our lands, but I would have received a small fiefdom as well. Like Siddhartha, we eschewed worldly pleasures to pursue enlightenment."

"How did you end up here, in these mountains?" I asked.

"Chasing Buddhas." Gaspar smiled. "I had heard that there lived a sage in these mountains. The locals called him the old man of the mountain. I came looking for the sage, and what I found was the yeti. Who knows how old he really was, or how long he'd been here? What I did know was that he was the last of his kind and that he would die before long without help. I stayed here and I built this monastery. Along with the monks who came here to study, I have been taking care of the yeti since you two were just infants. Now he is gone. I have no purpose, and I have learned nothing. Whatever there was to know here died under that lump of ice."

Joshua reached across the table and took the old man's hand. "You drill us every day in the same movements, we practice the same brush strokes over and over, we chant the same mantras, why? So that these actions will become natural, spontaneous, without being diluted by thought, right?"

"Yes," said Gaspar.

"Compassion is the same way," said Joshua. "That's what the yeti knew. He loved constantly, instantly, spontaneously, without thought or words. That's what he taught me. Love is not something you think about, it is a state in which you dwell. That was his gift."

"Wow," I said.

"I came here to learn that," said Josh. "You taught it to me as much as the yeti."

"Me?" Gaspar had been pouring the tea as Joshua spoke and now he noticed that he'd overfilled his cup and the tea was running all over the table.

"Who took care of him? Fed him? Looked after him? Did you have to think about that before you did it?"

"No," said Gaspar.

Joshua stood. "Thanks for the boat."

Gaspar didn't accompany us to the front gate. As he promised, Number Four was waiting for us with our clothes and the money we had when we arrived six years before. I picked up the ying-yang vial of poison that Joy had given me and slipped the lanyard over my head, then I pushed the sheathed black glass dagger into the belt of my robe and tucked my clothes under my arm.

"You will go to find Gaspar's brother?" Number Four asked. Number Four was one of the older monks, one of the ones who had served the emperor as a soldier, and a long white scar marked his head from the middle of his shaved scalp to his right ear, which had healed to a forked shape.

"Tamil, right?" Joshua said.

"Go south. It is very far. There are many dangers along the way. Remember your training."

"We will."

"Good." Number Four turned on his heel and walked into the monastery, then shut the heavy wooden gate.

"No, no, Four, don't embarrass yourself with a sappy good-bye," I said to the gate. "No, really, please, no scenes."

Joshua was counting our money out of a small leather purse. "It's just what we left with them."

"Good."

"No, that's not good. We've been here six years, Biff. This money should have doubled or tripled during that time."

"What, by magic?"

"No, they should have invested it." He turned and looked back at the gate. "You dumb bastards, maybe you should spend a little less time studying how to beat each other up and a little more time on managing your money."

"Spontaneous love?" I said.

"Yeah, Gaspar'll never get that one either. That's why they killed the yeti, you know that, don't you?"

"Who?"

"The mountain people. They killed the yeti because they couldn't understand a creature who wasn't as evil as they were."

"The mountain people were evil?"

"All men are evil, that's what I was talking to my father about."

"What did he say?"

"Fuck 'em."

"Really?"

"Yeah."

"At least he answered you."

"I got the feeling that he thinks it's my problem now."

"Makes you wonder why he didn't burn that on one of the tablets. 'HERE, MOSES, HERE'S THE TEN COMMANDMENTS, AND HERE'S AN EXTRA ONE THAT SAYS FUCK 'EM.' "

"He doesn't sound like that."

"FOR EMERGENCIES," I continued in my perfect impression-of-God voice.

"I hope it's warm in India," Joshua said.

And so, at the age of twenty-four, Joshua of Nazareth did go down into India.

Part IV

Spirit

He who sees in me all things, and all things in me, is
never far from me, and I am never far from him.

THE BHAGAVAD GITA

Chapter 20

The road was just wide enough for the two of us to walk side by side. The grass on either side was as high as an elephant's eye. We could see blue sky above us, and exactly as far along the path as the next curve, which could have been any distance away, because there's no perspective in an unbroken green trench. We'd been traveling on this road most of the day, and passed only one old man and a couple of cows, but now we could hear what sounded like a large party approaching us, not far off, perhaps two hundred yards away. There were men's voices, a lot of them, footsteps, some dissonant metal drums, and most disturbing, the continuous screams of a woman either in pain, or terrified, or both.

"Young masters!" came a voice from somewhere near us.

I jumped in the air and came down in a defensive stance, my black glass knife drawn and ready. Josh looked around for the source of the voice. The screaming was getting closer. There was a rustling in the grass a few feet away from the road, then again the voice, "Young masters, you must hide."

An impossibly thin male face with eyes that seemed a size and a half too large for his skull popped out of the wall of grass beside us. "You must come. Kali comes to choose her victims! Come now or die."

The face disappeared, replaced by a craggy brown hand that motioned for us to follow into the grass. The woman's scream hit crescendo and failed, as if the voice had broken like an overtightened lute string.

"Go," said Joshua, pushing me into the grass.

As soon as I was off of the road someone caught my wrist and started dragging me through the sea of grass. Joshua latched onto the tail of my shirt and allowed himself to be dragged along. As we ran the grass whipped and slashed at us. I could feel blood welling up on my face and arms, even as the brown wraith pulled me deeper into the sea of green. Above the rasping of my breath I heard men shouting from behind us, then a thrashing of the grass being trampled.

"They follow," said the brown wraith over his shoulder. "Run unless you want your heads to decorate Kali's altar. Run."

Over my shoulder to Josh, I said, "He says run or it will be bad." Behind Josh, outlined against the sky, I saw long, swordlike spear tips, the sort of thing one might use for beheading someone.

"Okey-dokey," said Josh.

It had taken us over a month to get to India, most of the journey through hundreds of miles of the highest, most rugged country we had ever seen. Amazingly enough, there were villages scattered all through the mountains, and when the villagers saw our orange robes doors were flung wide and larders opened. We were always fed, given a warm place to sleep, and welcomed to stay as long as we wished. We offered obtuse parables and irritating chants in return, as was the tradition.

It wasn't until we came out of the mountains onto a brutally hot and humid grassland that we found our mode of dress was drawing more disdain than welcome. One man, of obvious wealth (he rode a horse and wore silk robes) cursed us as we passed and spit at us. Other people on foot began to take notice of us as well, and we hurried off into some high grass and changed out of our robes. I tucked the glass dagger that Joy had given me into my sash.

"What was he going on about?" I asked Joshua.

"He said something about tellers of false prophecies. Pretenders. Enemies of the Brahman, whatever that is. I'm not sure what else."

"Well, it looks like we're more welcome here as Jews than as Buddhists."

"For now," said Joshua. "All the people have those marks on their foreheads like Gaspar had. I think without one of those we're going to have to be careful."

As we traveled into the lowlands the air felt as thick as warm cream, and we could feel the weight of it in our lungs after so many years in the mountains. We passed into the valley of a wide, muddy river, and the road became choked with people passing in and out of a city of wooden shacks and stone altars. There were humped-back cattle everywhere, even grazing in the gardens, but no one seemed to bear them any mind.

"The last meat I ate was what was left of our camels," I said.

"Let's find a booth and buy some beef."

There were merchants along the road selling various wares, clay pots, powders, herbs, spices, copper and bronze blades (iron seemed to be in short supply), and tiny carvings of what seemed to be a thousand different gods, most of them having more limbs than seemed necessary and none of them looking particularly friendly.

We found grain, breads, fruits, vegetables, and bean pastes for sale, but nowhere did we see any meat. We settled on some bread and spicy bean paste, paid the woman with Roman copper coin, then found a place under a large banyan tree where we could sit and look at the river while we ate.

I'd forgotten the smell of a city, the fetid mélange of people, and waste, and smoke and animals, and I began to long for the clean air of the mountains.

"I don't want to sleep here, Joshua. Let's see if we can find a place in the country."

"We are supposed to follow this river to the sea to reach Tamil. Where the river goes, so go the people."

The river—wider than any in Israel, but shallow, yellow with clay, and still against the heavy air—seemed more like a huge stagnant puddle than a living, moving thing. In this season, anyway. Dotting the surface, a half-dozen skinny, naked men with wild white hair and not three teeth apiece shouted angry poetry at the top of their lungs and tossed water into glittering crests over their heads.

"I wonder how my cousin John is doing," said Josh.

All along the muddy riverbank women washed clothes and babies only steps from where cattle waded and shat, men fished or pushed long shallow boats along with poles, and children swam or played in the mud. Here and there the corpse of a dog bobbed flyblown in the gentle current.

"Maybe there's a road inland a little, away from the stench."

Joshua nodded and climbed to his feet. "There," he said, pointing to a narrow path that began on the opposite bank of the river and disappeared into some tall grass.

"We'll have to cross," I said.

"Be nice if we could find a boat to take us," said Josh.

"You don't think we should ask where the path leads?"

"No," said Joshua, looking at a crowd of people who were gathering nearby and staring at us. "These people all look hostile."

"What was that you told Gaspar about love was a state you dwell in or something?"

"Yeah, but not with these people. These people are creepy. Let's go."

The creepy little brown guy who was dragging me through the elephant grass was named Rumi, and much to his credit, amid the chaos and tumble of a headlong dash through a leviathan marshland, pursued by a murderous band of clanging, shouting, spear-waving decapitation enthusiasts, Rumi had managed to find a tiger—no small task when you have a kung fu master and the savior of the world in tow.

"Eek, a tiger," Rumi said, as we stumbled into a small clearing, a mere depression really, where a cat the size of Jerusalem was gleefully gnawing away on the skull of deer.

Rumi had expressed my sentiments exactly, but I would be damned if I was going to let my last words be "Eek, a tiger," so I listened quietly as urine filled my shoes.

"You'd think all the noise would have frightened him," Josh said, just as the tiger looked up from his deer.

I noticed that our pursuers seemed to be closing on us by the second.

"That is the way it is usually done," said Rumi. "The noise drives the tiger to the hunter."

"Maybe he knows that," I said, "so he's not going anywhere. You know, they're bigger than I imagined. Tigers, I mean."

"Sit down," said Joshua.

"Pardon me?" I said.

"Trust me," Joshua said. "Remember the cobra when we were kids?"

I nodded to Rumi and coaxed him down as the tiger crouched and tensed his hind legs as if preparing to leap, which is exactly what he was doing. As the first of our pursuers broke into the clearing from behind us the tiger leapt, sailing over our heads by half again the height of a man. The tiger landed on the first two men coming out of the grass, crushing them under his enormous forepaws, then raking their backs as he leapt again. After that all I could see was spear points scattering against the sky as the hunters became, well, you know. Men screamed, the woman screamed, the tiger screamed, and the two men who had fallen under the tiger crawled to their feet and limped back toward the road, screaming.

Rumi looked from the dead deer, to Joshua, to me, to the dead deer, to

Joshua, and his eyes seemed to grow even larger than before. "I am deeply moved and eternally grateful for your affinity with the tiger, but that is his deer, and it appears that he has not finished with it, perhaps . . ."

Joshua stood up. "Lead on."

"I don't know which way."

"Not that way," I said, pointing in the direction of the screaming bad guys.

Rumi led us through the grass to another road, which we followed to where he lived.

"It's a pit," I said.

"It's not that bad," said Joshua, looking around. There were other pits nearby. People were living in them.

"You live in a pit," I said.

"Hey, ease up," Joshua said. "He saved our lives."

"It is a humble pit, but it is home," said Rumi. "Please make yourself comfortable."

I looked around. The pit had been chipped out of sandstone and was about shoulder deep and just wide enough to turn a cow around in, which I would find out was a crucial dimension. The pit was empty except for a single rock about knee high.

"Have a seat. You may have the rock," said Rumi.

Joshua smiled and sat on the rock. Rumi sat on the floor of the pit, which was covered with a thick layer of black slime. "Please. Sit," said Rumi, gesturing to the floor beside him. "I'm sorry, we can only afford one rock."

I didn't sit. "Rumi, you live in a pit!" I pointed out.

"Well, yes, that is true. Where do Untouchables live in your land?"

"Untouchable?"

"Yes, the lowest of the low. The scum of the earth. None of the higher caste may acknowledge my existence. I am Untouchable."

"Well, no wonder, you live in a fucking pit."

"No," Joshua said, "he lives in a pit because he's Untouchable, he's not Untouchable because he lives in a pit. He'd be Untouchable if he lived in a palace, isn't that right, Rumi?"

"Oh, like that's going to happen," I said. I'm sorry, the guy lived in a pit.

"There's more room since my wife and most of my children died," said Rumi. "Until this morning it was only Vitra, my youngest daughter and me, but now she is gone too. There is plenty of room for you if wish to stay."

Joshua put his hand on Rumi's narrow shoulder and I could see the effect it had, the pain evaporating from the Untouchable's face like dew under a hot sun. I stood by being wretched.

"What happened to Vitra?" Joshua asked.

"They came and took her, the Brahmans, as a sacrifice on the feast of Kali. I was looking for her when I saw you two. They gather children and men, criminals, Untouchables, and strangers. They would have taken you and day after tomorrow they would have offered your head to Kali."

"So your daughter is not dead?" I asked.

"They will hold her until midnight on the night of the feast, then slaughter her with the other children on the wooden elephants of Kali."

"I will go to these Brahmans and ask for your daughter back," Joshua said.

"They'll kill you," Rumi said. "Vitra is lost, even your tiger cannot save you from Kali's destruction."

"Rumi," I said. "Look at me, please. Explain, Brahmans, Kali, elephants, everything. Go slow, act as if I know nothing."

"Like that takes imagination," Joshua said, clearly violating my implied, if not expressed, copyright on sarcasm. (Yeah, we have Court TV in the hotel room, why?)

"There are four castes," said Rumi, "the Brahmans, or priests, Kshatriyas, or warriors; Vaisyas, who are farmers or merchants; and the Sudras, who are laborers. There are many subcastes, but those are the main ones. Each man is born to a caste and he remains in that caste until he dies and is reborn as a higher caste or lower caste, which is determined by his karma, or actions during his last life."

"We know from karma," I said. "We're Buddhist monks."

"Heretics!" Rumi hissed.

"Bite me, you bug-eyed scrawny brown guy," I said.

"You are a scrawny brown guy!"

"No, you're a scrawny brown guy!"

"No, you are a scrawny brown guy!

"We are all scrawny brown guys," Joshua said, making peace.

"Yeah, but he's bug-eyed."

"And you are a heretic."

"You're a heretic!"

"No, you are a heretic."

"We're all scrawny brown heretics," said Joshua, calming things down again.

"Well, of course I'm scrawny," I said. "Six years of cold rice and tea, and not a scrap of beef for sale in the whole country."

"You would eat beef? You heretic!" shouted Rumi.

"Enough!" shouted Joshua.

"No one may eat a cow. Cows are the reincarnations of souls on their way to the next life."

"Holy cow," Josh said.

"That is what I am saying."

Joshua shook his head as if trying to straighten jumbled thoughts. "You said that there were four castes, but you didn't mention Untouchables."

"Harijans, Untouchables, have no caste, we are the lowest of the low. We may have to live many lifetimes before we even ascend to the level of a cow, and then we may become higher caste. Then, if we follow our dharma, our duty, as a higher caste, we may become one with Brahma, the universal spirit of all. I can't believe you don't know this, have you been living in a cave?"

I was going to point out that Rumi was in no position to criticize where we had been living, but Joshua signaled me to let it go. Instead I said, "So you are lower on the caste system than a cow?" I asked.

"Yes."

"So these Brahmans won't eat a cow, but they will take your daughter and kill her for their goddess?"

"And eat her," said Rumi, hanging his head. "At midnight on the night of the feast they will take her and the other children and tie them to the wooden elephants. They will cut off the children's fingers and give one to the head of each Brahman household. Then they will catch her blood in a cup and everyone in the household will taste it. They may eat the finger or bury it for good luck. After that the children are hacked to death on the wooden elephants."

"They can't do that," Joshua said.

"Oh yes, the cult of Kali may do anything they wish. It is her city, Kalighat." ["*Calcutta*" on the *Friendly Flyer map*.] "My little Vitra is lost. We can only pray that she is reincarnated to a higher level."

Joshua patted the Untouchable's hand. "Why did you call Biff a heretic when he told you that we were Buddhist monks?"

"That Gautama said that a man may go directly from any level to join Brahma, without fulfilling his dharma, that is heresy."

"That would be better for you, wouldn't it? Since you're on the bottom of the ladder?"

"You cannot believe what you do not believe," Rumi said. "I am an Untouchable because my karma dictates it."

"Oh yeah," I said. "No sense sitting under a bodhi tree for a few hours when you can get the same thing through thousands of lifetimes of misery."

"Of course, that's ignoring the fact that you're a gentile and going to suffer eternal damnation either way," said Josh.

"Yeah, leaving that out altogether."

"But we'll get your daughter back," Joshua said.

Joshua wanted to rush into Kalighat and demand the return of Rumi's daughter and the release of all the other victims in the name of what was good and right. Joshua's solution to everything was to lead with righteous indignation, and there is a time and a place unto that, but there is also a time for cunning and guile (Ecclesiastes 9 or something). I was able to talk him into an alternate plan by using flawless logic:

"Josh, did the Vegemites smite the Marmites by charging in and demanding justice at the end of a sword? I think not. These Brahmans cut off and eat the fingers of children. I know there's no finger-cutting commandment, Josh, but still, I'm guessing that these people think differently than we do. They call the Buddha a heretic, and he was one of their princes. How do you think they'll receive a scrawny brown kid claiming to be the son of a god who doesn't even live in their area?"

"Good point. But we still have to save the child."

"Of course."

"How?"

"Extreme sneakiness."

"You'll have to be in charge then."

"First we need to see this city and this temple where the sacrifices will be held."

Joshua scratched his head. His hair had mostly grown back, but was still short. "The Vegemites smote the Marmites?"

"Yeah, Excretions three-six."

"I don't remember that. I guess I need to brush up on my Torah."

The statue of Kali over her altar was carved from black stone and stood as tall as ten men. She wore a necklace of human skulls around her neck and a girdle made of severed human hands at her hips. Her open maw was lined with a saw blade of teeth over which a stream of fresh blood had been poured. Even her toenails curved into vicious blades which dug into the pile of twisted, graven corpses on which she stood. She had four arms, one holding a cruel, serpentine sword, another a severed head by the hair; the third hand she held crooked, as if beckoning her victims to the place of dark destruction to which all are destined, and the fourth was posed downward, in a manner presenting the goddess's hand-girded hips, as if asking the eternal question, "Does this outfit make me look fat?"

The raised altar lay in the middle of an open garden that was surrounded by trees. The altar was wide enough that five hundred people could have stood in the shadow of the black goddess. Deep grooves had been cut in the stone to channel the blood of sacrifices into vessels, so it could be poured through the goddess's jaws. Leading to the altar was a wide stone-paved boulevard, which was lined on either side by great elephants carved from wood and set on turntables so they could be rotated. The trunks and front feet of the elephants were stained rusty brown, and here and there the trunks exhibited deep gouges from blades that had hewn through a child into the mahogany.

"Vitra isn't being kept here," Joshua said.

We were hiding behind a tree near the temple garden, dressed as natives, fake caste marks and all. Having lost when we drew lots, I was the one dressed as a woman.

"I think this is a bodhi tree," I said, "just like Buddha sat under! It's so exciting. I'm feeling sort of enlightened just standing here. Really, I can feel ripe bodhies squishing between my toes."

Joshua looked at my feet. "I don't think those are bodhies. There was a cow here before us."

I lifted my foot out of the mess. "Cows are overrated in this country. Under the Buddha's tree too. Is nothing sacred?"

"There's no temple to this temple," Joshua said. "We have to ask Rumi where the sacrifices are kept until the festival."

"He won't know. He's Untouchable. These guys are Brahmans—priests—they wouldn't tell him anything. That would be like a Sadducee telling a Samaritan what the Holy of Holies looked like."

"Then we have to find them ourselves," Joshua said.

"We know where they're going to be at midnight, we'll get them then."

"I say we find these Brahmans and force them to stop the whole festival."

"We'll just storm up to their temple and tell them to stop it?"

"Yes."

"And they will."

"Yes."

"That's cute, Josh. Let's go find Rumi. I have a plan."

hapter 21

"You make a very attractive woman," Rumi said from the comfort of his pit. "Did I tell you that my wife has passed on to her next incarnation and that I am alone?"

"Yeah, you mentioned that." He seemed to have given up on us getting his daughter back. "What happened to the rest of your family, anyway?"

"They drowned."

"I'm sorry. In the Ganges?"

"No, at home. It was the monsoon season. Little Vitra and I had gone to the market to buy some swill, and there was a sudden downpour. When we returned . . ." He shrugged.

"I don't mean to sound insensitive, Rumi, but there is a chance that your loss could have been caused by—oh, I don't know—perhaps the fact that you LIVE IN A FUCKING PIT!"

"That's not helping, Biff," Joshua said. "You said you had a plan?"

"Right. Rumi, am I correct in assuming that these pits, when someone is not living in them, are used for tanning hides?"

"Yes, it is work that only Untouchables may do."

"That would account for the lovely smell. I assume you use urine in the tanning process, right?"

"Yes, urine, mashed brains, and tea are the main ingredients."

"Show me the pit where the urine is condensed."

"The Rajneesh family is living there."

"That's okay, we'll bring them a present. Josh, do you have any lint in the bottom of your satchel?"

"What are you up to?"

"Alchemy," I said. "The subtle manipulation of the elements. Watch and learn."

When it was not being used, the urine pit was the home of the Rajneesh family, and they were more than happy to give us loads of the white crystals that covered the floor of their home. There were six in the family, father, mother, an almost grown daughter, and three little ones. Another little son had been taken for sacrifice at the festival of Kali. Like Rumi, and all the other Untouchables, the Rajneesh family looked more like skeletons mummified in brown leather than people. The Untouchable men went about the pits naked or wearing only a loincloth, and even the women were dressed in tatters that barely covered them—nothing as nice as the stylish sari that I had purchased in the market-place. Mr. Rajneesh commented that I was a very attractive woman and encouraged me to drop by after the next monsoon.

Joshua pounded chunks of the crystallized mineral into a fine white powder while Rumi and I collected charcoal from under the heated dying pit (a firebox had been gouged out of the stone under the pit) which the Untouchables used to render the flowers from the indigo shrub into fabric dye.

"I need brimstone, Rumi. Do you know what that is? A yellow stone that burns with a blue flame and gives off a smoke that smells like rotten eggs?"

"Oh yes, they sell it in the market as some sort of medicine."

I handed the Untouchable a silver coin. Go buy as much of it as you can carry."

"Oh my, this will be more than enough money. May I buy some salt with what is left?"

"Buy what you need with what's left over, just go."

Rumi skulked away and I went to help Joshua process the saltpeter.

The concept of abundance was an abstract one to the Untouchables, except as it pertained to two categories, suffering and animal parts. If you wanted decent food, shelter, or clean water, you would be sorely disappointed among the Untouchables, but if you were in the market for beaks, bones, teeth, hides, sinew, hooves, hair, gallstones, fins, feathers, ears, antlers, eyeballs, bladders, lips, nostrils, poop chutes, or any other inedible part of virtually any creature that walked on, swam under, or flew over the subcontinent of India, then the Untouchables were likely to have what you wanted lying around, conveniently stored beneath a thick blanket of black flies. In order to fashion the equipment I needed for my plan, I had to think in terms of animal parts. Fine unless you need, say, a dozen short swords, bows and arrows, and chain mail for thirty soldiers and all you have to work with is a stack of nostrils and three mismatched poop chutes. It was a challenge, but I made do. As Joshua moved among the Untouchables, surreptitiously healing their maladies, I barked out my orders.

"I need eight sheep bladders—fairly dry—two handfuls of crocodile teeth, two pieces of rawhide as long as my arms and half again as wide. No, I don't care what kind of animal, just not too ripe, if you can manage it. I need hair from an elephant's tail. I need firewood, or dried dung if you must, eight oxtails, a basket of wool, and a bucket of rendered fat."

And a hundred scrawny Untouchables stood there, eyes as big as saucers, just staring at me while Joshua moved among them, healing their wounds, sicknesses, and insanities, without any of them suspecting what was happening. (We'd agreed that this was the wisest tack to take, as we didn't want a bunch of healthy Untouchables athletically bounding through Kalighat proclaiming that they had been cured of all ills by a strange foreigner, thus attracting attention to us and spoiling my plan. On the other hand, neither could we stand there and watch these people suffer, knowing that we—well, Joshua—had the power to help them.) He'd also taken to poking one of them in the arm with his finger anytime anyone said the word "Untouchable." Later he told me that he just hated passing up the opportunity for palpable irony. I cringed when I saw Joshua touching the lepers among them, as if after all these years away from Israel a tiny Pharisee stood on my shoulder and screamed, "Unclean!"

"Well?" I said after I'd finished my orders. "Do you want your children back or not?"

"We don't have a bucket," said one woman.

"Or a basket," said another.

"Okay, fill some of the sheep bladders with rendered fat, and bundle the wool in some kind of hide. Now go, we don't have a lot of time."

And they all stood and looked at me. Big eyes. Sores healed. Parasites purged. They just looked at me. "Look, I know my Sanskrit isn't great, but you do know what I am asking?"

A young man stepped forward. "We do not want to anger Kali by depriving her of her sacrifices."

"You're kidding, right?"

"Kali is the bringer of destruction, without which there can be no rebirth. She is the remover of the bondage that ties us to the material world. If we anger her, she will deprive us of her divine destruction."

I looked at Joshua across the crowd. "Do you understand this?"

"Fear?" he said.

"Can you help?" I asked in Aramaic.

"I'm not good at fear," Joshua said in Hebrew.

I thought for a second as two hundred eyes pinned me to the sandstone on which I stood. I remembered the red-stained gashes on the wooden elephant statues at the altar of Kali. Death was their deliverance, was it?

"What is your name?" I asked the man who had stepped out of the crowd.

"Nagesh," he said.

"Stick out your tongue, Nagesh." He did, and I threw back the cloth that covered my head and loosened it around my neck. Then I touched his tongue.

"Destruction is a gift you value?"

"Yes," said Nagesh.

"Then I shall be the instrument of the goddess's gift." With that I pulled the black glass dagger from the sheath in my sash, held it up before the crowd. While Nagesh stood, passive, wide-eyed, I drove my thumb under his jaw, pushed his head back, and brought the dagger down across his throat. I lowered him to the ground as the red liquid spurted over the sandstone.

I stood and faced the crowd again, holding the dripping blade over my head. "You owe me, you ungrateful fucks! I have brought to your people the gift of Kali, now bring me what I ask for."

They moved really quickly for people who were on the edge of starvation.

Ａfter the Untouchables scattered to do my bidding, Joshua and I stood over the bloodstained body of Nagesh.

"That was fantastic," Joshua said. "Absolutely perfect."

"Thanks."

"Had you been practicing all that time we were in the monastery?

"You didn't see me push the pressure point in his neck then?"

"No, not at all."

"Gaspar's kung fu training. The rest, of course, was from Joy and Balthasar."

I bent over and opened Nagesh's mouth, then took the ying-yang vial from around my neck and put a drop of the antidote on the Untouchable's tongue.

"So he can hear us now, like when Joy poisoned you?" Joshua asked.

I pulled back one of Nagesh's eyelids and watched the pupil contract slowly in the sunlight. "No, I think he's still unconscious from me holding the pressure point. I didn't think the poison would work quickly enough. I could only get a drop of poison on my finger when I loosened my sari. I knew it would keep him down, I just wasn't sure it would put him down."

"Well, you are truly a magus, now, Biff. I'm impressed."

"Joshua, you healed a hundred people today. Half of them were probably dying. I did some sleight of hand."

My friend's enthusiasm was undeterred. "What's the red stuff, pomegranate juice? I can't figure out where you concealed it."

"No, actually I was going to ask you about that."

"What?"

I held my arm up and showed Joshua where I had slashed my own wrist (the source of blood for the show). I had been holding it against my leg and as soon as I removed the pressure the blood started spurting again. I sat down hard on the sandstone and my vision began to tunnel down to a pinpoint. "I was hoping you could help me out with this," I said before I fainted.

𝔜ou need to work on that part of the trick," Joshua said when I came to. "I might not always be around to fix your wrist." He was speaking Hebrew—that meant for my ears only.

I saw Joshua kneeling above me, then beyond him the sky was blotted out by curious brown faces. The recently murdered Nagesh was in the front of the crowd. "Hey, Nagesh, how'd the rebirth go?" I asked in Sanskrit.

"I must have strayed from my dharma in my last life," Nagesh said. "I have been reincarnated, once again, as an Untouchable. And I have the same ugly wife."

"You challenged master Levi who is called Biff," I said, "of course you didn't move up. You're lucky you're not a stink bug or something. See, destruction isn't the big favor you all thought it was."

"We brought the things you asked for."

I hopped to my feet feeling incredibly rested and energized. "Nice," I said to Joshua. "I feel like I just had one of those strong coffees you used to make at Balthasar's."

"I miss coffee," said Josh.

I looked at Nagesh, "I don't suppose you . . ."

"We have swill."

"Never mind," I said. Then I said one of those things that as a boy growing up in Galilee, you never think you'll hear yourself say: "Okay, Untouchables, bring me the sheep bladders!"

𝔯umi said that the goddess Kali was served by a host of black-skinned female demons, who sometimes during the feast would bring men to corners of the altar and copulate with them as blood rained down from the goddess's saw-tooth maw above.

"Okay, Josh, you're one of them," I said.

"What are you gonna be?"

"The goddess Kali, of course. You got to be God last time."

"What last time?"

"All of the last times." I turned to my intrepid minions. "Untouchables, paint him up!"

"They're not going to buy that a burr-headed Jewish kid is their goddess of destruction."

"O ye of little faith," I said.

Three hours later we were again crouched beneath a tree near the temple of Kali. We were both dressed as women, covered from head to toe by our saris, but I was looking much lumpier under mine due to Kali's extra arms and garland of severed heads, played tonight by painted sheep bladders filled with explosives and suspended around my neck by long strands of elephant tail hair. Any observers who might get close enough to notice my protrusions were quickly deterred by the smell coming off of Joshua and me. We had used the goo from the bottom of Rumi's pit to paint our bodies black. I didn't have the courage to ask what the substance had been in life, but if there was a place where they allowed vultures to ripen in the sun before pounding them into a smooth paste and mixing it with just the right amount of buffalo squat, then Rumi called it home. The Untouchables had also painted huge red rings around Joshua's eyes, fitted him with a ropey wig of oxtails, and affixed to his torso six pert little breasts fashioned from pitch.

"Stay away from any open flame. Your tits will go up like volcanos."

"Why did I have to have six and you only had to have two."

"Because I am the goddess and have to wear the garland of skulls and the extra arms."

We'd made my arms from rawhide, using my primary arms as models, then drying the molded arms in place over the fire. The women made a harness that held the extra arms in place under my own, then we painted the arms black with the same black goo. They were a little wobbly, but they were light and would look realistic enough in the dark.

It was still hours from the height of the ceremony at midnight, when the children would be hacked to death, but we wanted to be there in time to stop the revelers from cutting off the children's fingers if we could. Now, the wooden elephants were empty on their turntables, but the altar of Kali was already filling with gruesome tribute. The heads of a thousand goats had been laid on the altar before the goddess, and the blood ran slick over the stones and in the grooves that channeled it into large brass pots at the corners of the altar. Female acolytes carried the pots up a narrow ladder at the back of the great statue of Kali, then dumped them through some sort of reservoir that fed it through the goddess's jaws. Below, by torchlight, worshipers danced in the sticky shower as the blood flowed down upon them.

"Look, those women are dressed like me," Joshua said. "Except they only have two breasts each."

"Technically, they're not dressed, they're painted. You make a very attractive female demon, Josh. Did I tell you that?"

"This isn't going to work."

"Of course it's going to work."

I guessed that there were already ten thousand worshipers in the temple square, dancing, chanting, and beating drums. A procession of thirty men came down the main boulevard, each carrying a basket under his arm. As they reached the altar, each man dumped the contents of the basket over the rows of bloody goat heads.

"What are those?" Joshua asked.

"Those are exactly what you think they are."

"They're not the heads of the children?"

"No, I think those are the heads of strangers who happened down the road we were on before Rumi came along to pull us into the grass."

After the severed heads were dispersed across the altar, the female acolytes came out of the crowd dragging the headless corpse of a man, which they laid on the steps leading to the altar. Each one mimed having intercourse with the corpse, then rubbed their genitalia against the bloody stump of its neck before dancing away, blood and ochre dripping down the insides of their thighs.

"There's sort of a theme developing here," I said.

"I think I'm going to be sick," Joshua said.

"Mindful breath," I said, using one of the phrases that Gaspar was always barking at us when we were learning meditation. I knew that if Joshua could stay with the yeti for days at a time without freezing to death, he could certainly conjure up the bodily control to keep from throwing up. The sheer magnitude of the carnage was all that was keeping me from vomiting. It was as if the atrocity of the whole scene couldn't fit in my mind all at once, so I could only see just enough for my sanity and my stomach to remain intact.

A shout went up in the crowd now and I could see a torch-lit sedan chair being carried above the heads of the worshipers. On it reclined a half-naked man with a tiger skin wrapped around his hips, his skin painted light gray with ashes. His hair was plaited with grease and he wore the bones of a human hand as a skullcap. Around his neck hung a necklace of human skulls.

"High priest," I said.

"They aren't even going to notice you, Biff. How can you even get their attention after they've seen all this?"

"They haven't seen what I'm going to show them."

As the sedan chair emerged from the crowd in front of the altar, we could see a procession following it: tied to the back of the sedan chair was a line of naked children, most of them not more than five or six, their hands tied together, a less ornately dressed priest on either side of them to steady them. The priests began to untie the children and take them to the great wooden elephants lining the boulevard. Here and there in the crowd I could see people beginning to brandish edged weapons: short swords, axes, and the long-bladed spears Joshua and I had seen over the elephant grass. The high priest was sitting on the headless corpse, shouting a poem about the divine release of Kali's destruction or something.

"Here we go," I said, pulling the black glass dagger from under my sari. "Take this."

Joshua looked at the blade shimmering in the torchlight. "I won't kill anyone," he said. Tears were streaming down his cheeks, drawing long red lines through the black and if anything making him look more fierce.

"That's fine, but you'll need to cut them loose."

"Right." He took the knife from me.

"Josh, you know what's coming. You've seen it before. Nobody else here has, especially those kids. You can't carry all of them, so they have to have enough of their wits about them to follow you. I know you can keep them from being afraid. Put your teeth in."

Joshua nodded and slipped the row of crocodile teeth attached to a piece of rawhide under his upper lip, leaving the teeth to protrude like fangs. I put in my own false fangs, then ran into the dark to circle the crowd.

As I approached the rear of the altar I pulled the special torch I'd made from under my girdle of human hands. (Actually my girdle of human hands was made of dried goat's udders stuffed with straw, but the Untouchable women had done a pretty good job as long as no one bothered to count fingers.) Through Kali's stone legs I could see the priests tying each of the children on the trunk of a wooden elephant. As soon as the bonds were tight, each priest drew a bronze blade and held it aloft, ready to strike off a finger as soon as the high priest gave the signal.

I struck the tip of my torch on the edge of the altar, screamed for all I was worth, then threw my sari off and ran up the steps as the torch burst into dazzling blue flame that trailed sparks behind me as I ran. I hopped across the array of goat heads and stood between the legs of the statue of Kali, my torch held aloft in one hand, one of my severed heads swinging by the hair in the other.

"I am Kali," I screamed. "Fear me!" It came out sort of mumbled through my fake teeth.

Some of the drums stopped and the high priest turned around and looked at me, more because of the bright light of the torch than my fierce proclamation.

"I am Kali," I shouted again. "Goddess of destruction and all this disgusting crap you have here!" They weren't getting it. The priest signaled for the other priests to come around me from the sides. Some of the female acolytes were already trying to make their way across the dance floor of decapitations toward me.

"I mean it. Bow down to me!" The priests charged on. I did have the crowd's attention, though unfortunately they weren't cowering in fear at my angry goddessness. I could see Joshua moving around the wooden elephants, the guarding priests having left their posts to come after me. "Really! I mean it!" Maybe it was the teeth. I spit them out toward the nearest of my attackers.

Running across a sea of slick, bloody heads is evidently a pretty difficult task. Not if you've spent the last six years of your life hopping from the top of one post to another, even in ice and snow, but for the run-of-the-mill homicidal priest, it's a tough row to hoe. The priests and acolytes were slipping and sliding among the goat and human heads, falling over each other, smacking into the feet of the statue, one even impaling himself on a goat's horn when he fell.

One of the priests was only a few feet away from me now, trying not to fall on his own blade as he crawled over the mess. "I will bring destruction . . . oh, fuck it," I said. I lit the fuse on the severed head I held in my hand, then swung it between my legs and tossed it in a steep arch over my head. It trailed sparks on its way into the black goddess's open maw, then disappeared.

I kicked the approaching priest in the jaw, then danced across the goat heads, leapt over the head of the high priest, and was halfway to Joshua at the first wooden elephant when Kali, with a deafening report, breathed fire out over the crowd and the top of her head blew off.

Finally, I had the crowd's attention. They were trampling each other to get away, but I had their attention. I stood in the middle of the boulevard, swinging my second severed head in a circle, waiting for the fuse to burn down before I let it sail over the heads of the receding crowd. It exploded in the air, sending a circle of flame across the sky and no doubt deafening some of the worshipers who were close.

Joshua had seven of the children around him, clinging to his legs as he moved to the next elephant. Several of the priests had recovered and were storming down the steps of the altar toward me, knives in hand. I pulled another head from my garland, lit the fuse, and held it out to them.

"Ah, ah, ah," I cautioned. "Kali. Goddess of destruction. Wrath et cetera."

At the sight of the sparking fuse they stopped and began to backpedal. "Now that's the sort of respect you should have shown before."

I started whirling the head by the hair and the priests lost all semblance of courage and turned and ran. I hurled the head back up the boulevard onto the altar, where it exploded, sending a spray of real severed goat heads in all directions.

"Josh! Duck! Goat heads!"

Joshua pushed the children to the ground and fell over them until the pieces settled. He glared at me a second, then went on to free the other children. I hurled three more heads into different directions and now the entire temple square was nearly deserted but for Joshua, the children, a few injured worshipers, and the dead. I had built the bombs without any shrapnel in them, so those who had been injured had been trampled in the panic and the dead were those who had already been sacrificed to Kali. I think we pulled it off without killing anyone.

As Joshua led the children down the wide boulevard and out of the temple square, I covered our exit, backing down the boulevard, my last explosive head swinging in one hand, my torch in the other. Once I saw that Joshua and the children were safely away, I lit the fuse, whirled the head around and let it fly toward the black goddess.

"Bitch," I said.

I was out of sight when it exploded.

Joshua and I got as far as a limestone cliff overlooking the Ganges before we had to stop to let the children rest. They were tired and hungry, but mostly they were hungry, and we had brought nothing for them to eat. At least, after

Joshua's touch, they weren't afraid, and that gave them some peace. Josh and I were too jangled to sleep, so we sat up as the children lay down on the rocks around us and snored like kittens. Joshua held Rumi's little daughter, Vitra, and before long her face was smeared with black paint from nuzzling his shoulder. All through the night, as he rocked the child, all I heard Joshua say was, "No more blood. No more blood."

At first light we could see thousands, no, tens of thousands of people gathering at the banks of the river, all dressed in white, except for a few old men who were naked. They moved into the water and stood facing east, heads raised in anticipation, dotting the river as far as the eye could see. As the sun became a molten fingernail of light on the horizon, the muddy surface of the river turned golden. The gold light reflected off its surface onto the buildings, the shanties, the trees, the palaces, making everything in sight, including the worshipers, appear to have been gilded. And worshipers they were, for we could hear their songs from where we sat, and although we could not discern the words, we could hear that these were the songs of God.

"Are those the same people from last night?" I said.

"They would have to be, wouldn't they?"

"I don't understand these people. I don't understand their religion. I don't understand how they think."

Joshua stood and watched the Indians bowing and singing to the dawn, looking occasionally to the face of the child that slept on his shoulder. "This is testament to the glory of God's creation, whether these people know it or not."

"How can you say that? The sacrifices to Kali, the way the Untouchables are treated. Whatever they might believe, in practice their religion is hideous."

"You're right. It's not right to condemn this child because she was not born a Brahman?"

"Of course not."

"Then is it right to condemn her because she is not born a Jew?"

"What do you mean?"

"A man who is born a gentile may not see the kingdom of God. Are we, as Hebrews, any different from them? The lambs at the temple on Passover? The wealth and power of the Sadducees while others go hungry? At least the Untouchables can reach their reward eventually, through karma and rebirth. We don't allow any gentile to do so."

"You can't compare what they do to God's law. We don't sacrifice human beings. We feed our poor, we take care of the sick."

"Unless the sick are unclean," Joshua said.

"But, Josh, we're the chosen. It's God's will."

"But is it right? He won't tell me what to do. So I'll say. And I say, no more."

"You're not just talking about eating bacon, are you?"

"Gautama the Buddha gave the way to people of all births to find the hand of God. With no blood sacrifice. Our doors have been marked with blood for too long, Biff."

"So that's what you think you're going to do? Bring God to everyone?"

"Yes. After a nap."

"Of course, I meant after a nap."

Joshua held the little girl so I could see her face as she slept on his shoulder.

When the children awoke we led them back to their families at the pits, handing them into the arms of their mothers, who snatched each child away from us as if we were devils incarnate; they glared over their shoulders as they carried the babies back to their pits.

"Grateful bunch," I said.

"They are afraid that we've angered Kali. And we've brought them another hungry mouth."

"Still. Why did they help us if they didn't want their children back?"

"Because we told them what to do. That's what they do. What they are told. That's how the Brahmans keep them in line. If they do what they are told, then perhaps they will not be Untouchables next life."

"That's depressing."

Joshua nodded. We only had little Vitra to return to her father now, and I was sure that Rumi would be happy to see his daughter. His distress over losing her had basically been the reason he had saved our lives. As we came over the sandstone rise we could see that Rumi was not alone in his pit.

Rumi stood on his sitting rock, stark naked, sprinkling salt on his erect member as a large humpbacked cow, which nearly filled the rest of the pit, licked at the salt. Joshua held Vitra so she faced away from the pit, then backed away, as if he didn't want to disturb the moment of beefy intimacy.

"A cow, Rumi?" I exclaimed. "I thought you people had beliefs."

"That's not a cow, that's a bull," Joshua said.

"Oh, that's got to be your super-bonus abomination there. Where we come from whole cities get destroyed for that kind of thing, Rumi." I reached over and put my hand over Vitra's eyes. "Stay away from Daddy, honey, or you'll turn into a pillar of salt."

"But this is my wife, reincarnated."

"Oh, don't try that one on me, Rumi. For six years I lived in a Buddhist monastery where the only female company was a wild yak. I know from desperate."

Joshua grabbed my arm. "You didn't?"

"Relax, I'm just making a point. You're the Messiah here, Josh. What do you think?"

"I think we need to go to Tamil and find the third magus." He set Vitra down and Rumi quickly pulled up his loincloth as the child ran to him. "Go with God, Rumi," Joshua said.

"May Shiva watch over you, you heretics. Thank you for returning my daughter."

Joshua and I gathered up our clothes and satchels, then bought some rice in the market and set out for Tamil. We followed the Ganges south until we came to the sea, where Joshua and I washed the gore of Kali from our bodies.

We sat on the beach, letting the sun dry our skin as we picked pitch out of our chest hairs.

"You know, Josh," I said, as I fought a particularly stubborn gob of tar that had stuck in my armpit, "when you were leading those kids out of the temple square, and they were so little and weak, but none of them seemed afraid . . . well, it was sort of heartwarming."

"Yep, I love all the little children of the world, you know?"

"Really?"

He nodded. "Green and yellow, black and white."

"Good to know— Wait, green?"

"No, not green. I was just fuckin' with you."

Chapter 22

Tamil, as it turned out, was not a small town in southern India, but the whole southern peninsula, an area about five times the size of Israel, so looking for Melchior was akin to walking into Jerusalem on any given day and saying, "Hey, I'm looking for a Jewish guy, anyone seen him?" What we had going for us was that we knew Melchior's occupation, he was an ascetic holy man who lived a nearly solitary life somewhere along the coast and that he, like his brother Gaspar, had been the son of a prince. We found hundreds of different holy men, or yogis, most of them living in complete austerity in the forest or in caves, and usually they had twisted their bodies into some impossible posture. The first of these I saw was a yogi who lived in a lean-to on the side of a hill overlooking a small fishing village. He had his feet tucked behind his shoulders and his head seemed to be coming from the wrong end of his torso.

"Josh, look! That guy is trying to lick his own balls! Just like Bartholomew, the village idiot. These are my people, Josh. These are my people. I have found home."

Well, I hadn't really found home. The guy was just performing some sort of spiritual discipline (that's what "yoga" means in Sanskrit: discipline) and he wouldn't teach me because my intentions weren't pure or some claptrap. And he wasn't Melchior. It took six months and the last of our money and we both saw our twenty-fifth birthdays before we found Melchior reclining in a shallow stone nook in a cliff over the ocean. Seagulls were nesting at his feet.

He was a hairier version of his brother, which is to say he was slight, about sixty years old, and he wore a caste mark on his forehead. His hair and beard were long and white, shot with only a few stripes of black, and he had intense dark eyes that seemed to show no white at all. He wore only a loincloth and he was as thin as any of the Untouchables we had met in Kalighat.

Joshua and I clung to the side of the cliff while the guru untied from the human knot he'd gotten himself into. It was a slow process and we pretended to look at the seagulls and enjoy the view so as not to embarrass the holy man by seeming impatient. When he finally achieved a posture that did not appear as if it had been caused by being run over by an ox cart, Joshua said, "We've come from Israel. We were six years with your brother Gaspar in the monastery. I am—"

"I know who you are," said Melchior. His voice was melodic, and every sentence he spoke seemed as if he were beginning to recite a poem. "I recognize you from when I first saw you in Bethlehem."

"You do?"

"A man's self does not change, only his body. I see you grew out of the swaddling clothes."

"Yes, some time ago."

"Not sleeping in that manger anymore?"

"No."

"Some days I could go for a nice manger, some straw, maybe a blanket. Not that I need any of those luxuries, nor does anyone who is on the spiritual path, but still."

"I've come to learn from you," Joshua said. "I am to be a bodhisattva to my people and I'm not sure how to go about it."

"He's the Messiah," I said helpfully. "You know, *the* Messiah. You know, *Son of God.*"

"Yeah, *Son of God,*" Joshua said.

"Yeah," I said.

"Yeah," said Joshua.

"So what do you have for us?" I asked.

"And who are you?"

"Biff," I said.

"My friend," said Josh.

"Yeah, his friend," said I.

"And what do you seek?"

"Actually, I'd like to not have to hang on to this cliff a lot longer, my fingers are going numb."

"Yeah," said Josh.

"Yeah," said I.

"Find yourself a couple of nooks on the cliff. There are several empty. Yogis Ramata and Mahara recently moved on to their next rebirth."

"If you know where we can find some food we would be grateful," Joshua said. "It's been a long time since we've eaten. And we have no money."

"Time then for your first lesson, young Messiah. I am hungry as well. Bring me a grain of rice."

Joshua and I climbed across the cliff until we found two nooks, tiny caves really, that were close to each other and not so far above the beach that falling out would kill us. Each of our nooks had been gouged out of the solid rock and was just wide enough to lie down in, tall enough to sit up in, and deep enough to keep the rain off if it was falling straight down. Once we were settled, I dug through my satchel until I found three old grains of rice that had worked their way into a seam. I put them in my bowl, then carried the bowl in my teeth as I made my way back to Melchior's nook.

"I did not ask for a bowl," said Melchior. Joshua had already skirted the cliff and was sitting next to the yogi with his feet dangling over the edge. There was a seagull in his lap.

"Presentation is half the meal," I said, quoting something Joy had once said.

Melchior sniffed at the rice grains, then picked one up and held it between his bony fingertips.

"It's raw."

"Yes, it is."

"We can't eat it raw."

"Well, I would have served it up steaming with a grain of salt and a molecule of green onion if I'd known you wanted it that way." (Yeah, we had molecules in those days. Back off.)

"Very well, this will have to do." The holy man held the bowl with the rice grains in his lap, then closed his eyes. His breathing began to slow, and after a moment he appeared not to be breathing at all.

Josh and I waited. And looked at each other. And Melchior didn't move. His skeletal chest did not rise with breath. I was hungry and tired, but I waited. And the holy didn't move for almost an hour. Considering the recent nook vacancies on the cliff face, I was a little concerned that Melchior might have succumbed to some virulent yogi-killing epidemic.

"He dead?" I asked.

"Can't tell."

"Poke him."

"No, he's my teacher, a holy man. I'm not poking him."

"He's Untouchable."

Joshua couldn't resist the irony, he poked him. Instantly the yogi opened his eyes, pointed out to sea and screamed, "Look, a seagull!"

We looked. When we looked back the yogi was holding a full bowl of rice. "Here, go cook this."

So began Joshua's training to find what Melchior called the Divine Spark. The holy man was stern with me, but his patience with Joshua was infinite, and it was soon evident that by trying to be part of Joshua's training I was actually holding him back. So on our third morning living in the cliff, I took a long satisfying whiz over the side (and is there anything so satisfying as whizzing from a high place?) then climbed to the beach and headed into the nearest town to look for a job. Even if Melchior could make a meal out of three grains of rice, I'd scraped all the stray grains out of both my and Joshua's satchels. The yogi might be able to teach a guy to twist up and lick his own balls, but I couldn't see that there was much nourishment in it.

The name of the town was Nicobar, and it was about twice the size of Sepphoris in my homeland, perhaps twenty thousand people, most of whom seemed to make their living from the sea, either as fishermen, traders, or shipbuilders. After inquiring at only a few places, I realized that for once it wasn't my lack of skills that were keeping me from making a living, it was the caste system. It extended far deeper into the society than Rumi had told me. Subcastes of the larger four dictated that if you were born a stonecutter, your sons would be stonecutters, and their sons after them, and you were bound by your birth to never do any other job, regardless of how good or bad you were at it. If you were born a mourner, or a magician, you would die a mourner or a magician, and the only way you'd get out of death or magic was to die and be reincarnated as something else. The one skill that didn't seem to require a belonging to a caste was village idiot, but the Hindus seemed to thrust the more eccentric holy men into this role, so I found no openings there. I did have my bowl, and my experience at collecting alms for the monastery, so I tried my hand at begging, but every time I would get a good corner staked out, along would hop some one-legged blind guy to steal my action. By the late afternoon I had one tiny copper coin and the steward of the beggars guild had come along to warn me that if he caught me begging in Nicobar again, he'd see that I was admitted to the guild by the immediate removal of my arms and legs.

I bought a handful of rice at the market and was skulking out of town, my bowl before me and my head down, like a good monk, when I saw before me a most delicate set of toes, painted vermilion and followed by a dainty foot, an elegant ankle ajangle with copper bangles, an inviting calf decorated with hennaed designs as intricate as lace, and from there a bright skirt led me up the seam to a bejeweled navel, full breasts haltered in yellow silk, lips like plums, a nose as long and straight as a Roman statue's, and wide brown eyes, shaded in blue and lined to make them look the size of a tiger's. They drank me in.

"You're a stranger," she said. One long finger on my chest stopped me on the spot. I tried to hide my rice bowl in my shirt, and in a fabulous display of sleight of hand, ended up spilling the grains down my front.

"I'm from Galilee. In Israel."

"Never heard of it. Is it far?" She reached into my shirt and began to pick out the rice grains that had caught against my sash, running her fingernail along my stomach muscles and dropping the grains, one by one, into my bowl.

"Very far. I've come here with my friend to obtain sacred and ancient knowledge, that kind of thing."

"What is your name?"

"Biff—or Levi who is called Biff. We do that 'who is called' thing a lot in Israel."

"Follow me, Biff, I'll show you some ancient and sacred knowledge." She hooked her finger into my sash and walked into a nearby doorway, for some reason completely confident that I would follow.

Inside, amid piles of colorful pillows strewn about the floors and deep carpets the likes of which I hadn't seen since Balthasar's fortress, stood a carved camphorwood stand on which a large codex lay open. The book was bound in brass filigreed with copper and silver, and the pages were made of a parchment finer than I had ever seen.

The woman pushed me toward the book and left her hand on my back as I looked at the open page. The handwritten script was gilded and so ornate that I could barely make out the words, which didn't matter anyway, because it was the illustration that caught my eye. A man and a woman, nude, each perfect. The man had the woman facedown on a rug, her feet hooked over his shoulders, her arms held behind her as he entered her. I tried to call on my Buddhist training and discipline to keep from embarrassing myself in front of the strange woman.

"Ancient sacred wisdom," she said. "The book was a gift from a patron. The Kama Sutra, it's called. Thread of Desire."

"The Buddha said that desire is the source of all suffering," I said, feeling like the kung fu master that I knew I was.

"Do they look like they are suffering?"

"No." I began to tremble. I had been too long out of the company of women. Far too long.

"Would you like to try that? That suffering. With me?"

"Yes," I said. All the training, all the discipline, all the control, gone in a word.

"Do you have twenty rupees?"

"No."

"Then suffer," she said, and she stepped away.

"See, I told you."

Then she walked away, trailing the scent of sandalwood and roses behind her as she went to the door, her hips waving good-bye to me all the way across the room, the bangles on her arms and ankles ringing like tiny temple bells calling me to worship at her secret grotto. At the door she crooked a finger for me to follow her out, and I did.

"My name is Kashmir," she said. "Come back. I'll teach you ancient and sacred knowledge. One page at time. Twenty rupees each."

I took my stupid, pathetic, useless grains of rice and went back to my holy, stupid, useless, stupid male friends at the cliff.

Í brought some rice," I said to Joshua when I had climbed to my nook in the cliff. "Melchior can do his rice thing and we'll have enough for supper."

Josh was sitting on the shelf of his nook, his legs folded into the lotus position, hands in the mudra of the compassionate Buddha. "Melchior is teaching the path to the Divine Spark," Joshua said. "First you have to quiet the mind. That's why there's so much physical discipline, attention to breath, you have to be so completely in control that you can see past the illusion of your body."

"And how is that different from what we did in the monastery?"

"It's subtle, but it's different. There the mind would ride the wave of action, you could meditate while on the exercise posts, shooting arrows, fighting. There was no goal because there was no place to be but in the moment. Here, the goal is to see beyond the moment, to the soul. I think I'm getting a glimpse. I'm learning the postures. Melchior says that an accomplished yogi can pass his entire body through a hoop the size of his head."

"That's great, Josh. Useful. Now let me tell you about this woman I met." So I jumped over to Josh's ledge and began to tell him about my day, the woman, the Kama Sutra, and my opinion that this just might be the sort of ancient spiritual information a young Messiah might need.

"Her name is Kashmir, which means soft and expensive."

"But she's a prostitute, Biff."

"Prostitutes didn't bother you when you were making me help you learn about sex."

"They still don't bother me, it's just that you don't have any money."

"I got the feeling she likes me. I think maybe she'll do me pro bono, if you know what I mean?" I elbowed him in the ribs and winked.

"You mean *for the public good*. You forget your Latin? 'pro bono' means 'for the public good.' "

"Oh. I thought it meant something else. She's not going to do me for that."

"No, probably not," said Josh.

So the next day, first thing, I made may way back to Nicobar, determined to find a job, but by noon I found myself sitting on the street next to one of the blind, no-legged beggar kids. The street was packed with traders, haggling, making deals, exchanging cash for goods and services, and the kid was making a killing on the spare change. I was astounded at the amount in the kid's bowl; there must have been enough for three Kama Sutra pages right there. Not that I would steal from a blind kid.

"Look, Scooter, you look a little tired, you want me to watch the bowl while you take a break?"

"Get your hand out of there!" The kid caught my wrist (me, the kung fu master). He was quick. "I can tell what you're doing."

"Okay, fine, how about I show you some magic tricks. A little sleight of hand?"

"Oh, that'll be fun. I'm blind."

"Look, make up your mind."

"I'm going to call for the guild-master if you don't go away."

So I went away, despondent, defeated—not money enough to look at the edge of a page of the Kama Sutra. I skulked back to the cliffs, climbed up to my nook, and resolved to console myself with some cold rice left over from last night's supper. I opened my satchel and—

"Ahhh!" I leapt back. "Josh, what are you doing in there?" And there he was, his beatific old Joshua face with the sole of a foot on either side like big ears, a few vertebrae showing, one hand, my ying-yang amulet vial, and a jar of myrrh.

"Get out of there. How'd you get in there?"

I've mentioned our satchels before. The Greeks called them wallets, I guess you would call them duffel bags. They were made of leather, had a long strap we could throw over our shoulder, and I suppose if you'd asked me before, I would have said you could get a whole person in one if you had to, but not in one piece.

"Melchior taught me. It took me all morning to get in here. I thought I'd surprise you."

"Worked. Can you get out?"

"I don't think so. I think my hips are dislocated."

"Okay, where's my black glass knife?"

"It's at the bottom of the bag."

"Why did I know you were going to say that?"

"If you get me out I'll show you what else I learned. Melchior taught me how to multiply the rice."

A few minutes later Joshua and I were sitting on the ledge of my nook being bombarded by seagulls. The seagulls were attracted by the huge pile of cooked rice that lay between us on the ledge.

"That's the most amazing thing I've ever seen." Except that you really couldn't see it done. One minute you had a handful of rice, the next a bushel.

"Melchior says that it usually takes a lot longer for a yogi to learn to manipulate matter like this."

"How much longer?"

"Thirty, forty years. Most of the time they pass on before they learn."

"So this is like the healing. Part of your, uh, legacy?"

"This isn't like the healing, Biff. This can be taught, given the time."

I tossed a handful of rice into the air for some seagulls. "Tell you what. Melchior obviously doesn't like me, so he's not going to teach me anything. Let's trade knowledge."

Í brought rice to Joshua, had him multiply it, then sold the surplus in the market, and eventually I started trading fish instead of rice because I could raise twenty rupees in fewer trips. But before that, I asked Joshua to come to town with me. We went to the market, which was thick with traders, haggling, making deals, exchanging cash for goods and services, and over on the side, a blind and legless beggar was making a killing on the change.

"Scooter, I'd like you to meet my friend Joshua."

"My name's not Scooter," said the waif.

A half hour later Scooter could see again and miraculously his severed legs had been regenerated.

"You bastards!" said Scooter as he ran off on clean new pink feet.

"Go with God," Joshua said.

"Now I guess we'll see how easy it is to earn a living!" I shouted after the kid.

"He didn't seem very pleased," said Josh.

"He's only learning to express himself. Forget him, others are suffering as well."

And so it came to pass, that Joshua of Nazareth moved among them, healing them and performing miracles, and all the little blind children of Nicobar did see again, and all the lame did stand up and walk.

The little fuckers.

And so the exchange of knowledge began: what I was learning from Kashmir and the Kama Sutra for what Joshua was learning from the holy man Melchior. Each morning, before I went to town and before Joshua went to learn from his guru, we met on the beach and shared ideas and breakfast. Usually some rice and a fresh fish roasted over the fire. We'd gone long enough without eating animal flesh, we had decided, despite what Melchior and Gaspar tried to teach us.

"This ability to increase the bounty of food—imagine what we can do for the people of Israel, of the world."

"Yes, Josh, for it is written: 'Give a man a fish and he eats for a day, but teach a man to be a fish and his friends eat for a week.' "

"That is not written. Where is that written?"

"Amphibians five-seven."

"There's no friggin' Amphibians in the Bible."

"Plague of frogs. Ha! Gotcha!"

"How long's it been since you had a beating?"

"Please. You can't hit anyone, you have to be at total peace with all creation so you can find Sparky the Wonder Spirit."

"The Divine Spark."

"Whatever, th—ouch. Oh great, and what am I supposed to do, hit the Messiah back?"

"Turn the other cheek. Go ahead, turn it."

As I said, thus did the enlightened exchange of sacred and ancient teachings begin:

The Kama Sutra sayeth:

When a woman winds her small toes into the armpit hair of the man, and the man hops upon one foot, while supporting the woman on his lingam and a butter churn, then the achieved position is called "Rhinoceros Balancing a Jelly Donut."

"What's a jelly donut?" Joshua asked.

"I don't know. It's a Vedic term lost to antiquity, but it is said to have had great significance to the keepers of the law."

"Oh."

The Katha Upanishad sayeth:

Beyond the senses are the objects,
and beyond the objects is the mind.
Beyond the mind is pure reason,
and beyond reason is the Spirit in man.

"What's that supposed to mean?"

"You have to think about it, but it means that there's something eternal in everyone."

"That's swell. What's with the guys on the bed of nails?"

"A yogi must leave his body if he is going to experience the spiritual."

"So he leaves through the little holes in his back?"

"Let's start again."

The Kama Sutra sayeth:

When a man applies wax from the carnuba bean to a woman's yoni and buffs it with a lint-free cloth or a papyrus towel until a mirror shine is achieved, then it is call "Readying the Mongoose for Trade-in."

"Look, she sells me pieces of sheepskin parchment, and each time, after we're finished, I'm allowed to copy the drawings. I'm going to tie them all together and make my own codex."

"You did that? That looks like it hurts."

"This from a guy I had to break out of a wine jar with a hammer yesterday."

"Yeah, well, it wouldn't have happened if I'd remembered to grease my

shoulders like Melchior taught me." Joshua turned the drawing to get a different angle on it. "You're sure this doesn't hurt?"

"No, not if you keep your bottom away from the incense burners."

"No, I mean her."

"Oh, her. Well, who knows? I'll ask her."

> The Bhagavad Gita sayeth:
> I am impartial to all creatures,
> and no one is hateful or dear to me,
> but men devoted to me are in me,
> and I am in them.

"What's the Bhagavad Gita?"

"It's like a long poem in which the god Krishna advises the warrior Arjuna
as he drives his chariot into battle."

"Really, what's he advise him?"

"He advises him not to feel bad about killing the enemy, because they are
essentially already dead."

"You know what I'd advise him if I was a god? I'd advise him to get someone else to drive his friggin' chariot. The real God wouldn't be caught dead
driving a chariot."

"Well, you have to look at it as a parable, otherwise it sort of reeks of false
gods."

"Our people don't have good luck with false gods, Josh. They're—I don't
know—frowned upon. We get killed and enslaved when we mess with them."

"I'll be careful."

> The Kama Sutra sayeth:
> When a woman props herself up on the table and inhales the
> steam of the eucalyptus tea, while gargling a mixture of lemon, water,
> and honey, and the man takes the woman by the ears, and enters her
> from behind, while looking out the window at the girl across the
> street hanging out her laundry to dry, then the position is called "Dis-
> tracted Tiger Hacking Up a Fur Ball."

"I couldn't find that one in the book, so she dictated it to me from memory."

"Kashmir's quite the scholar."

"She had the sniffles, but agreed to my lesson anyway. I think she's falling for me."

"How could she not, you're a very charming fellow."

"Why, thank you, Josh."

"You're welcome, Biff."

"Okay, tell me about your little yoga thing."

> The Bhagavad Gita sayeth:
>> Just as the wide-moving wind
>> is constantly present in space,
>> so all creatures exist in me.
>> Understand it to be so!

"Is that the kind of advice you'd give someone who's riding into battle? You'd think Krishna would be saying stuff like, 'Look out, an arrow! Duck!' "

"You'd think," Joshua sighed.

> The Kama Sutra sayeth:
>> The position of "Rampant Monkey Collecting Coconuts" is achieved when a woman hooks her fingers into the man's nostrils and performs a hokey-pokey motion with her hips and the man, while firmly stroking the woman's uvula with his thumbs, swings his lingam around her yoni in a direction counter to that in which water swirls down a drain. (Water has been observed swirling down the drain in different directions in different places. This is a mystery, but a good rule of thumb for achieving Rampant Monkey is to just go in the direction counter to which your own personal drain swirls.)

"Your drawings are getting better," Joshua said. "In the first one I thought she had a tail."

"I'm using the calligraphy techniques we learned in the monastery, only using them to draw figures. Josh, are you sure it doesn't bother you, talking about this stuff when you'll never be allowed to do it?"

"No, it's interesting. It doesn't bother you when I talk about heaven, does it?"

"Should it?"

"Look, a seagull!"

The Katha Upanishad sayeth:
For a man who has known him,
the light of truth shines.
For one who has not known, there is darkness.
The wise who have seen him in every being
on leaving this life, attain life immortal.

"That's what you're looking for, huh, the Divine Spark thing?"
"It's not for me, Biff."
"Josh, I'm not a satchel of sand here. I didn't spend all of my time studying and meditating without getting some glimpse of the eternal."
"That's good to know."
"Of course it helps when angels show up and you do miracles and stuff too."
"Well, yes, I guess it would."
"But that's not a bad thing. We can use that when we get home."
"You have no idea what I'm talking about, do you?"
"Not a clue."

Our training went on for two years before I saw the sign that called us home. Life was slow, but pleasant there by the sea. Joshua became more efficient at multiplying food, and while he insisted on living an austere lifestyle so he could remain unattached to the material world, I was able to get a little money ahead. In addition to paying for my lessons, I was able to decorate my nook (just some erotic drawings, curtains, some silk cushions) and buy a few personal items such as a new satchel, an ink stone and a set of brushes, and an elephant.

I named the elephant Vana, which is Sanskrit for wind, and although she certainly earned her name, I regret it was not due to her blazing speed. Feeding Vana was not a difficulty with Joshua's ability to turn a handful of grass into a fodder farm, but no matter how hard Joshua tried to teach her yoga, she was not able to fit into my nook. (I consoled Joshua that it was probably the climb, and not his failure as a yoga guru that deterred Vana. "If she had fingers, Josh, she'd be snuggling up with me and seagulls right now.") Vana didn't like being on the beach when the tide came and washed sand between her toes, so she lived in a pasture just above the cliff. She did, however, love to swim, and some days rather than ride her on the beach all the way to Nicobar, I would have her swim into the harbor just under water, with only her trunk showing and me standing on her forehead. "Look, Kashmir, I'm walking on water! I'm walking on water!"

So eager was my erotic princess to share my embrace that rather than wonder at the spectacle as did the other townsfolk she could only reply:

"Park the elephant in back."

(The first few times she said it I thought she was referring to a Kama Sutra position that we had missed, pages stuck together perhaps, but it turned out such was not the case.)

Kashmir and I became quite close as my studies progressed. After we went through all the positions of the Kama Sutra twice, Kashmir was able to take things to the next level by introducing Tantric discipline into our lovemaking. So skillful did we become at the meditative art of coupling that even in the throes of passion, Kashmir was able to polish her jewelry, count her money, or even rinse out a few delicates. I myself had so mastered the discipline of controlled ejaculation that often I was halfway home before release was at last achieved.

It was on my way home from Kashmir's—as Vana and I were cutting through the market so that I could show my friends the ex-beggar boys the possible rewards for the man of discipline and character (to wit: I had an elephant and they did not)—that I saw, outlined on the wall of a temple of Vishnu, a dirty water stain, caused by condensation, mold, and wind-blown dust, which described the face of my best friend's mother, Mary.

Yeah, she does that," said Joshua, when I swung over the edge of his nook and announced the news. He and Melchior had been meditating and the old man, as usual, appeared to be dead. "She used to do it all the time when we were kids. She sent James and me running all over the place washing down walls before people saw. Sometimes her face would appear in a pattern of water drops in the dust, or the peelings from grapes would fall just so in a pattern after being taken out of the wine press. Usually it was walls."

"You never told me that."

"I couldn't tell you. The way you idolized her, you'd have been turning the pictures into shrines."

"So they were naked pictures?"

Melchior cleared his throat and we both looked at him. "Joshua, either your mother or God has sent you a message. It doesn't matter who sent it, the message is the same. It is time for you to go home."

We would be leaving for the north in the morning, and Nicobar was south, so I left Joshua to pack our things on Vana while I walked into town to break the news to Kashmir.

"Oh my," she said, "all the way back to Galilee. Do you have money for the journey?"

"A little."

"But not with you?"

"No."

"Well, okay. Bye."

I could swear I saw a tear in her eye as she closed the door.

The next morning, with Vana loaded with my drawings and art supplies; my cushions, curtains, and rugs; my brass coffeepot, my tea ball, and my incense burner; my pair of breeding mongooses (mongeese?), their bamboo cage, my drum set, and my umbrella; my silk robe, my sun hat, my rain hat, my collection of carved erotic figurines, and Joshua's bowl, we gathered on the beach to say good-bye. Melchior stood before us in his loincloth, the wind whipping the tails of his white beard and hair around his face like fierce clouds. There was no sadness in his face, but then, he had endeavored his entire life to detach from the material world, which we were part of. He'd already done this a long time ago.

Joshua made as if to embrace the old man, then instead just poked him in the shoulder. Once and only once, I saw Melchior smile. "But you haven't taught me everything I need to know," Josh said.

"You're right, I have taught you nothing. I could teach you nothing. Everything that you needed to know was already there. You simply needed the word for it. Some need Kali and Shiva to destroy the world so they may see past the illusion to divinity in them, others need Krishna to drive them to the place where they may perceive what is eternal in them. Others may perceive the Divine Spark in themselves only by realizing through enlightenment that the spark resides in all things, and in that they find kinship. But because the Divine Spark resides in all, does not mean that all will discover it. Your dharma is not to learn, Joshua, but to teach."

"How will I teach my people about the Divine Spark? Before you answer, remember we're talking about Biff too."

"You must only find the right word. The Divine Spark is infinite, the path to find it is not. The beginning of the path is the word."

"Is that why you and Balthasar and Gaspar followed the star? To find the path to the Divine Spark in all men? The same reason that I came to find you?"

"We were seekers. You are that which is sought, Joshua. You are the source. The end is divinity, in the beginning is the word. You are the word."

Part V

Lamb

I am light, now I fly, now I see
myself beneath myself, now a god dances
through me.

FRIEDRICH NIETZSCHE

Chapter 23

We rode Vana north toward the Silk Road, skirting the great Indian desert that had almost killed Alexander the Great's forces as they returned to Persia after conquering half of the known world, three centuries before. Although it would have saved a month to cut through the desert, Joshua was not confident about his ability to conjure enough water for Vana. A man should learn the lessons of history, and although I insisted that Alexander's men had probably been tired from all that conquering, while Josh and I had basically been sitting around at the beach for two years, he insisted we take the less hostile route through Delhi, and north into what is now Pakistan until we joined the Silk Road once again.

A little ways down the Silk Road I thought we received another message from Mary. We had stopped to have a short rest. When we resumed the journey, Vana happened to walk over where she had just done her business and the pile was pressed into the perfect likeness of a woman's face, dark poo against the light gray dust.

"Look, Josh, there's another message from your mother."

Josh glanced and looked away. "That's not my mother."

"But look, in the elephant poop, it's a woman's face."

"I know, but it's not my mother. It's distorted because of the medium. It doesn't even look like her. Look at the eyes."

I had to climb to the back of the elephant to get another angle on it. He was right, it wasn't his mother. "I guess you're right. The medium obscured the message."

"That's what I'm saying."

"I'll bet it looks like someone's mom, though."

With the detour around the desert, we were nearly two months getting to Kabul. Although Vana was an intrepid walker, as I have mentioned, she was a less than agile climber, so we often had to take long detours to get her through the mountains of Afghanistan. Josh and I both knew that we could not take her into the high, rocky desert once we passed Kabul, so we agreed to leave the elephant with Joy, if we could find the erstwhile courtesan.

Once in Kabul we asked around the market for any news of a Chinese woman named Tiny Feet of the Divine Dance of Joyous Orgasm, but no one had heard of her, nor had they seen a woman simply named Joy. After a full day of searching, Joshua and I were about to abandon the search for our friend when I remembered something she had once said to me. I asked a local tea seller.

"Is there a woman who lives around here, a very rich woman perhaps, who calls herself the Dragon Lady or something like that?"

"Oh, yes sir," the fellow said, and he shuddered as he spoke, as if a bug had run across his neck. "She is called the Cruel and Accursed Dragon Princess."

nice name," I said to Joy as we rode through the massive stone gates into the courtyard of her palace.

"A woman alone, it helps to have your reputation precede you," said the Cruel and Accursed Dragon Princess. She looked almost exactly as she had almost nine years ago when we had left, except perhaps that she wore a little more jewelry. She was petite, and delicate, and beautiful. She wore a white silk robe embroidered with dragons and her blue-black hair hung down her back almost to her knees, held in place by a single silver band that just kept it from sweeping around her shoulders when she turned. "Nice elephant," she added.

"She's a present," Joshua said.

"She's lovely."

"Do you have a couple of camels you can spare, Joy?" I asked.

"Oh, Biff, I had really hoped that you two would sleep with me tonight."

"Well, I'd love to, but Josh is still sworn off the muffin."

"Young men? I have a number of man-boys I keep around for, well, you know."

"Not those either," Joshua said.

"Oh Joshua, my poor little Messiah. I'll bet no one made you Chinese food for your birthday this year either?"

"We had rice," Joshua said.

"Well, we'll see what the Accursed Dragon Princess can do to make up for that," said Joy.

We climbed down from the elephant and exchanged hugs with our old friend, then a stern guard in bronze chain mail led Vana away to the stables and four guards with spears flanked us as Joy led us into the main house.

"A woman alone?" I said, looking at the guards that seemed to stand at every doorway.

"In my heart, darling," Joy said. "These aren't friends, family, or lovers, these are employees."

"Is that the Accursed part of your new title?" Joshua said.

"I could drop it, just be the Cruel Dragon Princess, if you two want to stay on."

"We can't. We've been called home."

Joy nodded dolefully and led us into the library (filled with Balthasar's old books), where coffee was served by young men and women who Joy had obviously brought from China. I thought of all the girls, my friends and my lovers, who had been killed by the demon so long ago, and swallowed my coffee around a lump in my throat.

Joshua was as excited as I had seen him in a long time. It might have been the coffee. "You won't believe the wonderful things I've learned since I left here, Joy. About being the agent of change (change is at the root of belief, you know), and about compassion for everyone because everyone is part of another, and most important, that there is a bit of God in each of us—in India they call it the Divine Spark."

He rambled on like that for an hour, and eventually my melancholy passed and I was infected by Joshua's enthusiasm for the things he had learned from the Magi.

"Yes," I added, "and Josh can climb inside a standard-size wine amphora. You have to bust him out with a hammer, but it's interesting to watch."

"And you, Biff?" Joy asked, smiling into her cup.

"Well, after supper I'll show you a little something I like to call Water Buffalo Teasing the Seeds out of the Pomegranate."

"That sounds—"

"Don't worry, it's not that hard to learn. I have pictures."

We were four days at Joy's palace, enjoying comfort, food, and drink such as we hadn't experienced since we'd last seen her. I could have stayed forever, but on the morning of the fifth day Joshua stood at the entrance to Joy's bedchamber, his satchel slung over his shoulder. He didn't say a word. He didn't have to. We shared breakfast with Joy and she met us at the gate to say good-bye.

"Thanks for the elephant," she said.

"Thanks for the camels," Joshua said.

"Thanks for the sex book," Joy said.

"Thanks for the sex," I said.

"Oh, I forgot, you owe me a hundred rupees," Joy said. I had told her about Kashmir. The Cruel and Accursed Dragon Princess grinned at me. "Just kidding. Be well, my friend. Keep that amulet I gave you and remember me, huh?"

"Of course." I kissed her and climbed on my camel's back, then coaxed him to his feet.

Joy embraced Joshua and kissed him on the lips, hard and long. He didn't seem to be trying to push her away.

"Hey, we had better go, Josh," I said.

Joy held the Messiah at arm's length and said. "You are always welcome here, you know that?"

Josh nodded, then climbed on his camel. "Go with God, Joy," he said. As we rode through the gates of the palace the guards shot fire arrows that trailed long tails of sparks over us until they exploded above the road ahead: Joy's last good-bye to us, a tribute to the friendship and arcane knowledge we had all shared. It scared the bejeezus out of the camels.

After we had been on the road awhile, Joshua asked, "Did you say good-bye to Vana?"

"I intended to, but when I went to the stable she was practicing her yoga and I didn't want to disturb her."

"No kidding?"

"Really, she was sitting in one of the postures you taught her."

Joshua smiled. It didn't hurt anything for him to believe that.

The journey on the Silk Road through the high deserts took us over a month, but it was fairly uneventful, except for one attack by a small group of bandits. When I caught the first two spears they flung at me and flung them right back, wounding the two who had thrown them, they turned and ran. The weather was mild, or as mild as one can expect in a deadly and brutal desert, but by now Joshua and I had traveled so much in this sort of harsh country that there was little that affected us. Just before we reached Antioch, however, a sandstorm whipped up out of the desert that left us hiding between our camels for two days, breathing through our shirts and washing the mud out of our mouths every time we took a drink. The storm settled enough to travel, and we were at a veritable gallop in the streets of Antioch when Joshua located an inn by impacting with its sign on his forehead. He was knocked back off his camel and sat up in the street with blood streaming down his face.

"Are you hurt badly?" I asked, kneeling beside him. I could barely see in the driving dust.

Joshua looked at the blood on his hands where he had touched his forehead. "I don't know. It doesn't hurt that badly, but I can't tell."

"Inside," I said, helping him to his feet and through the door of the inn.

"Shut the door," the innkeeper shouted as the wind whipped through the room. "Were you born in a barn?"

"Yeah," said Joshua.

"He was," I said. "Angels on the roof, though."

"Shut the damn door," said the innkeeper.

I left Joshua sitting there by the door while I went out and found shelter for the camels. When I returned Joshua was wiping his face with a linen cloth that someone had handed to him. A couple of men stood over him, eager to help. I handed the cloth to one of them and examined Josh's wounds. "You'll live. A big bump and two cuts, but you'll live. You can't do the healing thing on—"

Joshua shook his head.

"Hey, look at this," one of the travelers who had helped Joshua said, holding up the piece of linen Joshua had used to wipe his face. The dust and blood from Josh's face had left a perfect likeness on the linen, even handprints where he'd gotten blood from his head wound. "Can I keep this?" the fellow said. He was speaking Latin, but with a strange accent.

"Sure," I said. "Where are you fellahs from?"

"We're from the Ligurian tribe, from the territories north of Rome. A city on the Po river called Turin. Have you heard of it?"

"No, I haven't. You know, you fellahs can do what you want with that cloth, but out on my camel I've got some erotic drawings from the East that are going to be worth something someday. I can let you have them for a very fair price."

The Turinians went off holding their pathetic swath of muddy cloth like it was some kind of holy relic. Ignorant bastards wouldn't know art if you nailed them to it. I bandaged Joshua's wounds and we checked into the inn for the night.

In the morning we decided to keep our camels and take the land route home through Damascus. As we passed out of the gates of Damascus on the final leg home, Joshua started to worry.

"I'm not ready to be the Messiah, Biff. If I'm being called home to lead our people I don't even know where to start. I understand the things I want to teach, but I don't have the words yet. Melchior was right about that. Before anything you have to have the word."

"Well it's not just going to come to you in a flash here on the Damascus road, Josh. That sort of thing doesn't happen. You're obviously supposed to learn what you need to know in its own time. To everything a season, yada, yada, yada . . ."

"My father could have made learning all this easier. He could have just told me what I was supposed to do."

"I wonder how Maggie's doing. You think she got fat?"

"I'm trying to talk about God here, about the Divine Spark, about bringing the kingdom to our people."

"I know you are, so am I. Do you want to do all of that without help?"

"I guess not."

"Well, that's why I was thinking about Maggie. She was smarter than us before we left, she's probably smarter than us now."

"She was smart, wasn't she? She wanted to be a fisherman," said Josh, grinning. I could tell that the thought of seeing Maggie tickled him.

"You can't tell her about all the whores, Josh."

"I won't."

"Or Joy and the girls. Or the old woman with no teeth."

"I won't tell her about any of them, not even the yak."

"There was nothing with the yak. The yak and I weren't even on speaking terms."

"You know, she probably has a dozen children by now."

"I know." I sighed. "They should be mine."

"And mine." Joshua sighed back.

I looked at him as he rode beside me in a sea of gently loping camel waves. He was staring off at the horizon, looking forlorn. "Yours and mine? You think they should be yours *and* mine?"

"Sure, why not. You know I love all the little—"

"You are such a doofus sometimes."

"Do you think she'll remember us? I mean, how we all were back then?"

I thought about it and shuddered. "I hope not."

No sooner did we pass into Galilee than we began to hear about what John the Baptist was doing in Judea.

"Hundreds have followed him into the desert," we heard in Gischala.

"Some say he is the Messiah," one man told us in Baca.

"Herod is afraid of him," said a woman in Cana.

"He's another crazy holy man," said a Roman soldier in Sepphoris. "The Jews breed them like rabbits. I hear he drowns anyone who doesn't agree with him. First sensible idea I've heard since I was sent to this accursed territory."

"May I have your name, soldier?" I asked.

"Caius Junius, of the Sixth Legion."

"Thank you. We'll keep you in mind." To Josh I said, "Caius Junius: front of the line when we start shoving Romans out of the kingdom into the fiery abyss."

"What did you say?" said the Roman.

"No, no, don't thank me, you earned it. Right at the front of the line you go, Caius."

"Biff!" Josh barked, and once he had my attention he whispered, "Try not to get us thrown into prison before we get home, please."

I nodded and waved to the legionnaire as we rode away. "Just crazy Jew talk. Pay no attention. *Whimper Fidelis*," I said.

"We have to find John after we see our families," Joshua said.

"Do you think that he's really claiming to be the Messiah?"

"No, but it sounds like he knows how to get the word out."

We rode into Nazareth a half hour later.

I suppose we expected more upon our arrival. Cheering maybe, little children running at our heels begging for tales of our great adventures, tears and laughter, kisses and hugs, strong shoulders to bear the conquering heroes through the streets. What we'd forgotten was that while we were traveling, having adventures, and experiencing wonders, the people of Nazareth had been living through the same old day-to-day crap—a lot of days had passed, and a lot of crap. When we rode up to Joshua's old house, his brother James was working outside under the awning, shaving a piece of olive wood into a strut for a camel saddle. I knew it was James the moment I saw him. He had Joshua's narrow hooked nose and wide eyes, but his face was more weathered than Josh's, and his body heavier with muscle. He looked ten years older than Joshua rather than the two years younger that he was.

He put down his spoke shave and stepped out in the sunlight, holding up a hand to shield his eyes.

"Joshua?"

Joshua tapped his camel on the back of his knees with the long riding crop and the beast lowered him to the ground.

"James!" Joshua climbed off the camel and went to his brother, his arms out as if to embrace him, but James stepped back.

"I'll go tell mother that her favorite son has returned." James turned away and I saw the tears literally shoot out of Joshua's eyes into the dust.

"James," Joshua was pleading. "I didn't know. When?"

James turned and looked his half brother in the eye. There was no pity there, no grief, just anger. "Two months ago, Joshua. Joseph died two months ago. He asked for you."

"I didn't know," Joshua said, still holding his arms out for the embrace that wasn't going to come.

"Go inside. Mother has been waiting for you. She starts every morning wondering if this is the day you'll return. Go inside." He turned away as Joshua went past him into the house, then James looked up at me. "The last thing he said was 'Tell the bastard I love him.' "

"The bastard?" I said as I coaxed my camel to let me down.

"That's what he always called Joshua. 'I wonder how the bastard is doing. I wonder where the bastard is today?' Always talking about the bastard. And mother yammering on always about how Joshua did this, and Joshua did that, and what great things Joshua would do when he returned. And all the while I'm the one looking out for my brothers and sisters, taking care of them when Father got sick, taking care of my own family. Still, was there any thanks? A kind word? No, I was doing nothing more than paving Joshua's road. You have no idea what it's like to always be second to Joshua."

"Really," I said. "You'll have to tell me about that sometime," I said. "Tell Josh if he needs me I'll be at my father's house. My father *is* still alive, isn't he?"

"Yes, and your mother too."

"Oh good, I didn't want to put one of my brother's through breaking the painful news." I turned and led my camel away.

"Go with God, Levi," James said.

I turned. "James, it is written, 'To the work you are entitled, but not the fruits thereof.' "

"I've never heard that. Where is that written?"

"In the Bhagavad Gita, James. It's a long poem about going into battle, and this warrior's god tells him not to worry about killing his kinsmen in battle, because they are already dead, they just don't know it yet. I don't know what made me think of it."

my father hugged me until I thought he'd broken my ribs, then he handed me off to my mother, who did the same until she seemed to come to her senses, then she began to cuff me about the head and shoulders with her sandal, which she had whipped off with surprising speed and dexterity for a woman her age.

"Seventeen years you're gone and you couldn't write?"

"You don't know how to read."

"So you couldn't send word, smart mouth?"

I fended off the blows by directing their energy away from me, as I had been taught at the monastery, and soon two small boys who I didn't recognize were catching the brunt of the beating. Fearing lawsuits from small strangers, I caught my mother's arms and hugged them to her sides as I looked at my father, nodded to the two little ones, and raised my eyebrows as if to say, *Who are the squirts?*

"Those are your brothers, Moses and Japeth," my father said. "Moses is six and Japeth is five."

The little guys grinned. Both were missing front teeth, probably sacrificed to the squirming harpy I was currently holding at bay. My father beamed as if to say, *I can still build the aquaduct—lay a little pipe, if you know what I mean— when I need to.*

I scowled as if to say, *Look, I was barely able to hold on to my respect for you when I found out what you did to make the first three of us; these little fellows are only evidence that you've no memory for suffering.*

"Mother, if I let you go will you calm down?" I looked over her shoulder at Japeth and Moses. "I used to tell people she was besought by a demon, do you guys do that?" I winked at them.

They giggled as if to say, *Please, end our suffering, kill us, kill us now, or kill this bitch that plagues us like the torments of Job.* Okay, maybe I was just imagining that's what they were saying. Maybe they were just giggling.

I let my mother go and she backed off. "Japeth, Moses," mother said, "come meet Biff. You've heard your father and me talk about our oldest disappointment—well, this is him. Now run and get your other brothers, I'll go fix something nice."

My brothers Shem and Lucius brought their families and joined us for dinner and we all lay around the table as mother served us something nice, I'm not sure what it was. (I know I've said that I was the oldest of three brothers, and obviously, with the squirts, it was five, but dammit, by the time I met Japeth and Moses I was too old to have the time to torment them, so they never really paid their dues as brothers. They were more like, oh, pets.) "Mother, I've brought you a gift from the East," I said, running out to the camel to retrieve a package.

"What is it?"

"It's a breeding mongoose," I said, tapping on the cage. The little scamp tried to bite the pad off of my finger.

"But there's only one."

"Well, there were two, but one escaped, so now there's one. They'll attack a snake ten times their size."

"It looks like a rat."

I lowered my voice and whispered conspiratorially, "In India, the woman train them to sit on their heads like hats. Very fashionable. Of course the fad hasn't reached Galilee yet, but in Antioch, no self-respecting woman will go out of the house without wearing a mongoose."

"Really," said Mother, looking at the mongoose in a new light. She took the cage and stowed it gently away in the corner, as if it contained a delicate egg, rather than a vicious miniature of herself. "So," said Mother, waving to her two daughters-in law and the half-dozen grandchildren that loitered near the table, "your brothers married and gave me grandchildren."

"I'm happy for them, Mother."

Shem and Lucius hid their grins behind a crust of flatbread the same way they did when we were little and mother was giving me hell.

"All the places you traveled, you never met a nice girl you could settle down with?"

"No, Mother."

"You can marry a gentile, you know. It would break my heart, but why did the tribes almost wipe out the Benjamites if it wasn't so a desperate boy could marry a gentile if he needs to? Not a Samaritan, but, you know, some other gentile. If you have to."

"Thanks, Mother, I'll keep that in mind."

Mother pretended to find some lint or something on my collar, which she picked at while she said, "So your friend Joshua never married either? You heard about his little sister Miriam, didn't you?" Here her voice went to a conspiratorial whisper. "Started wearing men's clothes and ran off to the island of Lesbos." Back to normal nudging tone. "That's Greek, you know? You boys didn't go to Greece on your travels, did you?"

"No, Mother, I really have to go."

I tried to stand and she grabbed me. "It's because your father has a Greek name, isn't it? I told you, Alphaeus, change the name, but you said you were proud of it. Well, I hope you're proud of it now. What's next, Lucius here will start hanging Jews on crosses like the other Romans?"

"I'm not a Roman, Mother," Lucius said wearily. "Lots of good Jews have Latin names."

"Not that it matters, Mother, but how do you think they get more Greeks?"

To my mother's credit, she stopped for a second to think. I used the lull to escape.

"Nice to see you guys." I nodded to all of my relatives, old and new. "I'll come by and visit before I go. I have to go check on Joshua." And I was out the door.

I threw the door open at Joshua's old house without even knocking, nearly coldcocking Joshua's brother Judah in the process. "Josh, you've got to bring the kingdom soon or I'm going to have to kill my mother."

"She still plagued by demons?" asked Judah, who looked exactly as he had when he was four, except for the beard and the receding hairline, but he was as wide-eyed and goofy of smile as he had ever been.

"No, I was just being hopeful when I used to say that."

"Will you join us for supper?" said Mary. Thank God she had aged: gone a little thicker around the hips and waist, developed some lines at the corner of her eyes and mouth. Now she was just the second or third most beautiful creature on earth.

"Love to," I said.

James must have been home with his wife and children, as I guessed were the other sisters and brothers, except for Miriam, and I'd already been apprised of her whereabouts. At the table it was only Mary, Joshua, Judah, his pretty wife, Ruth, and two little redheaded girls that looked like their mother.

I expressed my condolences for the family's loss, and Joshua filled me in on the timing of events. About the time that I spotted Mary's portrait on the temple wall in Nicobar, Joseph had taken ill with some disease of the water. He started peeing blood, and in a week he was bedridden. He lingered only a week longer before he died. He'd been buried for two months now. I looked at Joshua as Mary related this part of the story and he shook his head, meaning, *too long in the grave, there's nothing I can do*. Mary had known nothing about a message calling us home.

"Even if you two had only been in Damascus you'd have been lucky to get here in time. He went so fast." She was strong, had recovered somewhat from the loss, but Joshua appeared to still be in shock.

"You have to go find Joshua's cousin John," Mary said. "He's been preaching about the coming of the kingdom, of preparing the way for the Messiah."

"We've heard," I said.

"I'll stay here with you, Mother," Joshua said. "James is right, I have responsibilities. I've shirked them too long."

Mary touched her son's face and looked in his eyes. "You will leave in the morning and you will find John the Baptist in Judea and you will do what God has ordained you do since he placed you in my womb. Your responsibilities are not to a bitter brother or an old woman."

Joshua looked at me. "Can you leave in the morning? I know it's soon after being gone so long."

"Actually, I thought I'd stay, Josh. Your mother needs someone to look after her, and she's still a relatively attractive woman. I mean, a guy could do worse."

Judah aspirated an olive pit and began coughing furiously until Joshua pounded him on the back and the pit shot across the room, leaving Judah gasping and staring at me through watery red eyes.

I put my hand on Joshua and Judah's shoulders. "I think I can learn to love you both as sons." I looked at the pretty but shy Ruth, who was tending the little girls. "And you, Ruth, I hope that you can learn to love me as a slightly older, but incredibly attractive close uncle. And you, Mary—"

"Will you go with Joshua to Judea, Biff?" Mary interrupted.

"Sure, first thing in the morning."

Joshua and Judah were still staring at me as if they'd both been smacked in the face with a large fish. "What?" I said. "How long have you guys known me? Jeez. Grow a sense of humor."

"Our father died," said Joshua.

"Yeah, but not today," I said. "I'll meet you here in the morning."

The next morning, as we rode through the square, we passed Bartholomew, the village idiot, who looked no worse or less filthy for the years gone by, and who seemed to have come to some sort of understanding with his doggy friends. Instead of jumping all over him as they always had, now they sat quietly before him in a group, as if listening to a sermon.

"Where have you been?" Bart called to us.

"In the East."

"Why did you go there?"

"We were looking for the Divine Spark," Joshua said. "But we didn't know that when we left."

"Where are you going?"

"To Judea, to find John the Baptist."

"He should be easier to find than the Spark. Can I come?"

"Sure," I said. "Bring your things."

"I don't have any things."

"Then bring your stench."

"That will follow on its own," Bartholomew said.

And thus we became three.

Chapter 24

I've finally finished reading these stories by Matthew, Mark, Luke, and John. These guys make the whole thing seem like an accident, like five thousand people just showed up on a hill one morning. If that was the case, getting them all there was the miracle, let alone feeding them. We busted our asses to organize sermons like that, and sometimes we even had to put Joshua in a boat and float him offshore while he preached, just to keep him from getting mobbed. That boy was a security nightmare.

And that's not all, there were two sides to Joshua, his preaching side and his private side. The guy who stood there railing at the Pharisees was not the same guy who would sit around poking Untouchables in the arm because it cracked him up. He planned the sermons, he calculated the parables, although he may have been the only one in our group that understood any of them.

What I'm saying is that these guys, Matthew, Mark, Luke, and John, they got some of it right, the big stuff, but they missed a lot (like thirty years, for instance). I'll try to fill it in, which is why, I guess, the angel brought me back from the dead.

And speaking of the angel, I'm about convinced that he's gone psycho. (No, psycho isn't a word I had back in my time, but enough television and I'll have a whole new vocabulary. It applies. I believe, for instance, that "psycho" was the perfect term for John the Baptist. More about him later.) Raziel took me to a place where you wash clothes today. A Laundromat. We were there all day. He wanted to make sure

I knew how to wash clothes. I may not be the sharpest arrow in the quiver, but it's laundry, for Christ's sake. He quizzed me for a hour about sorting whites and colors. I may never get this story told if the angel keeps deciding to teach me life lessons. Tomorrow, miniature golf. I can only guess that Raziel is trying to prepare me to be an international spy.

Bartholomew and his stench rode one camel while Joshua and I shared the other. We rode south to Jerusalem, then east over the Mount of Olives into Bethany, where we saw a yellow-haired man sitting under a fig tree. I had never seen a yellow-haired person in Israel, other than the angel. I pointed him out to Joshua and we watched the blond man long enough to convince ourselves that he wasn't one of the heavenly host in disguise. Actually, we pretended to watch him. We were watching each other.

Bartholomew said, "Is there something wrong? You two seem nervous."

"It's just that blond kid," I said, trying to look in the courtyards of the large houses as we passed.

"Maggie lives here with her husband," Joshua said, looking at me, relieving no tension whatsoever.

"I knew that," said Bart. "He's a member of the Sanhedrin. High up, they say."

The Sanhedrin was a council of priests and Pharisees who made most of the decisions for the Jewish community, as far as the Romans would allow them, anyway. Aside from the Herods and Pontius Pilate, the Roman governor, they were the most powerful men in Israel.

"I was really hoping Jakan would die young."

"They have no children," Joshua said. What Josh was saying was that it was strange that Jakan hadn't divorced Maggie for being barren.

"My brother told me," I said.

"We can't go see her."

"I know," I said, although I wasn't sure why not.

We finally found John in the desert north of Jericho, preaching on the bank of the Jordan River. His hair was as wild as ever and now he had a beard that was just as out of control. He wore a rough tunic that was belted with a sash of unscraped camel skin. There was a crowd of perhaps five hundred people there, standing in sun so hot that you had to check road signs to make sure you hadn't accidentally taken the turnoff to hell.

We couldn't tell what John was talking about from a distance, but as we got closer we heard him say, "No, I'm not the one. I'm just getting things ready. There's one that's coming after me, and I'm not qualified to carry his jockstrap."

"What's a jockstrap?" Joshua asked.

"It's an Essene thing," Bartholomew answered. "They wear them on their manhood, very tightly, to control their sinful urges."

Then John spotted us over the crowd (we were on camelback). "There!" said John, pointing. "You remember me telling you that one would come. Well, there he is, right there. I'm not kidding, that's him on the camel. On the left. Behold the Lamb of God!"

The crowd looked back at Josh and me, then laughed politely as if to say, *Oh right, he just happened along right when you were talking about him. What, we don't know from a shill when we see one?*

Joshua glanced nervously at me, then at Bart, then at me, then he grinned sheepishly (as one might expect from a lamb) at the crowd. Between gritted teeth he asked, "So am I supposed to give John my jockstrap, or something?"

"Just wave, and say, 'Go with God,' " Bart said.

"Waving here—waving there," Josh mumbled though a grin. "Go with God. Thank you very much. Go with God. Nice to see you. Waving—waving."

"Louder, Josh. We're the only ones who can hear you."

Josh turned to us so the crowd couldn't see his face. "I didn't know I was going to need a jockstrap! Nobody told me. Jeez, you guys."

Thus did begin the ministry of Joshua bar Joseph, ish Nazareth, the Lamb of God.

So, who's the big guy?" John asked, as we sat around the fire that evening. Night crawled across the desert sky like a black cat with phosphorus dandruff. Bartholomew rolled with his dogs down by the riverbank.

"That's Bartholomew," Joshua said. "He's a Cynic."

"And the village idiot of Nazareth for over thirty years," I added. "He gave up his position to follow Joshua."

"He's a slut, and he's the first one baptized in the morning. He stinks. More locusts, Biff?"

"No thanks, I'm full." I stared down at my bowl of roasted locusts and honey. You were supposed to dip the locusts in the honey for a sweet and nutritious treat. It was all John ate.

"So this Divine Spark, all that time away, that's what you found?"

"It's the key to the kingdom, John," Josh said. "That's what I learned in the East that I'm supposed to bring to our people, that God is in all of us. We are all brothers in the Divine Spark. I just don't know how to spread the word."

"Well, first, you can't call it the Divine Spark. The people won't understand it. This thing, it's in everyone, it's permanent, it's a part of God?"

"Not God the creator, my father, the part of God that's spirit."

"Holy Ghost," John said with a shrug. "Call it the Holy Ghost. People understand that a ghost is in you, and they understand that it goes on after you, and you'll just have to make them believe that it's God."

"That's perfect," Joshua said, smiling.

"So, this Holy Ghost," John said, biting a locust in half, "it's in every Jew, but gentiles don't have it, right? I mean what's the point, after the kingdom comes?"

"I was getting to that," said Josh.

It took John the better part of the night to deal with the fact that Joshua was going to let gentiles into the kingdom, but finally the Baptist accepted it, although he kept looking for exceptions.

"Even sluts?"

"Even sluts," Joshua said.

"Especially sluts," I said.

"You're the one who is cleansing people of their sins so they will be forgiven," Joshua added.

"I know, but gentile sluts, in the kingdom." He shook his head, assured now by the Messiah himself that the world was going to hell in a handbasket. Which really shouldn't have surprised him, since that had been his message for over ten years. That, and identifying sluts. "Let me show you where you'll be staying."

Shortly after I had met him on the road to Jerusalem, John had joined the Essenes. You couldn't be born an Essene, because they were all celibate, even in marriage. They also refrained from intoxicating drink, adhered strictly to Jewish dietary law, and were absolutely maniacal about cleansing themselves, physically, of sin, which had been the big selling point for John. They had a thriving community in the desert outside of Jericho called Qumran, a small city of stone and brick homes, a scriptorium for copying scrolls, and aqueducts that ran out of the mountains to fill their ritual baths. A few of them lived in the caves above the Dead Sea where they stored the jars that held their sacred scrolls, but the most zealous of the Essenes, which included John, didn't even allow themselves the comfort of a cave. He showed us accommodations near his own.

"It's a pit!" I screamed.

Three pits, to be exact. I suppose there's something to be said for having a private pit. Bartholomew, with his many canine pals, was already settling into his new pit.

"Oh, John," Josh said, "remind me to tell you about karma."

So, for over a year, while Joshua was learning from John how to say the words that would make people follow him, I lived in a pit.

It makes sense, if you think about it. For seventeen years Joshua had spent his time either studying or sitting around being quiet, so what did he know about communicating? The last message he'd gotten from his father was two words, so he wasn't getting his speaking skills from that side of the family. On the other hand, John had been preaching for those same seventeen years, and that squirrelly bastard *could* preach. Standing waist deep in the Jordan, he would wave his arms and roll his eyes and stir the air with a sermon that would make you believe the clouds were going to open and the hand of God Hisownself was going to reach down, grab you by the balls, and shake you till the evil rattled out of you like loose baby teeth. An hour of John's preaching and you were not only lining up to be baptized, you'd jump right in the river and try to breathe the bottom muck just to be relieved of your own wretchedness.

Joshua watched, and listened, and learned. John was an absolute believer in who Joshua was and what he was going to do, as far as he understood, anyway, but the Baptist worried me. John was attracting the attention of Herod Antipas. Herod had married his brother Philip's wife, Herodia, without her obtaining a divorce, which was forbidden by Jewish law, an absolute outrage by the more severe laws of the Essenes, and a subject that fit well into John's pervasive "slut" theme. I was starting to notice soldiers from Herod's personal guard hovering around the edge of John's crowds when he preached.

I confronted the Baptist one evening when he came out of the wilderness in one of his evangelical rages to ambush me, Joshua, Bartholomew, and a new guy as we sat around eating our locusts.

"Slut!" John shouted with his "thunder of Elijah" voice, waving a finger under Bart's nose.

"Yeah, John, Bartholomew's been getting laid a lot," I said, evangelizing for sarcasm.

"Almost," said Bart.

"I mean with another human being, Bart."

"Oh. Sorry. Never mind."

John wheeled on the new guy, who put his hands up. "I'm new," he said.

Thus rebuked, John spun to face Joshua.

"Celibate," Joshua said. "Always have been, always will be. Not happy about it."

Finally John turned to me. "Slut!"

"John, I'm cleansed, you baptized me six times today." Joshua elbowed me in the ribs. "What? It was hot. Point is, I counted fifty soldiers in the crowd today, so ease up a little on the slut talk. You're backed up or something. You really need to rethink this no marriage, no sex, no fun, ascetic thing."

"And the honey-and-locust living-in-a pit thing," said the new guy.

"He's no different than Melchior or Gaspar," Joshua said. "They were both ascetics."

"Melchior and Gaspar weren't running around calling the provincial governor a slut in front of hundreds of people. It's a big difference, and it's going to get him killed."

"I am cleansed of sin and unafraid," said John, sitting down by the fire now, some of his verve gone.

"Yeah, are you cleansed of guilt? Because you're going to have the blood of thousands on your hands when the Romans come to get you. In case you haven't noticed, they don't just kill the leaders of a movement. There's a thousand crosses on the road to Jerusalem where Zealots died, and they weren't all leaders."

"I am unafraid." John hung his head until the ends of his hair were dipping into the honey in his bowl. "Herodia and Herod are sluts. He's as close as we have to a Jewish king, and he's a slut."

Joshua pushed his cousin's hair out of his eyes and squeezed the wild man's shoulder. "If it be so, then so be it. As the angel foretold, you were born to preach the truth."

I stood up and tossed my locusts into the fire, showering sparks over John and Joshua. "I've only met two people whose births were announced by angels, and three-quarters of them are loony." And I stormed off to my pit.

"Amen," said the new guy.

That night, as I was falling asleep, I heard Joshua scrambling in the pit next to mine, as if a bug or an idea had roused him from his bedroll. "Hey!" he said.

"What?" I replied.

"I just did the math. Three quarters of two is—"

"One and a half," said the new guy, who had moved into the pit on the other side of Josh. "So John's either all crazy and you're half crazy, or you're three-quarters crazy and John's three-quarters crazy, or—well—actually it's a constant ratio, I'd have to graph it out for you."

"So what are you saying?"

"Nothing," said the new guy. "I'm new."

the next morning Joshua leapt out of his pit, shook off the scorpions, and after a long morning whiz, kicked some dirt clods into my pit to thunk me from my slumber.

"This is it," Joshua said. "Come down to the river, I'm going to have John baptize me today."

"Which will make it different from yesterday in what way?"

"You'll see. I have a feeling." And off he went.

The new guy prairie-dogged up out of his pit. He was tall, the new guy, and the morning sun caught on his bald scalp as he looked around. He noticed some flowers growing where Joshua had just relieved himself. Lush blossoms of a half-dozen vibrant colors stood surrounded by the deadest landscape on the planet. "Hey, were those there yesterday?"

"That always happens," I said. "We don't talk about it."

"Wow," said the new guy. "Can I tag along with you guys?"

"Sure," I said.

And thus did we become four.

at the river, John preached to a small gathering as he lowered Joshua into the water. As soon as Joshua went under the water a rift opened across the desert sky, which was still pink with the dawn, and out of the rift came a bird that looked to be fashioned from pure light. And everyone on the riverbank said "ooh" and "ahh," and a big voice boomed out of the heavens, saying, "This is my son, with whom I am well pleased." And as quickly as it had come, the spirit was gone. But the gatherers at the riverbank stood with their mouths open in amazement, staring yet into the sky.

And John came to his senses then, and remembered what he was doing, and lifted Joshua out of the water. And Joshua wiped the water out of his eyes, looked at the crowd who stood stunned with mouths hanging open, and he said unto them: "What?"

No, really, Josh, that's what the voice said, 'This is my son, with whom I am well pleased.' "

Joshua shook his head and chewed a breakfast locust. "I can't believe he couldn't wait until I came up. You're sure it was my father?"

"Sounded like him." The new guy looked at me and I shrugged. Actually it sounded like James Earl Jones, but I didn't know that back then.

"That's it," said Joshua. "I'm going into the desert like Moses did, forty days and forty nights." Joshua got up and started walking into the desert. "From here on out, I'm fasting until I hear something from my father. That was my last locust."

"I wish I could say that," said the new guy.

As soon as Joshua was out of sight I ran to my pit and packed my satchel. I was a half day getting to Bethany, and another hour asking around before someone could direct me to the house of Jakan, prominent Pharisee and member of the Sanhedrin. The house was made of the golden-tinged limestone that marked all of Jerusalem, and there was a high wall around the courtyard. Jakan had done very well for himself, the prick. You could house a dozen families from Nazareth in a house this size. I paid two blind guys a shekel each to stand by the wall so I could climb on their shoulders.

"How much did he say this was?"

"He said it was a shekel."

"Doesn't feel like a shekel."

"Would you guys quit feeling your shekels and stand still, I'm going to fall."

I peeped over the top of the wall and there, sitting under the shade of an awning, working at a small loom, was Maggie. If she had changed, it was only that she'd become more radiant, more sensuous, more of a woman and less of a girl. I was stunned. I guess I expected some sort of disappointment, thinking that my time and my love might have shaped a memory that the woman could never live up to. Then I thought, perhaps the disappointment was yet to come. She was married to rich man, a man who, when I knew him, had been a bully and a dolt. And what had always really made Maggie's memory in my mind was her spirit, her courage, and her wit. I wondered if those things could have survived all these years with Jakan. I started to shake, bad balance or fear, I don't know, but I put my hand on top of the wall to steady myself and cut myself on some broken pottery that had been set in mortar along the top.

"Ouch, dammit."

"Biff?" Maggie said, as she looked me in the eye right before I tumbled off the shoulders of the blind guys.

I had just climbed to my feet when Maggie came around the corner and hit me, full-frontal womanhood, full speed, leading with lips. She kissed me so hard that I could taste blood from my cut lips and it was glorious. She smelled the same—cinnamon and lemon and girl sweat—and felt better than memory could ever allow. When she finally relaxed her embrace and held me at arm's length, there were tears in her eyes. And mine.

"He dead?" said one of the blind men.

"Don't think so, I can hear him breathing."

"Sure smells better than he did."

"Biff, your face cleared up," Maggie said.

"You recognized me, with the beard and everything."

"I wasn't sure at first," she said, "so I was taking a risk jumping you like that, but in the midst of it all I recognized that." She pointed to where my tunic had tented out in the front. And then she grabbed that betraying rascal, shirtfront and all, and led me down the wall toward the gate by it.

"Come on in. You can't stay long, but we can catch up. Are you okay?" she said, looking over her shoulder, giving me a squeeze.

"Yeah, yeah, I'm just trying to think of a metaphor."

"He got a woman from up there," I heard one of the old blind guys say.

"Yeah, I heard her drop. Boost me up, I'll feel around."

In the courtyard, with Maggie, over wine, I said, "So you really didn't recognize me?"

"Of course I recognized you. I've never done that before. I just hope no one saw me, they still stone women for that."

"I know. Oh, Maggie, I have so much to tell you."

She took my hand. "I know." She looked into my eyes, past my eyes, her blue eyes looking for something beyond me.

"He's fine," I said, finally. "He's gone into the desert to fast and wait for a message from the Lord."

She smiled. There was a little of my blood in the corners of her mouth, or maybe that was wine. "He's come home to take his place as the Messiah then?"

"Yes. But I don't think the way people think."

"People think that John might be the Messiah."

"John is . . . He's . . ."

"He's really pissing Herod off," Maggie offered.

"I know."

"Are you and Josh going to stay with John?"

"I hope not. I want Joshua to leave. I just have to get him away from John long enough to see what's going on. Maybe this fast . . ."

The iron lock on the gate to the courtyard rattled, then the whole gate shook. Maggie had locked it behind us after we'd entered. A man cursed. Evidently Jakan was having trouble with his key.

Maggie stood and pulled me to my feet. "Look, I'm going to a wedding in Cana next month with my sister Martha, the week after Tabernacles. Jakan can't go, he's got some meeting of the Sanhedrin or something. Come to Cana. Bring Joshua."

"I'll try."

She ran to the closest wall and held her hand in a stirrup. "Over."

"But, Maggie . . ."

"Don't be a wuss. Step, hands—step, shoulders—and over. Be careful of the pottery on top."

And I ran—did exactly as she'd said: one foot in the stirrup, one on her shoulder, and over the wall before Jakan could get in the gate.

"Got one!" said one of the old blind guys as I tumbled down on top of them.

"Hold her still while I stick it in."

I was sitting on a boulder, waiting for Joshua when he came out of the desert. I held out my arms to hug him and he fell forward, letting me catch him. I lowered him to the rock where I had been sitting. He had been smart enough to coat all the exposed parts of his skin with mud, probably mixed from his own urine, to protect it from burning, but in a few spots on his forehead and hands the mud had crumbled away and the skin was gone, burned to raw flesh. His arms were as thin as a small girl's, they swam in the wide sleeves of his tunic.

"You okay?"

He nodded. I handed him a water skin I had been keeping cool in the shade. He drank in little sips, pacing himself.

"Locust?" I said, holding up one of the crispy torments between my thumb and forefinger.

At the sight of it I thought Joshua would vomit the water he had just drunk. "Just kidding," I said. I whipped open the mouth of my satchel, revealing dates, fresh figs, olives, cheese, a half-dozen flat loaves of bread, and a full wineskin. I'd sent the new guy into Jericho the day before to bring back the food.

Josh looked at the food spilling out of the satchel and grinned, then covered his mouth with his hand. "Ow. Ouch. Ow."

"What's wrong?"

"Lips . . . chapped."

"Myrrh," I said, pulling a small jar of the ointment from the satchel and handing it to him.

An hour later the Son of God was refreshed and rejuvenated, and we sat sharing the last of the wine, the first that Joshua had had since we'd come home from India over a year ago.

"So, what did you see in the desert?"

"The Devil."

"The Devil?"

"Yep. He tempted me. Power, wealth, sex, that sort of thing. I turned him down."

"What did he look like?"

"He was tall."

"Tall? The prince of darkness, the serpent of temptation, the source of all corruption and evil, and all you can say about him is he was tall?"

"Pretty tall."

"Oh, good, I'll be on the lookout then."

Joshua said, pointing at the new guy. "He's tall, too." I realized then that the Messiah might be a little tipsy.

"Not the Devil, Josh."

"Well, who is he then?"

"I'm Philip," said the new guy. "I'm going with you to Cana tomorrow."

Joshua wheeled around to me and almost fell off his rock. "We're going to Cana tomorrow?"

"Yes, Maggie's there, Josh. She's dying."

Chapter 25

Philip, who was called the new guy, asked that we go to Cana by way of Bethany, as he had a friend there that he wanted to recruit to follow along with us. "I tried to get him to join with John the Baptist," Philip said, "but he wouldn't stand for the eating-locusts, living-in-pits thing. Anyway, he's from Cana, I'm sure he'd love to have a visit home."

As we came into the square of Bethany, Philip called out to a blond kid who was sitting under a fig tree. He was the same yellow-haired kid that Joshua and I had seen when we first passed through Bethany over a year ago.

"Hey, Nathaniel," Philip called. "Come join me and my friends on the way to Cana. They're from Nazareth. Joshua here might be the Messiah."

"Might be?" I said.

Nathaniel walked out into the street to look at us, shading his eyes against the sun. He couldn't have been more than sixteen or seventeen. He barely had the fuzz of a beard on his chin. "Can anything good come out of Nazareth?" he said.

"Joshua, Biff, Bartholomew," Philip said, "this is my friend Nathaniel."

"I know you," Joshua said. "I saw you when we last passed through here."

Then, inexplicably, Nathaniel fell to his knees in front of Joshua's camel and said, "You are truly the Messiah and the Son of God."

Joshua looked at me, then at Philip, then at the kid, prostrating himself on camel's feet. "Because I've seen you before you believe that I'm the Messiah, even though a minute ago nothing good could come out of Nazareth?"

"Sure, why not?" said Nathaniel.

And Josh looked at me again, as if I could explain it. Meanwhile Bartholomew, who was on foot along with his pack of doggie followers (whom he had disturbingly begun to refer to as his "disciples"), went over to Nathaniel and helped the boy to his feet. "Stand up, if you're coming with us."

Nathaniel prostrated himself before Bartholomew now. "You are truly the Messiah and the Son of God."

"No, I'm not," Bart said, lifting the kid to his feet. "He is." Bart pointed to Joshua. Nathaniel looked to me, for some reason, for confirmation.

"You are truly a babe in the woods," I said to Nathaniel. "You don't gamble, do you?"

"Biff!" Joshua said. He shook his head and I shrugged. To Nathaniel he said, "You're welcome to join us. We share the camels, our food, and what little money we have." Here Joshua nodded toward Philip, who had been nominated to carry the communal purse because he was good at math.

"Thanks," said Nathaniel, and he fell in behind us.

And thus we became five.

"Josh," I said in a harsh whisper, "that kid is as dumb as a stick."

"He's not dumb, Biff, he just has a talent for belief."

"Fine," I said, turning to Philip. "Don't let the kid anywhere near the money."

As we headed out of the square toward the Mount of Olives, Abel and Crustus, the two old blind guys who'd helped me over Maggie's wall, called out from the gutter. (I'd learned their names after correcting their little gender mistake.)

"Oh son of David, have mercy on us!"

Joshua pulled up on the reins of his camel. "What makes you call me that?"

"You *are* Joshua of Nazareth, the young preacher who was studying under John?"

"Yes, I am Joshua."

"We heard the Lord say that you were his son with whom he was well pleased."

"You heard that?"

"Yes. About five or six weeks ago. Right out of the sky."

"Dammit, did everyone hear but me?"

"Have mercy on us, Joshua," said one blind guy.

"Yeah, mercy," said the other.

Then Joshua climbed down from his camel, laid his hands upon the old men's eyes, and said, "You have faith in the Lord, and you have heard, as evidently everyone in Judea has, that I am his son with whom he is well pleased." Then he pulled his hands from their faces and the old men looked around.

"Tell me what you see," Joshua said.

The old guys sort of looked around, saying nothing.

"So, tell me what you see."

The blind men looked at each other.

"Something wrong?" Joshua asked. "You can see, can't you?"

"Well, yeah," said Abel, "but I thought there'd be more color."

"Yeah," said Crustus, "it's kind of dull."

I stepped up. "You're on the edge of the Judean desert, one of the most lifeless, desolate, hostile places on earth, what did you expect?"

"I don't know." Crustus shrugged. "More."

"Yeah, more," said Abel. "What color is that?"

"That's brown."

"How about that one?"

"That would be brown as well."

"That color over there? Right there?"

"Brown."

"You're sure that's not mauve."

"Nope, brown."

"And—"

"Brown," I said.

The two former blind guys shrugged and walked off mumbling to each other.

"Excellent healing," said Nathaniel.

"I for one have never seen a better healing," said Philip, "but then, I'm new."

Joshua rode off shaking his head.

When we came into Cana we were broke and hungry and more than ready for a feast, at least most of us were. Joshua didn't know about the feast. The wedding was being held in the courtyard of a very large house. We could hear the drums and singers and smell spiced meat cooking as we approached the gates. It was a large wedding and a couple of kids were waiting outside to tend to our camels. They were curly haired, wiry little guys about ten years old; they reminded me of evil versions of Josh and me at that age.

"Sounds like a wedding going on," Joshua said.

"Park your camel, sir?" said the camel-parking kid.

"It is a wedding," said Bart. "I thought we were here to help Maggie."

"Park your camel, sir?" said the other kid, pulling on the reins of my camel.

Joshua looked at me. "Where is Maggie? You said she was sick?"

"She's in the wedding," I said, pulling the reins back from the kid.

"You said she was dying."

"Well, we all are, aren't we? I mean, if you think about it." I grinned.

"You can't park that camel here, sir."

"Look, kid, I don't have any money to tip you. Go away." I hate handing my camel over to the camel-parking kids. It unnerves me. I'm always sure that I'm never going to see it again, or it's going to come back with a tooth missing or an eye poked out.

"So Maggie isn't really dying?"

"Hey, guys," Maggie said, stepping out of the gate.

"Maggie," Joshua said, throwing his arms up in surprise. Problem was, he was so intent on looking at her that he forgot to grab on again, and off the camel he went. He hit the ground facedown with a thump and a wheeze. I jumped down from my camel, Bart's dogs barked, Maggie ran to Josh, rolled him over, and cradled his head in her lap while he tried to get his breath back. Philip and Nathaniel waved to people from the wedding who were peeping through the gate to see what all the commotion was about. Before I had a chance to turn, the two kids had leapt up onto our camels and were galloping around the corner off to Nod, or South Dakota, or some other place I didn't know the location of.

"Maggie," Joshua said. "You're not sick."

"That depends," she said, "if there's any chance of a laying on of hands."

Joshua smiled and blushed. "I missed you."

"Me too," Maggie said. She kissed Joshua on the lips and held him there until I started to squirm and the other disciples started to clear their throats and bark "get a room" under their breaths.

Maggie stood up and helped Joshua to his feet. "Come on in, guys," she said. "No dogs," she said to Bart, and the hulking Cynic shrugged and sat down in the street amid his canine disciples.

I was craning my neck to see if I could see where our camels had been taken. "They're going to run those camels into the ground, and I know they won't feed or water them."

"Who?" asked Maggie.

"Those camel-parking boys."

"Biff, this is my youngest brother's wedding. He couldn't even afford wine. He didn't hire any camel-parking boys."

Bartholomew stood and rallied his troops. "I'll find them." He lumbered off.

Inside we feasted on beef and mutton, all manner of fruits and vegetables, bean and nut pastes, cheese and first-pressed olive oil with bread. There was singing and dancing and if it hadn't been for a few old guys in the corner looking very cranky, you'd never have known that there wasn't any wine at the party. When our people danced, they danced in large groups, lines and circles, not couples. There were men's dances and women's dances and very few dances where both could participate, which is why people were staring at Joshua and Maggie as they danced. They were definitely dancing together.

I retreated to a corner where I saw Maggie's sister Martha watching as she nibbled at some bread with goat cheese. She was twenty-five, a shorter, sturdier version of Maggie, with the same auburn hair and blue eyes, but with less tendency to laugh. Her husband had divorced her for "grievous skankage" and now she lived with her older brother Simon in Bethany. I'd gotten to know her when we were little and she took messages to Maggie for me. She offered me a bite of her bread and cheese and I took it.

"She's going to get herself stoned," Martha said in slightly bitter, moderately jealous, younger sister tone. "Jakan is a member of the Sanhedrin."

"Is he still a bully?"

"Worse, now he's a bully with power. He'd have her stoned, just to prove that he could do it."

"For dancing? Not even the Pharisees—"

"If anyone saw her kiss Joshua, then . . ."

"So how are you?" I said, changing the subject.

"I'm living with my brother Simon now."

"I heard."

"He's a leper."

"Look, there's Joshua's mother. I have to go say hello."

There's no wine at this wedding," Mary said.

"I know. Strange, isn't it?"

James stood by scowling as I hugged his mother.

"Joshua is here too?"

"Yes."

"Oh good, I was afraid that you two might have been arrested along with John."

"Pardon me?" I stepped back and looked to James for explanation. He seemed the more appropriate bearer of bad news.

"You hadn't heard? Herod has thrown John in prison for inciting people to revolt. That's the excuse anyway. It's Herod's wife who wanted John silenced. She was tired of having John's followers refer to her as 'the slut.' "

I patted Mary's shoulder as I stepped away. "I'll tell Joshua that you're here."

I found Joshua sitting in a far corner of the courtyard playing with some children. One little girl had brought her pet rabbit to the wedding and Joshua was holding it in his lap, petting its ears.

"Biff, come feel how soft this bunny is."

"Joshua, John has been arrested."

Josh slowly handed the bunny back to the little girl and stood. "When?"

"I'm not sure. Shortly after we left, I guess."

"I shouldn't have left him. I didn't even tell him we were leaving."

"It was bound to happen, Joshua. I told him to lay off Herod, but he wouldn't listen. You couldn't have done anything."

"I'm the Son of God, I could have done something."

"Yeah, you could have gone to prison with him. Your mother is here. Go talk to her. She's the one that told me."

As Joshua embraced Mary, she said, "You've got to do something about this wine situation. Where's the wine?"

James tapped Joshua on the shoulder. "Didn't bring any wine with you from the lush vineyards of Jericho?" (I didn't like hearing sarcasm being used by James against Joshua. I had always thought of my invention as being used for good, or at least against people I didn't like.)

Joshua gently pushed his mother away. "You shall have wine," he said, then he went off to the side of the house where drinking water was stored in large stone jars. In a few minutes he returned with a pitcher of wine and cups for all of us. A shout went through the party and suddenly everything seemed to step up a level. Pitchers and cups were filled and drained and filled again, and those who had been near the wine jars started declaring a miracle had been performed, that Joshua of Nazareth had turned water into wine. I looked for him, but he was nowhere to be found. Having been free of sin all of his life, Joshua wasn't very good at dealing with guilt, so he had gone off by himself to try to numb the guilt he felt over John's arrest.

After a few hours of subterfuge and guile, I was able to get Maggie to sneak out the back gate with me.

"Maggie, come with us. You talked to Joshua. You saw the wine. He's the one."

"I've always known he was the one, but I can't come with you. I'm married."

"I thought you were going to be a fisherman."

"And I thought you were going to be a village idiot."

"I'm still looking for a village. Look, get Jakan to divorce you."

"Anything he can divorce me for he can also kill me for. I've seen him pass judgment on people, Biff. I've seen him lead the mobs to the stonings. I'm afraid of him."

"I learned to make poisons in the East." I raised my eyebrows and grinned. "Huh?"

"I'm not going to poison my husband."

I sighed, an exasperated sigh that I'd learned from my mother. "Then leave him and come away with us, far from Jerusalem where he can't reach you. He'll have to divorce you to save face."

"Why should I leave, Biff? So I can follow around a man who doesn't want me and wouldn't take me if he did?"

I didn't know what to say, I felt like knives were twisting in fresh wounds in my chest. I looked at my sandals and pretended to have something caught in my throat.

Maggie stepped up, put her arms around me, and laid her head against my chest. "I'm sorry," she said.

"I know."

"I missed both of you, but I missed just *you* too."

"I know."

"I'm not going to sleep with you."

"I know."

"Then please stop rubbing that against me."

"Sure," I said.

Just then Joshua stumbled through the gate and crashed into us. We were able to catch ourselves and him before anyone fell. The Messiah was holding the little girl's pet bunny, hugging it to his cheek with the big back feet swinging free. He was gloriously drunk. "Know what?" Josh said. "I love bunnies. They toil not, neither do they bark. Henceforth and from now on, I decree that whenever something bad happens to me, there shall be bunnies around. So it shall be written. Go ahead Biff, write it down." He waved to me under the bunny, then turned and started back through the gate. "Where's the friggin' wine? I got a dry bunny over here!"

"See," I said to Maggie, "you don't want to miss out on that. Bunnies!"

She laughed. My favorite music.

"I'll get word to you," she said. "Where will you be?"

"I have no idea."

"I'll get word to you."

𝑖t was midnight. The party had wound down and the disciples and I were sitting in the street outside of the house. Joshua had passed out and Bartholomew had put a small dog under his head for a pillow. Before he had left, James had made it abundantly clear that we weren't welcome in Nazareth.

"Well?" said Philip. "I guess we can't go back to John."

"I'm sorry I didn't find the camels," Bartholomew said.

"People teased me about my yellow hair," said Nathaniel.

"I thought you were from Cana," I said. "Don't you have family we can stay with?"

"Plague," said Nathaniel.

"Plague," we all said, nodding. It happens.

"You'll probably be needing these," came a voice out of the darkness. We all looked up to see a short but powerfully built man walking out of the darkness, leading our camels.

"The camels," said Nathaniel.

"My apologies," said the man, "my brother's sons brought them home to us in Capernaum. I'm sorry it's taken so long to get them back to you."

I stood and he handed the camel's reins to me. "They've been fed and watered." He pointed to Joshua, who was snoring away on his terrier. "Does he always drink like that?"

"Only when a major prophet has been imprisoned."

The man nodded. "I heard what he did with the wine. They say he also healed a lame man in Cana this afternoon. Is that true?"

We all nodded.

"If you have no place to stay, you can come home with me to Capernaum for a day or two. We owe you at least that for taking your camels."

"We don't have any money," I said.

"Then you'll feel right at home," said the man. "My name is Andrew."

And so we became six.

Chapter 26

You can travel the whole world, but there are always new things to learn. For instance, on the way to Capernaum I learned that if you hang a drunk guy over a camel and slosh him around for about four hours, then pretty much all the poisons will come out one end of him or the other.

"Someone's going to have to wash that camel before we go into town," said Andrew.

We were traveling along the shore of the Sea of Galilee (which wasn't a sea at all). The moon was almost full and it reflected in the lake like a pool of quicksilver. It fell to Nathaniel to clean the camel because he was the official new guy. (Joshua hadn't really met Andrew, and Andrew hadn't really agreed to join us, so we couldn't count him as the *official* new guy yet.) Since Nathaniel did such a fine job on the camel, we let him clean up Joshua as well. Once he had the Messiah in the water Joshua came out of his stupor long enough to slur something like: "The foxes have their holes and birds have their nests, but the son of man has nowhere to lay his head."

"That's so sad," said Nathaniel.

"Yes, it is." I said. "Dunk him again. He still has barf on his beard."

And so, cleansed and slung over a camel damply, Joshua did by moonlight come into Capernaum, where he would be welcomed as if it were his home.

Out!" screeched the old woman. "Out of the house, out of town, out of Galilee for all I care, you aren't staying here."

It was a beautiful dawn over the lake, the sky painted with yellow and orange, gentle waves lapped against the keels of Capernaum's fishing boats. The village was only a stone's throw away from the water, and golden sunlight reflected off the waves onto the black stone walls of the houses, making the light appear to dance to the calls of the gulls and songbirds. The houses were built together in two big clusters, sharing common walls, with entries from every which way, and none more than one story tall. There was a small main road through the village between the two clusters of homes. Along the way were a few merchant booths, a blacksmith's shop, and, on its own little square, a synagogue that looked as if it could contain far more worshipers than the three hundred residents of the village. But villages were thick along the shores of the lake, one running right into the next, and we guessed that perhaps the synagogue served a number of villages. There was no central square around the well as there was in most inland villages, because the people pulled their water from the lake or a spring nearby that bubbled clean chilly water into the air as high as two men.

Andrew had deposited us at his brother Peter's house, and we had fallen asleep in the great room among the children only a few hours before Peter's mother-in-law awoke to chase us out of the house. Joshua was holding his head with both hands as if to keep it from falling off his neck.

"I won't have freeloaders and scalawags in my house," the old woman shouted as she threw my satchel out after us.

"Ouch," said Joshua, flinching from the noise.

"We're in Capernaum, Josh," I said. "A man named Andrew brought us here because his nephews stole our camels."

"You said Maggie was dying," Joshua said.

"Would you have left John if I'd told you that Maggie wanted to see you?"

"No." He smiled dreamily. "It was good to see Maggie." Then the smile turned to a scowl. "Alive."

"John wouldn't listen, Joshua. You were in the desert all last month, you didn't see all of the soldiers, even scribes hiding in the crowd, writing down what John was saying. This was bound to happen."

"Then you should have warned John!"

"I warned John! Every day I warned John. He didn't listen to reason any more than you would have."

"We have to go back to Judea. John's followers—"

"Will become your followers. No more preparation, Josh."

Joshua nodded, looking at the ground in front of him. "It's time. Where are the others?"

"I've sent Philip and Nathaniel to Sepphoris to sell the camels. Bartholomew is sleeping in the reeds with the dogs."

"We're going to need more disciples," Joshua said.

"We're broke, Josh. We're going to need disciples with jobs."

An hour later we stood on the shore near where Andrew and his brother were casting nets. Peter was taller and leaner than his brother, and he had a head of gray hair wilder than even John the Baptist's, while Andrew pushed his dark hair back and tied it with a cord so it stayed out of his face when he was in the water. They were both naked, which is how men fished the lake when they were close to the shore.

I had mixed a headache remedy for Joshua out of tree bark, and I could tell it was working, but perhaps not quite enough. I pushed Joshua toward the shore.

"I'm not ready for this. I feel terrible."

"Ask them."

"Andrew," Joshua called. "Thank you for bringing us home with you. And you too, Peter."

"Did my mother-in-law toss you out?" asked Peter. He cast his net and waited for it to settle, then dove into the lake and gathered the net in his arms. There was one tiny fish inside. He reached in and pulled it out, then tossed it back into the lake. "Grow," he said.

"You know who I am?" said Joshua.

"I've heard," said Peter. "Andrew says you turned water into wine. And you cured the blind and the lame. He thinks that you are going to bring the kingdom."

"What do you think?"

"I think my little brother is smarter than I am, so I believe what he says."

"Come with us. We're going to tell people of the kingdom. We need help."

"What can we do?" said Andrew. "We're only fishermen."

"Come with me and I'll make you fishers of men."

Andrew looked at his brother who was still standing in the water. Peter shrugged and shook his head. Andrew looked at me, shrugged, and shook his head.

"They don't get it," I said to Joshua.

Thus, after Joshua had some food and a nap and explained what in the hell he meant by "fishers of men," we became seven.

These guys are our partners," Peter said, hurrying us along the shore. "They own the ships that Andrew and I work on. We can't go spread the good news unless they are in on it too."

We came to another small village and Peter pointed out two brothers who were fitting a new oarlock into the gunwale of a fishing boat. One was lean and angular, with jet-black hair and a beard trimmed into wicked points: James. The other was older, bigger, softer, with big shoulders and chest, but small hands and thin wrists, a fringe of brown hair shot with gray around a sunburned bald pate: John.

"Just a suggestion," Peter said to Joshua. "Don't say the fisher-of-men thing. It's going to be dark soon; you won't have time for the explanation if we want to make it home in time for supper."

"Yeah," I said, "just tell them about the miracles, the kingdom, a little about your Holy Ghost thing, but stay easy on that until they agree to join up."

"I still don't get the Holy Ghost thing," said Peter.

"It's okay, we'll go over it tomorrow," I said.

As we moved down the shore toward the brothers, there was a rustling in some nearby bushes and three piles of rags moved into our path.

"Have mercy on us, Rabbi," said one of the piles.

Lepers.

(I need to say something right here: Joshua taught me about the power of love and all of that stuff, and I know that the Divine Spark in them is the same one that is in me, so I should have not let the presence of lepers bother me. I know that announcing them unclean under the Law was as unjust as the Brahmans shunning the Untouchables. I know that even now, having watched enough television, you probably wouldn't even refer to them as lepers so as to spare their feelings. You probably call them "parts-dropping-off challenged," or something. I know all that. But that said, no matter how many healings I saw, lepers always gave me what we Hebrews call *the willies*. I never got over it.)

"What is it you want?" Joshua asked them.

"Help ease our suffering," said a female-sounding pile.

"I'll be over there looking at the water, Josh," I said.

"He'll probably need some help," Peter said.

"Come to me," Joshua said to the lepers.

They oozed on over. Joshua put his hands on the lepers and spoke to them very quietly. After a few minutes had passed, while Peter and I had seriously studied a frog that we noticed on the shore, I heard Joshua say, "Now go, and tell the priests that you are no longer unclean and should be allowed in the Temple. And tell them who sent you."

The lepers threw off their rags and praised Joshua as they backed away. They looked like perfectly normal people who just happened to be all wrapped up in tattered rags.

By the time Peter and I got back to Joshua, James and John were already at his side.

"I have touched those who they said were unclean," Joshua said to the brothers. By Mosaic Law, Joshua would be unclean as well.

James stepped forward and grabbed Joshua's forearm in the style of the Romans. "One of those men used to be our brother."

"Come with us," I said, "and we will make you oarlock makers of men."

"What?" said Joshua.

"That's what they were doing when we came up. Making an oarlock. Now you see how stupid that sounds?"

"It's not the same."

And thus we did become nine.

Philip and Nathaniel returned with enough money from the sale of the camels to feed the disciples and all of Peter's family as well, so Peter's screeching mother-in-law, who was named Esther, allowed us to stay, providing Bartholomew and the dogs slept outside. Capernaum became our base of operations and from there we would take one- or two-day trips, swinging through Galilee as Joshua preached and performed healings. The news of the coming of the kingdom spread through Galilee, and after only a few months, crowds began to gather to hear Joshua speak. We tried always to be back in Capernaum on the Sabbath so that Joshua could teach at the synagogue. It was that habit that first attracted the wrong sort of attention.

A Roman soldier stopped Joshua as he was making the short walk to the synagogue on Sabbath morning. (No Jew was permitted to make a journey of more than a thousand steps from sundown Friday until sundown Saturday—all at once, that is. One way. You didn't have to add up your steps all day and just stop when you got to a thousand. There would have been Jews standing all over the place waiting for Saturday sundown if that were the case. It would have been awkward. Suddenly I'm thankful that the Pharisees never thought of that.)

The Roman was no mere legionnaire, but a centurion, with the full crested helmet and eagle on his breastplate of a legion commander. He led a tall white horse that looked as if it had been bred for combat. He was old for a soldier, perhaps sixty, and his hair was completely white when he removed his helmet, but he looked strong and the wasp-waisted short sword at his waist looked dangerous. I didn't recognize him until he spoke to Joshua, in perfect, unaccented Aramaic.

"Joshua of Nazareth," the Roman said. "Do you remember me?"

"Justus," Joshua said. "From Sepphoris."

"Gaius Justus Gallicus," said the soldier. "And I'm at Tiberius now, and no longer an under-commander. The Sixth Legion is mine. I need your help, Joshua bar Joseph of Nazareth."

"What can I do?" Joshua looked around. All of the disciples except Bartholomew and me had managed to sneak away when the Roman walked up.

"I saw you make a dead man walk and talk. I've heard of the things you've done all over Galilee, the healings, the miracles. I have a servant who is sick. Tortured with palsy. He can barely breathe and I can't watch him suffer. I don't ask that you break your Sabbath by coming to Tiberius, but I believe you can heal him, even from here."

Justus dropped to his knee and kneeled in front of Joshua, something I never saw any Roman do to any Jew, before or since. "This man is my friend," he said.

Joshua touched the Roman's temple and I watched the fear drain out of the soldier's face as I had so many others.

"You believe it to be, so be it," said Joshua. "It's done. Stand up, Gaius Justus Gallicus."

The soldier smiled, then stood and looked Joshua in the eye. "I would have crucified your father to root out the killer of that soldier."

"I know," said Joshua.

"Thank you," Justus said.

The centurion put on his helmet and climbed on his horse. Then looked at me for the first time. "What happened to that pretty little heartbreaker you two were always with?"

"Broke our hearts," I said.

Justus laughed. "Be careful, Joshua of Nazareth," he said. He reined the horse around and rode away.

"Go with God," Joshua said.

"Good, Josh, that's the way to show the Romans what's going to happen to them come the kingdom."

"Shut up, Biff."

"Oh, so you bluffed him. He's going to get home and his friend will still be messed up."

"Remember what I told you at the gates of Gaspar's monastery, Biff? That if someone knocked, I'd let them in?"

"Ack! Parables. I hate parables."

Tiberius was only an hour's fast ride from Capernaum, so by morning word had come back from the garrison: Justus's servant had been healed. Before we had even finished our breakfast there were four Pharisees outside of Peter's house looking for Joshua.

"You performed a healing on the Sabbath?" the oldest of them asked. He was white-bearded and wore his prayer shawl and phylacteries wrapped about his upper arms and forehead. (What a jamoke. Sure, we all had phylacteries, every man got them when he turned thirteen, but you pretended that they were lost after a few weeks, you didn't wear them. You might as well wear a sign that said: "Hi, I'm a pious geek." The one he wore on his forehead was a little leather box, about the size of a fist, that held parchments inscribed with prayers and looked—well—as if someone had strapped a little leather box to his head. Need I say more?)

"Nice phylacteries," I said.

The disciples laughed. Nathaniel made an excellent donkey braying noise.

"You broke the Sabbath," said the Pharisee.

"I'm allowed," said Josh. "I'm the Son of God."

"Oh fuck," Philip said.

"Way to ease them into the idea, Josh," I said.

The following Sabbath a man with a withered hand came to the synagogue while Joshua was preaching and after the sermon, while fifty Pharisees who had gathered at Capernaum just in case something like this happened looked on, Joshua told the man that his sins were forgiven, then healed the withered hand.

Like vultures to carrion they came to Peter's house the next morning.

"No one but God can forgive sins," said the one they had elected as their speaker.

"Really," said Joshua. "So you can't forgive someone who sins against you?"

"No one but God."

"I'll keep that in mind," said Joshua. "Now unless you are here to hear the good news, go away." And Joshua went into Peter's house and closed the door.

The Pharisee shouted at the door, "You blaspheme, Joshua bar Joseph, you—"

And I was standing there in front of him, and I know I shouldn't have done it, but I popped him. Not in the mouth or anything, but right in the phylacteries. The little leather box exploded with the impact and the strips of parchment slowly settled to the ground. I'd hit him so fast that I think he thought it was a supernatural event. A cry went up from the group behind him, protesting—shouting that I couldn't do such a thing, that I deserved stoning, scourging, et cetera, and my Buddhist tolerance just wore a little thin.

So I popped him again. In the nose.

This time he went down. Two of his pals caught him, and another one at the front of the crowd started to reach into his sash for something. I knew that they could quickly overrun me if they wanted to, but I didn't think they would. The cowards. I grabbed the man who was pulling the knife, twisted it away from him, shoved the iron blade between the stones of Peter's house and snapped it off, then handed the hilt back to him. "Go away," I said to him, very softly.

He went away, and all of his pals went with him. I went inside to see how Joshua and the others were getting along.

"You know, Josh," I said. "I think it's time to expand the ministry. You have a lot of followers here. Maybe we should go to the other side of the lake. Out of Galilee for a while."

"Preach to the gentiles?" Nathaniel asked.

"He's right," said Joshua. "Biff is right."

"So it shall be written," I said.

James and John only owned one ship that was large enough to hold all of us and Bartholomew's dogs, and it was anchored at Magdala, two hours' walk south of Capernaum, so we made the trip very early one morning to avoid being stopped in the villages on the way. Joshua had decided to take the good news to the gentiles, so we were going to go across the lake to the town of Gadarene in the state of Decapolis. They kept gentiles there.

As we waited on the shore at Magdala, a crowd of women who had come to the lake to wash clothes gathered around Joshua and begged him to tell them of the kingdom. I noticed a young tax collector who was sitting nearby at his table in the shade of a reed umbrella. He was listening to Joshua, but I could also see his eyes following the behinds of the women. I sidled over.

"He's amazing, isn't he?" I said.

"Yes. Amazing," said the tax collector. He was perhaps twenty, thin, with soft brown hair, a light beard, and light brown eyes.

"What's your name, publican?"

"Matthew," he said. "Son of Alphaeus."

"No kidding, that's my father's name too. Look, Matthew, I assume you can read, write, things like that?"

"Oh yes."

"You're not married, are you?"

"No, I was betrothed, but before the wedding was to happen, her parents let her marry a rich widower."

"Sad. You're probably heartbroken. That's sad. You see those women? There's woman like that all the time around Joshua. And here's the best part, he's celibate. He doesn't want any of them. He's just interested in saving mankind and bringing the kingdom of God to earth, which we all are, of course. But the women, well, I think you can see."

"That must be wonderful."

"Yeah, it's swell. We're going to Decapolis. Why don't you come with us?"

"I couldn't. I've been entrusted to collect taxes for this whole coast."

"He's the Messiah, Matthew. The Messiah. Think of it. You, and the Messiah."

"I don't know."

"Women. The kingdom. You heard about him turning water into wine."

"I really have to—"

"Have you ever tasted bacon, Matthew?"

"Bacon? Isn't that from pigs? Unclean?"

"Joshua's the Messiah, the Messiah says it's okay. It's the best thing you've ever eaten, Matthew. Women love it. We eat bacon every morning, with the women. Really."

"I'll need to finish up here," Matthew said.

"You do that. Here, I'd like you to mark something for me," I looked over his shoulder at his ledger and pointed to a few names. "Meet us at the ship when you're ready, Matthew."

I went back over to the shore, where James and John had pulled the ship in close enough for us to wade out to. Joshua finished up blessing the women and sent them back to their laundry with a parable about stains.

"Gentlemen," I called. "Excuse me, James, John, you too Peter, Andrew. You will not need to worry about your taxes this season. They've been taken care of."

"What?" said Peter. "Where did you get the money—"

I turned and waved toward Matthew, who was running toward the shore. "This good fellow is the publican Matthew. He's here to join us."

Matthew ran up beside me and stood grinning like an idiot while trying to catch his breath. "Hey," he said, waving weakly to the disciples.

"Welcome, Matthew," Joshua said. "All are welcome in the kingdom." Joshua shook his head, turned, and waded out to the ship.

"He loves you, kid," I said. "Loves you."

Thus we did become ten.

Joshua fell asleep on a pile of nets with Peter's wide straw fishing hat over his face. Before I settled down to be rocked to sleep myself, I sent Philip to the back of the boat to explain the kingdom and the Holy Ghost to Matthew. (I figured that Philip's acumen with numbers might help out when talking to a tax collector.) The two sets of brothers sailed the ship, which was wide of beam and small of sail and very, very slow. About halfway across the lake I heard Peter say, "I don't like it. It looks like a tempest."

I sat bolt upright and looked at the sky, and indeed, there were black clouds coming over the hills to the east, low and fast, clawing at the trees with lightning as they passed. Before I had a chance to sit up, a wave broke over the shallow gunwale and soaked me to the core.

"I don't like this, we should go back," said Peter, as a curtain of rain whipped across us. "The ship's too full and the draft too shallow to weather a storm."

"Not good. Not good. Not good," chanted Nathaniel.

Bartholomew's dogs barked and howled at the wind. James and Andrew trimmed the sail and put the oars in the water. Peter moved to the stern to help John with the long steering oar. Another wave broke over the gunwale, washing away one of Bartholomew's disciples, a mangy terrier type.

Water was mid-shin deep in the bottom of the boat. I grabbed a bucket and began bailing and signaled Philip to help, but he had succumbed to the most rapid case of seasickness I had ever even heard of and was retching over the side.

Lightning struck the mast, turning everything a phosphorus white. The explosion was instant and left my ears ringing. One of Joshua's sandals floated by me in the bottom of the boat.

"We're doomed!" wailed Bart. "Doomed!"

Joshua pushed the fishing hat back on his head and looked at the chaos around him. "O ye of little faith," he said. He waved his hand across the sky and the storm stopped. Just like that. Black clouds were sucked back over the hills, the water settled to a gentle swell, and the sun shone down bright and hot enough to raise steam off our clothes. I reached over the side and snatched the swimming doggy out of the waves.

Joshua had laid back down with the hat over his face. "Is the new kid looking?" he whispered to me.

"Yeah," I said.

"He impressed?"

"His mouth is hanging open. He looks sort of stricken."

"Great. Wake me when we get there."

I woke him a little before we reached Gadarene because there was a huge madman waiting for us on the shore, foaming at the mouth, screaming, throwing rocks, and eating the occasional handful of dirt.

"Hold up there, Peter," I said. The sails were down again and we were rowing in.

"I should wake the master," said Peter.

"No, it's okay, I have the stop-for-foaming-madmen authority." Nevertheless, I kicked the Messiah gently. "Josh, you might want to take a look at this guy."

"Look, Peter," said Andrew, pointing to the madman, "he has hair just like yours."

Joshua sat up, pushed back Peter's hat and glanced to the shore. "Onward," he said.

"You sure?" Rocks were starting to land in the boat.

"Oh yeah," said Joshua.

"He's very large," said Matthew, clarifying the already clear.

"And mad," said Nathaniel, not to be outdone in stating the obvious.

"He is suffering," said Joshua. "Onward."

A rock as big as my head thudded into the mast and bounced into the water. "I'll rip your legs off and kick you in the head as you crawl around bleeding to death," said the madman.

"Sure you don't want to swim in from here?" Peter said, dodging a rock.

"Nice refreshing swim after a nap?" said James.

Matthew stood up in the back of the boat and cleared his throat. "What is one tormented man compared to the calming of a storm? Were you all in the same boat I was?"

"Onward," Peter said, and onward we went, the big boat full of Joshua and Matthew and the eight faithless pieces of shit that were the rest of us.

Joshua was out of the boat as soon as we hit the beach. He walked straight up to the madman, who looked as if he could crush the Messiah's head in one of his hands. Filthy rags hung in tatters on him and his teeth were broken and bleeding from eating dirt. His face contorted and bubbled as if there were great worms under the skin searching for an escape. His hair was wild and stuck out in a great grayish tangle, and it did sort of look like Peter's hair.

"Have mercy on me," said the madman. His voice buzzed in his throat like a chorus of locusts.

I slid out of the boat and the others followed me quietly up behind Joshua.

"What is your name, Demon?" Joshua asked.

"What would you like it to be?" said the demon.

"You know, I've always been partial to the name Harvey," Joshua said.

"Well, isn't that a coincidence?" said the demon. "My name just happens to be Harvey."

"You're just messing with me, aren't you?" said Josh.

"Yeah, I am," said the demon, busted. "My name is Legion, for there are a bunch of us in here."

"Out, Legion," Joshua commanded. "Out of this big guy."

There was a herd of pigs nearby, doing piggy things. (I don't know what they were doing. I'm a Jew, what do I know from pigs, except that I like bacon?) A great green glow came out of Legion's mouth, whipped through the air like smoke, then came down on the herd of pigs like a cloud. In a second it was sucked into the pigs' nostrils and they began foaming and making locust noises.

"Be gone," said Joshua. With that the pigs all ran into the sea, sucked huge lungfuls of water, and after only a little kicking, drowned. Perhaps fifty dead pigs bobbed in the swell.

"How can I thank you?" said the big foaming guy, who had stopped foaming, but was still big.

"Tell the people of your land what has happened," Joshua said. "Tell them the Son of God has come to bring them the good news of the Holy Ghost."

"Clean up a little before you tell them," I said.

And off he went, a lumbering monster, bigger even than our own Bartholomew, and smelling worse, which I hadn't thought possible. We sat down on the beach and were sharing some bread and wine when we heard the crowd approaching through the hills.

"The good news travels quickly," said Matthew, whose fresh-faced enthusiasm was starting to irritate me a little now.

"Who killed our pigs?"

The crowd was carrying rakes and pitchforks and scythes and they didn't look at all like they were there to receive the Gospel.

"You fuckers!"

"Kill them!"

"In the boat," said Josh.

"O ye of little—" Matthew's comment was cut short by Bart grabbing him by the collar and dragging him down the beach to the boat.

The brothers had already pushed off and were up to their chests in the water. They pulled themselves in and James and John helped set the oars as Peter and Andrew pulled us into the boat. We fished Bart's disciples out of the waves by the scruffs of their necks and set sail just as the rocks began to rain down on us.

We all looked at Joshua. "What?" he said. "If they'd been Jews that pig thing would have gone over great. I'm new at gentiles."

There was a messenger waiting for us when we reached Magdala. Philip unrolled the scroll and read. "It's an invitation to come to dinner in Bethany during Passover week, Joshua. A ranking member of the Sanhedrin requests your presence at dinner at his home to discuss your wonderful ministry. It's signed Jakan bar Iban ish Nazareth."

Maggie's husband. The creep.

I said, "Good first day, huh, Matthew?"

Chapter 27

The angel and I watched *Star Wars* for the second time on television last night, and I just had to ask. "You've been in God's presence, right, Raziel?"

"Of course."

"Do you think he sounds like James Earl Jones?"

"Who's that?"

"Darth Vader."

Raziel listened for a moment while Darth Vader threatened someone. "Sure, a little. He doesn't breathe that heavy though."

"And you've seen God's face."

"Yes."

"Is he black?"

"I'm not allowed to say."

"He is, isn't he? If he wasn't you'd just say he wasn't."

"I'm not allowed to say."

"He is."

"He doesn't wear a hat like that," said Raziel.

"Ah-ha!"

"All I'm saying is no hat. That's all I'm saying."

"I knew it."

"I don't want to watch this anymore." Raziel switched the channel. God (or someone who sounded like him) said, "This is CNN."

We came up to Jerusalem, in the gate at Bethsaida called the Eye of the Needle, where you had to duck down to pass through, out the Golden Gate, through the Kidron Valley, and over the Mount of Olives into Bethany.

We had left the brothers and Matthew behind because they had jobs, and Bartholomew because he stank. His lack of cleanliness had started to draw attention lately from the local Pharisees in Capernaum and we didn't want to push the issue since we were walking into the lair of the enemy. Philip and Nathaniel joined us on our journey, but stayed behind on the Mount of Olives at a clearing called Gethsemane, where there was a small cave and an olive press. Joshua tried to convince me to stay with them, but I insisted.

"I'll be fine," Joshua said. "It's not my time. Jakan won't try anything, it's just dinner."

"I'm not worried about your safety, Josh, I just want to see Maggie." I did want to see Maggie, but I was worried about Joshua's safety as well. Either way, I wasn't staying behind.

Jakan met us at the gate wearing a new white tunic belted with a blue sash. He was stocky, but not as fat as I expected him to be, and almost exactly my height. His beard was black and long, but had been cut straight across about the level of his collarbone. He wore the pointed linen cap worn by many of the Pharisees, so I couldn't tell if he'd lost any of his hair. The fringe that hung down was dark brown, as were his eyes. The most frightening and perhaps the most surprising thing about him was that there was a spark of intelligence in his eyes. That hadn't been there when we were children. Perhaps seventeen years with Maggie had rubbed off on him.

"Come in, fellow Nazarenes. Welcome to my home. There are some friends inside who wanted to meet you."

He led us through the door into a large great room, large enough in fact to fit any two of the houses we shared at Capernaum. The floor was paved in tile with turquoise and red mosaic spirals in the corners of the room (no pictures, of course). There was a long Roman-style table at which five other men, all dressed like Jakan, sat. (In Jewish households the tables were close to the ground and diners reclined on cushions or on the floor around them.) I didn't see Maggie anywhere, but a serving girl brought in large pitchers of water and bowls for us to wash our hands in.

"Let this water stay water, will you, Joshua?" Jakan said, smiling. "We can't wash in wine."

Jakan introduced us to each of the men, adding some sort of elaborate title to each of their names that I didn't catch, but which indicated, I'm sure, that they were all members of the Sanhedrin as well as the Council of Pharisees. Ambush. They received us curtly, then made their way to the water bowls to wash their hands before dinner, all of them watching as Joshua and I washed and offered prayer. This, after all, was part of the test.

We sat. The water pitchers and bowls were taken away by the serving girl, who then brought pitchers of wine.

"So," said the eldest of the Pharisees, "I hear you have been casting demons out of the afflicted in Galilee."

"Yes, we're having a lovely Passover week," I said. "And you?"

Joshua kicked me under the table. "Yes," he said. "By the power of my father I have relieved the suffering of some who were plagued by demons."

When Joshua said "my father" every one of them squirmed. I noticed movement in one of the doorways to Jakan's back. It was Maggie, making signals and signs like a madwoman, but then Jakan spoke. Attention turned to him and Maggie ducked out of sight.

Jakan leaned forward. "Some have said that you banish these demons by the power of Beelzebub."

"And how could I do that?" Joshua said, getting a little angry. "How could I turn Beelzebub against himself? How can I battle Satan with Satan? A house divided can't stand."

"Boy, I'm starving," I said. "Bring on the eats."

"With the spirit of God I cast out demons, that's how you know the kingdom has come."

They didn't want to hear that. Hell, I didn't want to hear that, not here. If Joshua claimed to bring the kingdom, then he was claiming to be the Messiah, which by their way of thinking could be blasphemy, a crime punishable by death. It was one thing for them to hear it secondhand, it was quite another to have Joshua say it to their faces. But he, as usual, was unafraid.

"Some say John the Baptist is the Messiah," said Jakan.

"There's nobody better than John," Joshua said. "But John doesn't baptize with the Holy Ghost. I do."

They all looked at each other. They had no idea what he was talking about. Joshua had been preaching the Divine Spark—the Holy Ghost—for two years, but it was a new way of looking at God and the kingdom: it was a change. These legalists had worked hard to find their place of power; they weren't interested in change.

Food was put on the table and prayers offered again, then we ate in silence for a while. Maggie was in the doorway behind Jakan again, gesturing with one hand walking over the other, mouthing words that I was supposed to understand. I had something I wanted to give her, but I had to see her in private. It was obvious that Jakan had forbidden her to enter the room.

"Your disciples do not wash their hands before they eat!" said one of the Pharisees, a fat man with a scar over his eye.

Bart, I thought.

"It's not what goes into a man that defiles him," Joshua said, "it's what comes out." He broke off some of the flatbread and dipped it into a bowl of oil.

"He means lies," I said.

"I know," said the old Pharisee.

"You were thinking something disgusting, don't lie."

The Pharisees passed the "no, your turn, no, it's your turn" look around the room.

Joshua chewed his bread slowly, then said, "Why wash the outside of the urn, if there's decay on the inside?"

"Yeah, like you rotting hypocrites!" I added, with more enthusiasm than was probably called for.

"Quit helping!" Josh said.

"Sorry. Nice wine. Manischewitz?"

My shouting evidently stirred them out of their malaise. The old Pharisee said, "You consort with demons, Joshua of Nazareth. This Levi was seen to cause blood to come from a Pharisee's nose and a knife to break of its own, and no one even saw him move."

Joshua looked at me, then at them, then at me again. "You forget to tell me something?"

"He was being an emrod, so I popped him." ("Emrod" is the biblical term for hemorrhoid.) I heard Maggie's giggling from the other room.

Joshua turned back to the creeps. "Levi who is called Biff has studied the art of the soldier in the East," Joshua said. "He can move swiftly, but he is not a demon."

I stood up. "The invitation was for dinner, not a trial."

"This is no trial," said Jakan, calmly. "We have heard of Joshua's miracles, and we have heard that he breaks the Law. We simply want to ask him by whose authority he does these things. This is dinner, otherwise, why would you be here?"

I was wondering that myself, but Joshua answered me by pushing me down in my seat and proceeding to answer their accusations for another two hours, crafting parables and throwing their own piety back in their faces. While

Joshua spoke the word of God, I did sleight-of-hand tricks with the bread and the vegetables, just to mess with them. Maggie came to the doorway and signaled me, pointing frantically to the front door and making threatening, head-bashing gestures which I took to be the consequences for my not understanding her this time.

"Well, I've got to go see a man about a camel, if you'll excuse me."

I stepped out the front door. As soon as I closed it behind me I was hit with the spraying girl-spit of a violently whispering woman.

"YoustupidsonofabitchwhatthefuckdidyouthinkIwastryingtosaytoyou?" She punched me in the arm. Hard.

"No kiss?" I whispered.

"Where can I meet you, after?"

"You can't. Here, take this." I handed her a small leather pouch. "There's a parchment inside to tell you what to do."

"I want to see you two."

"You will. Do what the note says. I have to go back in."

"You bastard." Punch in the arm. Hard.

I forgot what I was doing and entered the house still rubbing my bruised shoulder.

"Levi, have you injured yourself?"

"No, Jakan, but sometimes I strain a shoulder muscle just shaking this monster off."

The Pharisees hated that one. I realized that they were waiting for me to request water so I could go through the whole hand-washing ritual before I sat down to the table again. I stood there, thinking about it, rubbing my shoulder, waiting. How long could it possibly take to read a note? It seemed like a long time, with them staring at me, but I'm sure it was only a few minutes. Then it came, the scream. Maggie let go from the next room, long and high and loud, a virtuoso scream of terror and panic and madness.

I bent over and whispered into Joshua's ear, "Just follow my lead. No, just don't do anything. Nothing."

"But—"

The Pharisees all looked like someone had dropped hot coals into their laps as the scream went on, and on. Maggie had great sustain. Before Jakan could get up to investigate, there came my girl—still shrieking, I might add—a lovely green foam running out of her mouth, her dress torn and hanging in shreds on her blood-streaked body and blood running from the corners of her eyes. She screamed in Jakan's face and rolled her eyes, then leapt onto the table and growled as she kicked every piece of crockery off onto the floor where it shattered. The servant girl ran through screaming, "Demons have taken her, demons have taken her!" then bolted out the front door. Maggie started screeching again, then ran up and down the length of the table, urinating as she went. (Nice touch, I would never have thought of that.)

The Pharisees had backed up against the wall, including Jakan, as Maggie fell on her back on the table, thrashing and growling and screaming obscenities while splattering the front of their white cloaks with green foam, urine, and blood.

"Devils! She's been possessed by devils. Lots of them," I shouted.

"Seven," Maggie said between growls.

"Looks like seven," I said. "Doesn't it, Josh?"

I grabbed the back of Joshua's hair and sort of made him nod in agreement. No one was really watching him anyway, as Maggie was now spouting impressive fountains of green foam both out of her mouth and from between her legs. (Again, a nice touch I wouldn't have thought of.) She settled into a vibrating fit rhythm, with barking and obscenities for counterpoint.

"Well, Jakan," I said politely, "thank you for dinner. It's been lovely but we have to be going." I pulled Joshua to his feet by his collar. He was a little perplexed himself. Not terrified like our host, but perplexed.

"Wait," Jakan said.

"Festering dog penis!" Maggie snarled to no one in particular, but I think everyone knew who she meant.

"Oh, all right, we'll try to help her," I said. "Joshua, grab an arm." I pushed him forward and Maggie grabbed his wrist. I went around to the other side of the table and got hold of her other arm. "We have to get her out of this house of defilement."

Maggie's fingernails bit into my arm as I lifted her up and she pulled herself along on Josh's wrist, pretending to thrash and fight. I dragged her out the front door and into the courtyard. "Make an effort, Joshua, would you," Maggie whispered.

Jakan and the Pharisees bunched at the door. "We need to take her into the wilderness to safely cast out the devils," I shouted. I dragged her, and Joshua for that matter, into the street and kicked the heavy gate closed.

Maggie relaxed and stood up. A mound of green foam cascaded off of her chest. "Don't relax yet, Maggie. When we're farther away."

"Pork-eating goat fucker!"

"That's the spirit."

"Hi, Maggie," Joshua said, taking her arm and finally helping me drag.

"I think it went really well for short notice," I said. "You know, Pharisees make the best witnesses."

"Let's go to my brother's house," she whispered. "We can send word that I'm incurable from there.

"Rat molester!"

"It's okay, Maggie, we're out of range now."

"I know. I was talking to you. Why'd you take seventeen years to get me out of there?"

"You're beautiful in green, did I ever tell you that?"

"I've got to think that that was unethical," Joshua said.

"Josh, faking demonic possession is like a mustard seed."

"How is it like a mustard seed?"

"You don't know, do you? Doesn't seem at all like a mustard seed, does it? Now you see how we all feel when you liken things unto a mustard seed? Huh?"

𝕬t Simon the Leper's house Joshua went to the door first by himself so Maggie's appearance didn't scare the humus out of her brother and sister. Martha answered the door. "Shalom, Martha. I'm Joshua bar Joseph, of Nazareth. Remember me from the wedding in Cana? I've brought your sister Maggie."

"Let me see." Martha tapped her fingernail on her chin while she searched her memory in the night sky. "Were you the one who changed the water into wine? Son of God, was it?"

"There's no need to be that way," Joshua said.

I popped my head around Josh's shoulder. "I gave your sister a powder that sort of foamed her up all red and green. She's a bit nasty-looking right now."

"I'm sure that becomes her," said Martha, with an exasperated sigh. "Come in." She led us inside. I stood by the door while Joshua sat on the floor by the table. Martha took Maggie to the back of the house to help her clean up. It was a large house by our country standards, but not nearly as big as Jakan's. Still, Simon had done well for the son of a blacksmith. I didn't see Simon anywhere.

"Come sit at the table," Joshua said.

"Nope, I'm fine by the door here."

"What's the matter?"

"Do you know whose house this is?"

"Of course, Maggie's brother Simon's."

I lowered my voice. "imon-Say the eper-Lay."

"Come sit down. I'll watch over you."

"Nope. I'm fine here."

Just then Simon came in from the other room carrying a pitcher of wine and a tray of cups in his rag-wrapped hands. White linen covered his face except for his eyes, which were as clear and blue as Maggie's.

"Welcome, Joshua, Levi—it's been a long time."

We'd known Simon as boys, spending as much time as we did hanging around Maggie's father's shop, but he had been older, learning his father's craft then, and far too serious to be associating with boys. In my memory he was strong and tall, but now the leprosy had bent him over like an old woman.

Simon set the cups down and poured for the three of us. I remained against the wall by the door. "Martha doesn't take well to serving," Simon said, by way of apologizing for doing the serving himself. "She tells me that you turned water into wine at the wedding in Cana."

"Simon," Joshua said, "I can heal your affliction, if you'll allow me."

"What affliction?" He lay down at the table across from Joshua. "Biff, come sit with us." He patted a cushion next to him and I ducked in the event that fingers started flying. "I understand that Jakan used my sister as bait for a trap for you two."

"Not much of a trap," Joshua said.

"You expected that?" I asked.

"I thought there would be more, the whole Pharisee council perhaps. I wanted to answer them directly, not have my words passed through a dozen spies and rumormongers. I also wanted to see if there would be any Sadducees there."

Just then I realized what Joshua had already figured out: the Sadducees, the priests, weren't involved in Jakan's little surprise inquisition. They had been born to their power, and were not as easily threatened as the working-class Pharisees. And the Sadducees were the more powerful half of the Sanhedrin, the ones who commanded the soldiers of the Temple guard. Without the priests, the Pharisees were vipers without fangs, for now anyway.

"I hope we haven't brought the judgment of the Pharisees down on your head, Simon," Joshua said.

Simon waved a hand in dismissal. "Not to worry. There'll be no Pharisees coming here. Jakan is terrified of me, and if he really believes that Maggie is possessed, and if his friends believe it, well, I'd bet he's divorced her already."

"She can come back to Galilee with us," I said, looking at Joshua, who looked at Simon, as if to ask permission.

"She may do as she wishes."

"What I wish is to get out of Bethany before Jakan comes to his senses," Maggie said, coming from the other room. She wore a simple woolen dress and her hair was still dripping. There was still green goo on her sandals. She came across the room, knelt down, and gave her brother a huge hug, then a kiss on the eyebrow. "If he comes by or sends word, you'll tell him I'm still here."

I sensed Simon was smiling under the veil. "You don't think he'll want to come in and look around?"

"The coward," Maggie spat.

"Amen," I said. "How did you stay with a creep like that all of these years?"

"After the first year he didn't want to be anywhere near me. Unclean, don't you know? I told him I was bleeding."

"For all those years?"

"Sure. Do you think he would embarrass himself among the members of the Pharisee council by asking them about their own wives?"

Joshua said, "I can heal you of that affliction, if you'll allow me, Maggie."

"What affliction?"

"You should go," Simon said. "I'll send word about what Jakan has done as soon as I know. If he hasn't done it already, I have a friend who will plant the idea that if he doesn't divorce Maggie his place on the Sanhedrin might be questioned."

Simon and Martha waved to us from the doorway, Martha looking like a compact ghost of her older sister and Simon just looking like a ghost.

And thus did we become eleven.

there was a full moon and a sky full of stars thrown over us as we walked back to Gethsemane. From the top of the Mount of Olives we could see across the Kidron Valley to the Temple. Black smoke streamed into the sky from the sacrificial fires which the priests tended day and night. I held Maggie's hand as we walked through the grove of ancient olive trees and out into the clearing near the oil press where we camped. Philip and Nathaniel had built a fire and there were two strangers sitting by it with them. They all stood up as we approached. Philip glared at me, which baffled me until I remembered that he'd been with us at Cana, and seen Joshua and Maggie dancing at the wedding. He thought I was trying to steal Joshua's girl. I let her hand go.

"Master," said Nathaniel, tossing his yellow hair, "new disciples. These are Thaddeus and Thomas the Twins."

Thaddaeus stepped up to Joshua. He was about my height and age, and wore a tattered woolen tunic and looked especially gaunt, as if he might be starving. His hair was cut short like a Roman's, but it looked as if someone had cut it with a dull piece of flint. Somehow he looked familiar.

"Rabbi, I heard you preach when you were with John. I have been with him for two years."

A follower of John, that's where I knew him from, although I didn't remember meeting him. That explained the hungry look as well.

"Welcome, Thaddaeus," Joshua said. "These are Biff and Mary Magdalene, disciples and friends."

"Call me Maggie," Maggie said.

Joshua stepped over to Thomas the Twins, who was only one guy, younger, perhaps twenty, his beard still like soft down in places, his clothes finer than any of ours. "And Thomas."

"Don't, you're standing on Thomas Two," Thomas squealed.

Nathaniel pushed Joshua aside and whispered in his ear a little too loudly. "He sees his twin but no one else can. You said to show mercy, so I haven't told him that he's mad."

"And so you shall be shown mercy, Nathaniel," Joshua said.

"So we won't tell you that you're a ninny," I added.

"Welcome, Thomas," Joshua said, embracing the boy.

"And Thomas Two," Thomas said.

"Forgive me. Welcome, Thomas Two, as well," said Joshua to a perfectly empty spot in space. "Come to Galilee and help us spread the good news."

"He's over there," said Thomas, pointing to a different spot, equally empty.

And thus did we become thirteen.

❚n the trip back to Capernaum Maggie told us about her life, about the dreams she had set aside, and about a child that had died in the first year of her marriage. I could see Joshua was shaken when he heard of the child, and I knew he was thinking that if we hadn't taken off to the East, he would have been there to save it.

"After that," Maggie said, "Jakan didn't come near me. There was bleeding right after the baby died, and as far as he knew it never stopped. He's always been afraid that someone might think that there's a curse on his house, so my duties as a wife were public only. It's a double-edged sword for him. In order to appear dutiful I had to go to the synagogue and to the women's court in the Temple, but if they thought I was going there while I was bleeding I would have been driven out, maybe stoned, and Jakan would have been shamed. Who knows what he'll do now."

"He'll divorce you," I said. "He'll have to if he wants to save face with the Pharisees and the Sanhedrin."

Strangely enough, it was Joshua who I had trouble consoling about Maggie's lost child. She'd lived with the loss for years, cried over it, allowed it to heal as much as it would, but the wound was fresh for Joshua. He walked far behind us, shunning the new disciples who pranced around him like excited puppies. I could tell that he was talking to his father, and it didn't seem to be going well.

"Go talk to him," Maggie said. "It wasn't his fault. It was God's will."

"That's why he feels responsible," I said. We hadn't explained to Maggie about the Holy Ghost, the kingdom, all the changes that Joshua wanted to bring to mankind, and how those were at odds, at times, with the Torah.

"Go talk to him," she said.

I fell back in our column, past Philip and Thaddaeus, who were trying to explain to Nathaniel that it was his own voice he heard when he put his fingers in his ears and spoke, and not the voice of God, and past Thomas, who was having an animated discussion with empty air.

I walked along beside Joshua for a while before I spoke, and then I tried to sound matter-of-fact. "You had to go to the East, Joshua. You know that now."

"I didn't have to go right then. That was cowardly. Would it have been so bad to watch her marry Jakan? To see her child born?"

"Yes, it would have. You can't save everyone."

"Have you been asleep these last twenty years?"

"Have you? Unless you can change the past, you're wasting the present on this guilt. If you don't use what you learned in the East then maybe we shouldn't have gone. Maybe leaving Israel *was* cowardly."

I felt my face go numb as if the blood had drained from it. Had I said that? So, we walked along for a while in silence, not looking at each other. I counted birds, listened to the murmur of the disciples voices ahead, watched Maggie's ass move under her dress as she walked, not really enjoying the elegance of it.

"Well, I, for one, feel better," said Joshua finally. "Thanks for cheering me up."

"Glad to help," I said.

We arrived in Capernaum on the morning of the fifth day after leaving Bethany. Peter and the others had been preaching the good news to the people on the shore of Galilee and there was a crowd of perhaps five hundred people waiting for us. The tension had passed between Joshua and me and the rest of the journey had been pleasant, if for no other reason than we got to hear Maggie laugh and tease us. My jealousy of Joshua returned, but somehow it wasn't bitter. It was more like familiar grief for a distant loss, not the sword-in-the-heart, rending-of-flesh agony of a heartbreak. I could actually leave the two of them alone and talk to other people—think of other things. Maggie loved Joshua, that was assured, but she loved me as well, and there was no way to divine how that might manifest. By following Joshua we had already divorced ourselves of the expectations of normal existence. Marriage, home, family: they were not part of the life we had chosen, Joshua made that clear to all of his disciples. Yes, some of them were married, and some even preached with their wives at their sides, but what set them apart from the multitudes who would follow Joshua was that they had stepped off the path of their own lives to spread the Word. It was to the Word that I lost Maggie, not to Joshua.

As exhausted he was, as hungry, Joshua preached to them. They had been waiting for us and he wouldn't disappoint them. He climbed into one of Peter's boats, rowed out from the shore far enough for the crowd to be able to see him, and he preached to them about the kingdom for two hours.

When he had finished, and had sent the crowd on their way, two newcomers waited among the disciples. They were both compact, strong-looking men in their mid-twenties. One was clean-shaven and wore his hair cut short, so that it formed a helmet of ringlets on his head; the other had long hair with his beard plaited and curled in the style I had seen on some Greeks. Although they wore no jewelry, and their clothes we no more fancy than my own, there was an air of wealth about them both. I thought it might have been power, but if it was, it wasn't the self-conscious power of the Pharisees. If nothing else, they were self-assured.

The one with the long hair approached Joshua and kneeled before him. "Rabbi, we've heard you speak of the coming of the kingdom and we want to join you. We want to help spread the Word."

Joshua looked at the man for a long time, smiling to himself, before he spoke. He took the man by the shoulders and lifted him. "Stand up. You are welcome, friends."

The stranger seemed baffled. He looked back at his friend, then at me, as if I had some answer to his confusion. "This is Simon," he said, nodding toward his friend. "My name is Judas Iscariot."

"I know who you are," Joshua said. "I've been waiting for you."

And so we became fifteen: Joshua, Maggie, and me; Bartholomew, the Cynic; Peter and Andrew, John and James, the fishermen; Matthew, the tax collector; Nathaniel of Cana, the young nitwit; Philip and Thaddeus, who had been followers of John the Baptist; Thomas the twin, who was a loony; and the Zealots, Simon the Canaanite and Judas Iscariot. Fifteen went out into Galilee to preach the Holy Ghost, the coming of the kingdom, and the good news that the Son of God had arrived.

hapter 28

Joshua's ministry was three years of preaching, sometimes three times a day, and although there were some high and low points, I could never remember the sermons word for word, but here's the gist of almost every sermon I ever heard Joshua give.

> *You should be nice to people, even creeps.*
> *And if you:*
>   a) believed that Joshua was the Son of God (and)
>   b) he had come to save you from sin (and)
>   c) acknowledged the Holy Spirit within you (became as a little child, he would say) (and)
>   d) didn't blaspheme the Holy Ghost (see c),
> *then you would:*
>   e) live forever
>   f) someplace nice
>   g) probably heaven.
> *However, if you:*
>   h) sinned (and/or)
>   i) were a hypocrite (and/or)
>   j) valued things over people (and)
>   k) didn't do a, b, c, and d,
> *then you were:*
>   l) fucked

Which is the message that Joshua's father had given him so many years ago, and which seemed, at the time, succinct to the point of rudeness, but made more sense after you listened to a few hundred sermons.

That's what he taught, that's what we learned, that's what we passed on to the people in the towns of Galilee. Not everybody was good at it, however, and some seemed to miss the point altogether. One day Joshua, Maggie, and I returned from preaching in Cana to find Bartholomew sitting by the synagogue at Capernaum, preaching the Gospel to a semicircle of dogs that sat around him. The dogs seemed spellbound, but then, Bart was wearing a flank steak as a hat, so I'm not sure it was his speaking skills that held their attention.

Joshua snatched the steak off of Bartholomew's head and tossed it into the street, where a dozen dogs suddenly found their faith. "Bart, Bart, Bart," Josh said as he shook the big man by the shoulders, "don't give what's holy to dogs. Don't cast your pearls before swine. You're wasting the Word."

"I don't have any pearls. I am slave to no possessions."

"It's a metaphor, Bart," Joshua said, deadpan. "It means don't give the Word to those who aren't ready to receive it."

"You mean like when you drowned the swine in Decapolis? They weren't ready for it?"

Joshua looked at me for help. I shrugged.

Maggie said, "That's exactly right, Bart. You got it."

"Oh, why didn't you say so?" Bart said. "Okay guys, we're off to preach the Word in Magdala." He climbed to his feet and led his pack of disciples toward the lake.

Joshua looked at Maggie. "That's not what I meant at all."

"Yes it is," she said, then she took off to find Johanna and Susanna, two women who had joined us and were learning to preach the gospel.

"That's not what I meant," Joshua said to me.

"Have you ever won an argument with her?"

He shook his head.

"Then say amen and let's go see what Peter's wife has cooked up."

The disciples were gathered around outside of Peter's house, sitting on the logs we had arranged in a circle around a fire pit. They were all looking down and seemed to be caught in some glum prayer. Even Matthew was there, when he should have been at his job collecting taxes in Magdala.

"What's wrong?" asked Joshua.

"John the Baptist is dead," said Philip.

"What?" Joshua sat down on the log next to Peter and leaned against him.

"We just saw Bartholomew," I said. "He didn't say anything about it."

"We just found out," said Andrew. "Matthew just brought the news from Tiberius."

It was the first time since he'd joined us that I'd seen Matthew without the light of enthusiasm in his face. He might have aged ten years in the last few hours. "Herod had him beheaded," he said.

"I thought Herod was afraid of John," I said. It was rumored that Herod had kept John alive because he actually believed him to be the Messiah and was afraid of the wrath of God should the holy man perish.

"It was at the request of his stepdaughter," said Matthew. "John was killed at the behest of a teenage slut."

"Well, jeez, if he wasn't dead already, the irony would have killed him," I said.

Joshua stared into the dirt before him, thinking or praying, I couldn't tell. Finally he said, "John's followers will be like babes in the wilderness."

"Thirsty?" guessed Nathaniel.

"Hungry?" guessed Peter.

"Horny?" guessed Thomas.

"No, you dumbfucks, *lost.* They'll be *lost!*" I said. "Jeez."

Joshua stood. "Philip, Thaddeus, go to Judea, tell John's followers that they are welcome here. Tell them that John's work is not lost. Bring them here."

"But master," Judas said, "John has thousands of followers. If they come here, how will we feed them?"

"He's new," I explained.

The next day was the Sabbath, and in the morning as we all headed to the synagogue, an old man in fine clothes ran out of the bushes and threw himself at Joshua's feet. "Oh, Rabbi," he wailed, "I am the mayor of Magdala. My youngest daughter has died. People say that you can heal the sick and raise the dead, will you help me?"

Joshua looked around. A half-dozen local Pharisees watched us from different points around the village. Joshua turned to Peter. "Take the Word to the synagogue today. I am going to help this man."

"Thank you, Rabbi," the rich man gushed. He hurried off and waved for us to follow.

"Where are you taking us?" I asked.

"Only as far as Magdala," he said.

To Joshua I said, "That's farther than a Sabbath's journey allows."

"I know," Joshua said.

As we passed through all of the small villages along the coast on the way to Magdala, people came out of their houses and followed us for as long as they dared on a Sabbath, but I could also see the elders, the Pharisees, watching as we went.

The mayor's house was large for Magdala, and his daughter had her own sleeping room. He led Joshua into the bedchamber where the girl lay. "Please save her, Rabbi."

Joshua bent down and examined the girl. "Go out of here," he said to the old man. "Out of the house." When the mayor was gone Joshua looked at me. "She's not dead."

"What?"

"This girl is sleeping. Maybe they've given her some strong wine, or some sleeping powder, but she is not dead."

"So this is a trap?"

"I didn't see this one coming either," Joshua said. "They expect me to claim that I raised her from the dead, healed her, when she's only sleeping. Blasphemy *and* healing on the Sabbath."

"Let me raise her from the dead, then. I mean, I can do this one if she's only sleeping."

"They'll blame me for whatever you do as well. You may be their target too. The local Pharisees didn't devise this themselves."

"Jakan?"

Josh nodded. "Go get the old man, and gather as many witnesses as you can, Pharisees as well. Make a ruckus."

When I had about fifty people gathered in and around the house, Joshua announced, "This girl isn't dead, she's sleeping, you foolish old man." Joshua shook the girl and she sat up rubbing her eyes. "Keep watch on your strong wine, old man. Rejoice that you have not lost your daughter, but grieve that you have broken the Sabbath for your ignorance."

Then Joshua stormed out and I followed him. When we were a ways down the street he said, "Do you think they bought it?"

"Nope," I said.

"Me either," Joshua said.

In the morning a Roman soldier came to Peter's house with messages. I was still sleeping when I heard the shouting. "I can only speak to Joshua of Nazareth," someone said in Latin.

"You'll speak to me or you'll never speak again," I heard someone else say. (Obviously someone who had no desire to live a long life.) I was up and running in an instant, my tunic waving unbelted behind me. I rounded the corner at Peter's house to see Judas facing down a legionnaire. The soldier had partially drawn his short sword.

"Judas!" I barked. "Back down."

I put myself between them. I knew I could disarm the soldier easily, but not the legion that would follow him if I did. "Who sends you, soldier?"

"I have a message from Gaius Justus Gallicus, commander of the Sixth Legion, for Joshua bar Joseph of Nazareth." He glared at Judas over my shoulder. "But there is nothing in my orders to keep me from killing this dog while delivering it."

I turned to face Judas, whose face was on fire with anger. I knew he carried a dagger in his sash, although I hadn't told Joshua about it. "Justus is a friend, Judas."

"No Roman is the friend of a Jew," said Judas, making no effort whatever to whisper.

And at that point, realizing that Joshua hadn't reached our new Zealot recruit with the message of forgiveness for all men, and that he was going to get himself killed, I quickly reached up under Judas' tunic, clamped onto his scrotum, squeezed once, rapidly and extremely hard, and after he blasted a mouthful of slobber on my chest, his eyes rolled in his head and he slumped to his knees, unconscious. I caught him and lowered him to the ground so he didn't hit his head. Then I turned to the Roman.

"Fainting spells," I said. "Let's go find Joshua."

*J*ustus had sent us three messages from Jerusalem: Jakan had indeed divorced Maggie; the Pharisees' full council had met and they were plotting to kill Joshua; and Herod Antipas had heard of Joshua's miracles and was afraid that he might be the reincarnation of John the Baptist. Justus' only personal note was one word: *Careful.*

"Joshua, you need to hide," said Maggie. "Leave Herod's territory until things settle down. Go to Decapolis, preach to the gentiles. Herod Philip has no love for his brother, his soldiers won't bother you." Maggie had become a fiercely dedicated preacher herself. It was as if she had channeled her personal passion for Joshua into a passion for the Word.

"Not yet," said Joshua. "Not until Philip and Thaddeus return with John's followers. I will not leave them lost. I need a sermon, one that can serve as if it was my last, one that will sustain the lost while I'm gone. Once I deliver it to Galilee, I'll go to Philip's territory."

I looked at Maggie and she nodded, as if to say, *Do what you have to, but protect him.*

"Let's write it then," I said.

Like any great speech, the Sermon on the Mount sounds as if it just happened spontaneously, but actually Joshua and I worked on it for over a week—Joshua dictating and me taking notes on parchment. (I had invented a way of sandwiching a thin piece of charcoal between two pieces of olive wood so that I could write without carrying a quill and inkwell.) We worked in front of Peter's house, out in the boat, even on the mountainside where he would deliver the sermon. Joshua wanted to devote a long section of the sermon to adultery, largely, I realize now, motivated by my relationship with Maggie. Even though Maggie had resolved to stay celibate and preach the Word, I think Joshua wanted to drive the point home.

Joshua said, "Put in 'If a man even looks at a woman with lust in his heart, he has committed adultery.' "

"Really, you want to go with that? And this 'If a divorced woman remarries she commits adultery'?"

"Yeah."

"Seems a little harsh. A little Pharisee-ish."

"I had some people in mind. What do you have?"

" 'Verily I say unto you'—I know you like to say 'verily' when you're talking about adultery—anyway, 'Verily I say unto you, that should a man put oil upon a woman's naked body, and make her go upon all fours and bark like a dog, while knowing her, if you know what I mean, then he has committed adultery, and surely if a woman do the same thing right back, well she has jumped on the adultery donkey cart herownself. And if a woman should pretend to be a powerful queen, and a man a lowly slave boy, and if she should call him humiliating names and make him lick upon her body, then surely they have sinned like big dogs—and woe unto the man if he pretends to be a powerful queen, and—' "

"That's enough, Biff."

"But you want to be specific, don't you. You don't want people to walk around wondering, 'Hey, is this adultery, or what? Maybe you should roll over.' "

"I'm not sure that being that specific is a good idea."

"Okay, how 'bout this: 'Should a man or a woman have any goings-on with their mutual naughty bits, then it is more than likely they are committing adultery, or at least they should consider it.' "

"Well, maybe more specific than that."

"Come on, Josh, this isn't an easy one like 'Thou shalt not kill.' Basically, there you got a corpse, you got a sin, right?"

"Yes, adultery can be sticky."

"Well, yes . . . Look, a seagull!"

"Biff, I appreciate that you feel obliged to be an advocate for your favorite sins, but that's not what I need here. What I need is help writing this sermon. How we doing on the Beatitudes?"

"Pardon me?"

"The blesseds."

"We've got: Blessed are those who hunger and thirst after righteousness; blessed are the poor in spirit, the pure in heart, the whiners, the meek, the—"

"Wait, what are we giving the meek?"

"Let's see, uh, here: Blessed are the meek, for to them we shall say, 'attaboy.' "

"A little weak."

"Yeah."

"Let's let the meek inherit the earth."

"Can't you gave the earth to the whiners?"

"Well then, cut the whiners and give the earth to the meek."

"Okay. Earth to the meek. Here we go. Blessed are the peacemakers, the mourners, and that's it."

"How many is that?"

"Seven."

"Not enough. We need one more. How about the dumbfucks?"

"No, Josh, not the dumbfucks. You've done enough for the dumbfucks. Nathaniel, Thomas—"

"Blessed are the dumbfucks for they, uh—I don't know—they shall never be disappointed."

"No, I'm drawing the line at dumbfucks. Come on, Josh, why can't we have any powerful guys on our team? Why do we have to have the meek, and the poor, the oppressed, and the pissed on? Why can't we, for once, have blessed are the big powerful rich guys with swords?"

"Because they don't need us."

"Okay, but no 'Blessed are the dumbfucks.' "

"Who then?"

"Sluts?"

"No."

"How about the wankers? I can think of five or six disciples that would be really blessed."

"No wankers. I've got it: Blessed are those who are persecuted for righteousness' sake."

"Okay, better. What are you going to give them?"

"A fruit basket."

"You can't give the meek the whole earth and these guys a fruit basket."

"Give them the kingdom of heaven."

"The poor in spirit got that."

"Everybody gets some."

"Okay then, 'share the Kingdom of Heaven.'" I wrote it down.

"We could give the fruit basket to the dumbfucks."

"NO DUMBFUCKS!"

"Sorry, I just feel for them."

"You feel for everyone, Josh. It's your job."

"Oh yeah. I forgot."

We finished writing the sermon only a few hours before Philip and Thaddeus returned from Judea leading three thousand of John's followers. Joshua had them gather on a hillside above Capernaum, then sent the disciples into the crowd to find the sick and bring them to him. He performed miracles of healing all morning, then coming into the afternoon he gathered us together at the spring below the mountain.

Peter said, "There's at least another thousand people from Galilee on the hill, Joshua, and they are hungry."

"How much food do we have?" Joshua asked.

Judas came forward with a basket. "Five loaves and two fish."

"That will do, but you'll need more baskets. And about a hundred volunteers to help distribute the food. Nathaniel, you, Bartholomew, and Thomas go into the crowd and find me fifty to a hundred people who have their own baskets. Bring them here. By the time you get back we'll have the food for them."

Judas threw down his basket. "We have five loaves, how do you think—"

Joshua held up his hand for silence and the Zealot clammed up. "Judas, today you've seen the lame walk, the blind see, and the deaf hear."

"Not to mention the blind hear and the deaf see," I added.

Joshua scowled at me. "It will take little more to feed a few of the faithful."

"There are but five loaves!" shouted Judas.

"Judas, once there was a rich man, who built great barns and granaries so he could save all of the fruits of his wealth long into his old age. But on the very day his barns were finished, the Lord said, "Hey, we need you up here." And the rich man did say, "Oh shit, I'm dead." So what good did his stuff do him?"

"Huh?"

"Don't worry about what you're going to eat."

Nathaniel, Bart, and Thomas started off to their assigned duty, but Maggie grabbed Joshua and held him fast. "No," she said. "No one does anything until you promise us that you'll go into hiding after this sermon."

Joshua smiled. "How can I hide, Maggie? Who will spread the Word? Who will heal the sick?"

"We will," Maggie continued. "Now promise. Go into the land of the gentiles, out of Herod's reach, just until things calm down. Promise or we don't move." Peter and Andrew stepped up behind Maggie to show their support. John and James were nodding as she spoke.

"So be it," said Joshua. "But now we have hungry people to feed."

And we fed them. The loaves and the fish were multiplied, jars were brought in from the surrounding villages and filled with water, which was carried to the mountainside, and all the while the local Pharisees watched and growled and spied, but they hadn't missed the healings, and they didn't miss the Sermon on the Mount, and word of it went back to Jerusalem with their poison reports.

Afterward, at the spring by the shore, I gathered up the last of the pieces of bread to take home with us. Joshua came down the shore with a basket over his head, then pulled it off when he got to me.

"When we said we wanted you to hide we meant something a little less obvious, Joshua. Great sermon, by the way."

Joshua started helping me gather up the bread that was strewn around on the ground. "I wanted to talk to you and I couldn't get away from the crowd without hiding under the basket. I'm having a little trouble preaching humility."

"You're so good at that one. People line up to hear the humility sermon."

"How can I preach that the humble will be exalted and the exalted will be humbled at the same time I'm being exalted by four thousand people?"

"Bodhisattva, Josh. Remember what Gaspar taught you about being a bodhisattva. You don't have to be humble, because you are denying your own ascension by bringing the good news to other people. You're out of the humility flow, so to speak."

"Oh yeah." He smiled.

"But now that you mention it," I said, "it does seem a little hypocritical."

"I'm not proud of that."

"Then you're okay."

That evening, when we had all gathered again in Capernaum, Joshua called us to the fire ring in front of Peter's house and we watched the last gold of the sunlight reflecting on the lake as Joshua led us in a prayer of thanks.

Then he made the call: "Okay, who wants to be an apostle?"

"I do, I do," said Nathaniel. "What's an apostle?"

"That's a guy who makes drugs," I said.

"Me, me," said Nathaniel. "I want to make drugs."

"I'll try that," said John.

"That's an apothecary," said Matthew. "An apothecary mixes powders and makes drugs. Apostle means 'to send off.' "

"Is this kid a whiz, or what," I said, pointing a thumb at Matthew.

"That's right," said Joshua, "messengers. You'll be sent off to spread the message that the kingdom has come."

"Isn't that what we're doing now?" asked Peter.

"No, now you're disciples, but I want to appoint apostles who will take the Word into the land. There will be twelve, for the twelve tribes of Israel. I'll give you power to heal, and power over devils. You'll be like me, only in a different outfit. You'll take nothing with you except your clothes. You'll live only off the charity of those you preach to. You'll be on your own, like sheep among wolves. People will persecute you and spit on you, and maybe beat you, and if that happens, well, it happens. Shake off the dust and move on. Now, who's with me?"

And there was a roaring silence among the disciples.

"How about you, Maggie?"

"I'm not much of a traveler, Josh. Makes me nauseous. Disciple's fine with me."

"How 'bout you, Biff?"

"I'm good. Thanks."

Joshua stood up and just counted them off. "Nathaniel, Peter, Andrew, Philip, James, John, Thaddeus, Judas, Matthew, Thomas, Bartholomew, and Simon. You're the apostles. Now get out there and apostilize."

And they all looked at each other.

"Spread the good news, the son of man is here! The kingdom is coming. Go! Go! Go!"

They got up and sort of milled around.

"Can we take our wives?" asked James.

"Yes."

"Or one of the women disciples?" asked Matthew.

"Yes."

"Can Thomas Two go too?"

"Yes, Thomas Two can go."

Their questions answered, they milled around some more.

"Biff," Joshua said. "Will you assign territories for everybody and send them out?"

"Okey-dokey," I said. "Who wants Samaria? No one? Good. Peter, it's yours. Give 'em hell. Caesarea? Come on, you weenies, step up . . ."

Thus were the twelve appointed to their sacred mission.

The next morning seventy of the people who we'd recruited to help feed the multitude came to Joshua when they heard about the appointing of the apostles.

"Why only twelve?" one man asked.

"You all want to cast off what you own, leave your families, and risk persecution and death to spread the good news?" Joshua asked.

"Yes," they all shouted.

Joshua looked at me as if he himself couldn't believe it.

"It was a really good sermon," I said.

"So be it," said Joshua. "Biff, you and Matthew assign territories. Send no one to his hometown. That doesn't seem to work very well."

And so the twelve and the seventy were sent out, and Joshua, Maggie, and I went into Decapolis, which was the territory of Herod's brother, Philip, and camped and fished and basically hid out. Joshua preached a little, but only to small groups, and although he did heal the sick, he asked them not to tell anyone about the miracles.

After three months hiding in Philip's territory, word came by boat from across the lake that someone had intervened on Joshua's behalf with the Pharisees and that the death warrant, which had never really been formal, had been lifted. We went home to Capernaum and waited for the apostles to return. Their enthusiasm had waned some after months in the field.

"It sucks."

"People are mean."

"Lepers are creepy."

Matthew came out of Judea with more news of Joshua's mysterious benefactor from Jerusalem. "His name is Joseph of Arimathea," said Matthew. "He's a wealthy merchant, and he owns ships and vineyards and olive presses. He seems to have the ear of the Pharisees, but he is not one of them. His wealth has given him some influence with the Romans as well. They are considering making him a citizen, I hear."

"What makes him want to help us?" I asked.

"I talked to him for a long time about the kingdom, and about the Holy Ghost and the rest of Joshua's message. He believes." Matthew smiled broadly, obviously proud of his powerful convert. "He wants you to come to his house for dinner, Joshua. In Jerusalem."

"Are you sure it's safe for Joshua there?" asked Maggie.

"Joseph has sent this letter guaranteeing Joshua's safety along with all who accompany him to Jerusalem." Matthew held out the letter.

Maggie took the scroll and unrolled it. "My name is on this too. And Biff's."

"Joseph knew you would be coming, and I told him that Biff sticks to Joshua like a leech."

"Excuse me?"

"I mean, that you accompany the master wherever he travels," Matthew added quickly.

"But why me?" Maggie asked.

"Your brother Simon who is called Lazarus, he is very sick. Dying. He's asked for you. Joseph wanted you to know that you would have safe passage."

Josh grabbed his satchel and started walking that moment. "Let's go," he said. "Peter, you are in charge until I return. Biff, Maggie, we need to make Tiberius before dark. I'm going to see if I can borrow some camels there. Matthew, you come too, you know this Joseph. And Thomas, you come along, I want to talk to you."

So off we went, into what I was sure were the jaws of a trap.

Along the way Joshua called Thomas to walk beside him. Maggie and I walked behind them only a few paces, so we could hear their conversation. Thomas kept stopping to make sure that Thomas Two could keep up with them.

"They all think I'm mad," Thomas said. "They laugh at me behind my back. Thomas Two has told me."

"Thomas, you know I can lay my hands upon you and you will be cured. Thomas Two will no longer speak to you. The others won't laugh at you."

Thomas walked along for a while without saying anything, but when he looked back at Joshua I could see tears streaking his cheeks. "If Thomas Two goes away, then I'll be alone."

"You won't be alone. You'll have me."

"Not for long. You don't have long with us."

"How do you know that?"

"Thomas Two told me."

"We won't tell the others quite yet, all right, Thomas?"

"Not if you don't want me to. But you won't cure me, will you? You won't make Thomas Two go away?"

"No," Joshua said. "We may both need an extra friend soon." He patted Thomas on the shoulder, then turned to walk on ahead to catch up with Matthew.

"Well, don't step on him!" Thomas shouted.

"Sorry," said Joshua.

I looked at Maggie. "Did you hear that?"

She nodded. "You can't let it happen, Biff. He doesn't seem to care about his own life, but I do, and you do, and if you let harm come to him I'll never forgive you."

"But Maggie, *everyone* is supposed to be forgiven."

"Not you. Not if something happens to Josh."

"So be it. So, hey, once Joshua heals your brother, you want to go do something, get some pomegranate juice, or a falafel, or get married or something?"

She stopped in her tracks, so I stopped too. "Are you ever paying attention to anything that goes on around you?"

"I'm sorry, I was overcome by faith there for a moment. What did you say?"

When we got to Bethany, Martha was waiting for us in the street in front of Simon's house. She went right to Joshua and he held out his arms to embrace her, but when she got to him she pushed him away. "My brother is dead," she said. "Where were you?"

"I came as soon as I heard."

Maggie went to Martha and held her as they both cried. The rest of us stood around feeling awkward. The two old blind guys, Crustus and Abel, whom Joshua had once healed, came over from across the street.

"Dead, dead and buried four days," said Crustus. "He turned a sort of char-treuse at the end."

"Emerald, it was emerald, not chartreuse," said Abel.

"My friend Simon truly sleeps, then," Joshua said.

Thomas came up and put his hand on Joshua's shoulder. "No, master, he's dead. Thomas Two thinks it may have been a hairball. Simon was a leopard, you know?"

I couldn't stand it. "He was a LEPER, you idiot! Not a leopard."

"Well, he IS dead!" shouted Thomas back. "Not sleeping."

"Joshua was being figurative, he knows he's dead."

"Do you guys think you could be just a little more insensitive?" said Matthew, pointing to the weeping sisters.

"Look, tax collector, when I want your two shekels I'll ask—"

"Where is he?" Joshua asked, his voice booming over the sobs and protests.

Martha pushed out of her sister's embrace and looked at Joshua. "He bought a tomb in Kidron," said Martha.

"Take me there, I need to wake my friend."

"Dead," said Thomas. "Dead, dead, dead."

There was a sparkle of hope amid the tears in Martha's eyes. "Wake him?"

"Dead as a doornail. Dead as Moses. Mmmph . . ." Matthew clamped his hand over Thomas's mouth, which saved me having to render the twin uncon-scious with a brick.

"You believe that Simon will rise from the dead, don't you?" asked Joshua.

"In the end, when the kingdom comes, and everyone is raised, yes, I believe."

"Do you believe I am who I say I am?"

"Of course."

"Then show me where my friend lies sleeping."

Martha moved like a sleepwalker, her exhaustion and grief driven back just enough for her to lead us up the road to the Mount of Olives and down into the Kidron Valley. Maggie had been deeply shaken by the news of her brother's death as well, so Thomas and Matthew helped her along while I walked with Joshua.

"Four days dead, Josh. Four days. Divine Spark or not, the flesh is empty."

"Simon will walk again if he is but bone," said Joshua.

"Okey-dokey. But this has never been one of your better miracles."

When we got to the tomb there was a tall, thin, aristocratic man sitting outside eating a fig. He was clean-shaven and his gray hair was cut short like a Roman's. If he hadn't worn the two-striped tunic of a Jew I would have thought him a Roman citizen.

"I thought you would come here," he said. He knelt before Joshua. "Rabbi, I'm Joseph of Arimathea. I sent word through your disciple Matthew that I wanted to meet with you. How may I serve?"

"Stand up, Joseph. Help roll away this stone."

As with many of the larger tombs carved into the side of the mountain, there was a large flat stone covering the doorway. Joshua put his arms around Maggie and Martha while the rest of us wrestled with the stone. As soon as the seal was broken I was hit with a stench that gagged me and Thomas actually lost his supper in the dirt.

"He stinks," said Matthew.

"I thought he would smell more like a cat," said Thomas.

"Don't make me come over there, Thomas," I said.

We pushed the stone as far as it would go, then we ran away gasping for fresh air.

Joshua held his arms out as if waiting to embrace his friend. "Come out, Simon Lazarus, come out into the light." Nothing but stench came out of the tomb.

"Come forth, Simon. Come out of that tomb," Joshua commanded.

And absolutely nothing happened.

Joseph of Arimathea shifted uncomfortably from foot to foot. "I wanted to talk to you about the dinner at my house before you got there, Joshua."

Joshua held up his hand for silence.

"Simon, dammit, come out of there."

And ever so weakly, there came a voice from inside the tomb. "No."

"What do you mean, 'no'? You have risen from the dead, now come forth. Show these unbelievers that you have risen."

"I believe," I said.

"Convinced me," said Matthew.

"A no is as good as a personal appearance, as far as I'm concerned," said Joseph of Arimathea.

I'm not sure any of us who had smelled the stench of rotting flesh really wanted to see the source. Even Maggie and Martha seemed a little dubious about their brother's coming out.

"Simon, get your leprous ass out here," Joshua commanded.

"But I'm . . . I'm all icky."

"We've all seen icky before," said Joshua. "Now come out into the light."

"My skin is all green, like an unripe olive."

"Olive green!" declared Crustus, who had followed us into Kidron. "I told you it wasn't chartreuse."

"What the hell does he know? He's dead," said Abel.

Finally Joshua lowered his arms and stormed into the tomb. "I can't believe that you bring a guy back from the dead and he doesn't even have the courtesy to come out—WHOA! HOLY MOLY!" Joshua came backing out of the tomb, stiff-legged. Very calmly and quietly, he said, "We need clean clothes, and some water to wash with, and bandages, lots of bandages. I can heal him, but we have to sort of get all of his parts stuck back together first."

"Hold on, Simon," Joshua shouted to the tomb, "we're getting some supplies, then I'll come in and heal your affliction."

"What affliction?" asked Simon.

Chapter 29

When it was all finished, Simon looked great, better than I'd ever seen him look. Joshua had not only raised him from the dead, but also healed his leprosy. Maggie and Martha were ecstatic. The new and improved Simon invited us back to his house to celebrate. Unfortunately, Abel and Crustus had witnessed the resurrection and the healing, and despite our admonishments, they started to spread the story through Bethany and Jerusalem.

Joseph of Arimathea accompanied us to Simon's house, but he was hardly in a celebratory mood. "This dinner's not exactly a trap," he told Joshua, "it's more like a test."

"I've been to one of their trials by dinner," said Joshua. "I thought you were a believer."

"I am," said Joseph, "especially after what I saw today, but that's why you have to come to my house and have dinner with the Pharisees from the council. Show them who you are. Explain to them in an informal setting what it is that you are doing."

"Satan himself once asked me to prove myself," said Joshua. "What proof do I owe these hypocrites?"

"Please, Joshua. They may be hypocrites, but they have great influence over the people. Because they condemn you the people are afraid to listen to the Word. I know Pontius Pilate, I don't think anyone would harm you in my home and risk his wrath."

Joshua sat for a moment, sipping his wine. "Then into the den of vipers I shall go."

"Don't do it, Joshua," I said.

"And you have to come alone," said Joseph. "You can't bring any of the apostles."

"That's not a problem," I said. "I'm only a disciple."

"Especially not him," said Joseph. "Jakan bar Iban will be there."

"So I guess it's another night sitting home for me, too," said Maggie.

Later we all watched and waved as Joseph and Joshua left to go back to Jerusalem for the dinner at Joseph's house.

"As soon as they get around the corner you follow them," Maggie said to me.

"Of course."

"Stay close enough to hear if he needs you."

"Absolutely."

"Come here." She pulled me inside the door where the others wouldn't see and gave me one of those Maggie kisses that made me walk into walls and forget my name for a few minutes. It was the first in months. She released me and held me at arm's length, then, "You know that if there were no Joshua, I wouldn't love anyone but you," she said.

"You don't have to bribe me to watch over him, Maggie."

"I know. That's one of the reasons I love you," she said. "Now go."

My years of trying to sneak up on the monks in the monastery paid me back as I shadowed Joshua and Joseph through Jerusalem. They had no idea I was following, as I slipped from shadow to shadow, wall to tree, finally to Joseph's house, which lay south of the city walls, only a stone's throw from the palace of the high priest, Caiaphas. Joseph of Arimathea's house was only slightly smaller than the palace itself, but I was able to find a spot on the roof of an adjacent building where I could watch the dinner through a window and still have a view of the front door.

Joshua and Joseph sat in the dining room drinking wine by themselves for a while, then gradually the servants let in the other guests as they arrived in groups of twos and threes. There were a dozen of them by the time dinner was served, all of the Pharisees that had been at the dinner at Jakan's house, plus five more that I had never seen before, but all were severe and meticulous about washing before dinner and checking each other to make sure that all was in order.

I couldn't hear what they were saying, but I really didn't care. There seemed to be no immediate threat to Joshua, and that was all I was worried about. He could hold his own on the rhetorical battlefield. Then, when it seemed that it would end without incident, I saw the tall hat and white robe of a priest in the street, and with him two Temple guards carrying their long, bronze-tipped spears. I dropped down off the roof and made my way around the opposite side of the house, arriving just in time to see a servant lead the priest inside.

𝕒s soon as Joshua came through the door at Simon's house Martha and Maggie showered him with kisses as if he had returned from the war, then led him to the table and started interrogating him about the dinner.

"First they yelled at me for having fun, drinking wine, and feasting. Saying that if I was truly a prophet I would fast."

"And what did you tell them?" I asked, still a little winded from the running to get to Simon's house ahead of Joshua.

"I said, well, John didn't eat anything but bugs, and he never drank wine in his life, and he certainly never had any fun, and they didn't believe him, so what kind of standards were they trying to set, and please pass the tabbouleh."

"What did they say then?"

"Then they yelled at me for eating with tax collectors and harlots."

"Hey," said Matthew.

"Hey," said Martha.

"They didn't mean you, Martha, they meant Maggie."

"Hey," said Maggie.

"I told them that tax collectors and harlots would see the kingdom of God before they did. Then they yelled at me for healing on the Sabbath, not washing my hands before I eat, being in league with the Devil again, and blaspheming by claiming to be the Son of God."

"Then what?"

"Then we had dessert. It was some sort of cake made with dates and honey. I liked it. Then a guy came to the door wearing priest's robes."

"Uh-oh," said Matthew.

"Yeah, that was bad," said Joshua. "He went around whispering in the ears of all the Pharisees, then Jakan asked me by what authority I raised Simon from the dead."

"And what did you say?"

"I didn't say anything, not with the Sadducee there. But Joseph told them that Simon hadn't been dead. He was just sleeping."

"So what did they say to that?"

"Then they asked me by what authority I woke him up."

"And what did you say?"

"I got angry then. I said by all the authority of God and the Holy Ghost, by the authority of Moses and Elijah, by the authority of David and Solomon, by the authority of thunder and lightning, by the authority of the sea and the air and the fire in the earth, I told them."

"And what did they say?"

"They said that Simon must have been a very sound sleeper."

"Sarcasm is wasted on those guys," I said.

"Completely wasted," said Joshua. "Anyway, then I left, and outside there were two guards from the Temple. The shafts of their spears had been broken and they were both unconscious. There was blood on one's scalp. So I healed them, and when I saw they were coming around, I came here."

"They don't think you attacked the guards?" Simon asked.

"No, the priest followed me down. He saw them at the same time that I did."

"And your healing them didn't convince him?"

"Hardly."

"So what do we do now?"

"I think we should go back to Galilee. Joseph will send word if anything comes of the meeting of the council."

"You know what will come of it," Maggie said. "You threaten them. And now they have the priests involved. You know what will happen."

"Yes, I do," said Joshua. "But you don't. We'll leave for Capernaum in the morning."

Later Maggie came to me in the great room of Simon's house, where we were all bedded down for the night. She crawled under my blanket and put her lips right next to my ear. As usual, she smelled of lemons and cinnamon. "What did you do to those guards?" she whispered.

"I surprised them. I thought they might be there to arrest Joshua."

"You might have gotten him arrested."

"Look, have you done this before? Because if you have some sort of plan, please let me in on it. Personally, I'm making this up as I go along."

"You did good," she whispered. She kissed my ear. "Thank you."

I reached for her and she shimmied away.

"And I'm still not going to sleep with you," she said.

The messenger must have ridden through several nights to get ahead of us, but when we got back to Capernaum there was already a message waiting from Joseph of Arimathea.

Joshua:

Pharisee council condemned you to death for blasphemy. Herod concurs. No official death warrant issued, but suggest you take disciples into

*Herod Philip's territory until things settle down. No word from the priests
yet, which is good. Enjoyed having you at dinner, please drop by next time
you're in town.*

> *Your friend,*
> *Joseph of Arimathea*

Joshua read the message aloud to all of us, then pointed to a deserted mountaintop on the northern shore of the lake near Bethsaida. "Before we leave Galilee again, I am going up that mountain. I will stay there until all in Galilee who wish to hear the good news have come. Only then will I leave to go to Philip's territory. Go out now and find the faithful. Tell them where to find me."

"Joshua," Peter said, "there are already two or three hundred sick and lame waiting at the synagogue for you to heal them. They've been gathering for all the days you've been gone."

"Why didn't you tell me?"

"Well, Bartholomew greeted them and took their names, then we told them that you'd be with them as soon as you got the chance. They're fine."

"I lead the dogs back and forth by them occasionally so we look busy," said Bart.

Joshua stormed off to the synagogue waving his hands in the air as if asking God why he had been plagued by a gang of dimwits, but then, I might have been reading that into his gesture. The rest of us spread out into Galilee to announce that Joshua was going to be preaching a great sermon on a mountain north of Capernaum. Maggie and I traveled together, along with Simon the Canaanite and Maggie's friends Johanna and Susanna. We decided to take three days and walk a circle through northern Galilee that would take us through a dozen towns and bring us back to the mountain just in time to help direct the pilgrims that would be gathering. The first night we camped in a sheltered valley outside a town called Jamnith. We ate bread and cheese by the fire and afterward Simon and I shared wine while the women went off to sleep. It was the first time I'd ever had a chance to talk to the Zealot without his friend Judas around.

"I hope Joshua can bring the kingdom down on their heads now," Simon said. "Otherwise I may have to look for another prophet to pledge my sword to."

I nearly choked on my wine, and handed him the wineskin as I fought for breath.

"Simon," I said, "do you believe he's the Son of God?"

"No."

"You don't, and you're still following him?"

"I am not saying he's not a great prophet, but the Christ? the Son of God? I don't know."

"You've traveled with him. Heard him speak. Seen his power over demons, over people. You've seen him heal people. Feed people. And what does he ask?"

"Nothing. A place to sleep. Some food. Some wine."

"And if you could do those things, what would you have?"

Here Simon leaned back and looked into the stars, as he let his imagination unroll. "I would have villages full of women in my bed. I'd have a fine palace, and slaves to bathe me. I would have the finest food and wine and kings would travel from far away just to look at my gold. I would be glorious."

"But Joshua has only his cloak and his sandals."

Simon seemed to snap out of his reverie, and he wasn't happy about it. "Just because I am weak does not make him the Christ."

"That's exactly what makes him the Christ."

"Maybe he's just naive."

"Count on it," I said. I stood and handed him the wineskin. "You can finish it. I'm going to sleep."

Simon raised his eyebrows. "The Magdalene, she's a luscious woman. A man could lose himself there."

I took a deep breath and thought about defending Maggie's honor, or even warning Simon about making advances on her, but then I thought better of it. The Zealot needed to learn a lesson that I wasn't qualified to teach. But Maggie was.

"Good night, Simon," I said.

In the morning I found Simon sitting by the cold ashes of the fire, cradling his head in his hands. "Simon?" I inquired.

He looked up at me and I saw a huge purple goose egg on his forehead, just below the bangs of his Roman haircut. A spot of blood seeped out of the middle. His right eye was nearly swollen shut.

"Ouch," I said. "How did you do that?"

Just then Maggie came out from behind a bush. "He accidentally crawled into Susanna's bedroll last night," Maggie said. "I thought he was an attacker, so naturally, I brained him with a rock."

"Naturally," I said.

"I'm so sorry, Simon," Maggie said. I could hear Susanna and Johanna giggling behind the bush.

"It was an honest mistake," said Simon. I couldn't tell whether he meant his or Maggie's, but either way he was lying.

"Good thing you're an apostle," I said. "You'll have that healed up by noon."

We finished our loop of northern Galilee without incident, and indeed, Simon was nearly healed by the time we returned to the mountain above Bethsaida, where Joshua awaited us with over five thousand followers.

"I can't get away from them long enough to find baskets," Peter complained.

"Everywhere I go a there are fifty people following me," said Judas. "How do they expect us to bring them food if they won't let us work?"

I had heard similar complaints from Matthew, James, and Andrew, and even Thomas was whining that people were stepping all over Thomas Two. Joshua had multiplied seven loaves into enough to feed the multitude, but no one could get to the food to distribute it. Maggie and I finally fought our way to the top of the mountain where we found Joshua preaching. He signaled the crowd that he was going to take a break, then came over to us.

"This is excellent," he said. "So many of the faithful."

"Uh, Josh . . ."

"I know," he said. "You two go to Magdala. Get the big ship and bring it to Bethsaida. Once we feed the faithful I'll send the disciples down to you. Go out into the lake and wait for me."

We managed to pull John out of the crowd and took him with us to Magdala to help sail the ship back up the coast. Neither Maggie nor I felt confident enough to handle the big boat without one of the fishermen on board. A half-day later we docked in Bethsaida, where the other apostles were waiting for us.

"He's led them to the other side of the mountain," Peter said. "He'll deliver a blessing then send them on their way. Hopefully they'll go home and he can meet us."

"Did you see any soldiers in the crowd?" I asked.

"Not yet, but we should have been out of Herod's territory by now. The Pharisees are hanging on the edge of the crowd like they know something is going to happen."

We assumed that he would be swimming or rowing out in one of the small boats, but when he finally came down to the shore the multitude was still following him, and he just kept walking, right across the surface of the water to the boat. The crowd stopped at the shore and cheered. Even we were astounded by this new miracle, and we sat in the boat with our mouths hanging open as Joshua approached.

"What?" he said. "What? What? What?"

"Master, you're walking on the water," said Peter.

"I just ate," Joshua said. "You can't go into the water for an hour after you eat. You could get a cramp. What, none of you guys have mothers?"

"It's a miracle," shouted Peter.

"It's no big deal," Joshua said, dismissing the miracle with the wave of a hand. "It's easy. Really, Peter, you should try it."

Peter stood up in the boat tentatively.

"Really, try it."

Peter started to take off his tunic.

"Keep that on," said Joshua. "And your sandals too."

"But Lord, this is a new tunic."

"Then keep it dry, Peter. Come to me. Step upon the water."

Peter put one foot over the side and into the water.

"Trust your faith, Peter," I yelled. "If you doubt you won't be able to do it."

Then Peter stepped with both feet onto the surface of the water, and for a split second he stood there. And we were all amazed. "Hey, I'm—" Then he sank like a stone. He came up sputtering. We were all doubled over giggling, and even Joshua had sunk up to his ankles, he was laughing so hard.

"I can't believe you fell for that," said Joshua. He ran across the water and helped us pull Peter into the boat. "Peter, you're as dumb as a box of rocks. But what amazing faith you have. I'm going to build my church on this box of rocks."

"You would have Peter build your church?" asked Philip. "Because he tried to walk on the water."

"Would you have tried it?" asked Joshua.

"Of course not," said Philip. "I can't swim."

"Then who has the greater faith?" Joshua climbed into the boat and shook the water off of his sandals, then tousled Peter's wet hair. "Someone will have to carry on the church when I'm gone, and I'm going to be gone soon. In the spring we'll go to Jerusalem for the Passover, and there I will be judged by the scribes and the priests, and there I will be tortured and put to death. But three days from the day of my death, I shall rise, and be with you again."

As Joshua spoke Maggie had latched onto my arm. By the time he was finished speaking her nails had drawn blood from my biceps. A shadow of grief seemed to pass over the faces of the disciples. We looked not at each other, and neither at the ground, but at a place in space a few feet from our faces, where I suppose one looks for a clear answer to appear out of undefined shock.

"Well, that sucks," someone said.

We landed at the town of Hippos, on the eastern shore of the Sea of Galilee, directly across the lake from Tiberius. Joshua had preached here before when we had come over to hide the first time, and there were people in the town who would receive the apostles into their homes until Joshua sent them out again.

We'd brought many baskets of the broken bread from Bethsaida, and Judas and Simon helped me unload them from the ship, wading in and out of the shallows where we anchored, as Hippos had no dock.

"The bread stood piled like small mountains," Judas said. "Much more than when we fed the five thousand. A Jewish army could fight long days on that kind of supply. If the Romans have taught us anything its that an army fights on its stomach."

I stopped schlepping and looked at him.

Simon, who stood next to me, set his basket down on the beach, then lifted the edge of his sash to show me the hilt of his dagger. "The kingdom will be ours only when we take it by the sword. We've had no problem spilling Roman blood. No master but God."

I reached over and gently pulled Simon's sash back over the hilt of his dagger. "Have you ever heard Joshua talk about doing harm to anyone? Even an enemy?"

"No," Judas said. "He can't speak openly about taking the kingdom until he's ready to strike. That's why he always speaks in parables."

"That is a crock of rancid yak butter," said a voice from the ship. Joshua sat up, a net hung over his head like a tattered prayer shawl. He'd been sleeping in the bow of the ship and we'd completely forgotten about him. "Biff, call everyone together, here on the beach. I haven't made myself clear to everyone, evidently."

I dropped my basket and ran into town to get the others. In less than an hour we were all seated on the beach and Joshua paced before us.

"The kingdom is open to everyone," Joshua said. "Ev-ree-one, get it?"

Everyone nodded.

"Even Romans."

Everyone stopped nodding.

"The kingdom of God is upon us, but the Romans will remain in Israel. The kingdom of God has nothing to do with the kingdom of Israel, do you all understand that?"

"But the Messiah is supposed to lead our people to freedom," Judas shouted.

"No master but God!" Simon added.

"Shut up!" said Joshua. "I was not sent to deliver wrath. We will be delivered into the kingdom by forgiveness, not conquest. People, we have been over this, what have I not made clear?"

"How we are to cast the Romans out of the kingdom?" shouted Nathaniel.

"You should know better," Joshua said to Nathaniel, "you yellow-haired freak. One more time, we can't cast the Romans out of the kingdom because the kingdom is open to all."

And I think they were getting it, at least the two Zealots were getting it, because they looked profoundly disappointed. They'd waited their whole life for the Messiah to come along and establish the kingdom by crushing the Romans, now he was telling them in his own divine words that it wasn't going to happen. But then Joshua started with the parables.

"The kingdom is like a wheat field with tares, you can't pull out the tares without destroying the grain."

Blank stares. Doubly blank from the fishermen, who didn't know squat from farming metaphors.

"A tare is a rye grass," Joshua explained. "It weaves its roots amid the roots of wheat or barley, and there's no way to pull them out without ruining the crop."

Nobody got it.

"Okay," Joshua continued. "The children of heaven are the good people, and the tares are the bad ones. You get both. And when you're all done, the angels pick out the wicked and burn them."

"Not getting it," said Peter. He shook his head, and his gray mane whipped around his face like a confused lion trying to shake off the sight of a flying wildebeest.

"How do you guys preach this stuff if you don't understand it? Okay, try this: the kingdom of heaven is like, uh, a merchant seeking pearls."

"Like before swine," said Bartholomew.

"Yes! Bart! Yes! Only no swine this time, same pearls though."

Three hours later, Joshua was still at it, and he was starting to run out of things to liken the kingdom to, his favorite, the mustard seed, having failed in three different tries.

"Okay, the kingdom is like a monkey." Joshua was hoarse and his voice was breaking.

"How?"

"A Jewish monkey, right?"

"Is it like a monkey eating a mustard seed?"

I stood up and went to Joshua and put my arm around his shoulder. "Josh, take a break." I led him down the beach toward the village.

He shook his head. "Those are the dumbest sons of bitches on earth."

"They've become like little children, as you told them to."

"Stupid little children," Joshua said.

I heard light footsteps on the sand behind us and Maggie threw her arms around our necks. She kissed Joshua on the forehead, making a loud wet smacking sound, then looked as if she was going to do the same to me so I shied away.

"You two are the ninnies here. You both rail on them about their intelligence, when that doesn't have anything to do with why they're here. Have either one of you heard them preach? I have. Peter can heal the sick now. I've seen it. I've seen James make the lame walk. Faith isn't an act of intelligence, it's an act of imagination. Every time you give them a new metaphor for the kingdom they see the metaphor, a mustard seed, a field, a garden, a vineyard, it's like pointing something out to a cat—the cat looks at your finger, not at what you're pointing at. They don't need to understand it, they only need to believe, and they do. They imagine the kingdom as they need it to be, they don't need to grasp it, it's there already, they can let it be. Imagination, not intellect."

Maggie let go of our necks, then stood there grinning like a madwoman. Joshua looked at her, then at me.

I shrugged. "I told you she was smarter than both of us."

"I know," Joshua said. "I don't know if I can stand you both being right in the same day. I need some time to think and pray."

"Go on then," Maggie said, waving him on. I stopped and watched my friend walk into the village, having absolutely no idea what I was supposed to do. I turned back to Maggie.

"You heard the Passover prediction?"

She nodded. "I take it you didn't confront him."

"I don't know what to say."

"We need to talk him out of it. If he knows what awaits him in Jerusalem, why go? Why don't we go into Phoenicia or Syria? He could even take the good news to Greece and be perfectly safe. They have people running all over the place preaching different ideas—look at Bartholomew and his Cynics."

"When we were in India, we saw a festival in the city of their goddess Kali. She's a goddess of destruction, Maggie. It was the bloodiest thing I've ever seen, thousands of animals slaughtered, hundreds of men beheaded. The whole world seemed slick with blood. Joshua and I saved some children from being flayed alive, but when it was over, Joshua kept saying, no more sacrifices. No more."

Maggie looked at me as if she expected more. "So? It was horrible, what did you expect him to say?"

"He wasn't talking to me, Maggie. He was talking to God. And I don't think he was making a request."

"Are you saying that he thinks his father wants to kill him for trying to change things, so he can't avoid it because it's the will of God?"

"No, I'm saying that he's going to allow himself to be killed to show his father that things need to be changed. He's not going to try to avoid it at all."

For three months we begged, we pleaded, we reasoned, and we wept, but we could not talk Joshua out of going to Jerusalem for Passover. Joseph of Arimathea had sent word that the Pharisees and Sadducees were still plotting against Joshua, that Jakan had been speaking out against Joshua's followers in the Court of the Gentiles, outside the Temple. But the threats only seemed to strengthen Joshua's resolve. A couple of times Maggie and I managed to tie Joshua up and stash him in the bottom of a boat, using knots that we had learned from the sailor brothers Peter and Andrew, but both times Joshua appeared a few minutes later holding the cords that had bound him, saying things like, "Good knots, but not quite good enough, were they?"

Maggie and I worried together for days before we left for Jerusalem. "He could be wrong about the execution," I said.

"Yes, he could be," Maggie agreed.

"Do you think he is? Wrong about it, I mean?"

"I think I'm going to throw up."

"I don't see how that's going to stop him."

And it didn't. The next day we left for Jerusalem. On the way we stopped to rest along the road at a town along the Jordan River called Beth Shemesh. We were sitting there, feeling somber and helpless, watching the column of pilgrims move along the riverbank, when an old woman emerged from the column and beat her way through the reclining apostles with a walking staff.

"Out of the way, I need to talk to this fellow. Move, you oaf, you need to take a bath." She bonked Bartholomew on the head as she passed and his doggy pals nipped at her heels. "Look out there, I'm an old woman, I need to see this Joshua of Nazareth."

"Oh no, Mother," John wailed.

James got up to stop her and she threatened him with the staff.

"What can I help you with, Old Mother?" Joshua asked.

"I'm the wife of Zebedee, mother of these two." She pointed her staff to James and John. "I hear that you're going to the kingdom soon."

"If it be so, so be it," said Joshua.

"Well, my late husband, Zebedee, God rest his soul, left these boys a perfectly good business, and since they've been following you around they've run it into the ground." She turned to her sons. "Into the ground!"

Joshua put his hand on her arm, but instead of the usual calm that I saw come over people when he touched them, Mrs. Zebedee pulled away and swung her staff at him, barely missing his head. "Don't try to bamboozle me, Mr. Smooth Talker. My boys have ruined their father's business for you, so I want your assurance that in return they get to sit on either side of the throne in the kingdom. It's only fair. They're good boys." She turned to James and John. "If your father was alive it would kill him to see what you two have done."

"But Old Mother, it's not up to me who will sit next to the throne."

"Who is it up to?"

"Well, it's up to the Lord, my father."

"Well then go ask him." She leaned on her staff and tapped a foot. "I'll wait."

"But . . ."

"You would deny a dying woman her last request?"

"You're not dying."

"You're killing me here. Go check. Go."

Joshua looked at us all sheepishly. We all looked away, cowards that we were. It's not as if any of us had ever learned to deal with a Jewish mother either.

"I'll go up on that mountain and check," Joshua said, pointing to the highest peak in the area.

"Well go, then. You want I should be late for the Passover?"

"Right. Okay, then, I'll go check, right now." Josh backed away slowly, sort of sidled toward the mountain. Mount Tabor, I think it was.

Mrs. Zebedee went after her sons like she was shooing chickens out of the garden. "What are you, pillars of salt? Go with him."

Peter laughed and she whirled around with her staff ready to brain him. Peter pretended to cough. "I'd better go along, uh, just in case they need a witness." He scurried after Joshua and the other two.

The old woman glared at me. "What are you looking at? You think the pain of childbirth ends when they move away? What do you know? Does a broken heart know from a different neighborhood?"

They were gone all night, a very long night in which we all got to hear about John and James' father, Zebedee, who evidently had possessed the courage of Daniel, the wisdom of Solomon, the strength of Samson, the devotion of Abraham, the good looks of David, and the tackle of Goliath, God rest his soul. (Funny, James had always described his father as a wormy little guy with a lisp.) When the four came back over the hill we all leapt to our feet and ran to greet them—I would have carried them back on my shoulders if it would have shut the old woman up.

"Well?" she said.

"It was amazing," Peter said to us all, ignoring the old woman. "We saw three thrones. Moses was on one, Elijah was on another, and the third was ready for Joshua. And a huge voice came out of the sky, saying, 'This is my son, with whom I am well pleased.' "

"Oh yeah, he said that before," I said.

"I heard it this time," Joshua said, smiling.

"Just the three chairs then?" said Mrs. Zebedee. She looked at her two sons, who were cowering behind Joshua. "No place for you two, of course." She started to stagger away from them, a hand clutched to her heart. "I suppose one can be happy for the mothers of Moses and Elijah and this Nazareth boy, then. They don't have to know what it is to have a spike in the heart."

Down the riverbank she limped, off toward Jerusalem.

Joshua squeezed the brothers' shoulders. "I'll fix it." He ran after Mrs. Zebedee.

Maggie elbowed me and when I looked around at her there were tears in her eyes. "He's not wrong," she said.

"That's it," I said. "Well, ask his mother to talk him out of it. No one can resist her—I mean, I can't. I mean, she's not you, but . . . Look! Is that a seagull?"

art VI

Passion

Nobody's perfect. . . . Well, there was this one guy, but we killed him.

ANONYMOUS

Sunday

Joshua's mother and his brother James found us outside of the Golden Gate of Jerusalem, where we were waiting for Bartholomew and John, who were looking for Nathaniel and Philip to return with James and Andrew, who were off trying to find Judas and Thomas, who had been sent into the city to look for Peter and Maggie, who were looking for Thaddeus and Simon, who had been sent to look for a donkey.

"You'd think they'd have found one by now," Mary said.

According to prophecy, Joshua was supposed to enter the city on the colt of a donkey. Of course, no one was going to find one. That was the plan. Even Joshua's brother James had agreed to be part of the conspiracy. He'd gone ahead to wait inside the gate, just in case one of the disciples had missed the point and actually came back with a donkey.

About a thousand of Joshua's followers from Galilee had gathered on the road to the Golden Gate. They had lined the road with palm fronds for Joshua's entrance to the city, and they were cheering and singing hosannas all afternoon in anticipation of his triumphant entrance, but as the afternoon wore into evening, and no colt showed, the crowd gradually dispersed as everybody got hungry and went into the city to find something to eat. Only Joshua, his mother, and I were still waiting.

"I was hoping you might talk some sense into him," I said to Mary.

"I've seen this coming for a long time," Mary said. She wore her usual blue dress and shawl, and the usual light in her face seemed faded, not by age, but by grief. "Why do you think I sent for him two years ago?"

It was true, she had sent Joshua's younger brothers Judah and Jose to the synagogue at Capernaum to bring him home, claiming he was mad, but Joshua hadn't even gone outside to meet them.

"I wish you two wouldn't talk about me like I'm not here," Joshua said.

"We're trying to get used to it," I said. "If you don't like it, then give up this stupid plan to sacrifice yourself."

"What do you think we've been preparing for all of these years, Biff?"

"If I'd known it was this I wouldn't have helped. You'd still be stuck in a wine amphora in India."

He squinted to see through the gate. "Where is everyone? How hard can it be to find one simple ass?"

I looked at Joshua's mother, and although there was pain in her eyes she smiled. "Don't look at me," she said. "No one on my side of the family would ever sacrifice a straight line like that."

It was too easy, so I let it go. "They're all at Simon's house in Bethany, Josh. They aren't coming back tonight."

Joshua didn't say a word. He just climbed to his feet and walked off toward Bethany.

there is nothing you can do to stop this from happening!" Joshua screamed at the apostles, who were gathered in the front room of Simon's house. Martha ran from the room crying when Joshua glared at her. Simon looked at the floor, as did the rest of us. "The priest and the scribes will take me, and put me on trial. They will spit on me and scourge me and then they will kill me. I will rise from the dead on the third day and walk among you again, but you cannot stop what must happen. If you love me, you will accept what I'm telling you."

Maggie got up and ran out of the house, snatching the communal purse from Judas as she went. The Zealot started to rise to go after her but I pushed him back down on his cushion. "Let her go."

We all sat there in silence, trying to think of something to do, something to say. I don't know what everyone else was thinking, but I was still trying to formulate some way for Joshua to make his point without giving his life. Martha returned to the room with wine and cups and served each of us in turn, not looking at Joshua when she filled his cup. Joshua's mother followed her back out of the room, I presumed to help her prepare supper.

In time, Maggie came back, sliding through the door and going directly to Joshua, where she sat down at his feet. She took the communal purse out of her cloak and from it she pulled a small alabaster box, the sort that was used to store the precious ointments that women used to anoint the bodies of the dead at burial. She tossed the empty purse to Judas. Without a word, she broke the seal on the box and poured the ointment on Joshua's feet, then untied her long hair and began to wipe the oil from his feet with it. The rich aroma of spices and perfume filled the room.

In an instant Judas was on his feet and across the room. He snatched the box of ointment off the floor. "The money from this could have fed hundreds of the poor."

Joshua looked up at the Zealot and there were tears in his eyes. "You'll always have the poor, Judas, but I'm only here for a short while longer. Let her be."

"But . . ."

"Let her be," Joshua said. He held out his hand and Judas slammed the alabaster box into it, then stormed out of the house. I could hear him shouting out in the street, but I couldn't make out what he was saying.

Maggie poured the rest of the oil on Joshua's head and drew patterns on his forehead with her finger. Joshua tried to take her hand but she pulled it away from him and stepped back until he dropped his hand. "A dead man can't love," she said. "Be still."

When we followed Joshua to the Temple the next morning, Maggie was nowhere to be seen.

Monday

On Monday Joshua led us through the Golden Gate into Jerusalem, but this time there were no palm fronds laid on the road and no one was singing hosannas. (Well, there was this one guy, but he was always singing hosannas at the Golden Gate. If you gave him a coin he'd stop for a while.)

"It would be nice to be able to buy a little something for breakfast," Judas said. "If the Magdalene hadn't spent all of our money."

"Joshua smells nice, though," Nathaniel said. "Don't you think Joshua smells nice?"

Sometimes you find yourself grateful for the most unlikely things. Right then, when I saw Judas grit his teeth and the vein stand out on his forehead, I said a quick prayer of thanks for Nathaniel's naïveté.

"He does smell nice," said Bartholomew. "It makes one want to reassess one's values regarding the material comforts."

"Thank you, Bart," said Joshua.

"Yes, there's nothing like a good-smelling man," said John dreamily. Suddenly we were all very uncomfortable and there was a lot of throat-clearing and coughing and we all walked a few paces farther apart. (I haven't told you about John, have I?) Then John started to make a great and pathetic show of noticing the women as they passed. "Why, that little heifer would give a man some strong sons," John said in a booming and falsely masculine voice. "A man could surely plant some seed there, he could."

"Please shut up," James said to his brother.

"Maybe," said Philip, "you could have your mother come over and tell that woman to cleave unto you."

Everyone snickered, even Joshua. Well, everyone except James.

"You see?" he said to his brother. "You see what you've started? You little nancy."

"There's a nubile wench," exclaimed John unconvincingly. He pointed to a woman who was being dragged toward the city gates by a group of Pharisees, her clothes hanging in shreds on her body (which indeed appeared to be nubile, so credit to John for working outside of his element).

"Block the road," Joshua said.

The Pharisees came up to our human blockade and stopped. "Let us pass, Rabbi," the oldest of them said. "This woman has been caught in the act of adultery this very day and we're taking her out of the city to be stoned, as is the law." The woman was young and her hair fell in dirty curls around her face. Terror had twisted her face and her eyes were rolled back in her head, but an hour ago she had probably been pretty.

Joshua crouched and began writing in the dust at his feet. "What's your name?" he asked.

"Jamal," said the leader. I watched Joshua write the man's name, then next to it a list of sins.

"Wow, Jamal," I said. "A goose? I didn't even know that was possible."

Jamal dropped the adulteress's arm and stepped back. Joshua looked up at the other man who was holding the woman. "And your name?"

"Uh, Steve," said that man.

"His name is not Steve," said another man in the crowd. "It's Jacob."

Joshua wrote "Jacob" in the dust. "No," said Jacob. He let go of the woman, pushing her toward us. Then Joshua stood up and took the stone from the man nearest him, who surrendered it easily. His attention was focused on the list of sins written in the dirt. "Now let us stone this harlot," Joshua said. "Whoever of you is without sin, cast the first stone." And he held out the stone to them. They gradually backed away. In a moment they had all gone back the way they had come and the adulteress fell to Joshua's feet and hugged his ankles. "Thank you, Rabbi. Thank you so much."

"That's okay," said Joshua. He lifted her to her feet. "Now go, and sin no more."

"You really smell good, you know that?" she said.

"Yeah, thanks. Now go."

She started off. "I should make sure she gets home okay," I said. I started off after her, but Joshua caught the back of my tunic and pulled me back. "You missed the 'sin no more' part of my instructions?"

"Look, I've already committed adultery with her in my heart, so, you know, why not enjoy it?"

"No."

"You're the one who set the standards. By those rules, even John committed adultery with her in his heart, and he doesn't even like women."

"Do too," said John.

"To the Temple," Joshua said, pressing on.

"Waste of a perfectly good adulteress, if you ask me."

In the outer court of the Temple, where the women and the Gentiles were allowed to go, Joshua called us all together and began to preach the kingdom. Each time he would get started, a vendor would come by barking, "Get your doves. Get your sacrificial doves. Pure as the driven snow. Everybody needs one." Then Joshua would begin again and the next vendor would come by.

"Unleavened bread! Get your unleavened bread! Only one shekel. Piping hot matzo, just like Moses ate on the way out of Egypt, only fresher."

And a little girl who was lame was brought to Joshua and he started to heal her and ask about her faith when . . .

"Your denarii's changed to shekels, while you wait! No amount too large or small. Drachmas to talents, talents to shekels—all your money changed while you wait."

"Do you believe that the Lord loves you?" Joshua asked the little girl.

"Bitter herbs! Get your bitter herbs!" cried a vendor.

"Dammit all!" Joshua screamed in frustration. "You're healed, child, now get out of here." He waved off the little girl, who got up and walked for the first time in her life, then he slapped a dove vendor, ripped the top off his cage of birds, and released a cloud of doves into the sky.

"This is a house of prayer! Not a den of thieves."

"Oh no, not the moneychangers," Peter whispered to me.

Joshua grabbed a long low table where men were changing a dozen currencies into shekels (the only coin allowed for commerce inside the Temple complex) and he flipped it over.

"Oh, that's it, he's fucked," Philip said. And he was. The priests took a big percentage from the moneychangers. He might have slid by before, but now he'd interfered with their income.

"Out, you vipers! Out!" Joshua had taken a coil of rope from one of the vendors and was using it as a scourge to drive the vendors and the moneychangers out of the Temple gates. Nathaniel and Thomas had joined in Joshua's tirade, kicking at the merchants as they scampered away, but the rest of us sat staring or ministered to those who had come to hear Joshua speak.

"We should stop this," I said to Peter.

"You think you could stop this?" Peter nodded to the corner of the court-yard, where at least twenty priests had come out from the Inner Temple to watch the fracas.

"He's going to bring down the wrath of the priests on all of us," Judas said. He was looking at the Temple guards, who had stopped pacing the walls and were watching the goings-on below in the courtyard. To Judas' credit, he, Simon, and a few of the others had managed to calm the small crowd of the faithful who had gathered to be blessed and healed before Joshua's tantrum.

Beyond the walls of the Temple we could see the Roman soldiers staring down from the battlements of Herod the Great's old palace, which the governor commandeered during feast weeks when he brought the legions to Jerusalem. The Romans didn't enter the Temple unless they sensed insurrection, but if they entered, Jewish blood would be spilled. Rivers of it.

"They won't come in," Peter said, a tiny note of doubt in his voice. "They can see that this is a Jewish matter. They don't care if we kill each other."

"Just watch Judas and Simon," I said. "If one of them starts with that no-master-but-God thing, the Romans will come down like an executioner's blade."

Finally, Joshua was out of breath, soaked in sweat, and barely able to swing the coil of rope he was carrying, but the Temple was clear of merchants. A large crowd had started to follow him, shouting at the vendors as Joshua drove them out of the Temple. The crowd (probably eight hundred to a thousand people) was the only thing that kept the priests from calling the guards down on Joshua right then. Josh tossed the rope aside and led the crowd back to where we had been watching in horror.

"Thieves," he said to us breathlessly as he passed. Then he went to a little girl with a withered arm who had been waiting beside Judas.

"Pretty scary, huh?" Joshua said to her.

She nodded. Joshua put his hands over her withered arm.

"Are those guys in the tall hats coming over here?"

She nodded again.

"Here, can you make this sign with your finger?"

He showed her how to stick out her middle finger. "No, not with that hand, with this one."

Joshua took his hand away from her withered arm and she wiggled her fingers. The muscle and tendons had filled out until it looked identical to her other arm.

"Now," Joshua said, "make that sign. That's good. Now show it to those guys behind me with the tall hats. That's a good girl."

by whose authority do you perform these healings," said one of the priests, obviously the highest-ranking of the group.

"No master—" Simon began to shout but he was cut off by a vicious blow to the solar plexus from Peter, who then pushed the Zealot to the ground and sat on him while furiously whispering in his ear. Andrew had come up behind Judas and seemed to be delivering a similar lecture without benefit of the body blow.

Josh took a little boy from his mother's arms and held him. The boy's legs waved in the air as if they had no bones at all. Without looking away from the boy, Joshua said, "By what authority did John baptize?"

The priests looked around among themselves. The crowd moved in closer. We were in Judea, John's territory. The priests knew better than to challenge John's authority under God in front of a crowd this size, but they certainly weren't going to confirm it for Joshua's sake, either. "We can't say at this time," said the priest.

"Then I can't say either," said Joshua. He stood the little boy on his feet and held him steady as the boy's legs took his full weight, probably for the first time ever. The boy wobbled like a newborn colt and Joshua caught him and laughed. He took the boy's shoulders and helped him walk back to his mother, then he turned on the priests and looked at them for the first time.

"You would test me? Test me. Ask me what you will, you vipers, but I will heal these people and they shall know the word of God in spite of you."

Philip had moved up behind me during this speech and he whispered, "Can't you knock him out or something with your methods from the East? We have to get him out of here before he says any more."

"I think we're too late, John," I said. "Just don't let the crowd disperse. Go out into the city and bring more. The crowd is his only protection now. And find Joseph of Arimathea too. He might be able to help if this gets out of hand."

"This isn't out of hand?"

"You know what I mean."

The inquisition went on for two hours, with the priests concocting every verbal trap they could think of, and Joshua wiggling out sometimes, and blundering through at others. I looked for some way to get Joshua out of the Temple without him being arrested, but the more I looked, the more I noticed that the guards had moved down off the walls and were hovering around the gates to the courtyard.

Meanwhile the chief priest droned on: "A man dies and leaves no sons, but his wife marries his brother, who has three sons by his first wife . . . [and on] The three of them leave Jericho and head south, going three point three furlongs per hour, but they are leading two donkeys, which can carry two . . . [and on] So the Sabbath ends, and they are able to resume, adding on the thousand steps allowed under the law . . . and the wind is blowing southwest at two furlongs per hour . . . [and on] How much water will be required for the journey? Give your answer in firkins."

"Five," Joshua said, as soon as they stopped speaking. And all were amazed.

The crowd roared. A woman shouted, "Surely he is the Messiah."

"The Son of God has come," said another.

"You guys aren't helping," I shouted back at them.

"You didn't show your work, you didn't show your work," chanted the youngest of the priests.

Judas and Matthew had been scratching out the problem on the paving stones of the courtyard as the priest recited, but they had long since lost track. They looked up and shook their heads.

"Five," Joshua repeated.

The priests looked around among themselves. "That's right, but that doesn't give you authority to heal in the Temple."

"In three days, there will be no Temple, for I'll destroy it, and you nest of vipers with it. And three days after that, a new Temple shall be built in honor of my father."

And then I grabbed him around the chest and started dragging him toward the gate. The other apostles followed the plan and moved around us in a wedge. Beyond that, the crowd pressed in. Hundreds moved along with us.

"Wait, I'm not done!" Joshua yelled.

"Yes you are."

"Surely the true king of Israel has come to bring forth the kingdom," one woman shouted.

Peter smacked her on the back of the head. "Stop helping."

By the sheer mass of the crowd we were able to get Joshua out of the Temple and through the streets to Joseph of Arimathea's house.

Joseph let us in and led us to the upper room, which had a high arched stone ceiling, rich carpets on the floors and walls, piles of cushions, and a long low table for dining. "You're safe here, but I don't know for how long. They've already called a meeting of the Sanhedrin."

"But we just left the Temple," I said. "How?"

"You should have let them take me," Joshua said.

"The table will be set for the Passover feast of the Essenes," Joseph said. "Stay here for supper."

"Celebrate the Passover early? Why?" John asked. "Why celebrate with the Essenes?"

Joseph looked away from Joshua when he answered. "Because at the Essenes' feast, they don't kill a lamb."

Tuesday

We all slept that night in the upper room of Joseph's house. In the morning Joshua went downstairs. He was gone for a bit, then came back up the stairs.

"They won't let me leave," he said.

"They?"

"The apostles. My own apostles won't let me leave." He went back to the stairway. "You're interfering with the will of God!" he shouted down. He turned back to me. "Did you tell them not to let me leave?"

"Me? Yep."

"You can't do that."

"I sent Nathaniel to Simon's to fetch Maggie. He returned alone. Maggie wouldn't talk to him, but Martha did. Temple soldiers had been there, Josh."

"So?"

"What do you mean, so? They were there to arrest you."

"Let them."

"Joshua, you don't have to sacrifice yourself to prove this point. I've been thinking about it all night. You can negotiate."

"With the Lord?"

"Abraham did it. Remember? Over the destruction of Sodom and Gomorrah. He starts out getting the Lord to agree to spare the cities if he can find fifty righteous men, but by the end, he talks God down to ten. You can try something like that."

"That's not completely the point, Biff." Here he came over to me, but I found I couldn't look him in the eye, so I went to one of the large arched windows that looked down on the street. "I'm afraid of this— of what's going to happen. I can think of a dozen things I'd rather do this week than be sacrificed, but I know that it has to happen. When I told the priests that I would tear the Temple down in three days, I meant that all the corruption, all the pretense, all the ritual of the Temple that keeps men from knowing God would be destroyed. And on the third day, when I come back, everything will be new, and the kingdom of God will be everywhere. I'm coming back, Biff."

"Yeah, I know, you said that."

"Well, believe in me."

"You're not good at resurrections, Josh. Remember the old woman in Japhia? The soldier in Sepphoris, what did he last? Three minutes?"

"But look at Maggie's brother Simon. He's been back from the dead for months now."

"Yeah, and he smells funny."

"He does not."

"No, really, when you get close to him he smells spoiled."

"How would you know? You won't get close to him because he used to be a leper."

"Thaddeus mentioned it the other day. He said, 'Biff, I believe this Simon Lazarus fellow has spoiled.' "

"Really? Then let's go ask Thaddeus."

"He might not remember."

Joshua went down the steps to a low-ceilinged room with a mosaic floor and small windows cut high in the walls. Joshua's mother and brother James had joined the apostles. They all sat there against the walls, their faces turned to Joshua like flowers to the sun, waiting for him to say something that would give them hope.

"I'm going to wash your feet," he said. To Joseph of Arimathea, he said, "I need a basin of water and a sponge." The tall aristocrat bowed and went off to find a servant.

"What a pleasant surprise," Mary said.

James the brother rolled his eyes and sighed heavily.

"I'm going out," I said. I looked at Peter, as if to say, *Don't let him out of your sight.* He understood perfectly and nodded.

"Come back for the seder," Joshua said. "I have some things I have to teach you in the little time I have left."

there was no one home at Simon's house. I knocked on the door for a long time, then finally let myself in. There was no evidence of a morning meal, but the mikveh had been used, so I guessed that they had each bathed and then gone to the Temple. I walked the streets of Jerusalem, trying to think of some solution, but everything I had learned seemed useless. As evening fell I made my way back to Joseph's house, taking the long route so I didn't have to pass the palace of the high priest.

Joshua was waiting inside, sitting on the steps to the upper room, when I came in. Peter and Andrew sat on either side of him, obviously there to ensure that he didn't accidentally skip down to the high priest and turn himself in for blasphemy.

"Where have you been?" Joshua said. "I need to wash your feet."

"Do you have any idea how hard it is to find a ham in Jerusalem during Passover week?" I said. "I thought it would be nice, you know, some ham on matzo with a little bitter herb."

"He washed us all," Peter said. "Of course we had to hold Bart down, but even he's clean."

"And as I washed them, they will go out and wash others, by showing them forgiveness."

"Oh, I get it," I said. "It's a parable. Cute. Let's go eat."

We all lay around the big table, with Joshua at the head. Joshua's mother had prepared a traditional Passover supper, with the exception of the lamb. To begin the seder, Nathaniel, who was the youngest, had to ask a question. "Why is this night different from every other night of the year?"

"Bart's feet are clean?" said Thomas.

"Joseph of Arimathea is picking up the tab?" said Philip.

Nathaniel laughed and shook his head. "No. It's because other nights we eat bread and matzo, but tonight we only eat matzo. Jeez." He grinned, probably feeling smart for the first time in his life.

"And why do we only eat the matzo on this night?" asked Nathaniel.

"Skip ahead, Nate," I said. "We're all Jews here. Summarize. Unleavened bread because there was no time for it to rise with Pharaoh's soldiers on our tail, bitter herbs for the bitterness of slavery, God delivered us into the Promised Land, it was swell, let's eat."

"Amen," said everyone.

"That was pathetic," said Peter.

"Yeah, was it?" I said angrily. "Well, we sit here with the Son of God, waiting for someone to come and take him away and kill him, and none of us is going to do a damn thing about it, including God, so forgive me if I'm not peeing all over myself about having been delivered out of the hands of the Egyptians about a million years ago."

"You're forgiven," said Joshua. Then he stood up. "What I am, is in you all. The Divine Spark, the Holy Ghost, it unites you all. It is the God that is in you all. Do you understand that?"

"Of course God is part of you," James the brother said, "he's your father."

"No, in all of you. Watch, take this bread." He took a matzo and broke it into pieces. He gave a piece to everyone in the room and took a piece himself. Then he ate it. "Now, the bread is part of me, the bread is me. Now all of you eat it."

Everybody looked at him.

"EAT IT!" He screamed.

So we ate it. "Now it is part of you, I am part of you. You all share the same part of God. Let's try again. Hand me that wine."

And so it went like that, for a couple of hours, and I think that by the time the wine was gone, the apostles actually grasped what Joshua was saying to them. Then the begging started, as each of us pleaded for Joshua to give up the notion that he had to die to save the rest of us.

"Before this is finished," he said, "you will all have to deny me."

"No we won't," said Peter.

"You will deny me three times, Peter. I not only expect this, I command it. If they take you when they take me, then there is no one to take the good news to the people. Now, Judas, my friend, come here."

Judas went to Joshua, who whispered in his ear, then sent him back to his place at the table. "One of you will betray me this very night," said Joshua. "Won't you, Judas?"

"What?" Judas looked around at us, but when he saw no one coming to his defense, he bolted down the steps. Peter started after him, but Joshua caught the fisherman by the hair and yanked him back off of his feet.

"Let him go."

"But the high priest's palace isn't a furlong away," said Joseph of Arimathea. "If he goes there directly."

Joshua held his hand up for silence. "Biff, go directly to Simon's house and wait. Alone you can sneak by the palace without being seen. Tell Maggie and the others to wait for us. The rest of us will go through the city and through the Ben Hinnon valley so we don't have to pass the priest's palace. We'll meet you in Bethany."

I looked at Peter and Andrew. "You won't let him turn himself in?"

"Of course not."

I was off into the night, wondering even as I ran whether Joshua had changed his mind and was going to escape from Bethany into the Judean desert. I should have known right then that I'd been had. You think you can trust a guy, then he turns around and lies to you.

Simon answered the door and let me in. He held his finger to his lips, signally me to be quiet. "Maggie and Martha are in the back. They're angry with you. All of you. Now they'll be angry with me for letting you in."

"Sorry," I said.

He shrugged. "What can they do? It's my house."

I went directly through the front room into a second room that opened off to bedchambers, the mikveh, and the courtyard where food was prepared. I heard voices coming from one of the bedchambers. When I walked in, Maggie looked up from braiding Martha's hair.

"So, you've come to tell me that it's done," she said. Tears welled up in her eyes and I felt as if I would break down with her if she started sobbing now.

"No," I said. "He and the others are on their way here. Through Ben Hinnon, so it will be a few hours. But I have a plan." I pulled the ying-yang amulet that Joy had given me out of my tunic and waved it before them.

"Your plan is to bribe Joshua with ugly jewelry?" asked Martha.

I pointed to the tiny stoppers on either side of the amulet. "No, my plan is to poison him."

I explained how the poison worked to Mary and Martha and then we waited, counting the time in our imaginations, watching in our mind's eyes as the apostles made their way through Jerusalem, out the Essene gate, into the steep valley of Ben Hinnon, where thousands of tombs had been carved into the rock, and where once a river had run, but now was only sage and cypress and thistles clinging to the crevices in the limestone. After several hours we went outside to wait in the street, then when the moon started down and the night made way into early morning, we saw a single figure coming from the west, not the south as we had expected. As he got closer I could tell from heavy shoulders and the moon shining on his bald pate that it was John.

"They took him," he said. "At Gethsemane. Annas and Caiphais came themselves, with Temple guards, and they took him."

Maggie ran into my arms and buried her face in my chest. I reached out and pulled Martha close as well.

"What was he doing at Gethsemane?" I said. "You were supposed to be coming here through Ben Hinnon."

"He only told you that."

"That bastard lied to me. So they arrested everyone?"

"No, the others are hiding not far from here. Peter tried to fight the guards, but Joshua stopped him. Joshua negotiated with the priests to let us go. Joseph came too, he helped talk them into letting the rest of us go."

"Joseph? Joseph betrayed him?"

"I don't know," said John. "Judas was the one that led them to Gethsemane. He pointed Joshua out to the guards. Joseph came later, when they were about to arrest the rest of us."

"Where did they take him?"

"To the palace of the high priest. That's all I know, Biff. I promise."

He sat down hard in the middle of the street and began to weep. Martha went to him and cradled his head to her breast.

Maggie looked up at me. "He knew you would fight. That's why he sent you here."

"The plan doesn't change," I said. "We just have to get him back so we can poison him."

John looked up from Martha's embrace. "Did you change sides when I wasn't here?"

Wednesday

At first light Maggie and I were pounding on Joseph's door. A servant let us in. When Joseph came out from his bedchamber I had to hold Maggie back to keep her from attacking him.

"You betrayed him!"

"I did not," said Joseph.

"John said you were with the priests," I said.

"I was. I followed them up to keep them from killing Joshua for trying to escape, or in self-defense, right there at Gethsemane."

"What do you mean, 'in self-defense'?"

"They want him dead, Maggie," Joseph said. "They want him dead, but they don't have the authority to execute him, don't you understand that? If I hadn't been there they could have murdered him and said that he'd attacked them first. The Romans are the only ones who have the authority to have someone killed."

"Herod had John the Baptist killed," I said. "There were no Romans involved in that."

"Jakan and his thugs stone people all of the time," Maggie said. "Without Roman approval."

"Think, you two. This is Passover week. The city is crawling with Romans watching for rebellious Jews. The entire Sixth Legion is here, plus all of Pilate's personal guard from Caesarea. Normally there'd only be a handful. The high priests, the Sanhedrin, the Pharisee council, even Herod will think twice before they do anything outside the letter of Roman law. Don't panic. There hasn't even been a trial in the Sanhedrin yet."

"When will there be a trial?"

"This afternoon, probably. They have to bring everyone in. The prosecution is gathering witnesses against Joshua."

"What about witnesses for him?" I asked.

"That's not how it works," said Joseph. "I'll speak for him, and so will my friend Nicodemus, but other than that Joshua will have to defend himself."

"Swell," Maggie said.

"Who is prosecuting him?"

"I thought you'd know," Joseph said, cringing slightly. "The one who started the Sanhedrin plots against Joshua the other two times, Jakan bar Iban."

Maggie whirled around and glared at me. "You should have killed him."

"Me? You had seventeen years to push the guy down the steps or something."

"There's still time," she said.

"That won't help Joshua now," said Joseph. "Just hope that the Romans won't hear his case."

"You sound as if he's already convicted," I said.

"I'll do my best." Joseph didn't sound very confident.

"Get us in to see him."

"And let them arrest the two of you? I don't think so. You stay here. You can have the upper rooms to yourselves. I'll come back or send word as soon as anything happens."

Joseph hugged Maggie and kissed her on the top of the head, then left the room to get dressed.

"Do you trust him?" Maggie said.

"He warned Joshua before when they wanted to kill him."

"I don't trust him."

maggie and I waited all day in the upper room, jumping to our feet every time we heard footsteps going by in the street, until we were exhausted and shaking from worry. I asked one of Joseph's servant girls to go down to the palace of the high priest to see what was going on. She returned a short time later to report that the trial was still going on.

Maggie and I made a nest of the cushions under the wide arched window in the front, so we could hear the slightest noise coming from the street, but as night started to fall, the footsteps became fewer and farther between, the distant singing from the Temple faded, and we settled into each other's arms, a single lump of low, agonizing grief. Sometime after dark we made love together for the first time since the night before Joshua and I left for the Orient. All those years had passed, and yet it seemed familiar. That first time, so long ago, making love was a desperate way to share the grief we felt because we were each about to lose someone we loved. This time we were losing the same person. This time, we slept afterward.

Joseph of Arimathea didn't come home.

Thursday

It was Simon and Andrew who stormed up the steps to wake us Thursday morning. I threw my tunic over Maggie and jumped to my feet in just a loincloth. As soon as I saw Simon I felt the heat rise in my face.

"You treacherous bastard!" I was too angry to hit him. I just stood there screaming at him. "You coward!"

"It wasn't him," screamed Andrew in my ear.

"It wasn't me," said Simon. "I tried to fight the guards when they came to get Joshua. Peter and I both did."

"Judas was your friend. You and your Zealot bullshit!"

"He was your friend too."

Andrew pushed me away. "Enough! It wasn't Simon. I saw him face two guards with spears. Leave him be. We don't have time for your tantrum, Biff. Joshua is being flogged at the high priest's palace."

"Where's Joseph?" Maggie said. She'd dressed while I had been railing at Simon.

"He's gone on to the praetorium that Pilate set up at the Antonia Palace by the Temple."

"What the hell's he doing there if Joshua is being beaten at the palace in this end of the city?"

"That's where they'll take Joshua next. He was convicted of blasphemy, Biff. They want a death sentence. Pontius Pilate is the ruling authority in Judea. Joseph knows him, he's going to ask for Joshua's release."

"What do we do? What do we do?" I was starting to get hysterical. Since I could remember, my friendship with Joshua had been my anchor, my reason for being, my life; now it, he, was running toward destruction like a storm-driven ship to a reef, and I couldn't think of a thing to do but panic. "What do we do? What do we do?" I panted, the breath refusing to fill my lungs. Maggie grabbed me by the shoulders and shook me.

"You have a plan, remember." She tugged on the amulet around my neck.

"Right, right," I said, taking a deep breath. "Right. The plan." I grabbed my tunic and slipped it over my head. Maggie helped me wrap the sash.

"I'm sorry, Simon," I said.

He forgave me with the wave of a hand. "What do we do?"

"If they're taking Joshua to the praetorium, that's where we go. If Pilate releases him then we'll need to get him out of there. There's no telling what Josh will do to get them to kill him."

We were waiting along with a huge crowd outside the Antonia Palace when the Temple guards brought Joshua to the front gates. The high priest, Caiaphas, wearing his blue robes and with a jewel-encrusted chest piece, led the procession. His father, Annas, who had been the high priest previously, followed right behind. A column of guards surrounded Joshua in the middle of the procession. We could just see him amid the guards, and I could tell that someone had put a fresh tunic on him, but there were stripes of blood soaking through the back. He looked as if he was in a trance.

There was a great deal of posturing and shouting between the Temple guards, and from somewhere in the procession Jakan came forward and started arguing with the soldiers as well. It was obvious that the Romans were not going to let the Temple guards enter the praetorium, so the transfer of the prisoner was going to take place there at the gate or not at all. I was measuring whether I could sneak through the crowd, snap Jakan's neck, and sneak back out without jeopardizing our plan when I felt a hand on my shoulder. I looked around to see Joseph of Arimathea.

"At least it wasn't a Roman scourge they lashed him with. He took thirty-nine lashes, but it was just leather, not the lead-tipped whip that the Romans use. That would have killed him."

"Where were you? What took so long?"

"The prosecution took forever. Jakan went on half the night, taking testimony from witnesses who had obviously never even heard of Joshua, let alone seen any crime."

"What about the defense?" asked Maggie.

"Well, I put forth a defense of good deeds, but it was so overwhelmed by the accusations that it was lost in the noise. Joshua didn't say a word in his own defense. They asked him if he was the Son of God and he said yes. That confirmed the blasphemy charge. It's all they needed, really."

"What happens now? Did you talk to Pilate?"

"I did."

"And?"

Joseph rubbed the bridge of his nose as if fighting a headache. "He said he'd see what he could do."

We watched as the Roman soldiers took Joshua inside and the priests followed. The Pharisees, commoners in the eyes of the Romans, were left outside. A legionnaire almost caught Jakan's face in the gate when he slammed it.

I caught movement out of the corner of my eye, and I looked up to a high, wide balcony that was visible above the palace walls. It had obviously been designed by Herod the Great's architects as a platform from which the king could address the masses in the Temple without compromising his safety. A tall Roman in a lush red robe was standing on the balcony looking down on the crowd, and not looking particularly happy with their presence.

"Is that Pilate?" I asked Joseph, pointing to the Roman.

Joseph nodded. "He'll go downstairs to hold Joshua's trial."

But I wasn't interested at that point in where Pilate was going. What interested me was the centurion who stood behind him wearing the full-crested helmet and breastplate of a legion commander.

Not a half hour later the gate was opened and a squad of Roman soldiers brought Joshua out of the palace in bonds. A lower-rank centurion pulled Joshua along by a rope around his wrists. The priests followed along behind and were mobbed with questions by the Pharisees who had been waiting outside.

"Go find out what's going on," I said to Joseph.

We waded into the middle of the procession that followed. Most were screaming at Joshua and trying to spit on him. I spotted a few people in the crowd that I knew to be Joshua's followers, but they were going along silently, their eyes darting around as if any second they might be the next one arrested.

Simon, Andrew, and I followed behind at some distance, while Maggie fought the crowd to get close to Joshua. I saw her throw herself at her ex-husband, Jakan, who was trailing the priests, but she was stopped in mid-leap by Joseph of Arimathea, who caught her by the hair and pulled her back. Someone else was helping restrain her, but he wore a shawl over his head so I couldn't tell who it was. Probably Peter.

Joseph dragged Maggie back to us and handed her over to me and Simon. "She'll get herself killed."

Maggie looked up at me, a wildness in her eyes that I couldn't read, either anger or madness. I wrapped my arms around her and held her so her arms were pinned to her sides as we walked along. The man with the hood walked along beside me, his hand on Maggie's shoulder, steadying her. When he looked at me I could see it was Peter. The wiry fisherman seemed to have aged twenty years since I'd seen him Tuesday night.

"They're taking him to Antipas," Peter said. "As soon as Pilate heard Joshua was from Galilee he said it wasn't his jurisdiction and sent him to Herod."

"Maggie," I said into her ear, "please stop being a madwoman. My plan just went to hell and I could use some critical thinking."

Once again we waited outside of one of the palaces built by Herod the Great, but this time, because it was a Jewish king in residence, the Pharisees were let in and Joseph of Arimathea went in with them. A few minutes later he was back outside again.

"He's trying to get Joshua to perform a miracle," Joseph said. "He'll let him go if Joshua performs a miracle for him."

"And if Joshua won't do it?"

"He won't," said Maggie.

"If he won't do it," Joseph said, "we're back where we started. It will be up to Pilate to order the Sanhedrin's death sentence carried out or to release Joshua."

"Maggie, come with me," I said, tugging at her dress as I backed away.

"Why, where?"

"The plan's back on." I ran back to the praetorium, with Maggie in tow. I pulled up by a pillar across from the Antonia Palace. "Maggie, can Peter really heal? Really?"

"Yes, I told you."

"Wounds? Broken bones?"

"Wounds, yes. I don't know about bones."

"I hope so," I said.

I left her there while I went to the highest-ranking centurion stationed outside the gates.

"I need to see your commander," I said.

"Go away, Jew."

"I'm a friend. Tell him it's Levi from Nazareth."

"I'll tell him nothing."

So I stepped up and took the centurion's sword out of its scabbard, put the point under his chin for a split second, then replaced it in its scabbard. He reached for the sword and suddenly it was in my hand and under his chin again. Before he could call out the sword was back in its scabbard.

"There," I said, "you owe me your life twice. By the time you call to have me arrested I'll have your sword again and you'll not only be embarrassed but your head will be all wobbly from your throat being cut. Or, you can take me to see my friend Gaius Justus Gallicus, commander of the Sixth Legion."

Then I took a deep breath and waited. The centurion's eyes darted to the soldiers closest to him, then back to me. "Think, Centurion," I said. "If you arrest me, where will I end up anyway?" The logic of it seemed to strike him through his frustration.

"Come with me," he said.

I signaled to Maggie to wait and followed the soldier into Pilate's fortress.

Justus seemed uncomfortable in the lush quarters they had assigned him at the palace. He'd had shields and spears placed around the room in different places, as if he needed to remind anyone who entered that a soldier lived here. I stood in the doorway while he paced, looking up at me occasionally as if he wanted to kill me. He wiped the sweat from his closely cropped gray hair and whipped it so it drew a stripe across the stone floor.

"I can't stop the sentence. No matter what I want."

"I just don't want him hurt," I said.

"If Pilate crucifies him, he'll be hurt, Biff. That's sort of the point."

"Damaged, I mean. No broken bones, no cut sinew. Have them tie his arms to the cross."

"They have to use nails," Justus said, his mouth shaping into a cruel frown. "Nails are iron. They're inventoried. Each one is accounted for."

"You Romans are masters of supply."

"What do you want?"

"Okay, tie him then, only nail through the web of his fingers and toes, and put a board on the cross so he can support his weight with his feet."

"That's no kindness you're doing him. He could linger a week that way."

"No he won't," I said. "I'm going to give him poison. And I want his body as soon as he's dead."

At the word "poison," Justus had stopped pacing and looked up at me with open resentment. "It's not up to me to release the body, but if you want to make sure the body is unharmed I'll have to keep soldiers there until the end. Sometimes your people like to help the crucified die more quickly by throwing stones. I don't know why they bother."

"Yes, you do, Justus. You of all people do. You can spit that Roman bitterness toward mercy all you want, but you know. You were the one who sent for Joshua when your friend was suffering. You humbled yourself and asked for mercy. That's all I'm doing."

Now the resentment drained from his face and was replaced by amazement. "You're going to bring him back, aren't you?"

"I just want to bury my friend's body intact."

"You're going to bring him back from the dead. Like the soldier at Sepphoris, the one the Sicarii killed. That's why you need his body undamaged."

"Something like that," I nodded, looking at the floor to avoid the old soldier's eyes.

Justus nodded, obviously shaken. "Pilate has to authorize the body to be taken down. Crucifixion is supposed to stand as an example to others."

"I have a friend who can get the body released."

"Joshua could still be set free, you know?"

"He won't be," I said. "He doesn't want to be."

Justus turned from me then. "I'll give the orders. Kill him quickly, then take the body and get it out of my jurisdiction even quicker."

"Thank you, Justus."

"Don't embarrass any more of my officers or your friend will be asking for two bodies."

When I came out of the fortress Maggie ran into my arms. "It's horrible. They put a crown of thorns on his head and the crowd spit on him. The soldiers beat him." The crowd milled around us.

"Where is he now?"

The crowd roared and people began pointing up to the balcony. Pilate stood there next to Joshua, who was being held by two soldiers. Joshua stared straight ahead, still looking as if he were in a trance. Blood was running into his eyes.

Pilate raised his arms and the crowd went quiet. "I have no complaint with this man, yet your priests say that he has committed blasphemy. This is no crime under Roman law," said Pilate. "What would you have me do with him?"

"Crucify him!" screamed someone next to me. I looked over to see Jakan waving a fist. The other Pharisees began chanting, "Crucify him, crucify him." And soon the whole crowd seemed to join in. Among the crowd I saw the few of Joshua's followers that were left begin to slink away before the anger was turned on them. Pilate made a gesture as if he was washing his hands and walked inside.

ƒriday

Eleven apostles, Maggie, Joshua's mother, and his brother James gathered at the upper room of Joseph of Arimathea's house. The merchant had been to see Pilate and the governor agreed to release Joshua's body in honor of the Passover.

Joseph explained: "The Romans aren't stupid, they know our women prepare the dead, so we can't send the apostles to get him. The soldiers will give the body to Maggie and Mary. James, since you're his brother, they'll allow you to come along to help carry him. The rest of you should keep your faces covered. The Pharisees will be looking for Joshua's followers. The priests have already spent too much time on this during a feast week, so they'll all be at the Temple. I've bought a tomb near the hill where they'll crucify him. Peter, you will wait there."

"What if I can't heal him?" Peter said. "I've never even tried to raise the dead."

"He won't be dead," I said. "He just won't be able to move. I couldn't find the ingredients I needed to make a potion to kill the pain, so he'll look dead, but he'll feel everything. I know what it's like, I was in that state for weeks once. Peter, you'll have to heal the wounds from the lash and the nails, but they shouldn't be mortal. I'll give him the antidote as soon as he's out of sight of the Romans. Maggie, as soon as they give him to you, close his eyes if they're open or they'll dry out."

"I can't watch it," Maggie said. "I can't watch them nail him to that tree."

"You don't have to. Wait at the tomb. I'll send someone to get you when it's time."

"Can this work?" Andrew said. "Can you bring him back, Biff?"

"I'm not bringing him back from anything. He won't be dead, he'll just be hurt."

"We'd better go," said Joseph, looking out the window at the sky. "They'll bring him out at noon."

𝕬 crowd had gathered outside of the praetorium, but most were merely curious; only a few of the Pharisees, among them Jakan, had actually come out to see Joshua executed. I stayed back, almost a half-block away, watching. The other disciples were spread out, wearing shawls or turbans that covered their faces. Peter had sent Bartholomew to sit with Maggie and Mary at the tomb. No shawl could disguise his bulk or his stench.

Three heavy crossbeams leaned against the wall outside the palace gates, waiting for their victims. At noon Joshua was brought out along with two thieves who had also been sentenced to death, and the beams were placed upon their shoulders. Joshua was bleeding from a dozen places on his head and face, and although he still wore the purple robe that Herod had placed on him, I could see that blood from the flogging had run down and left streaks on his legs. He still looked like he was in some sort of trance, but there was no question that he was feeling the pain of his wounds. The crowd closed in on him, shouting insults and spitting on him, but I noticed that when he stumbled, someone always lifted him to his feet. His followers were still scattered among the crowd, they were just afraid to show themselves.

From time to time I looked around the periphery of the mob and caught the eye of one of the apostles. Always there was a tear there, and always a mix of anguish and anger. It took everything I had not to rush in among the soldiers, take one of their swords, and start hacking. Afraid of my own temper, I fell back from the crowd until I came alongside of Simon. "I can't do it either," I said. "I can't watch them put him on the cross."

"You have to," the Zealot said.

"No, you be there, Simon. Let him see your face. Let him know you're there. I'll come up once the cross is set." I had never been able to look at someone who was being crucified even when I didn't know them. I knew I wouldn't be able to stomach watching them do it to my best friend. I'd lose control, attack someone, and then we'd both be lost. Simon was a soldier, a secret soldier, but a soldier still. He could do it. The horrible scene at the temple of Kali ran through my head.

"Simon, tell him I said *mindful breath*. Tell him that there is no cold."

"What cold?"

"He'll know what it means. If he remembers he'll be able to shut out the pain. He learned to do that in the East."

"I'll tell him."

I wouldn't be able to tell him myself, not without giving myself away.

I watched from the walls of the city as they led Joshua to the road that ran by the hill called Golgotha, a thousand yards outside the Gennath Gate. I turned away, but even from a thousand yards I could hear him screaming as they drove the nails.

Justus had assigned four soldiers to watch Joshua die. After a half hour they were alone except for perhaps a dozen onlookers and the families of the two thieves, who were praying and singing dirges at the feet of the condemned. Jakan and the other Pharisees had only stayed to see Joshua hoisted upright and the cross set, then they went off to feast with their families.

"A game," I said, tossing a pair of dice in the air as I approached the soldiers. "Just a simple game." I had borrowed a tunic and an expensive sash from Joseph of Arimathea. He'd also given me his purse, which I held up and jingled in front of the soldiers. "A game, Legionnaire?"

One of the Romans laughed. "And where would we get money to gamble with?"

"We'll play for those clothes behind you. That purple robe at the foot of the cross."

The Roman lifted the robe with a spear point, then looked up at Joshua, whose eyes went wide when he saw me. "Sure, it looks like we'll be here a while. Let's have a game."

First I had to lose enough money to give the Romans something to gamble with, then I had to win it back slowly enough to keep me there long enough to accomplish my mission. (I silently thanked Joy for teaching me how to cheat at dice.) I handed the dice to the soldier nearest me, who was perhaps fifty years old, built short and powerfully, but covered with scar tissue and gnarled limbs, evidence of broken bones mishealed. He looked too old to be soldiering this far from Rome, and too beaten down to make the journey home. The other soldiers were younger, in their twenties, I guessed, all with dark olive skin and dark eyes, all lean, fit, and hungry-looking. Two of the younger soldiers carried the standard Roman infantry spear, a wooden shaft with a narrow iron spike as long as a man's forearm, tipped with a compact three-bladed point designed to be driven through armor. The other two carried the wasp-waisted Iberian short sword that I'd seen on Justus' belt so many times. He must have had them imported for his legion to fit his own preference. (Most Romans used a straight-bladed short sword.)

I handed the dice to the old soldier and dumped some coins out in the dirt. As the Roman threw the dice against the bottom of Joshua's cross I scanned the hills and saw the apostles watching from behind trees and over rocks. I gave a signal and it passed from one to the other, and finally to a woman who waited back on one of the city walls.

"Oh my, the gods have turned against me today," I said, rolling a losing combination.

"I thought you Jews only had one God."

"I was talking about your gods, Legionnaire. I'm losing."

The soldiers laughed and I heard a moan from above us. I cringed and felt as if my ribs would cave in on themselves from the pain in my heart. I ventured a glance at Joshua and he was looking right at me. "You don't have to do this," he said in Sanskrit.

"What nonsense is the Jew talking now?" asked the old soldier.

"I couldn't say, soldier. He must be delirious."

I saw two women approaching the foot of the cross on Joshua's left, carrying a large bowl, a jar of water, and a long stick.

"Hey there, get away from them."

"Just here to give a drink of water to the condemned, sir. No harm meant." The woman took a sponge from the bowl and squeezed it out. It was Susanna, Maggie's friend from Galilee, along with Johanna. They'd come down for the Passover to cheer Joshua into the city, now we'd conscripted them to help poison him. The soldier's watched as the women dipped the sponge, then attached it to the end of the stick and held it for the thief to drink from. I had to look away.

"Faith, Biff," Joshua said, again in Sanskrit.

"There, you shut up and die," barked one of the younger Romans.

I twitched and squinted at the dice in lieu of crushing the soldier's windpipe.

"Give me a seven. Baby needs new sandals," said another young Roman.

I couldn't look at Joshua and I couldn't look to see what the women were doing. The plan was that they would go to the two thieves first, so as not to raise suspicion, but now I was regretting the decision to delay.

Finally the Susanna brought the bowl to where we were gambling and set it down while Johanna poured some water over the sponge.

"Got any wine there for a thirsty soldier?" said one of the young soldiers. He smacked Johanna on the bottom. "Or some other relief?"

The old soldier caught the young soldier's arm and pushed him away. "You'll be up on that stick with this wretch, Marcus. These Jews take touching their women seriously. Justus won't tolerate it."

Susanna pulled her shawl around her face. She was pretty, lean with small facial features except for her wide brown eyes. She was too old not to be married, but I suspected that she had left a husband to follow Joshua. It was the same story with Johanna, except that her husband had followed along for a while, then divorced her when she wouldn't come home with him. She was more sturdily built, and she rolled like a wagon when she walked. She took the sponge and held it out to me.

"Drink, sir?" Here the timing was critical.

"Anyone want a sip of water?" I asked before taking the sponge. I was palming the ying-yang amulet as I said it.

"Drink after a Jewish dog. Not likely," said the old soldier.

"I'm getting the impression that my Jewish money might sully your Roman purse," I said. "Maybe I should go."

"No, your money's good enough," said a young soldier, punching my shoulder in good spirits. I was tempted to relieve him of his teeth.

I took the sponge and feigned taking a drink. When I raised the sponge to squeeze the water into my mouth I dumped the poison over it. Instantly I handed it back to Johanna so as not to poison myself. Without dipping it back in the water she affixed the sponge to the stick and raised it up to Joshua's face. His head rolled, and his tongue rolled out of the side of his mouth against the moisture.

"Drink," Johanna said, but Joshua didn't seem to hear her. She pushed the sponge harder against his mouth and it dripped on one of the Romans. "Drink."

"Move away from there, Marcus," said the old soldier. "When he goes he'll lose his fluids all over you. You don't want to sit too close." The old Roman laughed raucously.

"Drink it, Joshua," said Susanna.

Finally Joshua opened his eyes and pushed his face into the sponge. I held my breath as I heard him sucking the moisture out of it.

"Enough!" said the young soldier. He knocked the stick out of Susanna's hands. The sponge went flying off into the dirt. "He'll be dead soon."

"Not soon enough, though, with that block to stand on," said the old soldier.

Then time began to pass more slowly than I could ever remember. When Joy had poisoned me it had taken only seconds before I was paralyzed, then when I'd used the poison on the man in India he'd dropped almost immediately. I tried to pretend to pay attention to the game, but I was looking for some sign that the poison was working.

The women moved away and watched from a distance, but I heard one of them gasp and when I looked up, Joshua's head had lolled over. Drool ran out of his open mouth.

"How do you know when he's dead?" I asked.

"Like this." The young soldier named Marcus prodded Joshua in the thigh with his spear. Joshua moaned and opened his eyes and I felt my stomach sink. I could hear sobbing from Johanna and Susanna.

I threw the dice, and waited. An hour passed, and still Joshua moaned. I could hear him praying softly from time to time over the laughter of the soldiers. Another hour. I had begun to shake. Every sound from the cross was like a hot iron driven in my spine. I couldn't bring myself to look up at him. The disciples moved closer, less concerned now about staying hidden, but the Romans were too intent on their game to notice. Unfortunately, I was not intent enough.

"That's it for you," said the old soldier. "Unless you want to gamble for your own cloak now. Your purse is empty."

"Is this bastard ever going to die?" said one of the young soldiers.

"He just needs help," said the young soldier named Marcus, who had stood and was leaning on his spear. Before I could even get to my feet he thrust the spear upward into Joshua's side, the point went up under his ribs, and his heart blood pulsed down the iron in three great gushes, then ran out in a trickle. Marcus yanked the spear out. The entire hillside echoed with screaming, some of it my own. I stood transfixed, shaking, watching the blood run out of Joshua's side. Hands latched onto my arms and I was dragged back, away from the cross. The Romans started to pick up their things to head back to the praetorium.

"Loony," said the old soldier, looking at me.

Joshua looked at me one last time, then closed his eyes and died.

"Come away, Biff," a woman's voice said in my ear. "Come away." They turned me around and started marching me toward the city. I could feel a chill running over me as the wind came up and the sky started to darken under a sudden storm. There was still screaming, going on and on, and when Johanna clamped her hand over my mouth I realized it was me who had been screaming.

I blinked tears out of my eyes, again and again, trying to at least see where they were leading me, but as soon as my sight would clear another sob would rock my body and the water would rise again.

They were leading me to the Gennath Gate, that much I could tell, and there was a dark figure standing on the wall above the gate, watching us. I blinked and caught a single second of clarity as I saw who it was.

"Judas!" I screamed until my voice shattered. I shook off the women and ran through the gate, swung myself up on top of one of the huge doors, and leapt to the wall. Judas ran south along the wall, looking from side to side for a place to jump off.

There was no thought to what I was doing, nothing but grief gone to anger, love gone to hatred. I followed Judas across the roofs of Jerusalem, tossing aside anyone who got in my way, shattering pottery, crashing down rooftop chicken cages, pulling down lines of hanging clothes. When he came to a roof that led no further, Judas jumped two stories to the ground and came up limping as he ran down the street toward the Essene Gate at Ben Hinnon. I came off the roof full stride and landed without losing a step. Although I heard something tear in my ankle I couldn't feel it.

There was a line of people trying to get into the city at the Essene Gate, probably seeking shelter from the impending storm. Lightning crackled across the sky and raindrops as big as frogs began to plop onto the streets, leaving craters in the dust and painting the city with a thin coat of mud. Judas fought through the crowd as if he were swimming in pitch, pulling people past him on either side, moving a step forward only to be carried back a step.

I saw a ladder leaning against the city wall and ran up it. There were Roman soldiers stationed here on the wall and I brushed by them, ducking spears and swords as I made my way to the gate, then over it, then to the wall on the other side. I could see Judas below me. He'd broken out of the crowd and was making his way along a ridge that ran parallel to the wall. It was too far to jump, so I followed him from above until I came to the corner of the battlement, where the wall sloped down to accommodate the thickness required to hold the corner. I slid down the wet limestone on my feet and hands and hit the ground ten paces behind the Zealot.

He didn't know I was there. The rain came down now in sheets and the thunder was so frequent and loud that I could hear nothing myself but the roaring anger in my head. Judas came to a cypress tree that jutted over a high cliff with hundreds of tombs gouged into it. The path passed between a wall of tombs and the cypress tree; past the tree was a fifty-yard drop. Judas pulled a purse from his belt, pulled a small stone out of the opening to one of the tombs, then shoved the purse inside. I caught him by the back of the neck and he shrieked.

"Go ahead, put the stone back," I said.

He tried to wheel on me and hit me with the stone. I took it from him and fitted it back into the tomb, then kicked his feet out from under him and dragged him to the edge of the cliff. I clamped onto his windpipe and, holding the cypress tree with my free hand, I leaned him out over the cliff.

"Don't struggle!" I shouted. "You'll only free yourself to the fall."

"I couldn't let him live," Judas said. "You can't have someone like him alive." I pulled the Zealot back up on the cliff and whipped the sash from around his tunic.

"He knew he had to die," Judas said. "How do you think I knew he'd be at Gethsemane, not at Simon's? He told me!"

"You didn't have to give him up!" I screamed. I wrapped the sash around his neck, then pulled it tight over the crook of a cypress branch.

"Don't. Don't do this. I had to do it. Someone did. He would have just reminded us of what we'll never be."

"Yep," I said. I shoved him backward over the cliff and caught the end of the sash as it tightened around the branch. The sash twanged when it took his weight and his neck snapped with the sound of a knuckle cracking. I let go of the sash and Judas' body fell into the darkness. The boom of thunder concealed the sound of impact.

The anger ran out of me then, leaving me feeling as if my very bones were losing their structure. I looked forward, straight over the Ben Hinnon valley, into a sheet of lightning-bleached rain. "I'm sorry," I said, and I stepped off the cliff. I felt a bolt of pain, and then nothing.

That's all I remember.

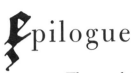

Epilogue

The angel took the book from him, then went out the door and across the hall, where he knocked on the door. "He's finished," the angel said to someone in the room.

"What, you're leaving? I can just go?" asked Levi who was called Biff.

The door across the hall opened, and there stood another angel, this one seeming to have more a female aspect than Raziel. She too held a book. She stepped into the hall to reveal a woman standing behind her, wearing jeans and a green cotton blouse. Her hair was long and straight, dark with reddish highlights, and her eyes were crystal blue and seemed to glow in contrast to her dark skin.

"Maggie," said Levi.

"Hi, Biff."

"Maggie finished her Gospel weeks ago," said Raziel.

"Really?"

The Magdalene smiled. "Well, I didn't have as much to write as you did. I didn't see you guys for sixteen years."

"Oh, right."

"It is the will of the Son that you two go out together into this new world," said the female angel.

Levi went across the hall and took her in his arms. They kissed for a long time until the angels began to clear their throats and murmur "Get a room" under their breaths.

They held each other at arm's length. Levi said, "Maggie, is this going to be like it always was? You know, you're with me, and you love me and everything, but it's only because you can't have Josh?"

"Of course."

"That's so pathetic."

"You don't want to be together?"

"No, I want to, it's just pathetic."

"I have money," she said. "They gave me money."

"That's good."

"Go," said Raziel, losing his patience. "Go, go, go. Go away." He pointed down the hallway.

They started walking down the hallway, arm in arm, tentatively, looking back at the angels every few steps, until at last they looked back and the angels were gone.

"You should have stuck around," the Magdalene said.

"I couldn't. It hurt too much."

"He came back."

"I know, I read about it."

"He was sad because of what you had done."

"Yeah, so was I."

"The others were angry with you. They said that you had the greatest reason to believe."

"That why they edited me out of their Gospels?"

"Good guess," she said.

They stepped into the elevator and the Magdalene pushed the button for the lobby. "By the way, it was Hallowed," she said.

"What was Hallowed?"

"The H. His middle name. It was Hallowed. It's a family name, remember, 'Our father, who art in heaven, Hallowed be thy name.' "

"Damn, I would have guessed Harvey," Biff said.

Afterword

Teaching Yoga to an Elephant

And there are also many other things which Jesus did, the which, if they should be written every one, I suppose that even the world itself could not contain the books that should be written. Amen.

JOHN 21:25

Can you really teach yoga to an elephant? Well no, *you* can't, but we're talking about Jesus here. Nobody knows what he could do.

The book you've just read is a story. I made it up. It is not designed to change anyone's beliefs or worldview, unless after reading it you've decided to be kinder to your fellow humans (which is okay), or you decide you really would like to try to teach yoga to an elephant, in which case, please get videotape.

I researched *Lamb*, I really did, but there is no doubt I could have spent decades researching and still managed to be inaccurate. (It's a talent, what can I say?) While I've made some attempt to paint an accurate picture of the world in which Christ lived, I changed things for my own convenience, and sometimes, obviously, there was no way of knowing what conditions really existed in the years 1 through 33.

The available written history about the peasant class, society, and the practice of Judaism in the first century in Galilee degenerates quickly into theory. The role of the Pharisees in peasant society, the Hellenistic influence, the influence of an international city like Joppa nearby: who knows how these things would have affected Christ as a boy? Some historians postulate that Yeshua of Nazareth would have been little more than an ignorant hillbilly, while others say that because of the proximity of Sepphoris and Joppa, he could have been exposed to Greek and Roman culture from an early age. I chose the latter because it makes for a more interesting story.

The historical life of Jesus, beyond a couple of references by Josephus, the Jewish historian of the first century, and the odd mention by Roman historians, is again mostly speculation. What we can know today of the life of Jesus of Nazareth is included in the four slim Gospels found in the New Testament: Matthew, Mark, Luke, and John. For those readers who know the Gospels (bear with me), you know that Matthew and Luke are the only two to mention Christ's birth, while Mark and John cover only the ministry part of Jesus' life. The wise men are mentioned only in one short passage in Matthew, and the shepherds are mentioned only in Luke. The slaughter of the innocents and the fleeing into Egypt are mentioned only in Matthew. In short, Jesus' infancy is a jumble, but the chronicle of his childhood is worse. Of the time from Jesus' birth to when he began his ministry in his thirties, the Bible gives us only one scene: Luke tells us of Jesus teaching in the Temple in Jerusalem at age twelve. Other than that, we have a thirty-year hole in the life of the most influential human being to ever walk the face of the earth. With *Lamb,* in my own goofy way, I attempted to fill that hole in history, but again, I am not trying to present history as it might really have been, I'm simply telling stories.

Some of the historical elements of *Lamb* are uncomfortable to work the modern mind around. The precocious sexuality comes to mind. That Maggie would have been betrothed by twelve and married by thirteen is almost certain from what we know of Jewish society in the first century, as are the facts that a Jewish boy of the time would have been learning his trade by age ten, would be betrothed at thirteen, and would be married by fourteen. Trying to create empathy for the adult roles of those whom we, today, would consider children, was of no small concern to me when I was writing that section of the book, but it may be the one section where the sexuality of the characters is not historically out of place. The average peasant in Galilee would have been lucky to live to the age of forty, so perhaps the children, by necessity, reached sexual maturity earlier than they would under less harsh conditions.

Although there are, I'm sure, many historical inaccuracies and improbabilities in this book, the most blatant that I have knowingly indulged is in the section where Biff and Joshua visit Gaspar in the mountains of China. While Gautama Buddha did indeed live and teach some five hundred years before the birth of Christ, and while his teachings were widespread in India by the time our heroes could have made it to the East, Buddhism didn't make it into China for almost five hundred years after Christ's death. The martial arts would not be developed by Buddhist monks until after that, but to remain historically accurate, I would have had to leave out an important question that I felt needed to be addressed, which is, "What if Jesus had known kung fu?"

The life of Gaspar, as described in *Lamb* (the nine years in the cave, etc.), is drawn from the legends of the life of the Buddhist patriarch Bodhidharma, the man who is said to have taken Buddhism to China around A.D. 500. Bodhidharma (or Daruma) is credited with the school of Buddhism that we know today as Zen. Buddhist legend does not mention Bodhidharma encountering a yeti, but they do have him cutting his eyelids off to avoid falling asleep and having them sprout into tea plants which later monks would brew to keep awake during meditation (which I left out), so I traded that story in on an abominable snowman and Biff's theory of natural selection. Seemed fair. Bodhidharma is also said to have invented and taught kung fu to the famous Shao Lin monks to condition them for the rigorous regimen of meditation he prescribed.

Most of the details of the festival of Kali, including the sacrifices and mutilations, come from Joseph Campbell's *Oriental Mythology*, from his *Masks of God* series. Campbell cites eyewitness accounts of the bloody ritual from nineteenth-century British soldiers and states that even today over eight hundred goats are beheaded for the festival of Kali in Calcutta. (Anyone who had trouble with this passage, please write to Campbell in his current incarnation.)

The cited verses from the Upanishads and Bhagavad Gita are actual translations of those revered writings. The verses from the Kama Sutra are completely from my imagination, but you'll finder weirder stuff in the actual book.

Theologically, I made certain assumptions about who Jesus was, mainly that he was who the Gospels say he was. While I used the Gospels heavily for reference, and there are a couple of references to the Acts of the Apostles (specifically the giving of the gift of tongues, without which Biff could not have told the story in modern American idiom), I tried *not* to draw on the rest of the New Testament, specifically the letters of Paul, Peter, James, and John, as well as Revelation, all written years after the Crucifixion (as were the Gospels). These missives eventually went on to define Christianity, but no matter what you may think of them, you have to agree that Jesus would not have been aware of them, or the events in them, or certainly the consequences of their teaching, so they had no place in this story. Joshua and Biff, as Jewish boys, would, however, have been familiar with the books of the Old Testament, the first five of which made up the base of their faith, the Torah, and the rest which were referred to by people of the time as Prophets and Writings, so I referred to these when I felt it was appropriate. As I understand it, however, the Talmud and most of the Midrash (illustrative stories explaining the law of God) had not yet been formulated and agreed upon, so they were not used as a reference for *Lamb*.

From the Gnostic Gospels (a set of manuscripts found at Nag Hammadi, Egypt, in 1945, but which actually may have been written earlier than the canonized Gospels) I've drawn only slightly on the Gospel of Thomas, a book of Christ's sayings, because it fit well with the Buddhist point of view (many of the sayings in the Gospel of Thomas are also found in Mark). The other Gnostic Gospels were either too fragmentary, or frankly, just plain creepy (the Infancy Gospel of Thomas describes Jesus, at age six, using his supernatural powers to murder a group of children because they tease him. Sort of *Carrie Goes to Nazareth*. Even I had to pass.)

Lamb is peppered throughout with biblical references, both real and made-up (i.e., Biff quotes liberally from nonexistent books of the Bible such as Dalmatians, Excretions, and Amphibians). My editor and I discussed the merit of footnoting these references and decided that footnotes would detract from the flow of the story. The problem arises, however, that if the reader knows the Bible well enough to recognize the real references, there's a good chance that he or she has decided not to read this book. Our final decision—well, my final decision, my editor wasn't really consulted on this because he might have said no—was to advise those who are not familiar with the Bible to find someone who is, sit them down, read them the passages in question, then say, "That one real? How 'bout that one?" If you don't know someone who is familiar with the Bible, just wait, someone will come to your door eventually. Keep extra copies of *Lamb* on hand so they can take one with them.

Another problem with telling a story that has been told so many times is that people are looking for elements with which they are familiar. Although I've glossed over many events that are chronicled in the Gospels, there are numerous elements which many people think are there, which simply are not. One is that Mary Magdalene was a prostitute. She's always portrayed that way in movies, but it doesn't ever say that she is in the Bible. She is mentioned by name eleven times in the synoptic Gospels (Matthew, Luke, Mark). Most references to her talk about her preparation for the burial of Jesus, and then being the first witness of his resurrection. It also says that Jesus cured her of evil spirits. No whore references, period. There are "Marys" without surnames all over the Gospels, and some of them, I suspect, may refer to the Magdalene, specifically the Mary who, soon before his death, anoints Jesus' feet with expensive ointment and wipes them with her hair, certainly one of the most tender moments in the Gospels and the primary basis for my rendering of Maggie's character. We know from letters that many of the leaders of the early church were women, but in first-century Israel, a woman who struck out on her own without a husband was not only considered uppity, but was very likely referred to as a harlot (as was a woman who was divorced). That could be where the myth originated.

Another Gospel misassumption is that the three wise men were kings, or, in fact, that there were even three of them. We make that assumption because there are three gifts given to the Christ child. Their names are never mentioned. The names Balthasar, Gaspar, and Melchior come to us from Christian tradition written hundreds of years after the time of Christ. We assume that Joseph of Nazareth, Jesus' stepfather, dies before the Crucifixion, yet it is never stated in the Gospels. He just may not have been involved. We make assumptions based on what we have been fed over the years at Christmas pageants and passion plays, but often, although inspired by faith, that material is little more than what you have just read: the product of someone's imagination. The Gospels do not agree on the order of the events that happen during the ministry, from Jesus' baptism by John to the Crucifixion, so I arranged events from all the Gospels in what seemed a logical, chronological order, while adding those elements that allow Biff's participation in the story. There are, of course, elements of the Gospels which I left out in the interest of brevity, but you can always find them in the Gospels if you want.

My sending Joshua and Biff to the East was motivated purely by story, not by basis in the Gospel or historical evidence. While there are indeed astounding similarities between the teachings of Jesus and those of Buddha (not to mention those of Lao-tzu, Confucius, and the Hindu religion, all which seem to have included some version of the Golden Rule), it's more likely that these stem from what I believe to be logical and moral conclusions that any person in search of what is right would come to, e.g.: that the preferable way to treat one another is with love and kindness; that pursuit of material gain is ultimately empty when measured against eternity; and that somehow, as human beings, we are all connected spiritually. While historians and theologians don't completely rule out the possibility that Christ may have traveled to the East, they seem to agree that he *could have* formulated the teachings we find in the Gospels with no more influence than the rabbinical teachings in Galilee and Judea. But what fun would that have been?

Finally, this story was set in a dire time, a deadly serious time, and the world of the first-century Jew under the rule of the Romans would not have been one that easily inspired mirth. It's more than a small anachronism that I portray Joshua having and making fun, yet somehow, I like to think that while he carried out his sacred mission, Jesus of Nazareth might have enjoyed a sense of irony and the company of a wisecracking buddy. This story is not and never was meant to challenge anyone's faith; however, if one's faith can be shaken by stories in a humorous novel, one may have a bit more praying to do.

My thanks to the many people who helped in the research and writing of this book, especially those who were generous enough to share their beliefs without judgment or condemnation.

Many thanks to Neil Levy, Mark Joseph, Professor William "Sundog" Bersley, Ray Sanders, and John "The Heretic" Campbell for their advice on religion, philosophy, and history. To Charlee Rodgers for putting up with the fits, starts, whining, and hubris of the process, as well as to Dee Dee Leichtfuss for readings and comments. Special thanks to Orly Elbaz, who was my tour guide through Israel and who showed infinite patience in answering my nitpicky historical questions. Also to my agent, Nick Ellison, and my editor, Tom Dupree, for their patience, tolerance, and advice.

Christopher Moore
Big Sur, California
November 2000

ﬃfterword II

When the Muse Sneezed

It's been five years since *Lamb* was first released, and during that time I've gotten a pretty good idea of what readers want to know about the book, and about me, that wasn't included in the original afterword, so here you go.

The first germ of inspiration for *Lamb* (a muse sneeze, if you will) came one night when I was reading a novel called *The Master and Margarita,* by Mikhail Bulgakov, which is essentially about life in the Stalinist Soviet Union in the 1930s, but includes an amazing scene from the trial of Jesus, in which Pontius Pilate has a migraine headache and just wants to get rid of this Hebrew troublemaker. Although I had read or watched numerous portrayals of the trial over the years, Bulgakov's depiction seemed extraordinarily vivid. This was because, I thought, of the human weakness of the witness, Pilate. I began to ponder the idea of how an eyewitness narrator might resurrect, so to speak, a well-worn story.

A week later, the PBS series *Frontline* ran a special called "From Jesus to Christ," in which archaeologists, historians, and theologians discussed the historical context of the life of Christ. Again and again the experts made the point that the story of the first thirty years of Christ's life was not covered in the canonical Gospels.

"Someone should write that story!" I said, talking sternly to myself as I am wont to do when no one is around to accuse me of being a nutter. "And since I know absolutely nothing about theology or history, I should be that someone!"

So I set about learning what I could about first-century Palestine (C.E.), as well as colonial Roman society, and generally what was going on around the world during the time of Christ. Turned out there was a lot to learn.

I had always done "field" research on my previous books—from living on a remote Pacific island to wandering the streets of San Francisco at all hours— but I thought that a trip to the Middle East would be a waste of time. After all, with my other books the main value of the research was to observe people in specific, extant environments, listen to their conversations, and figure out what their values were so I could construct agendas for my characters. With *Lamb*, all the characters would have been dead for two thousand years—what was there to listen to? And besides, things were hot—politically and literally—in the Middle East at the time.

It was my wifelike girlfriend of fourteen years, Charlee, who convinced me to go to Israel.

"You always find something you hadn't counted on that makes the books better," she said. "You need to go."

"You think so?"

"Absolutely," she said. "It will make for a richer story."

"You're probably right," I said. "Okay, I'll go."

"Good," she said. "And while you're away, I have to go to Hawaii so I won't worry about you."

So I called my travel agent, Large Carl, and I said, "I want the Footsteps of Jesus Tour. I want to get in, get out, and nobody gets hurt."

Three weeks later I was making my way across Israel on a bus full of English-speaking people (Brits, Americans, Aussies, Kiwis, and Canadians). I, of course, went as a Canadian (due to their relative worthlessness as hostages), sporting Toronto Maple Leafs T-shirts and ball caps, and being generally polite to enhance my cover.

From time to time, the air-conditioned coach would stop, and our guide, Orly, a frightfully intelligent woman from Jerusalem, would walk us out into the August sun to look at piles of brown stuff, mostly rocks. As it turned out, the piles of rocks had historical, often religious significance. Thanks to Orly's explanation, the rock piles quickly became portals to the past, giving context and meaning to my months of academic research and a lifetime of very sketchy religious education. (I was baptized Methodist as a baby, but raised First Church of NFL, as my father disapproved of anything that interfered with watching football on Sunday—so I was pretty much a seething heathen. To be honest, I have seldom actually seethed, but I like the sound of the phrase "seething heathen" and I believe that would be a terrific name for a Christian rock band. Because of the irony—duh. Most religions are way, way too short on irony. I mean, that's sort of what brought us all here, isn't it?) When Orly's narrative occasionally slowed a bit, it was fun to watch the British people blister in the sun.

We saw the ruins of a Crusader castle at Caesarea and learned how the Marmeluke warrior Saladin sacked it by sneaking guys in through the aqueduct to unlock the front door. (I know, I thought Marmelukes were snow dogs, too. How cool would it have been if the Crusaders had been turned back by snow dogs?) Evidently, this worked really well and he used the trick again and again. We saw the classical amphitheater built by Herod the Great in honor of Julius Caesar, who spared his life when the Romans first took Palestine. We saw Nazareth, a small city perched on hills strewn with giant basalt boulders, looking as if it had recently survived a meteor shower. It was very rough, hostile-looking country, and it was immediately obvious that the Jews in the time of Jesus would have had a difficult life here, even if they hadn't been under the foot of the Romans.

We stayed in a kibbutz near the Sea of Galilee (which is a freshwater lake, really) and the next day took a boat ride across the sea from Magdala (yes, where Maggie would have grown up) to Capernaum, where the apostle Peter lived. In Capernaum there was an excavation of houses that looked like ancient apartments, and it was here I first started seeing the way people would have lived, how the scenes from daily life would have played out. (To avoid defiling Peter's house, an order of monks—Dominicans, I think—has built a church over the excavation, a modern, disc-shaped thing that is cantilevered out over the lake; it looks as if aliens landed and wanted to dig up a two-thousand-year-old synagogue. Yes, that was there, the excavation of a synagogue from the time of Jesus, a carving of the menorah clearly visible on the stones.)

In Jesus' day, the lake would have been lined with villages, each no more than a hundred or so steps wide, leading from one to the next, but the hills above would have been desolate except for some brush and a few stubborn olive trees, just as they are today. Yes, today there is a church on the Mount of the Sermon, but still I could see it in my mind's eye—the people, five thousand strong, spread across the barren hillside, having come up from the lakeside villages to hear the rabbi speak. For all the churches, the shrines, the markers that have been laid down through history, *this* was where I got the greatest feeling of history, of "Yes, I can see it happening."

That hill is where Biff and Joshua would first formulate and reject "Blessed are the Dumbfucks" (which was, by the way, the first scene of the book I wrote, nearly a year and half before I actually started the manuscript). On the very mount where nearly two thousand years ago Jesus handed down the Beatitudes, I, the seething heathen, had a Moment.

Orly told us that some businessmen were building a platform out into the lake that would lie just below the surface, so people could go out and get a feel for what it was like to walk on water. I'm *not* kidding. Anything to simulate an epiphany, I guess. I felt a little ill, nonetheless. (But that just may have been caused by the odor of smoldering Brits.)

From there we went on to Jerusalem and Mount Moriah, where I saw the stone from which Mohammed ascended to heaven. It's in a big mosque called the Dome of the Rock, whose outstanding feature is a big gold dome. It's in every establishing shot of Jerusalem you've ever seen. I also saw the stone on which Abraham was almost allowed to sacrifice his son Isaac. And I saw the stone that marks the place where the Ark of the Covenant sat in the Great Second Temple during the time of Jesus, where the temple must rise once again before Jesus can return. The problem is, IT WAS THE SAME ROCK! One rock, three religions. And unless the giant mosque that houses that rock is destroyed, and a new, Jewish temple built on it, the Christian prophecy of Christ's return can never be fulfilled. So basically, the whole "Why don't those people in Jerusalem get their shit together?" question became a lot more complicated.

With all the tension in the old city today, I suddenly got a sense of just how oppressive life must have been for the people of Israel under Roman rule—how violated they must have felt. That feeling was underscored when we retraced Jesus' steps along the Via Dolorosa (Latin for "the Way of Grief") to Golgotha, where he was crucified.

The Via Dolorosa is an alley, really, barely ten feet wide in places, and it's constantly jammed with a steady stream of pilgrims scrabbling like they're trying to get into Wal-Mart for the Day After Thanksgiving sale. I mean, it's seriously jammed, a river of humanity. And set in the walls along the road there are signs, carved in stone and written in Latin, each marking a spot where Jesus was said to have fallen (called the Stations of the Cross). Nine of the stations are on the Via Dolorosa; the final five are in the Church of the Holy Sepulchre, which was built on the site where Jesus was crucified. Many of the pilgrims carry facsimile crosses. (I saw one church group from Kentucky carrying a cross that looked like it was made of carbon fiber and Styrofoam—like a Nike Sports Cross or something.)

As each group reached one of the station signs they would kneel, some doing fake falls to replicate Jesus' stumbles. From my somewhat higher perspective looking down on the kneeling/falling crowd, the whole tableau resembled a long, narcoleptic conga line, swooning and reviving, swooning and reviving. But they were having *their* Moment, each of them, as I had had mine on the mount above the Sea of Galilee. In a way, they were using their imaginations as time machines, taking themselves back to the time and place in which Jesus lived, was tortured, and was killed. The book I was going to write would be a time machine, too, and I wondered: Would people who had traveled seven thousand miles to reenact a torturous death in an ancient alley be able to take the retelling of Christ's life as a comedy? It didn't seem likely.

It seemed even less likely the next day as we went into Bethlehem, which was in Palestinian territory.

On the tour bus I shared a seat with a retired Baptist minister from Calgary, Alberta (let's call him Joe), who had lost his wife a year earlier and was taking a trip to the Holy Land as his "last hallelujah," so to speak. Each evening, as we got off the bus, I would ask Orly if we were going to visit Jewish or Palestinian territory the next morning. (There were practical reasons, like you couldn't wear shorts in a mosque, nor could you enter a synagogue without a hat, but there were other considerations as well.) So after the Via Dolorosa and the Church of the Holy Sepulchre day, as usual, I asked.

Orly told us that the next day we'd be going to Bethlehem, which was in Palestinian territory.

Bob bristled. "Why do you have to ask that every day?"

"Well, there's the hat thing, and, duh, the AK-47 factor," I said.

"Well, I don't care," Bob replied. "If I have to go, I'd just as soon go here in the Holy Land."

"Well, good," I said. "You can sit by the window tomorrow."

And from there on, that's how we decided where we would sit. To be fair, Bob was very tolerant of my particular brand of heresy. I think he was actually more offended by my fake Canadianess than by my searching for a comic perspective on Jesus, since I wasn't able to talk about hockey with any authority and was therefore not good company.

All around Bethlehem we saw Palestinian soldiers, sharply creased and spit-shined, looking very efficient and very, very angry in their blue desert camos. (We'd seen Israeli soldiers everywhere we'd been, but they just looked tired. These guys, well, they looked like they wanted to fight.)

Orly took us to the spot where St. Helena, mother of Constantine the Great, first marked the place of Christ's birth by building a church back in the third century. (She's also the lady who ordered the building of the church that became the Church of the Holy Sepulchre.) The Church of the Nativity, as it stands today, was built in 565, and far from being a rickety stable behind an inn, it's a massive medieval structure with walls ten feet thick and doors that are only four feet high to prevent Saracens from riding in on horseback and prying the golden tiles out of the ceiling (or so the story goes). If you go down a trapdoor into a cave, now lined with marble, you will see a silver star set in the floor, like a compass rose, marking the spot where Mary gave birth to Jesus. Right there, on the star. Yeah, right. It didn't feel like Galilee, or the Via Dolorosa, or even the Garden Tomb (the garden of Joseph of Arimathea, which some believe is the true site of Jesus' tomb)—places where you got a sense the events might have happened there. It felt artificial. Yet the Catholics in our group were visibly moved, and out of consideration for their faith I had to ponder this. So what if it took a Styrofoam cross or a silver star set in the floor for you to access your God? It didn't make it any less spiritually moving.

An hour later our group was allowed through a security door into a giant souvenir store where they sold all kinds of Nativity scenes stamped "Made in Bethlehem." One of our party, a Canadian air traffic controller, was accidentally locked out and got tear-gassed in the streets with a group that was protesting the peace talks that someone was trying to start at the time. He was thrilled. It was the most exciting thing that had ever happened to him, and seemed to border on a religious experience. Plus, his girlfriend scored a terrific Nativity scene carved out of olive wood. Hey, Jesus is where you find him. I guess that couple will find him on the mantel every year at Christmas, and He will always bring memories of being tear-gassed in the streets of Bethlehem.

I bought a silver Roman *dinar* from the first century, presumably a replica of one of the "pieces of silver" that Judas was given to betray Jesus. I had it set in a necklace for my wifelike girlfriend. ("Here, honey, if I screw this book up, we get twenty-nine more of these! It's the going rate.")

From Bethlehem we went south into Judea, to the Dead Sea and Masada, and it was here that I first envisioned what it must have been like for Jesus to heal the blind. Judea in August is the deadest-looking place I've ever seen, including Mars (I've seen pictures). Everything except the sky is a uniform shade of tan. There isn't a single green thing anywhere. I've been to the Sonora Desert and the Mojave Desert, and even those had a few cacti or Joshua trees, but here, nada. Anyone who suddenly regained his sight in Judea would think that the spectrum consisted of two colors: brown and bright. He'd think that sighted people had been lying to him all his life. So I shared this observation with Bob. He harrumphed, dismissing it with a single sound as blasphemous balderdash. It's evidently something they teach you at Canadian Baptist Seminary, because I have tried to harrumph as eloquently and gotten nowhere. When I do it, people think I'm trying to yack up a hairball.

At Masada, the great mountaintop fortress, you can see all the way across the Dead Sea into Jordan. And you can also see the earthen ramp that the Romans patiently built over a two-year period to raise their siege machines high enough to breach the fortress's walls. Here you can feel the inevitability of the Roman Empire, and, again, the desperation of all Jewish people. There is no little irony in the fact that the same Roman Empire that destroyed the Temple at Jerusalem, and ordered Jesus to the cross, would ultimately be the vehicle to bring the teachings of Christ to the rest of the world.

I returned from Israel and got to work on the book. I now had a much better understanding of what life in first-century Palestine must have been like, which served me well until I got to the part of the story where I would send Josh and Biff on a trip to the East in search of the wise men. To be truthful, I hadn't figured out what I was going to do in that part of the book—up till then it had always seemed so far into the story. But now there they were in Antioch, at the head of the Silk Road, and I had nowhere for them to go. I was stuck there, and, consequently, so were they, for six months.

The book was already overdue to my publisher, and I had spent my whole research budget on the Israel trip, so I was going to have to wing it on the entire continent of Asia. To compound the problem, construction had started on new homes on both sides of my house, and my life was invaded by the unending noise of nail guns and power saws. So, to write about Afghanistan, Nepal, and India, I went to Big Sur and checked into a concrete block motel with no phones in the room, no Internet, and limited TV reception. I took a suitcase full of books about Judaic practice in the first century, Joseph Campbell's *The*

Masks of God, historical maps, several annotated Bibles, and a marginally func-tioning laptop computer. I worked this way for two months, living on cups of soup, peanut butter sandwiches, coffee, vitamin C, and ibuprofen to keep my back from tweaking after sitting so many hours a day in a bad chair.

In the end, I had given myself an ulcer (who would'a figured a diet of coffee, vitamin C, and ibuprofen would be bad for your stomach?) and I had a manu-script.

When I finished writing *Lamb* in November 2000, I was relatively sure that after it was published I was going to have to hire a food taster and live in a secret studio apartment somewhere with Salman Rushdie. After all, at that time the country was surfing a wave of intolerance that seemed to be led by a group of Evangelical Christian political mercenaries, and the Supreme Court was about to choose a president who claimed to get messages from God about which peo-ple to bomb. It appeared that the only thing in short supply among America's faithful was a sense of humor, and I was about to release a comic retelling of the life of Christ into the wild. Despite my intent to simply tell a funny story that reflected the spirit of the man portrayed in the Gospels, the prospect of it being accepted as a non–attack book was growing increasingly grim. I steeled myself for battle, or at least for a giant game of Whack A Mole in which I would play the mole.

It was nearly eighteen months (February 2002) before the book was re-leased, and by then America had undergone a sea change in attitude. If any-thing, religious zealotry had been cranked *up* by the events of September 11, 2001, and Christian Americans (at least those who allowed themselves to be coopted politically) were calling for a smack-down with a younger, more nimble God who was, apparently, crazier than their own Old Testament psychopath. Faith and religion had somehow gotten balled up with patriotism and jingoism. While voices of reason were numerous, they were drowned out by scoundrels who saw the conflict as a way to further a political agenda. There is no group so united as one united by their god against a common enemy, and if you dis-agreed, you were not only their enemy, you were a traitor and an enemy of God hisownself.

And I had written a story about the Prince of Peace. I was pretty sure I was fucked.

But I was completely wrong.

Almost from the beginning, it appeared that people of faith who read *Lamb* responded to it in the most positive manner. People wrote me to say that they were giving it to their pastors. Pastors wrote to say that they wished that they could read it to their Sunday schools. As of this writing, there are at least three seminaries at which *Lamb* is taught, and many secular colleges as well. I've been asked to speak at numerous churches and sometimes I accept. (Me, a not particularly devout Buddhist with Christian tendencies!)

I've received more than twenty thousand e-mails from readers, many of whom say that the book has helped deepen their faith. Of all of those missives, only three have been negative: two, coincidentally, were from people in Alabama who hadn't actually read the book but were offended by the idea of it; the other from a retired Catholic monsignor in Toronto who wanted to challenge my religious scholarship (to which I respond, "Yeah, good point, Father."").

In short, the American public has surprised me, my family, and my publisher in the most pleasant way. They got it. It is interesting that in most of the letters I receive the writers also mention that they think the book will anger others, but not them. We are long on faith, just not in one another, apparently. And I certainly was guilty of lack of faith and understanding by fearing the reaction of the faithful. What a pleasant surprise.

Thanks.

Lamb has gone on to be published in twenty countries, and enthusiasm for the book has, if anything, grown over the years. People share it with their families, friends, clergy, and book groups. Every Christmas, Easter, and graduation season I'm bombarded with letters from people who want to purchase a hardcover as a gift, or at least replace their worn-out paperback, but don't want to pay the high prices on the auction sites. It's in response to these people that I asked my publisher to produce this special edition.

Thanks for getting it.

Christopher Moore
San Francisco, California
April 2007